A FATAL MOVE

THE DCI ALEX FLEMING SERIES #BOOK THREE

ROBERT MCNEIL

First published in 2022 by Bloodhound Books.

www.bloodhoundbooks.com

Print ISBN 978-1-5040-7259-5

ALSO BY ROBERT MCNEIL

1

If all went to plan, this would be the last day Her Majesty's Prison Service would keep Jack Kelso under lock and key.

He'd served four years of a twelve-year sentence for armed robbery. The man who planned it had avoided arrest. The police had found no hard evidence to link him to the crime. Kelso had not been so lucky and ended up in a category A prison. After four years, he'd moved to a category C. The authorities believed Kelso no longer posed a risk.

It was soon after the move that Kelso started to think of escape. He then discovered someone wanted to help him. A friend had suggested he complete a visiting order for someone he gave him a name and address for.

Curious, Kelso had filled in the VO and a man who called himself Oscar had turned up for the first visit. Kelso had taken an instant dislike to him and sensed the feeling was mutual. He noticed a hint of an Italian accent in Oscar. He had unruly black hair, a scar over his left eye, and an adenoidal-sounding voice.

'The boss says it's best you don't know who he is yet,' Oscar had wheezed, 'or why he wants you out. If you're caught you can't tell what you don't know. Okay? As for me, I've used a false name and address of an empty flat I was able to break into. No way the police will be able to link it to me.'

'Makes sense,' Kelso had replied. Despite his doubts, he couldn't turn down the chance of outside help.

Over the next few visits, they made detailed plans. It was now the day they would put them into action. After breakfast, Kelso walked down the long path leading to the prison workshops. There were a few winks from other inmates and one or two friendly slaps on the back. Five prison officers escorted the men enjoying the early morning June sunshine. They were trying to delay the time when the doors of the textiles workshop would clang shut behind them.

'Good luck, Kelso,' one inmate whispered as he walked past.

Kelso nodded his thanks and felt his stomach churning. Adrenaline was pumping through his body. The blue prison-issue T-shirt clung to his back with sweat. They reached the workshops building and an officer pulled out his keys. Unlocking the heavy metal door, he stood aside to watch the inmates enter. Once everyone was inside, he slammed the door shut with a loud metallic bang and turned the key. Having counted them out of the cell block and into the workshop, all were present and correct.

The workshop had four large cutting tables and tiers of sewing machines. A central aisle separated the two areas. Three civilian instructional officers occupied a small office in the top corner. They took turns to go round supervising procedures. Next to the office was an open entrance leading into a stores area. It was in this workshop that they made men's underwear for use in other prisons.

A private contractor delivered material which the inmates cut to shape. They then passed the cut parts to the men on the sewing machines to stitch together. It was the job of one man to go round collecting all the offcuts. Putting them into large sacks, he would take them to the storeroom. The contractor would then collect them for recycling.

The grey stubble on Kelso's head and face suggested an older man, but in fact Kelso had only turned forty-five. Life in prison had aged him, but looks belied the fact he kept himself fit. When he turned up for work for the first time, one of the instructional officers had noted his powerful build. He'd suggested Kelso would be most suited to the heavy work and put him on bagging offcuts.

Kelso had fixed his eyes on the man with a steely glare. 'Fine,' was all he said.

Colour had drained from the man's face. 'Great,' he muttered, then strode back to the safety of the office.

Smiling at the memory, Kelso had almost filled his first trolley full of offcut sacks. Shorty, one of the storeroom inmates, came up behind him. 'Lorry's in and we've started to fill it,' he whispered. 'Give it a few minutes before you come through.'

'Okay. Sure this will work?'

Shorty smiled. 'Trust me,' he said, then turned to stroll back into the storeroom.

Kelso watched the seconds tick by on the big clock on the wall and took five deep breaths as he looked around him. Sweat broke out on his forehead. He gave a subtle thumbs-up sign to the men who were getting ready to create a diversion. Pulling on the handle of the trolley, he steered it towards the entrance to the storeroom. *It's now or never*, he thought.

The argument started between two inmates. Their voices became more heated. One inmate was waving a pair of scissors in the face of the other man who knocked them out of his hand. The scissors skidded across the concrete floor. The hum of sewing machines had stopped and everyone looked on as the two men wrestled each other to the floor.

All hell let loose as inmates cheered and shouted while

banging tin mugs on their tables. The din in the workshop was deafening. Alarm bells rang as prison officers waded in to try to break up the fight. One of them fell over and the watching inmates howled with laughter.

In the ensuing chaos, Kelso slipped unseen into the storeroom. He glanced across and saw several inmates surrounding the civilian storeman. They were shouting and arguing to add to the bedlam in the workshop. Kelso ran up the concrete ramp to the loading area followed by Shorty. Kelso jumped into the back of the boxed lorry, made his way to the front and found the empty sack Shorty had left there for him.

With heart pounding and trembling hands, Kelso climbed inside the sack. Shorty crammed piles of offcuts around Kelso and pulled the ties tight. For good measure, he piled some full sacks on top. He then ran down the ramp to join the other inmates hounding the storeman.

More prison officers had rushed to the workshop to quell the riot. Three of them ran into the storeroom and pulled the inmates away from the storeman. 'Are all your men accounted for?' one of the officers shouted at the trembling man.

'Y-yes. They're all here.'

'Right, close the rear doors on the lorry and get it out of here – now!'

A few moments later, Kelso heard the driver's door slam shut and the engine spark into life. There was a harsh sound of grating gears and the lorry lurched forwards. *Just need to get past the front gate and I'm out!*

2

DCI Alex Fleming watched from an upstairs window to see the chief constable's car pulling into the car park. Superintendent Liz Temple, dressed in black suit and white shirt, had gone down to meet him. She strode across the tarmac as Matthew Upson climbed out of the rear passenger door.

'He's here,' Fleming said, coming out of his office to the open-plan area where DS Logan and DC Anderson sat.

'Invited to join them?' Logan asked Fleming.

'Not sure why, but yes. The super's going to call me.'

'Feel a bit sorry for him,' Logan said. 'They say the police and crime commissioner had it in for him from the day he was elected.'

Fleming shrugged. 'Too many unsolved murder cases, a few corrupt detectives, and a disgraced assistant chief constable all on Daubney's watch didn't help much.'

'Tough at the top, eh?'

'Of course, you wouldn't know about that, Sarge,' Anderson quipped.

'We only arrived in the office an hour ago and Naomi's already flinging insults at me,' Logan complained.

'Only joking, Sarge. You're far too sensitive.'

Logan screwed up a loose piece of paper and threw it across the adjoining desks at Anderson.

'Upson might wander round here after I've seen him, so be on your best behaviour. No fooling about.'

'When do we ever?' Logan asked with a smile.

'*We* don't,' Anderson said. 'It's just you.'

Fleming raised his eyes to the ceiling. 'All the same, Upson may be retiring but we still want to give a good impression.'

'As always,' Logan and Anderson said in unison.

Fleming laughed. 'Anyone for a coffee? Vending machine only. Round's on me.'

'Usual for me,' Logan said.

'Same,' came from Anderson. 'Thanks, sir.'

Fleming set off to the far end of the open-plan area to get the coffees.

When he returned, Logan was putting his phone down. 'Going to miss yours,' he said. 'Super's summonsed you.'

Fleming put the three coffees down on Anderson's desk. 'Looks like one of you gets two cups.'

'That'll be me,' Logan said. 'Seniority,' he added with a smile.

Fleming wagged a finger. 'Best behaviour, remember.' He laughed as he headed towards Temple's office.

~

Fleming knocked on Temple's door and heard her call him in. She was sitting at the small coffee table she used for informal meetings. Upson sat opposite her. 'Pull up a chair,' Temple said.

Upson rose from his chair and offered a hand. 'Good to see you, Fleming. I've heard good things about you. We need more like you on the force.'

'Thank you, sir.'

They took their seats as Temple poured coffee.

Upson looked at Fleming. 'I wanted to see you before I left. Wanted to thank you for the excellent work you're doing.' Upson coughed. 'Despite some rather awkward internal politics getting in the way at times.'

Fleming knew what he was talking about and wasn't sure how to respond. There had been a few hiccups during his first two cases since joining the major crime unit. 'I try never to let anything get in the way of a murder investigation.'

'Well... just so you know, I appreciate what you're doing.'

'Thanks. Looking forward to retirement, sir?' As soon as he said it, Fleming realised it wasn't the best thing to say.

Upson laughed. 'We all know it wasn't a matter of choice. Daubney more or less invited me to resign.' He tapped his hand on Fleming's arm. 'Remember that when the next police and crime commissioner elections are due.'

Fleming smiled. 'I will.'

'Matthew was telling me he and his wife are planning to move to Darmont,' Temple said.

Fleming raised an eyebrow. 'Oh?'

Upson stretched his legs. 'Yes, my daughter and the grandchildren live in London and Darmont has a station with a direct line. We can get there in less than an hour. It's also a picture-postcard village. Old church, pond, local butcher... and two good pubs.'

'Sounds good. Have you found somewhere yet?' Fleming asked.

'We've put an offer in which we're confident they'll accept. House prices there have fallen a bit.'

'Bit against the national trend. Any particular reason?'

'Property developer, Paul Canning, has put in a planning

application. It's for a major housing and shopping development on the outskirts of the village.'

'It's caused a bit of a stir by all accounts,' Temple said. 'It's on a greenfield site. The parish council has objected to it on the basis it flies in the face of the local neighbourhood plan. The district council seem to be in favour because it's in line with the county local plan for development. Things are getting a bit heated. Protests, death threats, and allegations of bribery and corruption.'

Upson sighed. 'Yes, all a bit unfortunate. Especially for local people trying to sell property.'

'Those on the edge of the site presumably,' Fleming guessed.

'Yes. The house we've made an offer on backs onto it. I do feel sorry for the people selling, but we can't offer more than the current market value.'

'And, if you ever decided to move again, you would have the same problem over the value of the house,' Fleming said.

'Exactly.'

'More coffee?' Temple asked.

Upson rose to his feet. 'No, thanks. Should get back to Kidlington. One or two people there I need to say cheerio to.' He shook Temple's hand before turning to Fleming. 'Carry on the good work, young man.' He grasped Fleming's hand with a firm grip.

Fleming took his leave, amused that Upson saw him as a young man. He'd turned thirty-nine a few months ago.

'We were all ready to be on our best behaviour,' Logan said, 'but he didn't come to see us.'

'Sorry, Harry. He had to go... people to see.'

'More important than us,' Logan mumbled.

Anderson laughed. 'A few minutes ago, you were saying you hoped he wouldn't come through. Can't do with all the forelock tugging, you said.'

Logan offered a shrug and grinned.

'He's moving to Darmont,' Fleming said. 'The super reckons there's trouble brewing there over a planning application.'

'Yes, I heard,' Anderson said. 'You never know, our next case may come from there.'

'Don't joke about things like that, Naomi,' Fleming said. 'Upson's going to live there.'

3

The lorry slowed and came to a stop. *This is it. Must be the front gate*, Kelso thought. Finding it airless inside the sack, he felt in his pocket for the scissors he'd picked up in the workshop. He felt tempted to slit the sack open. *Get through the gates first. Might check inside. Take no chances.*

'Just need to check in the back, mate,' Kelso heard a prison officer say. 'Bit of a commotion in the workshop, eh?'

Kelso's body tensed. It was stifling inside the sack and fluff from the offcuts made him want to sneeze. Sweat was running off his forehead. He heard the driver's door open and the sound of heavy boots crunching on the tarmac as the driver jumped down.

'Yeah,' the driver said. 'Don't know what happened. They were almost finished loading and alarm bells went off. Next thing I know, the storeman's slamming the rear doors shut and shouting at me to go.'

The sound of footsteps stopped at the back of the lorry.

'Never a dull moment here,' Kelso heard the prison officer say. 'Open the doors.'

Kelso's heart skipped a beat as the bolts slid back with a clang. He felt a blast of hot air as the doors opened and light filled the back of the vehicle. The lorry dipped on its suspension as a prison officer hauled himself inside. The officer was gasping with the effort and then there was silence. Boots scraped on the floor as the officer moved round what little space there was in the back. 'Full load you've got here,' the officer shouted out to the driver.

'Like I said, we'd about finished loading.'

Kelso heard a grunt and boots hitting the ground.

'All looks okay,' the officer said. 'See you next time.'

'Sure.'

The doors close with a thump and the driver rammed the bolts home.

A few seconds later, the driver's door slammed shut, the engine revved and the lorry lurched forward. Kelso could hear the metallic screeching of the prison gates swinging shut. He wasted no time getting the scissors out to cut the sack open. He breathed in hard, crawled out, and made his way to the rear of the lorry. If Oscar, or whatever his name was, got his part of the plan right, he'd be waiting for the lorry to appear.

Officers had brought the riot in the workshop under control. They'd decided to stop the inmates working for the day and send them back to their cells. One of the officers counted them all out. 'Where's Kelso?' he shouted.

No one spoke. Everyone looked blankly at one another.

The officer in charge was first to react. 'Fuck! The textiles lorry.' He pulled his radio off its clip on his shirt and radioed the front gate. 'Is the textiles lorry still there?' he shouted.

There was the sound of crackling before a voice came

through loud and clear. 'Left a few minutes ago. What's the problem?'

'We have an escapee. Jack Kelso's in it!'

'We checked. He wasn't there.'

'He bloody well was! He must have been buried under all the sacks.'

'Fuck!'

'Get some officers out in cars, chase after it, and ring the police. Tell them what's happened and give them the lorry reg number. We should catch them before they get too far.'

Kelso was standing ready at the back of the lorry when he heard the sudden squeal of brakes. The vehicle shuddered to a halt, throwing him into the rear doors. He fell to the floor, banging his head in the process. Only a few minutes had passed since they'd left the prison.

There was shouting outside and Kelso heard the driver's door open. 'Don't shoot!' he heard the driver call out.

Kelso opened his eyes wide. *They're armed!*

A few seconds later, the rear doors swung open. A terrified driver stood outside, held up by two hooded men armed with handguns.

'Out! Quick!' one of the men shouted.

Kelso recognised the faint Italian accent straight away.

Oscar prodded the driver with his gun. 'Mobile. Give me your mobile.'

The driver handed it over with shaking hands.

The other man had gone to the front of the lorry and pulled the ignition keys out.

'Get in the back,' Oscar ordered the driver who scrambled in.

Oscar slammed the doors shut and rammed the bolts home. 'In the car up front,' he shouted to Kelso.

Kelso flung himself in the back of a BMW X5 as Oscar and his accomplice jumped in the front. The accomplice took the driver's seat, gunned the engine and sped off, tyres spinning.

'Who are you?' Kelso asked the man he knew as Oscar.

'Guerra… Marco Guerra at your service,' he said, pulling his hood off.

'I take it the car's either stolen or has false number plates so the police can't trace it to you,' Kelso said. 'Chances are the lorry driver clocked the registration. The police will be patrolling the whole area in minutes.'

'What do you take me for, Kelso? I know what I'm doing. Don't try to tell me how to do my job. It's all taken care of.'

Kelso glared at Guerra. 'Just checking.'

'Yes, the car's stolen. We're only going half a mile. I've got a van parked off the road in a small clearing in the woods. We torch this one and take off in the van. After five miles and we're well clear, we transfer again to my car.'

'Right. You sure torching the car will destroy all forensic evidence?'

Guerra's eyes flashed. 'Fuck's sake, Kelso. It doesn't matter if they find your fingerprints or DNA. They know it was you who escaped.'

'I was thinking more that they might find evidence to link you to it.'

'Unlike you, Kelso, I have no criminal record. Police never managed to catch up with me. Anyway, if you hadn't noticed, me and my driver mate here are wearing gloves and we'll burn the clothes.'

'Got a change of clothes for me?'

'In the van. You can change in the back.'

Five minutes later, they were leaving the burning X5 behind.

~

Eight prison officers in two cars sped out of the prison car park. They headed off down the country road where they knew the textiles lorry would have gone. After a mile and a half, they found it. Black skid marks were visible behind the vehicle.

A senior officer called Thomas was first out of the cars. 'Looks like we've missed him,' he said. Running over to the rear doors of the vehicle, he heard the driver banging and shouting for help. 'It's okay, we're here,' Thomas shouted, pulling back the bolts. He yanked the doors open and found a shaking driver with sweat pouring down his face.

'There were two men... in masks... they had guns. Thought they were going to shoot me!' the man blurted out.

'Okay, take it easy,' Thomas said. 'What vehicle were they in and which way did they go?'

'It was a black car... BMW. They went that way,' the driver said, pointing a trembling finger.

Thomas nodded at one of the other officers. 'You stay here with the driver... and let the police know where you are. The rest of you get in the cars. Let's go!'

They saw the black smoke first, then the car, toxic gas and red flames still belching up into the sky.

The two cars screeched to a halt. Thomas was driving the first car and thumped his fists on the steering wheel. 'Fuck! We're too late. They must have had another vehicle and will be God knows where by now.'

4

It wasn't a dog walker or a jogger that found the body. It was two teenagers looking for a golf ball.

Deano and Chippy had set off early to walk to the playing fields in Darmont, down past the old church and village pond. When they got there, a sign at the entrance warned them golf practice wasn't allowed on the playing fields. They ignored it and carried on to the far end beyond the football pitch.

Chippy looked anxiously back towards the village hall. 'You see the car up there?'

'Yeah, why?'

'Can't see anyone about. Think someone's in the hall? Don't want to get caught playing golf.'

'Nah. It's Saturday. There won't be anyone there.'

Chippy was still uneasy. 'So where are they?'

'Look, if you're worried about playing, why didn't you say so before we walked all the way down here?'

'Sorry, Deano. Didn't think.'

Deano slapped Chippy on the back. He'd given his friend the nickname due to his love of chips, not because of his dubious skill at chipping a golf ball. 'Don't worry, mate,' he said, setting his golf bag down on the grass and pulling out a driver. 'They might have parked there to take a dog for a walk down by the woods. It won't be anyone official.'

'Okay. You're not going to use that thing here, are you?' Chippy asked.

'Yeah, why not? I won't hit it too far.'

Both boys had grown up in the village. It was a scenic place, off the beaten track with a population of around three thousand. No main roads passed through, just a network of narrow country lanes. There was a railway station which also served a local town five miles away. It was a direct line into London and you could be there in under an hour.

The Horse and Hounds pub was a popular eating place, while the Down Inn was more a traditional locals' pub. Villagers raved about the quality of meat and pies sold by the local butcher. The post office also served as a small convenience store. A medical practice sat in the centre of the village.

Deano bent down, stuck a long wooden tee in the grass, and placed a worn-looking golf ball on top.

'Bet you overhit it,' Chippy said.

Deano stood up and took a practice swing with his club. 'Watch and learn.'

He stood back from the ball, keeping it in line with the inside of his left foot and took a slow swing back. Unleashing the club with all his might he smashed it into the ball. It lifted into the air. Both boys watched as it veered to the right and dropped into the trees on the edge of the playing field.

'You see that?' Deano said. 'Must have hit it over a hundred and fifty yards!'

'Yeah,' Chippy agreed, 'but hardly a straight line. Doubt we'll find it.'

'Let's go look.'

Chippy giggled. 'Hope there isn't someone walking a dog in there. Might find a dead body with your ball next to it.'

'Ha, ha, very funny.'

The boys left their golf bags where they were and set off to look for the ball.

'Think I got a line on it,' Deano said. 'Came in about here.'

'Nah, much further to the right. Something wrong with your eyesight, mate,' Chippy said, disappearing into the trees.

'Course,' Deano shouted, 'once it hit a tree, it could have bounced anywhere.'

'Yeah, yeah. If I find it over here, you'll say it was deflected.'

Deano heard Chippy thrashing a club about in the bushes. Suddenly there was silence, then the sound of running feet.

Chippy appeared from behind a bush, ashen-faced.

Deano frowned. 'You find it?'

'Bloody hell, Deano, you've killed someone!'

Deano's mouth dropped open. 'Stop fucking about, Chippy. Not funny.'

'I'm not... not joking! There's a man lying under a bush. Oh, God, we're right in the shit now!'

Deano's eyes widened and the colour drained from his face. 'Where?'

Chippy turned. 'Over here.'

Deano followed him a few yards into the undergrowth. He saw the feet first and pushed the bushes to one side to reveal the rest of the body. After breathing out a sigh of relief that it wasn't his golf ball which had caused the damage, he vomited.

Chippy stood there helpless.

When Deano had stopped throwing up, he looked wide-eyed at Chippy. 'It wasn't my golf ball that put two holes in his head. He's been shot.'

Chippy was shaking. His eyes darted from side to side as though expecting someone with a gun to appear out of the bushes. 'Wha… what!'

Deano had recovered his senses and was pulling his mobile out of his pocket to dial 999.

5

Blue-and-white tape crossed the entrance to the village hall and playing fields. A uniformed officer stood guard and waved the marked Vauxhall Astra into the car park. Fleming and Logan climbed out and donned protective clothing and elasticated overshoes.

'Where's the body?' Fleming asked the young officer.

The officer pointed across the playing field. 'Far end, just inside the trees. You'll see the tape marking out the crime scene.'

'The super did reckon there was trouble brewing here, but I'll bet she didn't think it would be this,' Logan said.

They reached the inner cordon where another officer logged their names in a notebook. Ducking under the tape, the two detectives headed off into the edge of the woods. SOCOs were already at work searching the area around the body.

'DCI Fleming?' asked a man appearing from behind a bush.

'Yes, and this is DS Logan,' Fleming replied, pointing to his colleague.

'Right. I'm DI Oliver. Local CID. Pathologist hasn't arrived yet. No one's touched the body.'

Fleming nodded. 'Know who it is?'

'One of the uniforms knew. Local man by the name of Slater… Tom Slater. BMW up by the village hall is his.'

'SOCOs checking it?'

'They will when they're done here.'

'Was it locked or unlocked?'

'Locked.'

'CCTV up by the village hall?'

'Having it checked.'

'Right, let's have a look at the body.'

Slater was lying on his back, blank eyes staring up at them. There was one bullet hole in the centre of his forehead. A second had penetrated his cheekbone under the right eye. He wore casual clothes: jeans, blue shirt and a light-brown blazer. Fleming knelt down and checked his pockets.

There wasn't much apart from keys and a wallet. A quick look inside the wallet revealed a driving licence confirming the man's identity. Logan wandered round searching the ground nearby.

Fleming handed the contents over to Oliver. 'Get the SOCOs to bag these.'

'Right.'

'Who found the body?' Fleming asked.

'Two local boys,' Oliver said. 'Shook them up a bit.'

'Get statements though?'

'Down at the station now. Their parents are with them.'

'Send their statements over to me in the major crime unit when they're done.'

'Sure.'

'What were they doing here?'

Oliver shrugged and pursed his lips. 'It'll be in their statements.'

'Was Slater married?'

'Yes, a couple of my officers have been round to see his wife.'

'Let me have her address. I'll need to speak to her.'

'I'll send it over with the statements.'

'Thanks. I gather things have been getting a bit heated in the village over a proposed development.'

Oliver sighed. 'Yes. Protests, anger, even some death threats.'

'But not taken seriously?' Fleming guessed.

'No. People do and say things in the heat of the moment. There's been no physical assaults.'

'Until now,' Fleming said, looking down at Slater's body.

'You think it could be to do with the protests?'

'Ever had anything like this happen here before?'

'Not that I know of, no.'

'So I wouldn't rule it out.'

Logan strolled back into sight holding up a golf ball. 'Don't suppose it's worth getting the SOCOs to bag this,' he said with a smile.

Fleming chuckled. 'I know two boys who might have been looking for that.'

'Nathan's here,' Logan said, looking over Fleming's shoulder.

'Dr Nathan Kumar,' Fleming explained to Oliver. 'Home Office registered pathologist.'

'Hello, Alex. Got here before me, I see. Okay to have a look at the body?'

'Sure. Go ahead.'

Fleming looked at Logan and pointed up towards the village hall. 'I'm curious why Slater's BMW is up there,' he mused. 'He's a local man and it's not a big village. If he decided to go for a walk, why not go all the way?'

'Could be he preferred soft ground rather than pounding the streets.'

'He's wearing slip-ons, not walking boots or sturdy shoes.'

'So what are you thinking?'

'He wasn't going for a walk, and there's no sign of a struggle.

This has all the hallmarks of a professional hit. I reckon the killer arranged to meet Slater by the village hall for some reason. Then forced him over to the trees at gunpoint.'

'Or shot him someplace else and dumped him here.'

'Doesn't answer the question why Slater parked his BMW where he did. It would also be a bit difficult to manhandle a body all the way across the playing field. And, there are no vehicle tyre tracks.'

'Okay. Let's assume the killer did arrange to meet Slater at the village hall. That would suggest he knew the killer. Still begs the question why Slater came in his car.'

'Maybe he'd been some other place when he got the call, or the killer told him to come here.'

Logan's face lit up. 'Makes finding the killer a bit easier if Slater did know him... or her.'

'Depends on how many people he knew, and if they were aware who else he knew.'

Logan laughed. 'Beginning to sound like an extract from *Yes Minister.*'

'Nice to see a sense of humour maintained,' Kumar said as he approached.

'Logan coming out with one of his wisecracks,' Fleming said. 'Initial thoughts, Nathan?'

'Not much apart from the obvious. Shot twice through the head. Close range. The angle of entry and exit points of the bullets suggest the victim was standing facing the killer. Looks like he was holding the gun at roughly the same height as the victim's head.'

'So a man, or woman, of a similar height?'

'Could be. Death would have been almost instant. If the SOCOs recover the bullets, ballistics should be able to confirm what type of gun the killer used. I'd say a nine-millimetre handgun.'

'Approximate time of death?'

'About twelve to fifteen hours ago. I'll send you a full report once I get the body back to the mortuary.'

'Okay, thanks.'

Fleming waved Oliver over who was talking to one of the SOCOs. 'Can you put out an appeal for any witnesses to come forward? Get your men to conduct local house-to-house enquiries. Did anyone see or hear anything suspicious. Any sightings of vehicles nearby yesterday... late afternoon, evening.'

'On it.'

Fleming turned to Logan. 'We need contact details for Slater's family, friends and colleagues. Slater's phone would be a starting point. Forensics and pathology reports will help inform further lines of enquiry.'

'So this is the quiet village the chief constable wants to move to,' Logan muttered as they made their way back to their car.

6

Fleming was on his way to Liz Temple's office. He'd left Logan and Anderson setting up the small incident room. They didn't need a large one. Staff were in short supply these days. Logan had cleared the whiteboard of everything from a previous investigation. They'd stored all the details and files in archives.

Temple's door was open. Fleming gave a couple of knocks in any case and entered. She was sitting behind her desk looking at a newspaper. Fleming thought she looked older than her forty-eight years. She'd swept her black shoulder-length hair back into a bun and signs of grey were visible. He knew Temple was under a lot of pressure. Despite staff shortages, the police and crime commissioner still pressed for quick results.

'Seen this?' Temple asked.

'What is it, ma'am?'

'Reporter called Zoe Dunbar's written an article about local unrest over a planning application. Paul Canning submitted it for a major housing and shopping development in Darmont.'

'Zoe Dunbar, eh?'

'Know her?'

'I do. She's a freelance journalist. Came across her on my last case. She's persistent. Bit pushy.'

'Know a reporter who isn't?'

'Can't say I do. Anything interesting in the article?'

Temple shook her head. 'She's saying how it used to be a quiet little backwater and now it's all getting rather heated with feelings running high.'

'It's understandable if what the chief constable said about house prices is anything to go by.'

'One thing for people to get upset. But now we have a death in Darmont.'

'I'm sure it's not the first.'

'Don't play semantics with me, Alex. You know what I mean. I'm not in the mood for frivolity right now. First *murder* if you want to be pedantic.'

Fleming looked at Temple. She wasn't usually so tetchy. 'Sorry, ma'am. Everything okay?'

Temple offered a weak smile. 'I'm tired, that's all. Pressure being short-staffed.'

'Daubney appointed a new chief constable yet?'

'No word on that front.'

'Taking his time, isn't he?'

Temple shrugged. 'How did you and Logan get on in Darmont? Got initial thoughts on an investigative strategy?'

'First priority is safety of the public. As you say, feelings are running high and the killer used a firearm. We need to get bobbies visible on the streets over the next few days. Maybe have a short briefing meeting to reassure people. Could y–'

'You can do it,' Temple cut in. 'What else?'

'Victim's from Darmont... Tom Slater. I've got local CID arranging house-to-house. They're going to issue an appeal for any possible witnesses to come forward. And I've asked for a CCTV check on the car park where they found Slater's car.'

'Good.'

'Two boys discovered the body. CID are sending over the statements to me. I need to speak to Slater's wife as a priority. We'll also have to question Slater's friends, family and colleagues. Everyone he knew. Oh, and I'm waiting to see if Forensics find anything on Slater's mobile.'

'Thanks, Alex. Keep me informed.'

'Right. Sure you're okay?'

'Thanks for the concern. I'm fine.'

Fleming was almost out of the door when Temple called after him. 'You used to work for the Met before you came here, didn't you?'

Fleming stopped, turned. 'I did, yes. Why?'

'Ever come across a man by the name of Kelso... Jack Kelso?'

'If I recall, he's in prison for an armed robbery in London some years back. I may have interviewed him at some point.'

'You weren't the SIO then?'

'No. Why?'

'I heard he escaped from prison yesterday. Was going to warn you to watch your back if it was you who put him inside.'

'Thanks for telling me.'

Fleming was deep in thought as he made his way back to the incident room to see how Logan and Anderson were doing.

Logan had his mobile to his ear. 'Thanks for the heads-up. I'll let him know.'

'Him being me?' Fleming asked.

'Timely entrance, boss. That was an old mate who knows someone in the Met. Seems some guy you had dealings with a while back has escaped from prison.'

'Jack Kelso.'

'You've heard then?'

'Super told me.'

'Any need to watch your back?'

'Nah. I wasn't the SIO who nicked him. I did interview him once if I remember. Can I smell coffee?'

'You can,' Anderson confirmed. 'Want one?'

'That would be great,' Fleming said, turning to look at the whiteboard Logan had started writing on. He'd put Slater's name at the top with three lines drawn down to headings showing *opportunity*, *means*, and *motive*. There was a question mark under *opportunity*. Under *means*, he'd scribbled *handgun, type not yet confirmed*. The third line caught Fleming's attention. Logan had written *anger over the proposed development*, followed by another question mark.

Fleming pointed to the motive entry. 'Interesting you've marked that as a possible reason, Harry. Slater was a local man. If anything, he would be one of the angry residents. So why would someone shoot him?'

'I did wonder about that. At first, I thought he could have been stirring things up against the developer who had him silenced. I did a bit of checking while you were with the super.'

'And?'

'Slater was Paul Canning's personal assistant. Could have been a warning to Canning... or Slater was easier to target. Either way, he was on the developer's side. There may have been even more anger against him because he was a local.'

Fleming nodded his understanding. 'Seen as a traitor in the camp, eh?'

'That's what I was thinking.'

Anderson returned with Fleming's coffee. 'Who's the traitor then?'

Fleming took the coffee from Anderson. 'Thanks. Some residents in Darmont might have thought Slater was.'

7

The mansion was set in three acres of idyllic woodland a few miles from Henley-on-Thames. It had ten bedrooms, four reception rooms and eight bathrooms. Neat gardens surrounded the house and at the rear was a heated swimming pool and a tennis court. Millionaire property developer, Paul Canning, had purchased the property five years earlier. He'd paid the princely sum of five million pounds. Access to the house was off a small country lane through tall electronic gates. From there, a long gravel driveway wound its way through the grounds.

Canning's rich father had sent him to public school and he went on to Cambridge University to study economics. Having obtained a first-class degree, he started work for an estate agent friend of his father's. He stayed there until his father died of a heart attack, leaving Canning with a large fortune.

Using the money, Canning bought and refurbished some run-down flats in London. He then sold them for a massive profit. As the cash rolled in, he bought more flats and old terraced houses. He subdivided some of the larger properties into apartments and let rooms. He'd made his first million by the age of forty-two. Not satisfied with his little empire, Canning moved into planning major property developments. He then set up a complex network of companies to control his business interests.

After dinner, Canning had retired to a small reception room to read a local newspaper while puffing on a large cigar. After a day of video-conference meetings, phone calls and going through piles of paperwork, he'd decided to call it a day. His fifty-five-year-old wife, Jane, had taken a break from tidying up in the kitchen to come and pour him a brandy. Five years older than his wife, Canning still had a full head of white hair, brushed back from his forehead. The green eyes were still bright. But the double chin, wrinkled face and pallid features told a story of a man who had abused life over the years. An ample stomach showed he liked his food and didn't much like exercise. His stooped frame made him look shorter than his five foot ten.

'There you are,' Jane said, handing her husband the glass of brandy.

Canning looked at it, frowning. He lifted the glass. 'Top it up a bit. Can't abide pub measures.'

Jane shot him a dark glare.

Canning knew she disapproved, but he would do what he wanted. That's what he always did. 'About a third full will do.'

Jane poured until the glass was half full. 'I said a third, woman! Didn't you hear what I said?'

'I heard. Saving you the trouble of getting up to refill it later. And, by the way, I've told you before, I don't like you smoking in the house.'

Canning's eyes narrowed. 'I don't care what you don't like. I can do what I bloody well want in my own house. The one, I shouldn't have to remind you, I paid for.'

Chastised, Jane changed the subject. 'Are you reading the article about local opposition to your planning application?'

'I am indeed. As it happens, this reporter... Zoe Dunbar... wants to interview me about the plans.'

'You're not going to speak to her, are you?'

'I'm thinking about it.'

'Is that wise?'

Canning scowled. 'I don't need you to tell me what's wise.'

'Fine.'

'Anyway,' Canning added, 'it's a good way to get free publicity. I can get her to put a positive spin on it. Might bring some of the protesters round to my way of thinking. I could offer her a little... shall we say... cash incentive.'

'Well... if you think it might help.'

'It will. Didn't get to where I am today without knowing how to pull strings.'

'You didn't make your fortune by being nice to people, that's for sure.'

'I'm not in business to make friends. I'm in it to make money.'

Jane pointed to the newspaper. 'If the article's anything to go by, you're not making any friends in Darmont.'

'Do I give a fuck?'

Jane sighed. 'I doubt it. What time are you expecting Makayla?'

Canning looked at his watch. 'Any minute if she's on time,' he said, grabbing hold of the buffalo-horn handle of his ebony cane. He hauled himself out of the chair and hobbled over to the window. 'There, told you, she's just pulled into the driveway. Bang on time as usual. Go and let her in, there's a dear.'

~

Makayla Yamamura was Canning's accountant. She was forty, single, English, but of Japanese parentage. She pulled up by the front of Canning's mansion with the tyres of her bright-red Alfa Romeo Giulia crunching on the gravel.

Looking in the rear-view mirror, she checked her short copper hair. Satisfied it was in place, she topped up her red lipstick, and adjusted her silk teal-blue neck scarf. She liked to wear bright colours – they lifted the white pallor of her face. Content she looked presentable, she pushed the car door open and stepped out onto the gravel. She turned and walked up to the front door which opened before she reached it.

'Paul saw you arrive,' Jane said, holding the door open for Makayla. 'He's in the reception room through the hall on the left.'

Makayla smiled and walked over to Jane. 'Thanks. I just need to change my shoes.' She put a hand into her large bag and pulled out a pair of glossy red ones. They were a good match with her red suit and pink shirt. Putting her flat canvas driving shoes in the bag she made her way through the hallway.

Canning had returned to his chair and was taking a sip of his brandy when Makayla entered the room. 'Ah, Makayla! Help yourself to a drink.' He pointed to the drinks cabinet in the corner.

'I'm fine. Won't stay long. Have the police been to see you about Tom?'

'No, not yet. Dreadful business, eh?'

Makayla shuddered. 'Yes. Makes me nervous after the death threats you've had. Did Tom ever say anyone had threatened him?'

'He had a note. Shrugged it off.'

'All the same, bit scary.'

Canning showed no sympathy for the concern. 'I just wanted to confirm Tom's work on planning Isa Al Jameel's visit has paid off. Isa and his son, Dani, are coming to stay here for a few days. He's a wealthy Saudi businessman. What's important is, he's interested in investing in my development plans for Darmont. When he arrives, I want you to impress him with the finances we've managed to secure already. We need to convince him my scheme's going to reap big rewards.'

'We've still got to get planning approval.'

'I'm working on that.'

'By doing what, exactly?'

'The prime minister's had a cabinet reshuffle. He's appointed Walter Hammond as secretary of state for housing, communities and local government.'

Canning blew smoke from his cigar up towards the ceiling. 'Met Hammond at university. We were friends, but lost touch after graduating. He became an MP and I rekindled the friendship. Thought he might be a useful contact one day.'

'And?'

'Let's say I have a certain amount of persuasive influence over him.'

Makayla's eyes lit up. 'Talking of persuasion, I have something of interest for you.'

'Oh?'

'An accountant friend of mine told me about a failed business enterprise. The woman behind it happens to be the wife of the council planning officer, Eric Blunt. They're up to their necks in debt.'

Canning smiled. 'Is that so? I do believe Mr Blunt could be open to a bit of bribery.'

8

Fleming and Anderson found Gale Slater's house in a small cluster of eight new houses in the centre of Darmont. Builders had bought up every square foot of derelict land within the village. New builds had appeared everywhere over the past four years. There had been no objections to those but Canning's plan for a major housing and shopping development was another matter. It would be on greenfield land.

The Slaters' was a detached house with a small neat garden at the front. A two-year-old grey Mini Cooper sat on the red block-paving driveway. Fleming assumed it belonged to Mrs Slater. Forensics had taken her husband's BMW away for examination.

Fleming paused for a second at the front door before ringing the bell. He glanced at Anderson. 'Ready? Can be a little awkward at times questioning a spouse so soon after someone has killed their partner.'

Anderson smiled. 'I'm okay, sir.'

Fleming pushed the bell and a minute later a slim, frail-looking woman with a gaunt, lined face opened the door. She had shoulder-length unkempt auburn hair and wore jeans and a white shirt. The green cardigan matched the colour of her eyes. Fleming guessed she was in her fifties, but thought recent events had most likely aged her.

'Mrs Slater? DCI Fleming and DC Anderson. I phoned.'

'Oh, yes, do come in. It's Gale, by the way. Mrs Slater is far too formal.'

Fleming smiled. 'We won't take up too much of your time. But I'm afraid we do need to ask you some questions if that's okay?'

'Yes, fine.' Gale led them through into a large rectangular lounge. A long settee with a grey velvet cover sat in front of the window with matching chairs on each side. 'Have a seat. Can I get you both anything?'

'No, we're okay. Don't go to any bother,' Fleming said, sitting on the settee. Anderson took a chair and pulled out her notebook.

Fleming saw the redness in Gale's eyes. 'I hope this isn't too painful for you, but it would be good if we can get a few details about Tom.'

A clock chimed somewhere in the background as Gale spoke. 'You have a job to do. I'll be as helpful as I can.'

Fleming nodded. 'Okay. When did you last see Tom?'

Tears welled up in Gale's eyes and she dabbed at them with a handkerchief. 'Last... last Friday. He said he was going to meet Paul.'

'Mr Canning?'

'Yes.'

'He went in his car?'

'Yes.'

'So why would he park it at the village hall?'

Gale dabbed at her eyes again. 'I've no idea.'

Anderson looked up from her notebook. 'Is it possible he was with Mr Canning and got a phone call from someone who asked to meet him at the village hall? If that were the case, he might have driven straight there rather than come home first.'

Gale shrugged. 'I suppose so.'

'What did you do when he didn't come home on Friday night?'

'Tom said he might stay over, which was odd because he wasn't getting on very well with Paul lately.'

Fleming creased his brow. 'Why was that?'

Gale sighed. 'Tom was a heavy gambler. He'd lost a lot of money and asked Paul for a pay rise. Paul refused. Things became strained between them.'

'How had Tom been, apart from that. Was he his normal self?'

Gale's forehead creased as though she was deep in thought. 'He went to London a couple of weeks ago. Said he had a meeting with someone. Told me it was to do with the development. He went again last week and seemed a bit more relaxed after the second meeting. He stayed overnight in a hotel in Leicester Square.'

'Know which one?'

'I made a note of it.' Gale went over to a bureau and pulled out a piece of paper. She handed it to Anderson with a shaking hand.

'Do you know who he went to see?' Fleming asked.

'No. He was very secretive about it all. I didn't ask too much. I had a feeling he was going back to some of his old gambling haunts. He used to live in London. Worked for a letting agency there before he went to work for Paul.' Gale blew her nose. 'Tom was married, but they divorced. We got together, married and moved up here to Darmont a few years later.'

'Was there anything else about his behaviour which seemed out of the ordinary in the last couple of weeks or so?'

'He was concerned about the death threats he and Paul had both received.'

'By email, letter... phone calls?'

'A note pushed through the letter box.'

'Have you still got it?'

'Afraid not. Tom threw it in the bin. He was worried though. Not only about the note. It was the relationship with Paul that was bothering him. Paul can be an arrogant sod. He's used to getting his own way and is quick to dismiss people who disagree with him.'

'Dismiss, as in, sack?'

'The thought had crossed Tom's mind, but no, it was more like have nothing more to do with people he fell out with.'

'Working relationships had become untenable?'

'I suppose so. Tom had started talking about packing his job in and us moving to Spain.'

'Sounds like he might have feared for his life.'

'I don't think I can stay here now. I don't know what to do,' Gale sobbed.

'Do you have any family? Anyone who can be around to support you for a while.'

'My parents are no longer with us. Tom's mum and dad still live in London, but they're both in their eighties. I was never very close to them.'

'Any children?'

'I have a son from a previous marriage, Rashad.'

'Your ex-husband was foreign?'

'Iranian. Abdul Yousefi. We lived in London. Abdul left us and went back to Iran. He was killed in a car accident.'

'Where is your son now?'

'He's a bit of a hippie. He lives with some squatters in a small commune in west London. It's an old disused factory building.'

'I'll need to speak to him. Have you got the address and a photo I can take?'

Gale went over to the bureau again and pulled out an address book and a photo album.

Anderson held out her hand to take them. 'Still using his father's surname?' she asked as she scribbled the address in her notebook.

'Yes. I ought to tell you though, he and Tom never got on.'

'Oh?'

'Tom thought he was lazy. Rashad left school with no qualifications and got a job as an apprentice plumber. Didn't last long. He got into drugs and his boss sacked him. Tom and Rashad used to argue all the time. Then, one day, Tom blew his top and told Rashad he was cutting him out of his will and told him to leave.'

'What did you do about that?' Fleming asked.

'I tried to calm things down, but the damage had been done. Tom wouldn't relent and Rashad packed a bag and left.'

'How old is he?'

'Twenty-two.'

'Are you still in touch with him though?'

'We speak from time to time.'

'Does he know what happened to Tom?'

'Yes. I rang him.'

'What was his reaction?'

Gale started to cry again. 'He... he said, good riddance.'

While Fleming was asking questions, Anderson had pulled out her mobile and had taken a picture of Yousefi's photo. She returned the album and address book to Gale and put a hand on her shoulder. 'I'm so sorry.'

Fleming coughed. 'One more question, Gale. Is there anyone you can think of who might have sent the death threat?'

'There's a local man. Nasty piece of work. He's a self-employed electrician. Happens to be one of the men leading the protests against Paul's planning application. He had a big row with Tom at the parish council office after a public information meeting. Then there was a bit of a scuffle outside a pub a few days later. They say he has a previous conviction for assault.'

'His name?'

'Quinn, Vic Quinn.'

'Thank you so much for your time,' Fleming said, rising to go. 'One last thing. Some officers will need to come round to search the house if that's okay.'

Gale nodded and dabbed at her eyes once more.

'Rashad Yousefi and Vic Quinn are definitely two men we need to question,' Fleming said to Anderson as they shut the front door behind them.

9

Fleming and Anderson left Gale Slater's house and walked back to Fleming's old Porsche 911. 'I'd like to have a quick look at the proposed development site. Then we'll go to see Mrs Lamb,' Fleming said, holding the passenger door open for Anderson.

'Be interesting to see what it's all about,' Anderson agreed.

Fleming walked round the car, climbed into the driving seat and turned the ignition key. The engine turned over with a few grating noises before bursting into life. 'Might need to think of changing this soon. It's beginning to sound a bit rough.'

'It's a lovely car though,' Anderson said. 'How old?'

'Seventeen. Served me well.'

'What would you get, sir?' Anderson asked as Fleming eased out of the cul-de-sac where he'd parked and turned right.

'Might get an Audi Q5.'

Fleming carried on through the centre of the village, past the church and pond. The playing fields and village hall were on the left. After a few hundred yards, he saw a sign for the train station. He followed the signs and drove past the entrance, noting the car park full of vehicles. 'Presumably commuters,'

Fleming guessed. 'The chief constable reckoned you can get into London in less than an hour.'

'Could be why Paul Canning thought it would be an ideal place for a housing and shopping development.'

Past the station, Fleming followed the road round the village, turned right and parked. They could see the area earmarked for the planned building. At the far end they saw a line of houses which would be right on the edge of the development.

'I guess those are the homes over there which are losing value,' Fleming said, pointing over the field.

'Not sure I would want a house there,' Anderson said. 'It's not only because it's spoiling their view of farm fields to the hills. It's going to be the noise and disruption during the building phase.'

'Reckon you're right, Naomi. Let's go see if we can find Mrs Lamb.'

They found Kathy Lamb's 1930s semi-detached house a hundred yards down from the village hall. Fleming saw the curtains twitch as they climbed out of the car and walked up the driveway. He rang the bell and, after a few seconds, the door opened to reveal a woman in her sixties with short grey hair. She wore a blue top and a long silver necklace hung from her neck. The flat black shoes matched the colour of her loose-fitting trousers.

Fleming flashed his warrant card. 'DCI Fleming and DC Anderson.'

'Yes, yes. Do come in.' Fleming noticed the gravelly voice of a heavy smoker.

Kathy showed them into a large living room with tasteful

furnishings. 'Have a seat.' She waved at the settee and an array of chairs in the room.

'Thanks. You told local CID you think you might have seen something on the day Tom Slater was murdered,' Fleming prompted.

'Yes, I saw the notice on the road outside the village hall. It was asking for anyone who saw anything suspicious last Friday to come forward.'

'What exactly did you see?' Fleming asked.

'Well, I was cleaning the front window when I heard a squeal of tyres. Mind you, that's not so unusual. Lots of youngsters on motorbikes go racing around. Mark my words, someone's going to get killed one of these days.'

'And after the squeal of tyres?'

'A car... it went past at such a speed. I knocked on the window and shouted for him to slow down.' Kathy laughed. 'Then I realised that wasn't going to do much good. He was hardly going to hear me, was he?'

'It was definitely a man?'

'Oh, yes.'

'Can you describe him?'

'Not really. He'd turned his face away from me and he was gone in an instant.'

'What kind of car was it?' Fleming asked.

'I'm not very good with car makes.'

'Big or small?' Anderson asked.

'It was quite big.'

'Colour?' Anderson prompted.

'Black, could have been dark grey.'

'Did you get a glimpse of the vehicle registration by any chance?' Fleming asked.

'There was a number. Think it was seventeen.'

'Remember any letters?'

'The first letter could have been an L. Sorry, it all happened so fast.'

'Don't worry, Mrs Lamb. You've been very helpful. By the way, where is the parish council office?'

'Oh, just down the road. It's attached at the end of the village hall. Been some commotion out there, I can tell you.'

'Protesters?' Fleming prompted.

'Yes, but not against the parish council. They're as angry as anyone over the plans. It's at odds with the local neighbourhood plan. It's the district council and the developer everyone is upset with. People have been writing to them, and the local MP.'

'Did you know Mr Slater?'

'Knew of him, but not personally, no. I know he worked for the developer. Took a lot of stick I gather.'

'From anyone in particular?'

'Wouldn't want to tell tales, but there's a village man whose mother is affected by the threat of the development being approved. She's trying to sell her house and has already had to knock thousands off the asking price. Still can't find a buyer. The back of her house looks over to where they're planning to build hundreds of houses. She's right on the edge of the village and has beautiful views over to the hills. Bloody disgrace if they approve the application. It's greenfield land. Mrs Quinn is on the verge of a nervous breakdown.'

'Her son is Vic Quinn?'

'Yes. He's one of the most vocal of the protesters. He goes to all the meetings at the parish council. Had a run-in with Mr Slater after a public information meeting held in the village hall. Heard there was a bit of a skirmish as well... outside the Down Inn.'

10

There was only a light breeze and a few white clouds drifted across the sky. Canning was leaning against the bonnet of his blue Land Rover Discovery. 'Over there,' he said, pointing his walking cane, 'is the top end of the development.' He swept the cane round in a wide arc. 'And all over those two fields will be the first phase of 480 detached and semi-detached houses.'

Eric Blunt, the council planning officer, shielded his eyes against the glare of the sun. The cream baseball cap he was wearing didn't quite go with the white shirt, red tie and grey trousers. But it did keep the sun off his balding head. He'd flung his suit jacket onto the back seat of his car and rolled up his shirtsleeves. He was a scrawny man in his mid-forties, of medium height, and his chin sported the hint of a stubble beard. 'It's useful to see the land as opposed to looking at a plan on paper,' he said.

'Couldn't agree more, Eric. Okay if I call you Eric?'

Blunt smiled. 'It's my name.' There was a slight lisp in his voice.

Canning pointed his cane again. 'Down at the bottom end

over there, there'll be a play area for children. There'll also be a small wooded park and gardens with a pond.'

Blunt was nodding. 'That ought to go down well with local residents.'

The cane swung round again over the other side of the road. 'Over there,' Canning continued, 'will be phase two.'

'More houses if I recollect from the plans.'

'Not only more houses, Eric. There'll be a supermarket. Locals won't have to drive to the nearest town five miles away to do their shopping. And... the swimming pool will be next to it.'

Blunt took off his large black-framed glasses. He mopped his forehead with a handkerchief. 'From memory of the plans, the shops, café and restaurant will be around there.' He pointed to the far left of the site for phase two. 'Right?'

'Correct.'

A car crept past and the front window slid down. 'Fucking property developers. Don't give a fuck about local people. Only interested in money. Bastard!' the driver shouted and sped off.

Canning lifted a finger in the air, hoping the driver would see it in his rear-view mirror. He turned his thoughts to the conversation he'd had with Blunt over his dire financial situation. Canning had taken a chance and offered the bribe. He thought he was safe in doing so. Blunt wouldn't want information about his debts made public. If he refused to take the money, Canning could threaten to reveal everything. And, he could always deny he had offered it, saying Blunt was out to destroy his reputation for some reason. The gamble had paid off. Blunt had agreed to accept money in return for using his position to push Canning's application through.

'Aren't we all?' Blunt muttered after the car.

'What?'

'Interested in money. Been thinking about what you

proposed. From what I see here, this is worth millions. Any way you could increase the offer?'

Canning tapped his cane on the ground. 'How about we leave it as it is, but if the application gets approved, I give you a bonus of another ten thousand. That do?'

Blunt offered a thin smile. 'Fair enough.'

'I don't know why local residents are so opposed to the development. Think about it. There may be a temporary slump in some house prices,' Canning said. 'But think long term. Chances are, they'll increase in value again if people in London think about moving out of the city. Why? Because they'll have the benefit of living in a rural location, but be able to commute into London. Darmont will become a desirable place to live and house prices will start to rise, mark my words.'

'You have a point,' Blunt agreed. 'Anyway, seen all I need to see for now. Thanks.' He shook Canning's hand, climbed into his car and drove off with a wave through the open window.

Canning lingered for a few more minutes, surveying the land he was going to build his dream on. A dream that would boost his wealth by millions. *Yes, things are going very much to plan.*

11

Kelso looked through the rear windows of the van as it careered out of the small clearing in the woods. Angry red and yellow flames engulfed the BMW, and dense black smoke billowed up into the sky.

The van swung to the right, throwing Kelso across the floor. 'Fuck's sake! Go a bit steadier!'

Guerra turned and leaned a chubby arm over the passenger seat. 'Hold on. Five minutes or so in this old wreck and then we transfer to the luxury of my Volvo XC60.'

'Why didn't you park it where we left the BMW?'

'Too near the textiles lorry. Didn't want to run the risk of anyone spotting my car anywhere nearby.'

'Makes sense, I suppose.'

'Damned right it does. Not taking any chances. I only hope the boss knows what he's doing breaking you out of prison. I tried to tell him we didn't need you.'

'For what?'

'That can wait. The boss'll come to see you tomorrow. He'll explain all.'

'And who is your boss?'

'Inquisitive bugger, aren't you, Kelso.'

'Like to know who has my interests at heart.'

'You'll find out tomorrow. Just a precaution... in case the police catch us. Don't want you blabbing to them who was behind your escape.'

'What makes you think you don't need me?'

'Boss seems to think you're the man to lead the operation... ex-army, handy with guns and all that crap.'

'Whatever it is, it sounds big.'

'It is. But let me tell you something, I think me and my sidekick here would have been capable of doing the job on our own. Don't want you trying to take over.'

'Listen, mate. I don't give a fuck what this operation is. You're welcome to do it on your own. All I wanted was to get out of prison.'

Guerra turned in his seat. 'There's a leather holdall in the back there with a change of clothes. Better get into them in case we get stopped.'

Kelso was stuffing his prison clothing into the bag when he heard the sound of sirens. He leaned forwards between Guerra and the driver. Two police cars were speeding towards them with blue lights flashing.

'Best duck down behind the seats,' Guerra advised. 'Should be okay though. They're on their way to where we came from.'

Kelso did as Guerra told him. His heart was pounding. He glanced through the van's rear windows and saw the blue lights disappear round a bend in the road. Turning back to look out of the front windscreen, Kelso tapped the driver on the shoulder. 'Don't say very much, do you, mate?'

'Concentrating on driving, that's all.'

Kelso slapped him on the back. 'Good man.'

'About half a mile ahead, there's a turn-off down a narrow

lane. My car's parked in a bit of a lay-by walkers sometimes use. We do a quick swap and we're on our way,' Guerra said.

'What're you doing about the van?'

Guerra flicked a thumb towards the driver. 'Taffy here will take care of it, don't worry.'

After a minute, the van screeched to a halt by Guerra's Volvo. After swapping vehicles, Kelso watched Taffy speed off down the lane. Guerra turned on the ignition, revved up, slipped the car into gear and followed the van for a mile then turned left.

'Where are we going?' Kelso asked.

'Boss's got a little holiday home the other side of Oxford. Uses it a lot for entertainment and as a retreat from time to time.'

'He's not there now then?'

Guerra looked puzzled.

'You said I would find out who he is tomorrow. Not going to take a day to get to Oxford,' Kelso explained.

Guerra grunted and stayed silent for the rest of the journey.

Fifty minutes later, the car turned right off a country lane and up a brown gravel driveway to the house.

Kelso whistled. 'Thought you said a little holiday home.' It was a two-storey stone house with red ivy covering the façade. By the number of windows on the first floor, Kelso guessed it must have at least six bedrooms.

Guerra laughed as he parked the car. 'By the boss's standards, this is little. It has eight bedrooms, six bathrooms, and a games room.'

Kelso pulled the leather holdall containing his prison clothing off the back seat and followed Guerra to the front door.

Inside, Guerra pointed up a central staircase. 'Your bedroom is along the landing, first on the left. There's a wardrobe with some casual clothes you can use.'

Kelso now realised why Guerra had asked for his sizes when he visited him in prison. 'Slick operation, I have to say. I'm impressed with the attention to detail. Down to you or your boss?'

'The boss. He's the one with the brains.'

'Is that why he doesn't trust you to handle this job you're on about?'

Guerra swung round and looked as though he was about to throw a punch at Kelso. 'You trying to wind me up?'

Kelso gave Guerra a warning stare. 'Bit touchy, aren't you? Only joking.'

'Kitchen is down there.' Guerra pointed along a hallway to the right of the staircase. 'You can grab yourself some food while I change. If you let me have the bag, I'll burn the clothes I'm wearing and your prison gear.'

'Okay. When do we expect your boss to arrive tomorrow?'

'When he feels like it.'

'You going to tell me who he is now we're clear of the police?'

Guerra shook his head. 'You'll find out when he arrives. Just remember, he did you a favour breaking you out of prison, so don't piss him off. He's big in the London criminal underworld. A few clubs are the face of his legitimate business, but he has a finger in a lot of pies.'

'Mostly illegal ones, eh?'

Guerra narrowed his eyes. 'A word of advice. Don't mess with him.'

12

Zoe Dunbar's London flat was on the fourth floor of a new block in Colindale. It was small with two bedrooms and an open-plan kitchen and living room, but it suited her. She lived on her own and it was handy to be near to the city where she had important contacts.

Dunbar was a freelance reporter. Nearing forty, she was tall with shoulder-length auburn hair and green eyes. She was a clever, feisty woman who exuded confidence. Having to press people for answers went with the job. Born in Glasgow, she'd studied journalism at the University of Strathclyde. On graduating, she was a trainee reporter for a Glasgow newspaper. She then moved to London for a national newspaper. Married at twenty-five, she divorced seven years later. Late nights and pressure of work had taken their toll. After the divorce, she decided to start working for herself.

Dunbar had always got on well with her old editor, Bob Inman. She kept in touch and still wrote the odd report for him. He'd liked the article she'd written about local unrest at Darmont. It had covered Paul Canning's planning application, and now there was the murder of Tom Slater. Dunbar had decided to arrange a meeting with Inman to discuss her plans for a bigger story.

With some time to spare before she left for her meeting, Dunbar poured herself a coffee. She blew steam from the top of her mug and the bitter aroma of fresh coffee wafted across the room. Standing by her balcony window, she looked down at the streets below. The sound of wailing sirens filled the air and two marked police cars, followed by an ambulance, sped by. *Could be another story*, she thought. Dunbar turned to the side table and switched on the radio. A news programme caught her attention.

'Local people in the sleepy village of Darmont are in shock after the murder of Tom Slater,' a reporter was saying. 'Rumours over who might have killed him are rife. Slater was employed by Paul Canning, the millionaire property developer. There have been protests over his plan to build more houses and a shopping complex in Darmont. DCI Alex Fleming is in charge of the murder enquiry.'

Dunbar smiled. *Fleming again.* She recalled him as a fellow Scot. A tall, slim, good-looking man about her age. He had short black hair that was starting to show some signs of greying. *Probably the job,* she mused.

Looking at her watch, Dunbar took a last sip of her coffee and turned the radio off. Grabbing a light jacket to match her skirt, she left the flat and took the lift to the ground floor. She passed through the security gates outside and set off on foot towards the Tube station. Seeing a free taxi, she changed her mind and flagged it down.

'Canary Wharf?'

'Sure, jump in.'

It was about fourteen miles to Bob Inman's offices, but traffic was heavy. It took over fifty minutes to get there. Dunbar paid the driver, walked into the tall building and took the lift to the third floor. Arriving at reception, she met someone she hadn't seen before. 'I'm here to see Bob Inman. He's expecting me. Zoe Dunbar.'

'Take a seat. I'll let him know you're here.'

Dunbar smiled her thanks and wandered over to where there were a few easy chairs round a large coffee table.

A few minutes later, Inman arrived looking his usual harassed self. No tie, top buttons of his shirt undone, and sleeves rolled up halfway to his elbows. Hair had long since gone from his head, but he'd compensated by having a short beard, albeit very grey. 'Zoe, how good to see you. Let's go to my office and you can fill me in on this story you want to cover.'

Inman's office was at the end of an open-plan area where admin staff and reporters were busy at their computers. Some were deep in conversation on their phones, while the phones not in use rang incessantly. As Dunbar and Inman strode up the central aisle, Dunbar received several nods of recognition. Reaching Inman's office, he closed the door and the hubbub from outside subdued. 'Coffee?'

'Thanks, don't mind if I do.'

Inman pointed to a small table with two chairs in the corner. 'Take a seat,' he said, turning to the coffee machine. 'White, one sugar?'

'Amazed you remember.'

'Good memory and attention to detail. It's why I got to where I am today.'

'That's what you always say, Bob.'

Inman laughed and brought two coffees over to sit beside Dunbar.

'Right, let's get down to the purpose of your visit. I liked your piece on Darmont. Especially your coverage of allegations of bribery and corruption. Love a bit of scandal.'

'They're only wild claims. No proof. Understandable though, given the proposed development takes no account of the neighbourhood plan. The site also happens to be on greenfield land.'

'And now… just to spice things up, we have a murder. So what's your angle on this, Zoe?'

'I want to dig deeper. How does a proposed development impact on a local community? Is there ever a good case for building on greenfield land? Is there any truth in the allegations of corruption? That sort of thing.'

'What about Slater?'

'I'll cover a bit about him as well. Was he killed by a protester? Did someone kill him because he was about to blow the whistle on Canning?'

'Or the council,' Inman added.

'Indeed. Lot of potential material there and I want to get right to the heart of what's going on at Darmont.'

'Any interviews lined up yet?'

'I've asked Paul Canning. I told him I wanted to do a piece based on government housing policy. Hinted I wanted to put a slant on how his proposed development will benefit the village.'

'But that's not your angle, right?'

'Far from it. Once I've got him onside, so to speak, I'll start to quiz him on Slater's murder and the allegations of corruption.'

'If he has got something to hide, he's hardly likely to tell you.'

'No, but I can gauge his reaction. I can always use the ploy of threatening to write that Canning refused to deny any impropriety.'

Inman slapped his thigh. 'You didn't get to–'

'Where I am today without being pushy,' Dunbar cut in to finish the sentence for Inman.

'Right. Has he agreed to see you?'

'Not yet. Might give him another prod. Tell him a national newspaper is interested in his story.'

'You need to speak to the parish council and the local planning authority as well.'

'On my list.'

'Get a feel for local anger. Speak to some of the protesters.'

'I will. Might see if Slater's wife will talk to me.'

'Worth a shot at Walter Hammond? Just promoted to secretary of state for housing, communities and local government. Be good to get his take on it all.'

'Okay.'

'And see if you can speak to the detective leading the investigation into Slater's murder. Heard on the radio this morning it's a DCI Fleming.'

'So did I. Came across him before. Not one for offering information freely, but I'll see what I can get from him.'

'Good luck with it all, Zoe. I look forward to seeing your report.'

Dunbar left to find a taxi to take her home. On the way back to her flat, Dunbar was deep in thought. *First job... get in touch with Canning about an interview.*

13

Logan looked round the small room and shook his head. 'What happened to incident rooms which used to be full of detectives?' he asked Fleming. 'I seem to remember, not so long ago, there'd be a room filled with people.'

'You've been watching too many films, Harry.'

'But there was, wasn't there?'

'Yes, you're right,' Fleming agreed, 'but manpower is a bit of an issue at the moment. Budget cuts are beginning to bite and things are a little tight.'

Logan looked round the empty room they intended to use. 'Tight is the right word, boss. There's only you, me, and Naomi. I take it we're not expecting anyone else?'

'Afraid not.'

'Should just have used your office,' Logan grumbled.

'Who needs anyone else when we've got you, Sarge,' Anderson quipped.

Logan's face lit up. 'Thank you for the vote of confidence, Naomi. You're right of course.'

Fleming smiled at his two colleagues. 'We *are* getting some help from local CID. DI Oliver has feet on the ground with bobbies doing house-to-house.'

'Oh well, at least *we* don't have to go plodding round the streets,' Logan said, looking at Anderson.

'Do you good to get some exercise, Sarge.'

'You implying I look unfit?'

'Would I ever. Just saying... exercise is good.'

'I'll have you know I'm at the peak of physical fitness, Naomi.'

Anderson laughed. 'I suppose you're not in bad condition... for someone over fifty.'

Logan screwed up an overtime form and threw it at Anderson. 'You need to replace that one with an updated one. I can see my hours are about to increase.'

'That's a point. How come we're short of staff due to budget cuts, but they can afford to pay us overtime, sir?' Anderson asked Fleming.

'Politics, Naomi. Top brass reckon we can cut numbers through efficiencies. It's all coming from the government wanting to reduce the deficit.'

'Having to pay overtime isn't exactly going to help, is it?' Logan asked.

'Paying a bit of overtime is cheaper than the cost of employing full-time staff,' Fleming said.

'I guess so.' Logan put on his serious face and looked at his notebook. 'Have you got anything back from DI Oliver yet on house-to-house enquiries and CCTV?' he asked Fleming.

'No. He sent over the statements from the two boys who found the body, but they don't throw much light on matters.'

'Next steps?' Logan asked.

Fleming looked at the whiteboard. 'We have some early leads to go on. Local guy called Quinn. He's a vociferous protester by all accounts and had a couple of run-ins with Slater.

We need to speak to him. Then there's Slater's stepson. There was no love lost between them. He had a big row with Slater and Slater threw him out. Cut him out of his will as well. We need to question him soon.'

Anderson looked at her notes. 'He lives in a commune in London.'

'Trip there for someone then?' Logan said. 'Budget permitting of course,' he added with a wry smile.

'We'll go,' Fleming said, looking at Logan. 'We also need to speak to Canning about the death threats. Then there's Slater's fall out with him over a pay rise he didn't get.'

'We have Slater's two recent visits to the hotel in London,' Anderson reminded Fleming.

'Right. We know which one, so we need to go and talk to them.' Fleming looked at Anderson. 'Can you go? See what you can find out.'

'Sure, no problem, sir. I'm happy to do that.'

'No taking in the sights and claiming it on expenses,' Logan joked. 'Remember the budget.'

Anderson picked up the screwed-up overtime form Logan had tossed at her and threw it back at him.

'I'm working up a list of all other family, friends and colleagues,' Logan said, ducking to avoid the missile. 'Made a start from Slater's mobile.'

'Super wants me to hold a briefing meeting, so I'll get that arranged,' Fleming said.

'Anything back on the search of Slater's house?' Anderson asked Fleming.

'SOCOs have searched it. They found nothing to suggest who the killer might have been.'

Anderson frowned. 'What about the car the witness saw?'

'I need you to get in touch with the Driver and Vehicle Licensing Agency. Give them what little we've got. Ask them to give us a list of all cars matching the colour and partial registration we have, and who owns them. We'll get local forces' CID officers to check them all out.'

'Ah! A very good example of the efficiencies the boss was talking about,' Logan announced. 'Comes out of someone else's budget.'

'Should have been an accountant, Sarge.'

'Very droll, Naomi.'

Fleming smiled. 'Verbal sparring aside, anything else?'

Logan and Anderson shook their heads.

'Okay. First thing. Let's go and speak to Vic Quinn.'

14

After a short wait, the doors of the Airbus A380 opened and Canning and Yamamura climbed out onto the steps. There was an instant blast of hot air. It hit them like they'd opened an oven door. There wasn't a cloud in the clear blue sky. It was thirty-nine degrees, and humid in Dubai.

They'd flown over to meet Isa Al Jameel. Canning had thought it would be a good idea to come to see him in person. He wanted to impress on Al Jameel how important he was for his plans. The Saudi's investment in Canning's housing and shopping development was crucial. It was also a good chance to finalise things for Al Jameel's visit to England to discuss business.

Al Jameel had reserved a table for three at the Al Dawaar revolving restaurant on the twenty-fifth floor of Hyatt Regency Dubai. Inside, it was a pleasant twenty-two degrees. Welcome relief from the heat outside. It was busy, and diners occupied most of the tables sitting round the outer edge of the restaurant. From there, they enjoyed stunning views of the Dubai skyline as the restaurant turned. Burj Khalifa, Dubai Creek and the sea were all in plain view.

Al Jameel was in his mid-fifties, a tall, sturdy man with a neatly trimmed black beard and moustache. He wore a white thawb and a red-and-white chequered keffiyeh with a black band round his head. Born in Saudi Arabia of rich parents, he'd moved into banking in his twenties. Using funds from his father, he invested in the oil and gas industry. It wasn't long before he made his first million. Later, he ploughed money into major skyscraper developments in Dubai. He'd married and had a son, Dani, but was now on his own.

Canning ordered margoogat, a meaty tomato-based stew cooked with turmeric, cumin and bezar. Yamamura decided to try machboos, a rice dish made from local spices, mixed with dried lemon. It was served with locally caught shrimp. Al Jameel chose the oysters and salad.

Al Jameel had decided sparkling water would be fine to go with the meal. Canning opted for a bottle of expensive white wine.

'How was your flight?' Al Jameel asked Canning as they sipped at their drinks.

'On time. Good service,' Canning said. 'We came business class. It's the only way to travel long distance.'

'Only took a little over seven hours,' Yamamura added.

Al Jameel smiled. 'You will find a bit of a difference in weather compared to England. I hope you don't find the heat too much.'

'Outside is far too hot, but in here it's fine,' Canning said.

'Do you live in Dubai itself?' Yamamura asked, changing the subject.

'I have a luxury penthouse in Dubai Marina. It's in one of the high-rise blocks I invested in.'

'Sounds nice,' Yamamura said.

Small talk continued over dinner. Al Jameel told them about Dubai and how he'd gone into business. Canning told Al Jameel how he'd ended up in the property industry. Yamamura took time to tell Al Jameel about all the finances so far secured for Canning's development plans.

'Good food, good company,' Canning said when they'd finished eating.

'And a great place to eat, I should add,' Yamamura said, dabbing at her lips with a napkin.

'Thank you, Makayla. May I call you by your first name?' Al Jameel asked, looking at Yamamura with dark-brown eyes.

'Of course, please do. I must say I enjoyed the meal. How were the oysters and salad?'

'One of my favourite dishes,' Al Jameel said.

'In which case, I'll make sure my wife cooks it for you when you come over to visit us,' Canning said.

'You don't have a cook?'

Canning laughed. 'It's my wife.'

Al Jameel smiled. 'I will look forward to meeting her.'

'I'm so pleased you're coming to England to stay with us. We wanted to come over to see you face to face so we can assure you our plans are still on track.'

'I did hear there is a certain amount of opposition to your proposed development,' Al Jameel said. 'And rather disturbing that someone has murdered your employee, Mr Slater.'

'Yes, regrettable indeed.'

'It has not affected your plans?'

'No, no, of course not. Tom's death, although most unfortunate, will have no effect on my application. It was a random act of violence by some disturbed individual. As they say, life goes on.'

'Have the police any idea who did it?'

'No, not yet. It's very early, but I'm sure they will find the culprit soon.'

'And you're certain this is nothing to do with your planning application?'

'No doubt in my mind,' Canning said. 'I'm very excited about the project. We're all going to reap very big rewards from it.'

Al Jameel smiled. 'In which case, I look forward to investing in your scheme. But, of course, the authorities have yet to approve it.'

Canning beamed. 'Excellent! Very good news. And, let me assure you, I am doing everything possible to make sure it is approved.'

Emirates flight EK30 from Dubai to London Heathrow was high over the Alps. Canning and Yamamura were enjoying a glass of champagne in business class of the Airbus A380.

'The dinner with Al Jameel seemed to go well,' Canning said. 'At least he's still coming over. I must admit, I was a bit worried he might change his mind.'

'Yes,' Yamamura agreed. 'He seems a very astute businessman. His investment will be a major boost to the project.'

Canning took a sip of his champagne. 'Indeed. All we need to do is get my application approved.'

Yamamura nodded. 'Have you decided yet whether to give an interview to the reporter, Zoe Dunbar?'

'I intend to. Bit of good publicity could work to our benefit.'

'You're assuming she'll write with a positive slant on the development. But I'm sure she'll write something about Tom's murder.'

'She may, but bearing in mind the death threats I've had, it might attract a certain amount of sympathy.'

'Forever the optimist, eh?'

'I'll use her to get some good publicity about Al Jameel's visit and potential investment.'

'Sounds like a fine idea.'

'There's one slight problem though. I had a phone call from Eric Blunt the day after I saw him. Seems the parish council have written to Walter Hammond. They want to get my application called in.'

'You didn't mention that to Al Jameel.'

'No. I didn't want to worry him. As I told you, Hammond is a friend. I'll have a word with him. It won't be a problem.'

15

The marked police car drew up outside Vic Quinn's terraced house on a quiet lane near the middle of the village. There was no front garden. Fleming stepped out of the passenger side of the car onto the narrow path in front of the house. Logan climbed out of the driver's side as Fleming went to ring the doorbell.

After a few seconds, the door opened to reveal an anxious-looking woman who looked to be in her thirties. She peered at Fleming with a quizzical look on her face and waited for him to speak.

Fleming showed his warrant card. 'Sorry to bother you. DCI Fleming and DS Logan. Is your husband here?'

The woman peered at Fleming. 'No. Is something wrong?'

'I just want to ask him a few questions. Only routine. Nothing to worry about.'

'Oh... I see. He's at his mother's house doing some electrical work. I can call him on his mobile to get him to come home if it's urgent.'

'No, that won't be necessary. If you let us have the address, we'll pop round and see him there.'

'It's number ten, Friars Court. Carry on down this road, turn left at the bottom, left again by the church and you'll find Friars Court on your right.'

Fleming smiled. 'Thanks.'

~

Quinn's mother's detached house had a small lawned area in front. A few shrubs lined a border by the pavement and a block-paving driveway led to a blue garage door.

Fleming rang the bell and a grey-haired woman who looked to be in her sixties opened the door. She gasped when she saw the marked police car and the two plain-clothed officers standing on the doorstep. 'What's happened? It's not Vic, is it? Has there been an accident?' she asked with a pained look on her face.

'There's no accident.' Fleming showed his warrant card. 'DCI Fleming and DS Logan. 'We thought your son was with you. His wife told us a few minutes ago.'

'He was. Had to go out to get some parts an hour ago. He's fitting some new kitchen ceiling lights for me.'

'Can we come in and wait? We wanted to ask him a few questions.'

Mrs Quinn drew in a deep breath and lifted a shaking hand to her mouth. 'I... I suppose so.' She turned on unsteady legs and showed the two detectives into a tidy living room. 'Have a seat.'

'We gather you're having a bit of trouble on the housing front,' Fleming said.

'Yes. This place is too big for me.'

'You're on your own?'

'My husband died five years ago. Heart attack.'

'I'm sorry to hear that,' Fleming said.

'Yes... well, I finally decided to sell. I wanted to get somewhere smaller so I could give any money left over to Vic. Then Paul Canning put in his application for planning permission to build on the land behind me. It was at the very time I decided to put the house on the market. I had some initial interest, but people were worried about the development. Not only because it'll spoil the views over the back. It's the noise and disruption during the building.'

'How are the estate agents managing the problem?' Fleming asked.

Mrs Quinn frowned. 'Not very well. They said I should reduce the asking price.'

'And you have?'

'Twenty thousand, and I still haven't been able to sell.'

'Ouch! Not good,' Logan remarked.

'Vic's angry. He says the parish council have written to the secretary of state to ask him to call in the application.'

'Call in?' Logan queried.

'The secretary of state has the power to direct the local planning authority to refer the application to him. If he calls it in, it'll go to a public inquiry,' Mrs Quinn explained.

'I didn't know that,' Logan admitted.

'I can see why your son's angry,' Fleming said. 'There may not be as much money after you've had to reduce your asking price.'

'It's not only the money. He thinks the development will ruin the village. And... he hates rich men like Canning who make their millions at the expense of others.'

As if on cue, the front door burst open and Vic Quinn stormed into the room. 'What are you doing here?' he demanded, his piercing green eyes darting between Fleming and Logan.

Fleming stood to offer a hand to Quinn, wondering if the

ruddy complexion was normal or due to anger. 'I wanted to ask you a few questions. Your mother very kindly said we could come in to wait for you.'

Quinn ignored the hand and looked at his mother. 'You all right?'

'Yes, but now you're here, I think I'll go upstairs for a rest. I'm tired.'

'Okay, Mum. I'll bring you some tea later.'

Quinn sank his sturdy frame into the chair his mother had vacated. 'What's this about?' he demanded in a broad Irish accent.

Fleming took in Quinn's thick red hair with matching beard and moustache. For a moment he had visions of what he thought might have passed for Rob Roy.

'We're investigating the murder of Tom Slater,' Fleming said. 'We want to question everyone who knew him.'

'So why me?'

'We hear you had a couple of run-ins with him... over the development.'

'I'm not the only one. The whole bloody village hates Canning and anyone who works for him.'

'You had a row with Slater outside the parish council office after a meeting.'

Quinn stared at Fleming and laughed. 'And that makes me a suspect? I lost count of how many angry people there were at the meeting.'

'I didn't say you were a suspect. I just need to be clear what happened.'

'The man was a devious, conniving bastard. Rubbed me up the wrong way. Things got a bit heated, as they always do at meetings where Canning and his cronies are involved.'

'And the skirmish outside the Down Inn. What was that all about?'

'Same thing. I'd had a few drinks. He goaded me. Look, I admit there was no love lost between us. I hated the man. But I didn't kill him if that's what you're thinking.'

'If I thought you did, you would be under arrest. You have a previous conviction for assault, don't you?'

'Fuck's sake, man. Doesn't make me a murderer.'

'Did you hate Mr Slater enough to drop a death threat through his letter box?'

Quinn shook his head. 'No way! Look, should I have a solicitor, the way these questions are going?'

'Only if we take you in for questioning under caution. You are free to decline to answer my questions, but we'd appreciate your cooperation.'

Logan had got up to stretch his legs and walked over to the window. 'That your car outside?'

'Yes, why?'

'Just curious.'

Quinn sighed and got up from his chair. 'Listen, I'm busy and I think we're done here, if you don't mind. I need to get back to work on my mother's lights.'

'Okay, Mr Quinn. Thank you for your time,' Fleming said. 'By the way... for the record, where were you last Friday night?'

'At home... with my wife.'

Fleming nodded. 'We'll be in touch if we have any more questions,' he said, making to leave.

'Check it out, Harry,' Fleming said, as they reached the car.

'Right.' Logan pointed toward Quinn's car. 'Notice something...? His car is black... and has a seventeen reg.'

16

The sunshine of the last few days had given way to thunderstorms. Canning and Yamamura had landed at Heathrow after their visit to Dubai. After picking up their luggage, Canning received a text message from Blunt.

'He wants to discuss something on neutral territory,' Canning said.

'What?' Yamamura asked.

'I don't know. Says he can meet us on our way back to Henley at a service station just off the M4.'

'Should we go?'

'Yes. It sounded urgent.'

'Okay.' Torrential rain hit the windscreen as soon as Yamamura pulled out of the car park. She switched the wipers on to full speed and cursed. It was mid-morning and the sky was black, lit only by the odd flash of lightning. 'Should have stayed in Dubai,' she muttered.

'Quite so,' Canning agreed. 'Wonder what Blunt wants though.'

'Why am I convinced it's not good news. If it was, he would

have said so in the text message. An urgent clandestine meeting sounds ominous.'

'Better not be bad news. That's not what I'm paying him to deliver.'

'Don't forget you've got the reporter, Zoe Dunbar, coming to see you tomorrow. Wouldn't be good if she was to publish anything negative.'

'Come on, Makayla! Why are you so damned pessimistic? It'll be fine.' Canning settled back in his seat and wasn't so sure. He stayed silent for the rest of the journey to the service station.

Yamamura kept quiet and stared at the road ahead.

They pulled into the service station and grabbed a coffee while they were waiting for Blunt. The storm had passed and there was only the odd drop of rain. The sky had lightened and patches of blue appeared behind racing clouds.

Back in the car, Canning looked at his watch. 'Where the hell is the man? We've come from bloody Dubai and we're here before him.'

'You didn't get the text from him until we landed,' Yamamura reminded him.

'Okay, okay! I don't like anyone keeping me waiting, that's all.'

Yamamura glanced out of her side window. 'Looks like he's here. Don't go upsetting him, will you. We need to keep him onside.'

Canning grunted.

Blunt pulled in next to them, got out of his car and eased himself into the back seat of Canning's car behind Yamamura. He spoke in short bursts as though out of breath. 'Hope I haven't kept you waiting. Traffic down here was awful. Accident on the road. Bad visibility in the downpour.'

'You're here now,' Canning said, showing no sympathy. 'What's so urgent?'

'You know I told you the other day that the parish council wrote to Walter Ham–'

'You don't need to remind me what you've already told me,' Canning cut in. 'What's new?'

'I'm afraid he's called in your application.'

'What!'

'Sorry. There's nothing I can do about it.'

'Why's he called it in?'

'I guess it's due to local concern. The application doesn't reflect the wishes of the neighbourhood plan and is more than what's proposed. The development is also on greenfield land.'

'So there'll be a public inquiry?'

'Afraid so.'

'But you can still lobby Hammond to press for approval. And you'll get your say at the inquiry.'

'I'll do my best.'

'Don't forget, you have an extra ten thousand riding on it.'

'Thought you ought to know,' Blunt said. 'Wanted to tell you face to face before you heard of it elsewhere.'

'Very thoughtful of you. Just make sure it's approved.'

Blunt had left and Canning and Yamamura were back on the road heading for Henley. Canning was silent and deep in thought on the way home. *Looks like I need to pay my old friend Walter Hammond a visit.*

17

It took Fleming and Logan over an hour to drive from the office to west London. Finding the old disused factory building where Gale Slater's son lived proved difficult. After asking some people for directions, they found the squatters' commune.

The detectives received some odd looks from the people they asked where the old factory building was. When they arrived, they knew the reason for the looks. The streets around were desolate. Steel roller shutters, padlocked at the bottom, hid shops that had once thrived. The old factory was at the end of a street next to a railway bridge spanning the road.

It started with a trickle of squatters moving in. A few waifs and strays and dropouts followed. It was now an established hippie commune. They'd long since removed wooden boards to reveal broken and cracked windows. Rusty gates hung open and weeds pushed up through the tarmac parking area in front of the building. Someone had rigged up a rope between a rusting drainpipe and a hook on the wall opposite. Drying clothes flapped in the breeze.

'Think it's safe to park in here?' Logan asked as he drove past the gates.

'Let's just say I'm glad I didn't bring the old Porsche,' Fleming said.

A young woman wearing denim jeans and a long yellow T-shirt came out of an open door. She was carrying a plastic laundry basket full of clothes. Seeing the police car and the two detectives getting out, she froze.

'Don't worry,' Fleming called across to her, 'we only need to see someone. We have some news for him.'

The woman brushed a strand of long brown hair from her eyes and pointed to the door. 'Everyone who's here is up the stairs on the first floor.'

'Thanks.'

Through the door, there was what was once a reception office on the right. A wide passageway led to a large area with a concrete floor. 'Looks like this was the main place of work, whatever it was,' Logan said, his voice echoing in the emptiness.

On their left, there were a couple of black wheelie bins against the wall. Their lids bulged open with the rubbish crammed inside. A scrawny black-and-white cat was slinking round the bins looking for scraps. It stopped and looked at the two men over its shoulder before scampering off out the door.

A metal staircase with open treads was at the end of the passageway. Their shoes clanged as they climbed the stairs. At the top, there was a short landing with three small offices. Along the landing, there was a large room with wooden floorboards.

'Would you look at this,' Logan whispered. Several makeshift huts constructed of chipboard and plywood lined the walls. A few large tents occupied some of the floor space. In the centre of the room, metal drums supported old doors to form a crude table.

'This isn't residential property,' a man's voice came from behind them. 'We're not breaking any laws by staying here as long as we don't cause any damage. You may have noticed on your way in what years of neglect has already done. If anything, we've improved the look of the place. And... a court has never told us to leave.'

Fleming turned to see a man coming towards him. He was tall, slim, and had greasy black hair tied back into a ponytail. The stud pierced through one eyebrow seemed to match his image. He was wearing torn jeans, no shoes and no shirt. The only top he had on was an old black waistcoat. Coloured beads dangled round his neck and down his chest.

'Needn't have dressed up for us,' Logan muttered.

'Don't worry, we're not here to tell you to move,' Fleming said. 'We're looking for Rashad Yousefi.'

Defiance flashed in the man's eyes. 'He's not here.'

'His mother told us this is where he lives. We need to speak to him.'

The man shrugged. 'Bit difficult, on account of the fact he's not here.'

'His stepfather's been killed. It's important we see Rashad.'

The man's eyes softened to show a hint of compassion. 'That's bad, man.'

'Any idea where he might be?' Logan asked.

'Said he was going to the jobcentre.'

'Whereabouts?' Fleming asked.

'Half hour's walk, four... five minutes by car.'

Logan reversed out between the gates of the yard. Turning left, he followed the directions the man in the commune had given them. They hadn't been driving long when Fleming pointed to a man trudging along the pavement. He was about a hundred yards in front of them.

'That's him! Pull over.'

'How do you know it's him?' Logan asked.

'Naomi got a photo from his mother when we went to see her.'

'Ah, right.'

As they approached and slowed, Yousefi glanced up in alarm. He turned and looked as though he was about to run.

Fleming slid his window down and shouted, 'Rashad! Your mother told us where to find you. We need to have a quick word.'

Yousefi stopped. He was of medium height, thin, and had short black hair. He had a serious, tight-lipped look on his face which the black stubble on his chin did nothing to hide. He was wearing faded blue jeans and a grubby white T-shirt with sweat stains under the armpits. His dark-brown eyes stared at Fleming. 'What do you want?'

'I want to ask you about your stepfather. Why don't you get in the car rather than stand out there?'

Yousefi scowled and climbed into the back seat.

'One of your friends in the commune told us he thought you'd gone to the jobcentre,' Fleming said.

'That supposed to be a question?'

'No. Any luck?' Fleming paused. 'That *is* a question.'

'What do you think?'

'From the look on your face, I'd say no.'

'Don't know why you bothered asking then.'

'You always this cheerful?' Logan chipped in.

Yousefi glared at him. 'Fuck you.'

'Your mother phoned you to let you know what had happened to your stepfather, didn't she?' Fleming asked.

'Yes.'

'She reckoned you weren't exactly beat up about it.'

'I wasn't.'

'Told us you'd said good riddance. Any particular reason?'

'It's no secret. We never got on. My father went back to Iran when I was seven. He was killed there in a car accident. My mother met Slater and married him when I was twelve.'

'Why didn't you get on?'

'He was a snob. Didn't like me because my father was Iranian. I didn't do well at school and he wasn't pleased. Kept telling me I was lazy and useless. I got a job as an apprentice plumber, but got the sack and he was even more pissed off.'

'Why did you get sacked?'

'Got into drugs. By then Slater was getting really angry. We argued all the time and, about two years ago, we had a massive row. He told me he was cutting me out of his will and asked me to leave.'

'Did you have any more to do with him afterwards? Did you ever speak to him again?'

'I tried to phone my mother a couple of weeks ago and he answered. I needed some money. He told me to fuck off and hung up.'

'Do you drive?'

'No, why?'

'Do you have any friends with cars?'

'I have one friend. He can't afford a car. His uncle can't drive anymore so gave it to him.'

'What is it?'

'Skoda something or other.'

'Colour?'

'What the fuck does it matter?'

'Be useful if you could just answer the question,' Logan said.

Yousefi shrugged. 'Black, if you must know.'

'A witness saw a black car speeding away from where your stepfather was murdered.'

'Whoa there... you saying it could have been my friend?'

'What's the registration number?'

'You're joking, right? You expect me to know that?'

'Where were you last Friday night?'

'In the commune. If you're done, I need to be somewhere else.'

'One more question,' Fleming said.

'You think I killed him, don't you?' Yousefi blurted.

'Did you?'

'No!' Rashad pulled the car door open.

'Know anyone who would want to kill him?' Fleming asked.

Rashad got out and leaned through Fleming's window. 'Ask every fucking man in Darmont!'

18

It was hot on the streets of London, but even hotter deep down in the Underground at Westminster. Paul Canning made his way along the platform, heading for the escalator. He'd caught an early train from Henley-on-Thames, changing twice. In a somewhat irritable mood, he arrived at London Paddington. Mingling with the masses was something he would avoid if at all possible. He was not a patient man. Jostling with the morning commuters had done nothing to improve his mood.

Breathing hard and sweating, he made his way up to the street. He leaned on his walking cane and looked across the busy road towards the Houses of Parliament. Glancing at his watch, he realised he was early for his meeting with Walter Hammond. *Just as well*, he thought as he watched the constant flow of traffic. *Take me forever to get over this bloody road.*

After what seemed an age, the traffic lights changed and Canning stepped off the pavement. A cyclist who had ignored the red lights swerved round him and stood up on the pedals to speed away. 'Idiot!' Canning shouted after him, waving his cane. 'Hope you get yourself killed!'

The man raised a middle finger in the air and carried on cycling.

'Some of them don't give a shit,' someone nearby shouted to Canning.

Canning grunted and made his way over the road. He decided to see if he could find a free bench in Victoria Tower Gardens next to the Palace of Westminster. *Need to gather my thoughts before I meet Walter.*

Canning had arranged to see his friend in the Central Lobby of the Palace of Westminster. He wanted to speak face to face with Hammond. It was the first part of Canning's devious strategy to make sure he got the support he needed. The pressure he could exert on Hammond would come later if required.

Knowing what he hoped to achieve from the meeting, Canning made his way back to the Houses of Parliament. Hammond had told him he would have to come through St Stephen's Entrance. To his dismay, there was a long queue outside. It took thirty minutes to go through the security checks and get his visitor pass. He then walked through St Stephen's Hall to the Central Lobby. Armed police were patrolling, the sound of their boots echoing round the hall. MPs, peers and other visitors milled about on the ornately tiled floor. Members came and went through the large arches where corridors led to the Lords and Commons.

Canning was admiring the statues of English and Scottish monarchs when he heard Hammond's voice.

'Paul, so good to see you. Have a good journey down?'

Hammond was the same age as Canning, but had aged less. He was tall and slim with short grey hair, though the hair was starting to show signs of receding. His dark eyes and thin smile had once prompted a colleague to describe him as the smiling assassin.

'Bloody awful,' Canning replied. 'Crowded trains, ghastly Underground, and a lungful of traffic fumes as soon as you get out on the street.'

'City life I'm afraid, old boy. How's Jane?'

'Fine. Listen, I came to congratulate you on your new appointment. Very well deserved, I'm sure.'

'Thanks, Paul. But you didn't come all the way down here just to say that, did you? Something on your mind I can help you with?'

'As it happens, yes. I was wondering why you called in my application for the housing and shopping development at Darmont.'

'Ah, yes. Might have guessed that's what you would want to talk about.'

'Well? Why did you?'

'The parish council wrote asking me to call it in.'

'You could have refused.'

'Hands tied, old boy. Given the extent of local opposition and concern, it would have looked odd if I hadn't.'

'And here was me thinking government policy was to increase housing supply and release land for developers like me. I'm doing my best to help you lot out, and all I get is obstruction at every turn. Doesn't make sense. Can't you change your mind and say you're happy for the local planning authority to decide?'

'Afraid not. I was under pressure from the prime minister to call it in.'

'But you do appoint the planning officer to chair the public inquiry that'll be held?'

'I do.'

'So, you could get someone who is likely to recommend approval of the development?'

'I–'

'And,' Canning cut in, 'the final decision rests with you, does it not?'

'It does, but you'll have every chance at the inquiry to challenge the parish council and local residents. You can stress why the planning officer should recommend acceptance of your application.'

'I will be making a very strong case, mark my words.'

Hammond smiled slyly. 'There you are then. Nothing to worry about.'

Canning tapped his cane on the tiled floor. 'Just thought I'd mention it. I won't take up any more of your time. Nice to see you.'

Hammond offered a hand. 'You too, Paul. Good luck.'

Canning shook Hammond's hand. 'By the way, a rich Saudi Arabian businessman is interested in investing in the development. He's coming over with his son to discuss it. They'll be staying with me at my place. Having a bit of a bash with him and other potential investors. You're very welcome to come. Chance to network with an influential Saudi.'

Hammond's eyes lit up. 'As it happens, the government are having talks with the Saudis over a trade deal and arms sale. It's worth about one and a half billion. Be useful to talk to him. You know, put a word in and all that.'

'Sure.' Canning turned to leave. 'I'll let you know the details.'

He chuckled as he left. *I still have another card to play.*

19

The silver Audi A5 turned right through the big gates and along the gravel driveway to Paul Canning's house. Zoe Dunbar had made good time from Colindale and was a few minutes early for her late-afternoon meeting. She parked in front of the house and rang the doorbell. After a few seconds, Jane Canning opened the door.

Dunbar showed her press card. 'Zoe Dunbar. Mr Canning is expecting me.'

Jane smiled. 'Ah, yes. It's such a nice afternoon, Paul's sitting round the back by the swimming pool. If you follow me, I'll take you to him.'

Dunbar followed Canning's wife along a gravel path past neat flower beds to the back of the house. There was a large patio area with steps leading down to a well-kept lawn. The pool was over to the right. Canning was sitting there, dressed in cream slacks and an open-necked white shirt.

Dunbar approached with an outstretched hand. 'Hello, Mr Canning, thank you for seeing me.'

Canning stood and shook her hand. 'Not at all. Good to get a chance to offer my view on things.' He removed his wide-brimmed Panama hat and waved it in front of his face. 'Still damned hot, isn't it? Can I get Jane to fetch you a drink?' He pointed to a glass on the table by his side. 'I'm having a large gin and tonic... loads of ice.'

Dunbar turned to Jane. 'Iced water would be fine, thank you.'

'Take a seat,' Canning said, pointing at the chair opposite his.

Dunbar sat and pulled a small digital recorder out of her handbag. 'Mind if I record this? So much easier than taking notes.'

Canning looked dubious and hesitated for a second. 'No, not at all. Before you do though, there's just one thing.'

'Yes?'

I saw the last article you did on Darmont. It didn't exactly paint a positive picture. You wrote about local opposition to my application. You also reported about unrest, and how feelings were running high. Even said people were claiming officials must be on the take.'

He paused as Jane arrived with Dunbar's glass of water and put it on the table beside her husband's gin. 'Can I get you anything else?' she asked Dunbar.

'No, that's fine. Thank you,' Dunbar said. She turned to face Canning. 'I only reported what people were telling me. I was very careful to say it was local people who were suggesting there had to be corrupt officials. I didn't say it was a matter of fact. I could have been sued for libel.'

'This time you'll report my side of things?'

'I intend to take a balanced approach. I always think there are two sides to every story and like to keep my reports fair. That's why I asked you for an interview. I wanted to look at it from a different perspective. Something like how a new development can have a positive impact on a local community.'

'Music to my ears.'

'Good.' Dunbar looked at Canning with her finger paused over the record button.

Canning nodded and Dunbar started the recording.

'Why did you choose Darmont as the site for your proposed development?'

'I knew the planning authority had a local plan. They argued the case for sustainable development. They did recognise government policy was to have more new homes. It was clear to me there was an appetite for more houses, but they didn't go far enough.'

'How so?'

'I thought they were missing a real opportunity. Darmont is within commuting distance of London and has no shops of note. There's no doubt there's a need for new houses. My vision is of a thriving village which has the dual benefits of being rural, yet near to London.'

'What about the argument that new homes ought not to be built on greenfield land?'

'There isn't enough suitable land within the existing boundary. Even the local plan allows for development on the surrounding fields.'

'But not for as many houses and shops as you propose.'

'No, but my plan will add improvements to the place.'

'In what way?'

'There's only a network of minor country roads into Darmont. There'll need to be some road-widening work to cater for more traffic.'

'You see increased traffic as a benefit?'

'The benefit will be to the local economy. With better access roads, there'll be more visitors to a thriving shopping complex.'

'There'll be a need for a bigger school,' Dunbar guessed.

'For sure. May even get a secondary school so kids don't have to catch a bus into the nearest town.'

'You seem convinced your proposed development will enhance the village. How will you bring local people round to your way of thinking?'

'Three ways. One, I'm hoping you *will* write a balanced report outlining the benefits I'm talking about. Two, I'll get my chance at the public inquiry to argue my case and get people to realise it's not all bad.'

'And the third?'

'The housing estate will have detached and semi-detached houses. There'll be a mix of styles in small clusters rather than long streets. We'll also have pedestrian paths and seating areas. Next to a small wooded park and pond, there'll be a play area for children. People don't get it yet. But they will.'

'What about investment? Are the plans affordable?'

'No doubt about it. I have several investors already on board. Next week, I have a rich Saudi businessman coming to stay here for a few days. He wants to discuss my application with a view to significant investment. His adult son will be with him. He's interested in getting involved in the project.'

'Do you think the murder of Tom Slater will put him off?'

'No, it won't. I got back from Dubai the other day. I went to see him. He agreed it was all a bit tragic, but is still interested.'

'You think your application will be approved?'

'I'm confident, yes.'

'Have you any idea who might have wanted to kill Tom Slater?'

Canning hesitated, then pointed to the recorder. He pulled a finger across his throat by way of saying he wanted the recording to stop.

Dunbar obliged.

'Some of the protesters have been getting out of hand.

There's one, name of Quinn, who had a couple of run-ins with Tom.'

'Have you spoken to the police about him?'

'They haven't been to see me yet. Expecting them any time.'

'One final question. Do you think it's possible Tom Slater tried to blackmail someone into supporting your application?'

'Ridiculous!'

'And is there any reason to suspect there might be some truth in the claims of bribery and corruption?'

Canning's eyes narrowed. 'Miss Dunbar, I do hope you are not going to revisit that angle in your report.'

'Sounds a little like a threat.'

'We're done here. Find your own way out.'

20

'His wife said he had someone with him, but he should be free by six,' Fleming said. He looked at his watch. 'I guess we should get there by then.'

They were on their way to see Paul Canning. Logan had decided to take the scenic route and they were on the A4130 heading towards Henley. 'Bang on six,' Logan agreed.

'Did you and Naomi get any results from the SOCOs on Slater's car?' Fleming asked.

'Nothing inside to suggest he had anyone with him. No sign of any violent struggle. Packet of mint sweets in the glove compartment with the car manual and service book, a pen and a couple of CDs.'

'Not much help. Fingerprints?'

'Yes, but only Slater's, and others not yet identified.'

'What about CCTV?'

'Again, not very helpful,' Logan said. 'It wasn't working, so we have no coverage of Slater arriving at the village hall car park or of who he met there.'

'Right. Wonder if Canning will be able to throw any light on matters.'

'We'll find out soon enough.'

Fifteen minutes later, Logan was turning into Canning's driveway when a silver Audi A5 drove out.

'Well, would you believe it,' Fleming exclaimed.

'What?'

'That was Zoe Dunbar.'

Logan frowned, then it dawned on him. 'Oh, yes, I remember. She took an interest in our last case. Didn't take her long to get here, did it?'

Canning came round the corner of the house as the two detectives were climbing out of the car. 'Thought I heard a car coming. You must be DCI Fleming and DS Logan.'

'That's right.'

'I was in the garden, but think we should go in the house if that's okay?'

'Sure,' Fleming said. 'Show the way.'

Canning took them through the front door and down the hall to the room he'd used for his brief meeting with Yamamura.

'Nice place you have here,' Logan said, taking in the obvious opulence. Two settees and four easy chairs sat on a rich cream carpet. Blue wallpaper adorned the walls. A large bay window looked out over the rear lawn. Curtain tie-backs fastened golden drapes to the sides. A long glass coffee table occupied the space between the two facing settees.

'Thank you,' Canning said, heading for the drinks cabinet. 'Think I need a drink after my last visitor.'

'Zoe Dunbar,' Fleming said.

Canning stopped and gave Fleming a quizzical look. 'You know her?'

'I've come across her before.'

'Bloody pushy if you ask me.'

'Sounds like her,' Fleming agreed.

'Get you two anything?' Canning asked, pointing at the array of bottles.

'No, thanks,' both detectives said.

Canning poured himself a large gin and tonic and waved at the available chairs. 'Help yourself,' he said, settling himself into one of the easy chairs.

'I'd like to ask a few questions if you don't mind,' Fleming said.

'Go ahead. I hope I can be of some help.'

'How long had Mr Slater worked for you?'

'About ten years.'

'And he was your personal assistant?'

'Yes.'

'What exactly did his job entail?'

Canning laughed. 'Just about everything. Organising my time and scheduling meetings, planning events, and taking my phone calls.'

'And planning events would include organising information meetings for your proposed development?'

'Yes.'

'And it was outside one of those meetings he had a row with a local man, the same man he had a bit of a spat with at a pub?'

'You're talking about Vic Quinn. Nasty piece of work. He's one of the most vocal of all the protesters. Ask Norman Read about him. He was with Tom at the pub that night.'

'Norman Read?'

'One of Tom's big golfing friends.'

'Did Mr Slater ever say he'd had a death threat from Quinn?'

'No, but he did get an anonymous note. Dismissed it. Told me he threw it away.'

Logan looked up from the notebook he'd been scribbling in. 'Did Mr Slater have an office?'

'He either worked from home, here, or in my office in London.'

'Did he keep any files here?' Fleming asked.

'Yes. There's a small room he used as an office.'

'We'll need to have a look if that's okay, and I'll have to get someone to check his workspace in your London office.'

'No problem.'

'When did you last see Mr Slater?'

'That would be Friday.'

'The day he was killed?'

Alarm flickered for a moment in Canning's eyes. 'Well... yes, I guess it would be.'

'And what time did you see him?'

Canning puffed out his cheeks. 'Six, seven o'clock.'

'Did he take a telephone call when you saw him?'

'Yes, as a matter of fact he did. No idea who it was. It was very brief.'

'Did he look alarmed when he took the call?'

'Don't know. He went out of the room to take it.'

'Any idea why he would have parked his car at the village hall?'

'No.'

'He went to London for two meetings recently. What were they about?'

Canning frowned. 'I don't recollect there were any meetings in London he had to go to. Surprise to me.'

'So you've no idea who he went to see?'

'None at all.'

'His wife told us her husband was a heavy gambler. Did you know that?'

Canning shook his head. 'No.'

'She told us things had become strained between you and Slater.'

'I don't like where this is going.'

'He asked you for a pay rise and you refused.'

Canning's hand shook as he sipped the last of his gin. 'I did. There were no grounds to offer him more money. I hope you're not suggesting I'm a suspect because things became awkward when I refused to pay him more.'

'I'm not suggesting anything of the kind, Mr Canning. Trying to get a feel for the last few days and weeks of his life, that's all.'

Canning put his empty glass on the coffee table. 'Are we done here?'

'Yes. Mind if we have a quick look in the room Mr Slater used for work here?'

They found nothing of any help amongst Slater's files and were on the way back to the office. 'What did you think of Canning?' Fleming asked Logan.

'Got a bit touchy when you mentioned his relationship with Slater had become strained. I noticed a shake of his hand when you brought the subject up.'

'Hmm. Perhaps he got a touch of nerves. People do when they're questioned and think a finger is being pointed at them. Thing is, as far as we know, he was the last person to see Slater alive...'

21

The Airbus A380 was high over the Alps when Isa Al Jameel and his son felt the first shudder. It was as though a giant sledgehammer had pounded the plane from underneath.

They'd boarded Emirates flight EK008 at Dubai International Airport for London Heathrow. On arrival, a chauffeur-driven limousine would take them to Canning's house. They were travelling business class, enjoying the ultimate in comfort and style. The first leg of the non-stop flight had been uneventful.

Now over the Alps, they were flying at a comfortable 34,000 feet when the turbulence started. A quick succession of jolts followed the first shudder. The plane lurched up and down on the air currents. The fasten seat belts sign flashed on the screens in front of them. Dani looked with alarm at his father.

'Don't worry, Dani,' Al Jameel said. 'It's only turbulence. Quite normal.'

But as he spoke the captain made an announcement over the tannoy system. 'Cabin crew to seats please.'

'You sure?' Dani asked.

Al Jameel tried to hide his own concern as the plane juddered. 'Relax.'

The captain's voice came over the tannoy again. 'This is your captain speaking. Sorry about the bumps. I'm going to take the plane up to 38,000 feet where we should be over it. There'll be less turbulence. Might be a bit shaky for a little while. Nothing to worry about.'

Dani looked at his father. His eyes were wide open.

Al Jameel smiled. 'It'll be fine,' he said as there was a noticeable increase in engine noise.

Dani gripped his seat belt and grimaced as the sky below flashed white with lightning. 'Allah be with us,' he muttered.

Al Jameel started to relax when he felt the plane level off and the sound of the engines returned to a steady drone. He closed his eyes and tried to get some sleep for the rest of the journey. He must have been in a deep sleep because the next thing he knew, Dani was shaking his arm.

'We're beginning our descent to Heathrow, Father.'

Not long after, the plane landed with a slight jolt and the engines roared as they went into reverse thrust. It took a while for the plane to taxi to its parking bay. Several minutes later, the doors opened for passengers to disembark.

After going through passport control, they collected their baggage. Outside, a chauffeur in a grey uniform and peaked cap met them. He showed them the way to a sleek silver limousine and put their bags in the boot.

On their way out of Terminal 3, the driver checked their final destination. 'Should be there in under forty minutes.'

They'd arrived at Canning's house and had enjoyed a dinner of oysters and salad. Afterwards, Al Jameel, Dani and Canning retired to the reception room Canning liked to use when he had visitors.

Canning poured himself a brandy, wondering if Al Jameel and Dani would approve. 'What can I get you both?' he asked.

'Sparkling water is fine, thank you,' Dani's father said.

Canning looked at Dani with raised eyebrows.

'Same for me.'

'Your wife is a very good cook,' Al Jameel said.

'Yes, she always excels when we have visitors. I told her your favourite dish was oysters and salad and she decided she would do that for you.'

'Very kind of her,' Al Jameel said.

Al Jameel and Dani had settled down into one of the settees and Canning sat opposite. 'How was your flight?'

'It was rather, how do you say... bumpy over the Alps. Dani was convinced we were about to crash,' Al Jameel said.

Dani smiled. He was a tall, slender man with brown eyes. He looked like his father, but the beard and moustache were thinner. In contrast to his father's white thawb, Dani wore a black one. Both men had on the same red-and-white chequered keffiyehs. 'I can't say that particular part of the journey was enjoyable,' Dani said.

'I'm very pleased you didn't crash,' Canning said. 'Wouldn't have done much for our potential business partnership.' He laughed. 'Your investment would be missed.'

'Have your police made any progress in finding your friend's killer?' Al Jameel asked.

'He wasn't actually my friend, just an employee. But no, I don't think they have.'

'And local resistance to your application?'

'There's still opposition. Always will be when change is afoot, but I'm sure people will come round to accepting it'll be for the good of the village.'

'Can we have a look at the site?' Dani asked. 'It would be good to see it so my father can get a feel for whether he thinks it is worthy of investment.'

'Of course. I'd intended to show you so you can visualise from the plans where we'll build everything. I'll also get my accountant to go over the finances we have already secured. Subject, that is, to the approval of the application.'

'And is there any news on that front?' Al Jameel asked.

Canning took a slow sip of his brandy. 'There is... but I'm sure it won't be a problem.'

Al Jameel raised an eyebrow. 'Problem?'

'It appears the secretary of state has called in my application.'

'What does that mean?' Dani asked.

'It's a term we use here. Usually, the local planning authority would approve applications. But in this case, it means the secretary of state will make the final decision.'

'Why has it been taken out of the hands of your planning authority?' Al Jameel asked.

'Local concern. Totally unfounded of course.'

'I see.'

Canning held up a hand. 'Let me reassure you, this will make no difference to my application. They'll hold a public inquiry and I'll get a chance to make my case while tearing apart the parish council one. It could work to my benefit. As it happens, the secretary of state is a good friend of mine. And... I have a certain amount of influence over him.'

Al Jameel smiled. 'Then we have nothing to worry about, do we?'

'Nothing at all,' Canning said, hoping very much that would be the case.

22

Anderson had caught an early train down from Oxford. She then took the Tube to Leicester Square Underground station. Emerging onto the street, she took several moments to work out which way to go. She set off after a quick check of the address Gale Slater had given her. The route she chose would, Anderson hoped, be the quickest way to get there.

The streets were busy, hot and noisy. Anderson felt overwhelmed by the constant flow of cars, lorries and London buses. The smell of exhaust fumes filled the air. She decided to seek temporary refuge by popping into a café. The aroma of fresh coffee was a welcome escape from the foul air outside.

A man with brown eyes and long black hair was behind the counter. He smiled at Anderson. 'You like to see the menu?' he asked in an Italian accent.

'Just a coffee please... latte,' Anderson replied, returning the smile.

'No problem. Take a seat and I bring it to you.'

'Thanks.' Anderson showed him the hotel address. 'Is this far?'

'No, not far at all. Turn right out of the door, follow the road for a few hundred yards then go left. The hotel is along the street on your left. You staying there?'

'No.' Anderson didn't offer any more information.

'Ah, okay. I bring your coffee in a minute.'

Anderson settled herself by a window and looked out on the busy street. There was the occasional short blast of a car horn. The sound of wailing sirens filled the air in the distance. The roar of plane engines passed overhead. *Couldn't live here*, Anderson thought.

The young man brought her latte and she thought about how she was going to approach her task as she sipped at it. After a few minutes she got up to leave.

'Have a nice day,' the young man called across to her as she reached the door.

'You too.'

It was only a six-minute walk to the hotel from the café. A selection of flags flew from the second floor of the grand three-storey building. Anderson took in the luxurious main entrance and large rectangular windows. *Has to be five-star.*

Anderson looked up as she went through the entrance and noted the presence of a CCTV camera. *Plus point.* The long reception desk was on the right, but there was only one young receptionist on duty. On the left there was a circular seating area where a man dressed in a smart suit sat reading a newspaper.

Anderson walked over to the receptionist and showed her warrant card. 'DC Anderson from Thames Valley Police. May I have a quick word?'

The receptionist's eyes widened and her face reddened. 'Yes... of course. Is there a problem?'

Anderson smiled. 'No, don't worry. I just need to ask about a customer who stayed here not long ago.'

'Oh, I see. Who was that?'

'Mr Slater, Tom Slater.' Anderson gave the receptionist the date of his first stay at the hotel.

The receptionist turned to a computer screen and tapped on the keyboard. 'Yes, got him. He stayed one night. Took a double room but he was on his own.'

'We have reason to believe he might have met someone here. Did he mention he was expecting anyone or book a dinner table for two?'

'He ate alone, but I remember him saying he was expecting someone at around six. He said to tell his visitor he could find him in the bar.'

'And you saw this visitor?'

'Yes. I told him where to find Mr Slater. That's all I remember.'

'Can you describe him?'

'Gosh, I see so many people. Let me think now. He sounded Italian.'

'Age?'

'Could have been in his thirties.'

The man with the newspaper butted in from behind Anderson. 'Sorry to intrude, but can I have my bill?'

Anderson turned and frowned. 'We're busy.'

'Busy chatting if you ask me. You youngsters can carry on chinwagging after I've paid my bill.'

'You can wait,' Anderson said, showing her warrant card. 'This is police business. Wouldn't want to obstruct a police officer in the course of her duties, would you?'

The man took a step back, a look of horror on his face. 'No... no, of course not.' He turned and strode off towards the lifts.

The receptionist giggled. 'Glad you put him in his place. He's a bit of a knob, sorry.'

Anderson smiled. 'Mr Slater had a second stay here more recently. Do you know if he saw the same man again?'

'Yes, he did. They met in the bar again. Is Mr Slater and the other man in some sort of trouble?'

'Mr Slater was murdered.'

'My god! You... you mean by the man who came to see him here?'

'That's taking a big leap in the dark. At this stage, we're only trying to establish Mr Slater's movements and who he came into contact with.'

'I see.'

'Could I have a word with the barman who was on duty on those evenings.'

'Afraid not. He's on sick leave. Had an accident. Knocked off his bike by a car.'

'Ouch! I'll need his address. Oh, and I notice there's a CCTV camera at the entrance. Is there more CCTV inside?'

'There is.'

'Can you arrange for any footage on those two nights to be sent over to me?'

Anderson gave the receptionist details of where to send the footage. She got the barman's address, offered her thanks and left to face the fume-filled streets again.

23

Fleming walked into the incident room to find Logan and Anderson engaged in a healthy debate, though it was nothing to do with the case.

'It was Steve McQueen,' Anderson said.

'No, it was James Coburn,' Logan countered.

'Nah. Had to be Steve McQueen, Sarge. Everyone knows he had a big part in *The Great Escape*.'

'He did, but it was Coburn who played Sedgwick.'

'I bow to your superior knowledge. I suppose the film was more in your time,' Anderson joked.

'I'll have you know, young woman, I was born four years *after* the film was made.'

'Still more your era than mine, Sarge.'

'Talking of escapes. Either of you heard any more about Jack Kelso?' Fleming asked.

'He escaped in a lorry collecting stuff from the prison. Transferred to a car which prison officers found ablaze. Kelso, and whoever sprung him out, then switched to another vehicle. They haven't found him yet.' Logan ran a hand through his receding grey hair. There was a hint of concern in his brown eyes. 'You think there's any chance he'll come after you?'

'Doubt it. The SIO who put him away has long since died. If I recall, I only questioned him once. Anyway, let's go through where we are.'

Logan looked at his notes. 'Had details back from the SOCOs and I've now got a list of all Slater's contacts off his mobile phone and from his wife. There was a call to his mobile on the evening he was murdered, but it can't be identified or traced to anyone. Whoever called used a burner phone.'

'Your briefing meeting is arranged for this afternoon,' Anderson reminded Fleming. 'Mrs Slater will be there. Do you want me to come?'

'Could be a good idea.'

'I should come as well,' Logan suggested. 'You know... in case the theory that the killer sometimes returns to the scene of the crime is right.'

'Only the briefing meeting isn't the scene of the crime,' Anderson said with a laugh.

Logan smiled. 'It might well be the scene of another one if you're not careful.'

'Returning to the case,' Fleming said, 'how did you get on in London, Naomi?'

'Slater saw the same man on his two visits to the hotel. They met in the bar, but the barman who was on duty both nights is off on sick leave. The receptionist is arranging to send over CCTV footage of the entrance and inside the hotel on the two nights in question. I've got the barman's address so I can go and see him at home once we have some still photos. See if he can pick out the man who met Slater.'

'Good.' Fleming looked at the whiteboard Logan had been scribbling on. 'It seems we have three main lines of enquiry to follow. One, there's Vic Quinn. One of the more vocal protesters and prone to violence. Had a couple of run-ins with Slater. He said he was with his wife at home on the night of the murder. Any joy with checking all that, Harry?'

'Still working on it,' Logan said. 'There's also the partial car registration match.'

'Anything from DVLA, Naomi?'

'Not yet, I guess they will need to run it all through the system. There could be thousands.'

'Hmm. We should ask them if they can do a search for the surrounding counties around Darmont first. Might speed things up a bit.'

'Okay, sir.'

'Right. Two, we have Slater's stepson, Rashad Yousefi. There was no love lost between them, and Slater threw him out. Have we checked his alibi out yet?'

'Still working on it, boss,' Logan said. 'What's the third line?'

'We need to find out more about this mystery man who Slater went to see in London. Could he be the killer? Maybe someone who Slater owed gambling debts to.'

'With a bit of luck, we'll have a photo of this man once I get the CCTV footage from the hotel,' Anderson said.

'Other actions still outstanding then,' Fleming said. 'I want to speak to Slater's parents next, and we ought to get the pathology and forensic reports any time. And... we carry on questioning everyone who knew Slater. Oh, almost forgot, we need to get someone to check Slater's workspace in Canning's London office.'

'I could do it when I go back to see the barman from the hotel,' Anderson offered.

'Great. Think that's all for now. Let's have a coffee before we go to Darmont for the briefing meeting.'

A row of desks had been set up at the front of the village hall. Fleming sat on one side with Gale Slater on his left and Anderson next to her. Canning and Yamamura were there, as was Vic Quinn. He sat at the rear with eyes boring into Canning's back. Logan was sitting amongst the press. It was hot outside. The parish council clerk had opened all the windows and doors to let in what little breeze there was.

Fleming eyed the expectant audience and began to speak. 'Before I begin, Mrs Slater wants to say a few words.' He glanced sideways at Gale Slater and smiled encouragement.

Gale's hands were shaking as she tried to steady the piece of paper she was clutching. She cleared her throat. 'I know Tom had his detractors in the village, but he was my husband. It's not easy for someone to lose a partner. Having to cope with their murder is... is something I would not wish on anyone.' Gale's voice faltered. 'If anybody has any information they think might be of help to the police, please let them know.' Gale pulled a handkerchief out of her sleeve and blew her nose. 'I also want to say thank you for the kindness and support I've received.' She looked at Fleming to signal she had finished what she wanted to say.

Fleming surveyed the listeners and noticed Zoe Dunbar had slipped in the open door to take a seat at the rear. 'Thank you, Gale. I want to stress that we are doing all we can to ensure the safety of the public. We have no reason though to believe people are at risk. That said, a firearm was involved, so we're treating this with the utmost seriousness. For the time being there will be more police patrols round the village. I hope that will put people's minds at rest.'

Vic Quinn stood up. 'What will put people's minds at rest is if Mr Canning and his cronies do the decent thing and scrap their plans for the housing and shopping development.'

One or two other locals voiced their support and the hall filled with shouts of approval.

Fleming stood and held his hands up. 'Can we have order please. This is not a meeting to discuss the planning application. I shouldn't have to remind everyone that this is a murder investigation. If there's any more disturbance I'll call the meeting off.'

The rumblings subsided and Fleming sat to resume proceedings. 'I'd like to repeat what Mrs Slater said and appeal for anyone who may have seen anything suspicious on the day of the murder to come forward. We have several lines of enquiry we are currently following and hope we can bring this investigation to a speedy conclusion. Any questions?'

A reporter near the front put up a hand. 'Can you be specific about the lines of enquiry you're following?'

'Not at this stage, no.'

Dunbar stood at the rear. 'Do you expect to make an arrest soon?'

Fleming smiled. 'Good to see you again, Miss Dunbar. It's too early to say.'

Dunbar continued standing. 'Still less than helpful with your answers I see,' she quipped. 'Do you think Mr Slater's murder could be linked in some way to the planning application?'

'It's a possibility we haven't ruled out.'

'What about motive? Any early indications?'

'There are a few possibilities we're looking at.'

'Have you reason to believe there's any truth in the allegations of bribery and corruption surrounding the application?'

'No.'

Dunbar sighed and sat down.

'If there are no more questions, we'll wrap the meeting up here,' Fleming said, rising to his feet.

When he left, Fleming could see Dunbar locked in conversation with some of the local residents.

24

Fleming hadn't slept well and had woken up with red eyes and a headache. Breakfast had been two cups of black coffee, scrambled eggs with bacon, and two aspirin. He'd been running late and skipped shaving.

It was only a twenty-three-minute drive to the office. Logan and Anderson were already there. Logan was studying a file on his desk and Anderson was scanning her computer screen.

'Anything new to report before I go to see the super?' Fleming asked.

Logan gazed up at a weary-looking Fleming. 'You okay, boss? Don't look too good if you ask me.'

'I'm fine, just tired. Had a bad night.'

Anderson looked up from her computer screen. 'Get you a coffee, sir?'

'That would be good. Thanks, Naomi.'

'What about me?' Logan complained.

'You've had one.'

'Another wouldn't go amiss. How about I make the next ones?' Logan tapped the file in front of him. 'I want to fill the boss in on the autopsy report on Slater.'

'I don't know. Any excuse,' she muttered as she left to get the coffees.

Logan looked closely at Fleming. 'You sure you're okay? I can always go and brief the super. Tell her you weren't feeling well and had to go home.'

'Thanks, Harry. I'm fine.'

Logan had given Fleming the gist of what was in the pathology and ballistics reports by the time Anderson returned with the coffees. Fleming took his and retired to his office to study everything before his meeting with Temple.

Temple's door was open as usual, but Fleming knocked anyway.

'Come in, Alex. Take a seat.'

Fleming thought she looked better than she had during his last meeting. *Typical, when I'm feeling crap.*

Temple gave Fleming a quizzical look. 'Are you all right? You look a bit pale.'

'Second person to ask me that today. Had a bad night and woke with a headache. I'm fine.'

'We can do this tomorrow if you want to go home and get some rest.'

'No, let me give you an update now, ma'am. I'll see how things are afterwards.'

'Okay. How did your briefing meeting go?'

'As well as can be expected. One of our possible suspects was there and caused a bit of a stir.'

'Really? Who was that?'

'Local man. Vic Quinn. He's one of the more vocal protesters and has a record of violence. Done for assault some years back.'

'What did he do to cause this hoo-ha?'

'He started slagging Canning off and things got a little heated.'

'Any more than the fact he's got previous and is a local protester to make him a suspect?'

'He has a lot of pent-up anger. His mother is finding it hard to sell her house because of the proposed development. She's had to knock thousands off the asking price. And... he had a couple of run-ins with Slater.'

'That it?'

'A witness saw a black car driving fast away from the village hall on the night of the murder. She remembered part of the registration and it matches Quinn's car.'

'You've questioned him?'

'Yes, but not under caution at this stage. We've got DVLA making a list of all cars with the partially recognised number plate and we're checking his alibi.'

Temple nodded. 'You said he was one of your possible suspects.'

'There's also Slater's stepson. No love lost between them. In fact, it would be fair to say his stepson hated him.'

'You've questioned him?'

'Yes. Checking his alibi. He doesn't have a car, but a friend does... and it's black.'

'Anything else?'

'House-to-house enquiries haven't come up with anything and the CCTV at the village hall wasn't working. I've received the pathologist's report and got details back from ballistics.'

'Anything useful?'

'The autopsy report is full of technical medical stuff, but doesn't help much in finding the killer. Cause of death, two bullets through the head at close range. The angle of entry and exit points suggest the killer was standing in front of Slater and could be about the same height. Time of death between eight and eleven on the Friday night. The SOCOs found the two bullets and some clothes fibres. Ballistics confirm a nine-millimetre handgun was the murder weapon. That's about it for now.'

'Okay. Thanks, Alex. Go home if you don't feel well.'

Fleming ignored Temple's advice and stayed in the office, but he did decide a trip to London to see Slater's parents might not be a great idea that day. It could wait until the following day. Passing the incident room, he noticed Logan and Anderson there. Logan was starting to write something on the whiteboard.

'Hey, boss,' Logan said. 'Bit of a result. Guess what I've just found out.'

25

The parish council office was a small affair attached to the end of Darmont village hall. Next to the clerk's office there was a room where they held council meetings. Paul Canning sat across the table from councillor Kim Ogilvie.

'The thing is,' Canning said, 'residents seem to be on a different planet... if you don't mind me saying so. They don't like the neighbourhood plan you put together. Neither do they, nor you, like the local council plan for Darmont. But the council do now seem to be in favour of my proposed housing and shopping development. The reality of the situation is they can't avoid change.'

Ogilvie sighed. 'We have tried to convince them that the neighbourhood plan is the best option for Darmont. Doesn't matter what we say though, there is strong opposition to any kind of development.'

'Unrealistic if I may say so. They'll have a chance at the forthcoming public inquiry to air their views. The parish council will as well of course, but development *will* take place, mark my words.'

'It's true we will have an opportunity to state our case, and that will be to press for the neighbourhood plan to take precedence over any other plan.'

'Let me put this to you. The position of local people is untenable as we both know. You oppose the council pla–'

'And your application,' Ogilvie cut in.

'Indeed. But it is almost certain that the secretary of state will lean towards major development. It's in line with current housing policy. There is a national need for thousands more houses. And I know the council are now going to support my application. Under the circumstances, it seems unlikely they will support your plans.'

'We can but hope.'

'I admire your optimism, but the truth of the matter is that the public inquiry has to decide on one thing only. That is whether to recommend in favour of my application or not.'

'And if your application is reject–'

'The council will decide to put their local plan in place,' Canning cut in.

Ogilvie shook her head. 'That will be a sad day for Darmont.'

Canning placed the palms of his hands on the table and fixed his eyes on Ogilvie. 'The parish council would be in a better position were it to lobby support for my application at the public inquiry.'

'What makes you say that?'

'You should back a winning team. I see your medical centre could do with a revamp, as could the village hall and your office. I'm sure my people could tweak our plans to include new builds for all three. Think about it.'

'I'll put what you said to the next parish council meeting.'

Canning left Kim Ogilvie to ponder over his offer. He felt sure he could bring the parish council round to supporting his application. His next port of call was to join Yamamura who was with Al Jameel and his son. She was going through the finances and showing them the proposed development site.

Steadying himself with his walking cane, Canning hobbled round the corner of the village hall to go to his car but stopped when he saw Vic Quinn dragging a screeching knife along the side of it. 'What the hell!'

Quinn turned with a wicked grin. 'Just walking by and couldn't believe my luck when I saw your car here.'

Canning's face turned puce. 'They should lock morons like you up and throw the fucking key away!' he shouted as he shuffled towards Quinn. 'You'll pay for this!'

Quinn ignored him and turned back to his work. 'Makes quite a good job, don't you think, you rich obnoxious bastard. Take your fucking car, your plans, and piss off out of Darmont. And don't come back!'

Canning swung has cane over his head and brought it down hard behind Quinn's knees.

Quinn cried out in pain and spun round to face Canning. He waved his knife menacingly in front of him. 'How about I do a job on your face, you fat bastard!'

Canning stepped back, fear in his eyes.

Quinn took a step closer and grabbed Canning's coat by the lapels. 'So help me, I'll put an end to your fucking plans right now!' He raised the knife towards Canning's face, but then recovered his composure. He released Canning and pushed him away, shaking his head. 'Hope you rot in hell, Canning.'

The window of the parish council office flew open and a frightened-looking Kim Ogilvie stuck her head out. 'I saw what happened. I've phoned the police.'

Quinn glared at her, turned and strode off.

Canning leaned against his car and drew deep breaths as Ogilvie rushed out to check he was okay.

'Look what he's done to my car. I thought he was going to kill me!'

'They told me a police car was patrolling the village. They should be here any minute.'

'They need to get that maniac and lock him up,' Canning said as he heard the wailing of police sirens not far away.

26

'No guessing, just tell me what you've found out, Harry,' Fleming said.

'Our man, Vic Quinn. His alibi doesn't stack up.'

Fleming raised an eyebrow. 'How come?'

'He told us he was at home with his wife on the night of the murder.'

'He wasn't?'

'His wife went out with friends in the village that night.'

'Okay. Maybe he got it wrong. Could be he forgot what night she went out and he was at home on his own.'

'I checked with neighbours and one of them swears she saw Quinn leave home in his car around eight o'clock the night of the murder and come back about nine.'

Fleming frowned. 'Doesn't make sense. That fits with the estimated time of death in the autopsy report, but if he's the killer, why would he take his car when he lives in the village? And why would he arrange to meet Slater at the village hall?'

'It's possible it wasn't him who phoned Slater,' Anderson chipped in. 'It could have been an impromptu thing. He might have gone out in his car for some reason, saw Slater, took a chance and killed him on the spur of the moment.'

'Problem with that theory,' Logan said, 'is you're assuming he had a gun with him, just in case. Bit unlikely, Naomi.'

'Only a thought, Sarge.' Anderson was beginning to sound doubtful. 'Maybe he kept a gun in his car,' she added without any real conviction.

'Full marks for trying, Naomi,' Logan said. 'Mind you... stranger things have happened in murder cases. And... it doesn't alter the fact that he lied about his alibi, and his car matches the partial registration the witness remembered. Not to mention his run-ins with Slater and that he's *very* angry over the proposed development.'

Fleming was about to respond when his mobile phone indicated an incoming call. 'Okay, we need to have another chat with Quinn,' he said, before taking the call. He looked at Logan. 'Need to take this. It's DI Oliver from local CID.'

Fleming tapped the answer icon and listened intently. 'Right. Make sure you get DNA samples and his fingerprints.' He ended the call.

'Development?' Logan queried.

'Quinn's been arrested.'

'What!'

'Seems he was vandalising Canning's car. There was a bit of a scuffle between him and Canning. Quinn is under arrest for causing criminal damage and assault. Chair of the parish council, Kim Ogilvie, saw it all.'

'We need to speak to him again.'

'Yes, but I'd rather wait to see if his fingerprints match the ones found on Slater's car. And... I'd like to have a word with Kim Ogilvie first.'

'Okay. Are you going to see Slater's parents today?'

'No. Think I'll give it a miss. I'll go tomorrow and take Naomi with me.'

~

Fleming felt better the next day. He decided it was the extra glass of whisky the night before which had tipped him over the edge. Anderson lived in Oxford as well, so it made sense to take the Porsche and pick her up to drive down to London. It was easier than both of them going into HQ to get a squad car. Slater's parents' semi-detached house was on an estate just off the A5 near Edgware. Fleming spotted a space in a long line of cars parked on the side of the road and managed to squeeze his car into the gap.

A frail old woman in her eighties, dressed in trousers, blouse and a thin cotton cardigan opened the door. She peered at Fleming with watery eyes.

Fleming showed his warrant card. 'DCI Fleming and DC Anderson. We spoke on the phone.'

'Oh, yes. We were expecting you. I'm Eva. Come in and meet my husband. Arthur's a bit older than me and he's a little deaf,' she explained.

Eva showed Fleming and Anderson along a narrow hallway into a long rectangular sitting room. Arthur was slouched on an easy chair to one side of an electric fire mounted on the wall. Another chair where Eva had been sitting was opposite with an open book balanced over one arm. A two-seater settee was against the wall facing the fire.

Fleming and Anderson took the settee, Anderson getting her notebook out at the ready.

'This is DCI Fleming and DC Anderson,' Eva told her husband in a rather loud voice.

Arthur nodded. 'Sorry I didn't get up. Bit frail these days.'

'Not at all,' Fleming said. 'I'm so sorry about your son. If it's okay we'd like to ask you both a few questions.'

Eva took her seat and closed the book. 'Of course. I hope we can help. Dreadful business. My own son, murdered. It's awful.' Tears formed in her eyes.

'Yes,' Fleming agreed. 'We're doing everything we can to find the culprit. Your son's wife told us he'd received a death threat. Did he ever tell you about that?'

Eva dabbed at her eyes with a handkerchief. 'He did, but he dismissed it. Said it was normal for people involved in new developments. Said not to worry about it.'

'Did he mention a man called Quinn at any time?'

Eva shook her head. 'No, can't say he did.'

'Did your son ever talk about moving to Spain?'

'He did, but it came to nothing,' Eva said.

'Did he tell you about a fall out he had with his boss, Paul Canning?'

'Yes. He'd asked for a pay rise, but Mr Canning refused. Tom was a bit upset. I think that's why he was talking about packing the job in and moving to Spain. But as I said, it came to nothing.'

'Do you think he asked for more money because he was in debt... gambling debts?'

Eva gasped. 'Gambling? I didn't know he gambled. Did you, Arthur?'

Arthur was nodding off. 'Gamble? Who's that. Never heard of him.'

'No, dear. Not a person. Tom had been *gambling*,' Eva shouted.

Arthur shrugged and closed his eyes again.

'Your son had two recent meetings in London which Paul Canning knew nothing about. Did Tom happen to say anything to you about meeting someone?'

'No.' It was Eva answering all the questions. Arthur's chin had dropped onto his chest.

'His wife told us Tom used to live in London.'

'Yes. He worked here for a letting agency before he started work for Mr Canning.'

'Gale Slater thought he might have been coming to London to some of his old gambling haunts.'

'This is all news to me,' Eva said. 'We never knew he gambled. Do you think it might be something to do with why someone killed him?'

'I don't know,' Fleming admitted. 'Maybe he had gambling debts and he was meeting the man he owed money to. We just need to follow up on every lead. I want to find the person he was meeting if for no other reason than to eliminate them from our enquiries.'

'I see.'

'I gather Tom never saw eye to eye with his stepson.'

'No, he didn't. Gale used to be married to an Iranian. They had a son, Rashad. When Tom and Gale got married, Tom and Rashad were always arguing. Tom thought he was lazy and would never make anything of his life. Turned out to be true. He got into drugs and lost his job. Tom threw him out.'

Fleming looked at Anderson who had been scribbling in her notebook. 'Anything you want to ask, Naomi?'

Anderson smiled at Eva. 'Is there anyone you can think of who might have had a grudge against your son?'

Eva paused. 'No... no, I can't think there is... except...'

'Yes?'

'Tom did sack a man recently. I don't know what it was about. But surely that wouldn't be a reason to kill someone?'

Fleming rose to leave. 'Stranger things have happened, Mrs Slater. Do you know this man's name?'

'No, but Mr Canning will know.'

'Of course. Thank you for your time. Don't get up. We'll let ourselves out.'

On the way back to Oxford, Fleming was thinking they'd found nothing new, except about the man Slater had fired.

27

Guerra had left Kelso saying he would return with his boss the next day. Kelso had thought of doing a runner, but two things held him back. One, he had no money and nowhere else to go. Two, he was curious over who it was who had facilitated his escape from prison. Then there was the operation Guerra's boss had thought Kelso was the man to head because he was ex-army and handy with guns. *How had he known that?* Whatever it was, it sounded big.

Kelso was walking round the grounds exploring while thinking. The house was set in private gardens of over an acre. Tall trees and hedges hid the house from view from the country lane leading to it. A sweeping gravel driveway opened up to a large circular parking space in front of the house.

Walking up the driveway to the lane, Kelso noted it wasn't a busy road. Heading back up the drive, he wandered across a lawn round to the right of the house. A tall yew hedge bordered the lawn extended all the way round the house. At the back there was a large patio edged with a low wall. Beyond the wall, another lawn surrounded by flower borders led to a small wooded area forming the rear boundary. Going back to the front door, Kelso satisfied himself that the property was a perfect place to hide out. It was completely secluded.

Guerra was another issue. Kelso had reservations about him. Guerra had struck him as being cocky, impulsive and quick to anger. It was clear Guerra didn't welcome his boss's desire to bring Kelso on board to run the operation, whatever it might be. *I think me and my sidekick here would have been capable of doing the job on our own. Don't want you trying to take over,* he'd said. Yes, Guerra was going to be someone to keep a very close eye on.

Going back into the house, Kelso went down the hallway to the kitchen. Guerra had stocked it with a few basic foodstuffs. After getting himself some breakfast, Kelso retired to the living room. He sat by the front window looking out over the gravel driveway.

He whiled the time away thinking and leafing through a few country magazines. After a couple of hours, Guerra's Volvo swung round the driveway and crunched to a halt on the gravel in front of the house. Kelso looked in surprise when he saw the tall silver-haired man with a black patch over his left eye get out. Sixty now, Ulrick Zimmerman was overweight, but stocky. Grey suits with matching waistcoat were still his taste in fashion.

Kelso had first come across him while they were both serving in Afghanistan. Kelso had been a sergeant and Zimmerman a captain. After leaving the army, Kelso had worked as a London nightclub bouncer for four years. It was there he stumbled across Zimmerman again. He'd started working for him as a minder when Zimmerman took over a club and became involved in the London gangland scene. It was Zimmerman who had masterminded the armed robbery. Kelso had been caught and convicted, but he'd stayed loyal to the man who had planned it all and had never implicated him.

Throwing the magazine he'd been reading onto the coffee table, Kelso rose, strode to the front door, pulled it open and looked over Guerra's shoulder. 'Well, well, if it isn't Ulrick Zimmerman. I might have guessed it was you who arranged my escape.'

'How are you, Jack?' Zimmerman asked. 'Took a bit longer than I thought it would to get you out.'

Guerra shook his head. He looked at Kelso, then turned round to look at his boss. 'You two know each other? I thought you only knew about Kelso, not that you knew him personally.'

Zimmerman's one cold grey eye held Guerra in a steady gaze. 'It's a long story. Let's go inside,' he mumbled in a hoarse voice.

Once inside, sitting in the living room, Guerra spoke first. 'What's the deal, boss? You didn't tell me you knew Kelso.'

'The name's Jack,' Kelso reminded him.

'Since when were we on first-name terms?' Guerra snapped.

Zimmerman glared at Guerra, and a corner of his mouth twitched. 'Keep your hair on, Marco. I need you two to get on together.'

Guerra scowled. There was no mistaking the sarcasm in his voice. 'Sorry, boss. I'll try to be nice to him.'

'You'd better,' Zimmerman warned. He then went on to recount how he and Kelso had first met and how Kelso had come to work for him in London.

'I didn't know all that,' Guerra said.

'Something else you don't know,' Zimmerman said. 'Jack here took the rap for an armed robbery I masterminded. He never snitched on me, and I vowed I would repay his loyalty one day.'

'When was all this? News to me.'

'Before your time, Marco. When they transferred Jack to a

category C training prison from the high security one, I saw there was a better chance of organising an escape. And here we all are.'

'Right,' Kelso said, 'now that's all out of the way. Marco told me you had a job in mind you thought you needed me for. What exactly does it entail?'

Zimmerman smiled through closed lips. 'Your transfer to a category C was most timely. It happened to coincide with some information that came my way.'

'Information which was going to be beneficial to you, only you need my help to realise the benefit,' Kelso guessed.

'Exactly.'

'Care to explain?'

'A man by the name of Paul Canning's submitted an application for a major housing and shopping development at Darmont.'

'How does that benefit you? Can't be you've offered to invest in it. That would be legal, and my guess is the job involved is definitely not legal.'

'Right again. The information I came across involves a rather wealthy man who is interested in investing in the development.'

'And you aim to rob him. Is that the plan?'

'In a way, yes.'

Kelso frowned. 'There's more than one way?'

'Isa Al Jameel is a rich Saudi businessman. I found out he was coming over to stay with Canning to discuss his possible investment. And... he's bringing his son with him.'

'I think I know where this is going,' Kelso said.

'I plan to kidnap the son and ask for a ransom of two million pounds.'

Kelso looked at Guerra. 'And you thought you and your driver mate, Taffy could handle this on you own?'

Guerra scowled. 'We could.'

'I don't think so,' Zimmerman said. 'Anyway, I've decided. Jack leads the actual kidnap and works out the how.' He glared at Guerra. 'And you do what you're told.'

Kelso saw the look on Guerra's face and somehow doubted whether he would.

28

They'd cleared the M25 on the way back to Oxford after speaking to Tom Slater's parents, Eva and Arthur Slater in London. Fleming flicked on the wipers of his Porsche as the first spots of rain hit the windscreen. 'Could be worth popping into Darmont to see if Kim Ogilvie is about. It's more or less on the way.'

'She'll have spoken to the local police. Are we likely to find out anything new?' Anderson asked.

'Maybe not, but as we're passing, it might be worth a quick word.'

'We didn't get much new from the Slaters, did we?'

'Not a lot,' Fleming agreed. 'Particularly poor old Arthur. He was finding it hard to stay awake. We need to speak to Paul Canning about the man Tom Slater sacked.'

The rain had eased and the wipers were beginning to scrape on the Porsche's windscreen as they pulled into the village hall car park. There was a light on in the parish council office. 'Might be in luck,' Fleming said.

They got out of the car and walked round the side of the building where they found the office door propped open. Kim Ogilvie was behind a desk tapping away on a keyboard while looking at the computer screen. She looked up as Fleming tapped on the door. 'Can I help you?'

Fleming showed his warrant card. 'DCI Fleming and DC Anderson. Mind if we come in to ask you a few questions?'

Ogilvie frowned. 'Is this to do with Vic Quinn and Paul Canning? I've given a statement to the local police.'

'We were passing through and thought we'd pop in on the off-chance you were here. Thought it would be a good opportunity to speak to you.'

'Oh, right. You'd better come in then and find yourselves a seat. Bit cramped I'm afraid.'

Fleming pulled up a chair and sat opposite Ogilvie while Anderson found a spare one by the window. She rummaged in her bag and fished out a notebook, pen at the ready.

Fleming looked across the desk at Ogilvie. 'You were here in the office when you saw the incident involving Vic Quinn and Paul Canning?'

'Yes. As I said, I told the police everything.'

'Do you mind if we go over things again... for my benefit?'

Ogilvie shrugged. 'Go ahead.'

'Can you talk me through what happened?'

'Mr Canning was leaving the office and I heard a loud scraping noise outside, like something scratching across metal. I got up to have a look and saw Mr Quinn pulling a knife along the side of Mr Canning's car. Mr Canning came round the corner and shouted out to Quinn. He turned to face Mr Canning and there was an exchange of words.'

'Did you hear what they were saying?'

'Quinn said something to the effect he'd been passing and couldn't believe his luck he'd found Mr Canning's car there.'

'And how did Mr Canning respond?'

'He shouted how morons like Quinn should be locked up and that he'd pay for it.'

'Then what happened?'

'Quinn turned his back on Mr Canning and carried on scratching the car while muttering some obscenities. Next thing, Canning hit Quinn over the back of his legs with his walking cane. Quinn spun round and waved his knife in front of Mr Canning. He shouted he would do a job on Mr Canning's face, then grabbed hold of him. Said something about putting an end to Mr Canning's plans, but then pushed him away saying he hoped he would rot in hell.'

'Can you describe the knife Quinn was holding?'

'It was only a small penknife.'

'When did you call the police?'

'I called them on my mobile while I was watching what was going on. I then opened the window and shouted out that I'd phoned the police.'

'What happened then?'

'Quinn strode off and I went out to check Mr Canning was okay. I told him the police were on their way. They'd told me a car was in the vicinity and would be here soon. It was part of the regular patrols since Mr Slater's murder.'

'They took statements from you and Mr Canning before going after Quinn?'

'That's right, I gather they arrested him at home later.'

'Why was Mr Canning here in the office?'

'He'd come to try to persuade me to get the parish council to support his application at the public enquiry.'

'He doesn't know you've asked for the application to be called in?'

'Oh, yes, he knows.'

'So why did he think he could get you to support his application when you've written to the secretary of state to oppose it?'

'He thought he could get us to change our minds.'

'By doing what?'

'He suggested he could include new builds for our medical centre, village hall and parish council office.'

'And that might sway the parish council?'

'It could. Our neighbourhood plan doesn't allow for those improvements. Neither does the council local plan.'

'And do you think he's offered benefits to the planning authority for supporting his application?'

Ogilvie pursed her lips. 'It's why some residents are making allegations of bribery and corruption.'

'You mean involving the council planning office?'

'It's what they claim, though there's no proof.'

'Have you any reason to believe they might have a point?'

'I can see no evidence to suggest so, no.'

Anderson had been busy scribbling in her notebook. She looked up at Ogilvie. 'I suppose Mr Canning is thinking he's already got the support of the council planning office. With your support the only objection to his application will be the local residents.'

Ogilvie nodded. 'And... their position is untenable because they object to any kind of development.'

On the drive back to HQ, Fleming was thinking about Paul Canning and his offer to the parish council. *He's either an astute businessman, or capable of bribery.*

29

Darmont Golf Club was a few miles out of the village, up a country lane and along a narrow potholed road. Fleming had checked to see if Tom Slater's friend would be at home or at work. It turned out he was at neither. He was playing golf and Fleming had agreed to meet him at the course clubhouse at midday. Fifteen minutes early, he swung his Porsche into the car park.

Anderson had collared him before he left the office to say she'd had a result from DVLA. They'd narrowed the list of all black cars registered in 2017 in the counties surrounding Darmont down to those starting with the letter L. It was still a big list, but she and Logan had liaised with local police forces to arrange for them to question every owner. It was one of those painstaking tasks police often had to carry out in the course of a murder investigation. Sometimes this detailed work produced results and Fleming was hoping the effort would not be in vain.

Norman Read had described himself to Fleming. 'Look out for a small stocky man wearing grey shorts, a blue golf T-shirt, white socks and a red baseball cap. Otherwise, anyone in the clubhouse will point me out,' he'd said.

As he was early, Fleming sat in the car for a while watching the golfers approach the eighteenth hole. After about ten minutes, Fleming saw him. Norman Read striding up the fairway, dressed as he'd described and wearing a bright-red baseball cap. He was with three other men. Fleming watched as they finished their game, shook hands and made their way to the car park pushing their golf trolleys.

Fleming waited until Read had put his clubs and trolly into his car boot before getting out of the Porsche to go over to him. 'Mr Read?'

Read turned and saw the warrant card Fleming was holding up for him to see. 'Ah! DCI Fleming. Been waiting long?'

'No, about ten minutes. Enjoyed watching a few missed pitches onto the green and a few angry golfers.'

Read laughed. 'Yes, I'm afraid some take it a bit too seriously and get quite upset if they play a bad shot. Would you like to go into the clubhouse and have a cup of tea?'

'Sure, that is if you don't mind me asking questions with other people around.'

'No problem. I told the guys you wanted to ask me about Tom. We can always sit in a corner out of earshot of others.'

Read led the way into a rather spacious area littered with tables and chairs. At the far end of the room there was a bar where golfers could order beer, soft drinks and snacks. Read pointed to a table near a window where no one else was sitting nearby. 'Take a seat and I'll get us a drink. Tea okay?'

'Fine, thanks. Let me–'

Read held up a hand. 'I'll get them. I've got a card and get a discount.'

Fleming smiled. 'Okay.'

A few minutes later, Read came to the table holding a tray with a pot of tea, two cups, milk and sugar. 'Help yourself.'

'Paul Canning told me you and Tom were big golfing friends,' Fleming said as he poured tea for both of them.

'Yes. I miss him. He was a good friend. Tragic affair.'

'Indeed. Mr Canning said you were with Tom at the pub the night there was a bit of a scuffle between him and Vic Quinn.'

'I was, yes. We were in the Down Inn having a quiet drink, just the two of us, and who should walk in but Quinn on his own. He was a regular there, everyone seemed to know him. He ordered a drink and started talking out loud for the benefit of everyone in the bar. It was embarrassing.'

'What was he saying?'

'He was spouting off about the planning application. He waved a hand towards Tom as he was saying how he didn't know how people involved in it had the audacity to drink in a local pub.'

'But Tom was a local man himself, wasn't he?'

'Yes, but in Quinn's eyes, that made it all the more galling.'

'What happened then?'

'We ignored him, but he kept on and on about how people in the council planning department must be on the take. Tom stuck it for a while, but then suggested we go somewhere else.'

'You left and Quinn followed you outside?'

'Yes.' Read sipped at his tea and looked thoughtful. 'He came barging out after us shouting at Tom, saying he'd get his comeuppance. Started slagging him off and said he didn't know how Tom had the nerve to come into a local pub when his boss wanted to destroy the village.'

'Then what happened?'

'Tom turned round and gave him a mouthful. Told him to piss off. Quinn flew into a rage and pushed Tom against the wall. Some other customers had come out and managed to pull Quinn off. Tom was quite shaken.'

'No one called the police?'

'No. It was over in a flash and no one was hurt.'

Fleming finished his tea, put his cup back on the saucer and looked across at Read. 'There was another incident involving Quinn. It was outside the parish council office after a public information meeting in the village hall. Were you there?'

'I was. It was a few days earlier. Same thing. Quinn shouting at Tom as he left. There wasn't a scuffle then, but Quinn did shout abuse at Tom. He said it was because of him and Canning that his mother couldn't sell her house. Tom ignored him and walked away with Quinn shouting after him saying he was a dead man.'

'Did Tom think he was serious?'

'No. But Quinn is an angry, aggressive man.'

Fleming nodded. 'Angry people sometimes do say things they don't really mean.'

'Tom did get murdered though.'

'Did Tom tell you he'd received a death threat?'

'Yes, but he shrugged it off.'

'Was he a gambling man?'

Read put his cup down and looked deep in thought before answering. 'Yes, he betted on the horses. And used to frequent a casino in London.'

'Did he ever tell you he had gambling debts?'

'He lost more than he won, for sure, but I'm not aware he had massive debts.'

'Did he ever talk about his stepson?'

'Complete waste of space, he used to say. They never got on and Tom threw him out after a massive row. Reckoned Rashad threatened him and said he would get even with him.'

Fleming didn't stay much longer. He thanked Read for his time and left thinking the threats against Tom Slater were mounting up.

30

Interview room one was a small, cramped affair comprising a table and four chairs. A digital recorder was on the end of the table, up against the wall. Fleming and Logan were sitting opposite Vic Quinn. Logan switched on the DIR and Fleming went through the formalities stating where they were, the date, time, and who was present.

Fleming looked across the table at Quinn. 'You are not under arrest and you're not obliged to remain at the station so you can leave at any time. You do not have to say anything. But it may harm your defence if you do not mention when questioned something which you later rely on in court. Anything you do say may be given in evidence. Free, independent legal advice is available if you want it.'

Quinn glowered at Fleming, ran a hand through his thick red hair and slouched back in his chair. 'I've already taken legal advice. Police have charged me with the damage on Canning's car. They dropped the assault charge because Canning assaulted me first. My solicitor tells me you can't ask me more questions about any of that.'

'Your solicitor is right. I want to ask you about something else, the murder of Tom Slater.'

Quinn's eyes shot open. 'You can't pin that on me because I had a couple of run-ins with him!'

'I'm not pinning anything on you, Mr Quinn. I just want to ask you a few more questions. If you want a solicitor present, I can arrange it.'

'I don't need one. I had nothing to do with it.'

'One of the run-ins you had with Mr Slater was at the Down Inn pub. You said you'd had a few drinks and he goaded you.'

'He did, yes.'

'Only we have an eyewitness who says something different.'

Quinn sneered. 'One of his few friends no doubt.'

'You came into the pub and started shouting your mouth off about the development.'

'Thought we had freedom of speech in this country.'

Fleming ignored the comment. 'You made accusations of people in the planning department being on the take. Have you any proof, or were you just trying to stir things up?'

'Stands to reason, doesn't it? Powerful men with loads of money and influence. Bet there is some kind of offer going on under the table.'

'Mr Slater and his friend ignored you, but then decided to leave. You followed them outside and started shouting at Mr Slater. You said something to the effect he would get his comeuppance.'

'Can't remember exactly what I said. I'd had a few drinks and... let me remind you... so had they.'

'You then pushed Mr Slater up against the pub wall.'

'Like I told you before at my mother's house, he goaded me. I lost my temper for a second.'

'It took a few onlookers to pull you off.'

'It was nothing. No one got hurt.'

'After a meeting outside the parish council office you shouted to Mr Slater. You told him he was a dead man.'

Quinn shrugged. 'Only said in the heat of the moment.'

'And a few days later, someone murdered Mr Slater.'

Before Quinn could respond, there was a knock on the interview room door and Anderson entered to pass a note to Fleming. He glanced at it before speaking into the recording machine. 'For the purposes of the DIR, DC Anderson has entered the room. Interview suspended at ten thirty am.'

Fleming signalled for Anderson to stay while he scribbled something on a notepad, shielding it from Quinn's view with his hand. He passed it to Anderson who looked at it, nodded her understanding, and left the room.

Fleming glanced at Logan and tipped his head towards the recording machine. Logan switched it back on.

'Interview resumed at ten thirty-two am. DC Anderson has left the room,' Fleming said.

An anxious-looking Quinn rested his elbows on the table and put his head in his hands. 'I didn't kill him,' he mumbled through his fingers.

Fleming slipped the note Anderson had passed him into a folder lying on the table.

'You have a black car with a seventeen reg. A witness saw a similar car speeding away from the village hall on the night of the murder. You said you were at home with your wife, so it couldn't have been you, right?'

There was a look of relief on Quinn's face. 'Yeah, that's right,' he said with more than a hint of defiance.

'Only we know you lied about your alibi. Your wife was out with friends that night.'

Quinn was silent for a moment before answering. 'Okay, so I got the days mixed up. She went out, so it must have been the night I was on my own.'

'And you didn't go out?'

Quinn shook his head and said nothing.

'For the purposes of the DIR, Mr Quinn is shaking his head.'

Fleming looked in his folder. 'The thing is, a neighbour said she saw you leave home in your car around eight and come back about nine. Happens to coincide with the approximate time of death of Mr Slater.'

Quinn's eyes darted between Logan and Fleming and drops of sweat appeared on his forehead. 'Okay, I did go out. The only reason I didn't let on was because it would look bad if I was out the night Slater was killed.'

'So where did you go?'

'I was hungry and decided to go to the nearby town to get a takeaway curry. I came straight back.'

'Where did you get the curry from?'

'The Rising Sun.'

Logan made a note to check it out.

Fleming reached inside his folder and pulled out the note Anderson had handed him. 'Forensics have identified fingerprints on Slater's car door handle. They happen to match the prints the police took when they arrested you for vandalising Canning's car.'

Quinn's head slumped onto his chest. 'It's not what it seems. I know it looks bad. That's why I didn't mention it.'

'Mention what, Mr Quinn?'

'When I went out to get a curry, I drove past the village hall and saw Slater's car parked there. It was late and he wasn't in the car. I don't know why, but I stopped and tried to open the door. He'd locked it. I thought I heard two shots from down in the woods and left in a hurry.'

'Why didn't you come forward when the police issued an appeal for any witnesses?'

'Because I knew I'd be a suspect if I was anywhere near the scene. Especially after my run-ins with Slater.'

'Okay, Mr Quinn, that's all for now. You're free to go.'

Quinn looked perplexed. 'You're not arresting me?'

'No, but don't plan on going anywhere. Interview terminated at eleven thirty am.'

31

The aroma of coffee filled the room next to interview room one. Quinn had gone and Logan eyed Fleming with a quizzical look. 'Why did you decide not to arrest him, boss? Evidence is mounting up.'

'True,' Fleming agreed, 'but if I'd arrested him, I'd have to have either charged or released him without charge after twenty-four hours. I wanted to check his story out first.'

'Right. What was in the note Naomi passed you?'

'She discovered the fingerprints found on Slater's car that Forensics hadn't been able to identify yet are Quinn's.'

'Ah, that's where you got the information from when you questioned him.'

'Remember I asked for the locals to take Quinn's prints when I got the call to say they'd arrested him for vandalising Canning's car?'

Logan nodded.

'They phoned Naomi to tell her they matched.'

'So, what next?'

'We question Quinn's wife. Get a warrant for Forensics to search his house to see if he has a gun, or evidence he had one there. They can also check for bloodstains on his clothing.'

'By the time we pull her in, Quinn will have told her what to say to back up his story.'

'That's why I slipped a note to Naomi. I asked her to bring Mrs Quinn in for questioning before we let Quinn go, and get a warrant to search the house. We'll also need to check with The Rising Sun to see if they can remember Quinn calling in for a curry. Check if there's any CCTV in the area as well.'

'Wondered what you were scribbling down to pass to Naomi.'

'Let's go see if Naomi's managed to get her.'

Quinn's wife was sitting in interview room one having a cup of tea with Anderson when Fleming and Logan walked in.

Fleming smiled at her. 'I'm grateful you agreed to come in to assist with our enquiries.' He noticed Mrs Quinn's hand shake and saw the anxious look on her face. Realising the presence of three detectives was going to overwhelm her, Fleming made a decision. 'This is just an informal chat so my colleagues can leave us to it,' he said, looking at Logan and Anderson.

They both took the hint and left.

Fleming sat down. 'Can I get you more tea?'

'No... no thanks, I'm fine.'

'Look, I know this is difficult for you, but I need to ask you a few questions if that's okay?'

Her voice was a mere whisper. 'Yes. Will Vic go to prison?'

Fleming wasn't sure if she was thinking of the vandalism charge on Canning's car or Slater's murder. He played safe. 'As Mr Canning assaulted Vic first, he wasn't charged with assault. The cost of damage to Canning's car was less than a thousand pounds so he'll get away with a fine, suspended sentence, or fine and community order. Three months imprisonment is possible, but unlikely.'

'I couldn't bear it if he went to prison.'

'Mrs Quinn, you volunteered to come here so you are free to leave at any time. It would help, though, if you could answer my questions.'

'I'll try.'

'Did your husband tell you about a bit of a skirmish he had with Tom Slater by the Down Inn pub?'

'Yes, he did. Said he was sorry it happened, but he reckoned Mr Slater was provoking him.'

'Were you with your husband when he confronted Mr Slater by the parish council office after a meeting in the village hall?'

'Yes.'

'Is it true he shouted after Mr Slater that he was a dead man?'

'Oh, God! Yes, he did, but he was angry after the meeting. He can be a bit hot-headed. You don't think...'

'I just need to be certain of all the facts. Your husband told us he was at home with you on the night someone killed Tom Slater, but we know you'd gone out with friends.'

'He must have got mixed up with the dates.'

'He told us he didn't leave the house, but a neighbour saw him drive off in his car. Did you know that?'

Mrs Quinn dabbed a handkerchief against her eyes. 'Yes, he told me.'

'What exactly did he tell you?'

'He said he went for a curry and, on the way out of the village, he saw Mr Slater's car, but he wasn't in it. Vic thought it odd because the parish council office and village hall were both closed. He stopped and was trying the door to Mr Slater's car when he heard what he thought were shots. Not knowing what to do, he left in a hurry.'

'Why did neither of you report this?'

'You think he did it, don't you?'

'I only want to establish the facts, Mrs Quinn. There is a certain amount of circumstantial evidence against your husband. He hasn't done himself any favours by lying over his whereabouts on the night of the murder. It doesn't help matters having had public confrontations with Mr Slater.'

Mrs Quinn started to cry. 'He didn't do it. I know he didn't. He's strong-minded and can be a bit volatile if he's angry, but he'd never kill anyone.'

'Mrs Quinn, I have to tell you that we have a warrant to search your house. If your husband is innocent and has nothing to hide, you should have no reason to worry.'

Fleming thanked Quinn's wife again for agreeing to come in and wondered if she did have reason to be concerned about her husband.

32

Guerra and Zimmerman had left Kelso on his own to think about a draft plan for the kidnap of Al Jameel's son. It had come as a surprise to Kelso to find his old boss had been the man behind his prison escape. But when he thought it over, it made sense. Kelso had taken the rap for the armed robbery Zimmerman had planned. Kelso had kept his mouth shut and Zimmerman escaped arrest. The man owed him and had repaid the debt.

Kelso had given a lot of thought over how they would abduct Dani. The first thing he had to do was get the lay of the land around Canning's mansion before Al Jameel and his son arrived. Next on the agenda was to put the place under surveillance. Once Canning's guests arrived, Kelso would see what security, if any, was in place. He would then establish whether Dani had any set routines.

There had been one more very important thing to take care of. Using the burner phone Guerra had given him, he'd phoned an old army friend he knew as The Supplier. He'd earned the title on account he could supply handguns and false papers. It was The Supplier who had provided the gun for the ill-fated armed robbery.

'There's a three-year-old Range Rover in the double garage,' Zimmerman had told Kelso. 'Keys are hanging on a hook inside the front door and there's fuel in the tank if you need wheels.'

It was handy, but Kelso had been reluctant to use it. He was growing a beard to disguise himself, but he still wanted to keep his exposure to the outside world to a minimum. It wasn't worth taking chances while the search for him was still hot. But Kelso knew it was a risk he had to take. The Supplier had a gun ready for him. Zimmerman and Guerra didn't need to know about this. Neither did they need to know anything about plans he was making to escape the country after he had his share of the ransom money.

Kelso rummaged around in the wardrobe where Guerra had left him some casual clothes. He picked out a pair of faded blue jeans, brown shoes, and a sleeveless black polo shirt. Hooking the arms of some sunglasses into the neck of his shirt, he made his way downstairs. He collected the car keys and pulled on a blue baseball cap off a hook next to the keys and jammed it on his head. *Best I can do for disguise.*

Turning left onto the country lane that ran past the house, Kelso made his way towards the A40. It was about twenty-five minutes to Thornhill Park & Ride at Headington on the east side of Oxford. He'd arranged to meet The Supplier there. Kelso parked and got a ticket. He was taking no chances of getting a parking fine, even though he didn't intend to stay around too long.

He waited half an hour before he saw The Supplier's black Mercedes GLC. It pulled into the large car park and headed for the far end where there were fewer cars. Kelso eased out of his space, followed the Mercedes and parked next to it. The Supplier saw him and waved, indicating for Kelso to climb into the passenger seat next to him. It was clear he wasn't going to bother with details like getting a parking ticket.

Kelso got into the Mercedes and leaned across to shake hands with his old friend. 'Good to see you, man. How you doing?' Kelso asked with a big grin.

'I'm good, Jack. How about you? Enjoying your freedom?'

'Hell yes. Never been better.'

'There's a big manhunt on the go for you. Lot of stuff in the news with your photo. The police have asked the public to be on the lookout, but warned people not to approach.'

'I'm hoping it'll calm down after a few days. I've got a great place to hide and I'm keeping a low profile.'

The Supplier laughed and slapped Kelso on the leg. 'Today being an exception, eh?'

'Today being an exception,' Kelso agreed. 'Important things to see to.'

'What do you want a gun for, if you don't mind me asking? Need to rob somewhere to get your escape money?'

'Kind of. The less you know the better. Have you got it?'

'Under your seat. Have a look.'

Kelso bent forwards to lean under his seat and pulled out a black plastic gun box. He flicked it open and there was a Glock 17 inside. 'Just the job. Nice one, mate.'

'It's got a full magazine with seventeen rounds. Take it you don't need any more than that?'

'Shouldn't think so, thanks. You sure you're okay waiting for payment? All being well, I should get the money in the next couple of weeks or so.'

'For you, not a problem. I trust you completely. You can pay me when you collect your false ID papers and passport.'

'How'll you do the passport?'

'A friend of mine. They call him The Forger. He's bloody good. His usual trick is to steal the identity of a deceased person about your age and change the photo. Otherwise, he'll use a stolen passport and do the same.'

'Bit tricky to do these days, isn't it?'

'Yes, but he's an expert. Trust me. To be on the safe side, we intend to smuggle you out on a boat to Antwerp. You'll then go by car to Brussels where you get a flight to Brazil.'

'Sounds good. I owe you one.'

'I'll phone you when the documents are ready. Should be in your timescale within the next two weeks. Okay?' The Supplier paused. 'This robbery... think you can pull it off this time?'

'I'm sure. There's one weak link, but I can take care of it.'

33

Before getting in his car to drive to Luton Airport, Fleming called Logan in the office. 'Harry? Change of plan, I'll not be in today. I've managed to get a flight from Luton to Edinburgh this morning.'

'Looking up old friends or something in your old home town?'

'No. I spoke to Paul Canning and he told me the guy who Slater sacked now works for an estate agent in Edinburgh. Thought I pay him a visit.'

'Okay. By the way, Rashad Yousefi lied about his alibi. He said he was in the commune on the night of Slater's murder. Not true. He left there around six in the evening and arrived back about ten.'

'We need to bring him in to question him under caution. See if you can get something fixed up at a local police station in London near the commune. We'll pick it up as soon as we can after I get back from Edinburgh.'

'Will do. Enjoy the trip.'

Fleming ended the call and set off for Luton. Driving down the M40 going south to link up with the M25, he decided to switch the radio on. He found a news programme and tuned in as a reporter was giving an update on the Jack Kelso prison escape. There had been no progress or sightings of him. He'd vanished. *Any need to watch your back?* Logan had asked.

Fleming pushed the thought from his mind as he took the exit for the M25 going north. He would then join the M1 before taking the A1081 to Luton Airport.

After parking in the mid-stay car park and checking in for easyJet flight EZY12, Fleming went for a coffee.

An hour later he was in the air for the one-and-a-quarter-hour flight.

On landing, Fleming took a taxi into Edinburgh and asked the driver to drop him off in Princes Street. He was early for his meeting so went for a walk before heading up to George Street to find Gilchrist and Loggie's office.

Half an hour later, Fleming walked into Nash's office. A young woman sat behind one of two desks. Wishing to be discreet, Fleming didn't show his warrant card. 'I'm here to see Mr Nash. He's expecting me. My name's Fleming.'

'Ah, he told me. I'll buzz him.' She picked up a handset from her desk and tapped in three numbers. 'Mr Fleming is here.' She put the phone down and smiled. 'He's coming right away.'

A tall lanky Nash appeared through a door at the back of the office and offered a bony hand to Fleming. He looked like a man who had once had a full head of hair, but it had long since deserted him, as was the ability to smile. Fleming wasn't sure if Nash had bulging eyes or whether it was the thick lenses in his glasses which magnified them. He wore grey suit trousers and the collar on his white shirt looked as though it was one size too big.

Fleming shook the offered hand. *Weak grip.*

Nash turned to his colleague. 'Okay if I leave you for a few minutes to hold the fort?'

'Sure, no problem.'

'There's a nice coffee shop a few doors along,' Nash said, looking at Fleming. 'Can I get you one while we chat?'

'Fine.'

The coffee shop formed a long rectangle with a row of tables along one wall. It wasn't busy and there was a free table by the front window overlooking the street. Nash went to the counter to order the coffees while Fleming took the seat by the window.

'You've come a long way to see me,' Nash said, joining Fleming and placing folded hands on the table. 'How can I help you?'

'I'm investigating the murder of Tom Slater, an old colleague of yours.'

'You said on the phone. I read about it in the papers. Protests there seem to be getting out of hand.'

'What made you come all the way here after you lost your job with Paul Canning? It's a far cry from London.'

'I used to live here before I moved south. Thought I'd like to come back... and, Gilchrist and Loggie offered me a job. From your accent, would I be right in thinking you're based a long way from home?'

'Born and bred here in Edinburgh as it happens. Worked in a solicitor's office for a couple of years after graduating, then joined the Met. I transferred to Thames Valley Police later.'

A young waiter arrived at the table with their coffees. 'Shout if you want anything else.' He didn't wait for a reply before returning behind the counter.

Fleming took a sip from his coffee and looked across the table at Nash.

'You think one of the protesters killed him?'

'Pretty obvious, isn't it?'

'At this stage, no. It's just a possibility. What exactly led to your dismissal, Mr Nash?'

Nash sighed out loud. 'Tom Slater and Canning's scheming accountant, Makayla Yamamura, stitched me up.'

'Oh, how?'

'I was a project manager and had to recruit some senior consultants. I budgeted them at a thousand pounds a day each. Turns out Yamamura put them through the books as junior consultants on five hundred a day. The budget was underspent by three thousand and the surplus money ended up in an account that later found its way into Slater's pocket.'

'So, they accused you of fraud because you said the consultants would cost a thousand a day, but you only paid them five hundred?'

'No, a thousand a day was what I estimated. *Makayla* paid them five hundred a day.'

'They wouldn't want to get the police involved if they were behind the fraud, so how did they explain to you why they weren't going to call the police?'

'They didn't, which is why I knew they were behind it.'

'So why didn't *you* call the police or report it to Canning?'

Nash took a last sip from his coffee before placing the cup back in its saucer. 'Because I knew they were clever enough to cover their tracks and it *was* me who had requested the budget. As for Canning... he didn't like me. He's a bully. Fell out with me because I had the gall to disagree with him over something. We had a massive row and he threatened to get rid of me. I was... as they say... fucked.'

'Why do you think Slater stole the money?'

'Debts. Gambling debts.'

34

Eric Blunt was in a difficult position. Refusing to speak to the press wouldn't look good. Especially when they said they wanted to talk about the council's local plan. *Why would he refuse to do that?* Taking no chances, he'd phoned Canning to let him know. It transpired that Zoe Dunbar had already spoken to Canning. He'd told Blunt to be wary of any questions she might ask about allegations of bribery. But it seemed Canning was content she would put a positive slant on the planning application. Blunt felt reassured.

Five minutes before she was due to arrive, Blunt took the call from reception. Dunbar was there. He went down to the large atrium and saw a tall slim woman with shoulder-length auburn hair standing at the desk. She looked to be in her late thirties and wore a grey suit with a blue shirt. As Blunt approached, she turned and smiled. 'Mr Blunt?'

'Yes. No trouble finding us?'

'Not at all. Satnav took me straight here.'

'Great. Let's go up to my office.' Blunt pointed across the atrium towards the lifts at the far end.

Blunt's office was a spacious affair with a large window

behind his desk looking out over the street below. The desk had nothing on it other than a computer screen on one corner and a stack of wire baskets on the other side. There was a small coffee table and two chairs by the wall to the left of the desk. Pinned to a board on the wall next to the table was a large outline sketch of Canning's proposed development. 'Please, take a seat,' Blunt said. 'I'll get my secretary to bring us a drink.'

'Thanks.' Dunbar sat and looked up at the board. 'Is this it? The plan for Darmont?'

Blunt was on his way to the door and turned. 'Yes, it is. Have a look while I pop my head out to ask Wendy if she'll get us some coffee.'

Blunt came back into the office and sat across from Dunbar. 'Looks impressive, don't you think?'

'Yes, it does.'

'I gather you want to report on the Canning planning application and the council local plan.'

'Yes, but I also wanted to know the story behind the parish council neighbourhood one.'

'They prepared it with some involvement from Darmont residents, but there were different agendas.'

'How come? Weren't they supposed to work together?'

'They were, but residents objected to everything the parish council proposed. They couldn't agree.'

Dunbar nodded. 'Yes, I've talked to locals who're against *any* kind of development.'

'They are, I'm afraid, hence the current protests over the planning application.' Blunt was about to say something else when there was a knock on his door. The secretary came in with a tray containing two coffees and a plate of biscuits. 'Thanks, Wendy,' Blunt said as she placed the tray on the table in front of them.

Wendy smiled. 'You're welcome.'

'Help yourself,' Blunt said, looking at Dunbar.

'I thought councils were cutting back on hospitality these days,' Dunbar said with a wry smile.

'Refreshments aren't allowed if meetings are with internal staff, only if there are visitors.'

'In which case, I'll have one of those chocolate biscuits.'

Blunt helped himself to one as well before continuing with what he was going to say when Wendy came in. 'To be fair, the parish council saw the need for some development. But they didn't... in our view... go far enough with the proposed neighbourhood plan.'

'Due to pressure from residents?'

'I guess so.'

'And so you prepared one which involved building more houses in Darmont?'

'Yes. We were mindful of the need to build more homes. Every council had to prepare a strategy. That's what we did.'

'But at odds with the parish council neighbourhood one.'

'Neighbourhood planning is part of the Localism Act. It aimed to give local communities the chance to influence development in their area. As you've found out, the wishes of Darmont residents were not in keeping with the aim to provide more houses.'

'Okay, but it seems the parish council are also not happy to accept major development in Darmont. As you said, they didn't go far enough with their proposals.'

'No. It's all a bit unfortunate. It was bad enough both local residents and the parish council opposing our plan. But we now have both parties opposed to the Canning application as well.'

'Because that goes even further than you wanted?'

'It does, yes.'

'In what way?'

'It includes even more houses, a shopping development, café, restaurant, supermarket and a swimming pool.'

'And you are now supporting Canning's application?'

'We are, yes.'

'Why?'

'Because, on reflection, we do think it offers more benefits to the local community.'

'Despite the fact the development will be on greenfield land?'

'There isn't enough land within the village boundary. It's inevitable, I'm afraid.'

Dunbar locked eyes with Blunt. 'It's clear people oppose the Canning application and protests are becoming violent. Do you think that's why someone killed Tom Slater?'

Blunt frowned. 'To say protests are becoming violent is going a bit too far. There's strong opposition, that's for sure. But I doubt someone would see that as a reason to kill Tom Slater. Bit extreme, don't you think?'

'Stranger things have happened. Someone could have been so angry that they wanted to lash out and kill Canning, or anyone who worked for him. I hear there have been death threats.'

Blunt shifted uncomfortably in his seat. 'So I believe.'

'Have you had a death threat?'

'Look, are we not straying from your brief?'

Dunbar ignored Blunt and continued to press. 'Is there any truth in the allegations that someone on the council is being bribed by Canning? Isn't that why the council now seem to be in support of his application?'

'This is preposterous! I hope you are not going to publish anything along those lines.'

'I notice you didn't actually refute the claims. Can I say a council official declined to deny the allegations?'

'No, you may not! There has been no impropriety! If you don't mind, I have another meeting I need to prepare for.'

Dunbar looked as though she knew the interview was over and left, leaving Blunt looking like he wished he hadn't agreed to speak to her.

35

Anderson took an early morning train from Oxford to London Paddington and then the Tube to St James's Park. It was a nice summer's day and she decided to walk up through the park toward Piccadilly to her first port of call.

Canning's London office was in a block up a small side street. She went into the reception area and saw from a board that Canning's office was on the third floor. Ignoring the lifts, Anderson took the stairs and came out onto a landing. The stairs continued upwards off to the right. On the left, the writing on the glass window of a door told her she'd arrived at her destination.

She entered to find a small reception area where a young woman sat behind a desk with a phone to her ear. While listening, she looked up when Anderson came in and put her hand over the mouthpiece. 'Be with you in a minute.'

Anderson waited until the receptionist ended the call. 'DC Anderson, Thames Valley Police. Mr Canning is expecting me.'

'Oh, yes. I'll let him know you're here.'

It was five minutes before Canning appeared out of his

office, stooped over his walking cane. 'Sorry to keep you waiting. Important business call.'

Anderson remembered seeing Canning at the briefing meeting and had thought then that he looked like a man used to getting his own way. She somehow doubted he was sorry for keeping her waiting, but did it because he could. *Arrogant sod.* Anderson smiled. 'No problem. I've come to check Mr Slater's office.'

'It's this way.' Canning turned to hobble along a short corridor.

'I take it no one has touched or removed anything?' Anderson asked as she followed Canning.

'Not yet, but I need to clear it out when you're done. Need to get it ready for when I recruit a replacement.' They reached the door to Slater's office and Canning turned to give Anderson a disparaging look. 'Mind you, I've no idea what you think you might find in there to help with your enquiries, but go ahead.'

'Thank you.'

'Let my secretary in reception know when you're finished. No need to bother me again.'

Don't worry. I've no intention of doing so. 'Shouldn't be too long. I'm not sure I expect to find anything of importance, but we need to check.'

'Hmm.' Canning turned to shuffle back towards reception.

Anderson entered Slater's office and closed the door behind her. Canning had lied. Slater's desk was empty apart from a photograph on a stand and a computer screen. Someone had been in to clear the desk. She walked round it and pulled up a chair. The photograph was of Slater and his wife. No stepson.

The top-right desk drawer had a key in it. Anderson turned the key and opened it to find a few stationery items and another set of keys. She tried them all in the other three desk drawers. All she found was some printer paper, a card system of reminders, and a drawer full of suspension files. A quick flick through revealed nothing of immediate interest.

Looking under the desk, Anderson saw a wastepaper bin. It was empty. Someone had cleared that as well. The last key opened a metal filing cabinet. Anderson scanned through the contents. All she found was papers on developments, building regulations and copies of applications. A thought then struck Anderson. She went back to the desk and opened the drawer with the card system in it. Each card had a date on a protruding flap. She flicked through until she found the dates matching Slater's London meetings. Nothing.

She thought for a moment, then looked at earlier cards. She saw it there, two days in front of the date of the second meeting. A note saying: *Re meeting. Ask for a larger share!*

Anderson slipped the note into her notebook and went back to reception. 'I'm finished here, but I'll be getting someone to come and take Mr Slater's computer away for forensic examination.'

The secretary's eyes flashed concern. 'I'll get Mr Canning to come and see you to authorise it.'

'No need to bother him. He has no say in the matter. It's a police murder enquiry. Just tell him to make sure no one touches it in the meantime.'

Anderson left wondering why Slater wanted to ask for a larger share of something. *Of what?*

Anderson's next port of call was to see the barman who worked at the hotel where Slater met the mystery man. She took the Tube down to Victoria and then a train to Croydon. It was only a short walk to the block of flats where Fabio Enrico lived. His apartment was on the third floor. It was compact with a combined kitchen and living room, a bathroom, and one bedroom. Anderson's first impression was that Enrico was not the tidiest of people. But on second thoughts, it could have been due to his injuries.

Anderson put Enrico in his late twenties. He was tall, slim, and had a stubble beard running along the jawline. A moustache curved around his upper lip to join the stubble. Enrico looked fashionable. He wore casual clothes. Tight black jeans hugged his thin legs. A matching short-sleeved silk shirt was open at the neck.

'Sorry about the mess,' Enrico said. 'I'm normally much tidier. Used to everything being neat and tidy. Comes with working for a five-star hotel I guess.' He laughed.

Anderson smiled. 'No worries. How are you after your accident? The receptionist at the hotel said you were knocked off your bike by a car.'

'It was a motorbike.'

'Not a car then?'

'No, I mean a car knocked me off my motorbike.' Enrico laughed again. 'Easy how things get misconstrued.'

Anderson smiled. 'Tell me about it.'

'Anyway, to answer your question, I'm on the mend.'

'Good. What were the extent of your injuries?'

'I was lucky. No broken bones, just loads of cuts and bruises.'

'Ouch!'

'You wanted to ask me about a man who stayed at the hotel twice in the last couple of weeks or so and met someone at the bar?'

'Yes, I'm sure you get lots of guests meeting other people at the bar so you might not remember. The man staying at the hotel was Tom Slater. The receptionist thought his visitor might have had an Italian accent. Ring any bells?'

'I do remember because the man was Italian, like me. Mr

Slater asked me to put the drinks on his bill and gave me his name.'

'Did you hear what they were talking about?'

'No, sorry.'

'Did you get a name for the other man?'

Enrico lifted his shoulders. 'Sorry.'

Anderson got her laptop out and logged on to show Enrico the CCTV footage taken on the nights of both visits. 'Can you pick him out?' she asked, turning the laptop screen towards Enrico.

'Yes, yes! That's him.' Enrico pointed at the screen. 'Are they in trouble?'

'Mr Slater isn't. He's dead. Murdered.'

'Oh, my god! That's bad, man. You think this Italian...?'

'No idea at this stage. Just trying to trace everyone who was in contact with Mr Slater in the last few weeks.'

Anderson thanked Enrico who had identified the same man on both meetings with Slater. She left wishing him a speedy recovery.

On the way back to Oxford, Anderson felt elated. She now had a photograph of the man Slater met at the London hotel... the man he wanted to ask for a larger share!

36

The temperature had risen to thirty degrees and there wasn't a cloud in the sky. Cars had been rolling in up the gravel driveway to park as best they could in front of Canning's mansion. Once the parking places there were full, cars parked on an overspill area marked out on the lawn. Canning didn't mind if there was any damage. He could afford to pay someone to renew it. In any case, today was a day for getting on best terms with all those who would support him and help finance his project.

'This is a great day for Isa and Dani's welcome party,' Canning had said to his wife earlier. 'About forty people if they all turn up.'

'Good job we got a marquee,' Jane said. 'Bloody hot out there. At least people will be able to get out of the sun for some shade.'

'Caterers all set up?' Canning checked.

Jane nodded. 'Barbeque's all arranged. Lots of strawberries and cream as well!'

'Good. I may have ordered too much champagne, wine, and beer. I'd rather have too much than run short though. We can use any left over for the celebration party if Walter Hammond approves my application.'

'Do you think there'll be any trouble from protesters?'

'I'm not taking any chances, especially with Isa and Dani here. We can't afford any setbacks with them, so I've decided to increase security. The company use former royal marines you know. More than a match for any threat.'

'You sound as though you're expecting world war three.'

'Can't be too careful. There's a lot at stake.'

'Suppose not. Who's coming?'

'Lots of people with power, influence and wealth. A few of my most senior executives will be here, Makayla, and key investors.'

'Walter Hammond?'

'Yes, he'll be here with his wife. Stuck-up bitch.'

'Paul! I do hope you don't introduce her like that!'

'Hammond told me the government are in talks with Saudi Arabia over a trade deal and arms sale. No doubt he'll want to ingratiate himself with Isa. He won't miss the chance to impress the prime minister. Networking with an influential Saudi businessman will earn him some points.'

'You're so cynical.'

'Eric Blunt and his bankrupt wife will be here as well.'

'Paul!'

'Invited Kim Ogilvie, chair of the parish council, but she declined.'

'Any reason?'

'I asked her to put an offer to the parish council as an incentive for them to support my application.'

'And?'

'They declined. Thought it would look as though it was going beyond good business. They worried it would look like they were accepting suspect incentives.'

'What did you offer?'

'A new medical centre, village hall and parish council office.'

'They thought it was a bribe, for God's sake!'

'Not at all. There's no doubt the village needs it. Existing buildings are in a state of bad repair. Quite legitimate. Anyway... their loss.'

~

The party was in full swing. Champagne, wine and beer were flowing and guests were tucking into the barbeque food. Canning had given a short speech to welcome everyone, in particular Al Jameel and his son. Canning was now going round to introduce them to his other guests.

He spotted Yamamura talking to three key investors over by the pool and steered Al Jameel and Dani over to them.

'May I introduce Isa Al Jameel and his son, Dani,' Canning said as he approached. Turning to Al Jameel, 'You've met Makayla, my accountant.'

Al Jameel bowed his head. 'Of course. Since our arrival here she has been most helpful showing us round the site and explaining the finances you have secured.'

'Ah, yes!' Canning said. 'These three good men are a few of the people who have already signed up to invest in the development.'

He went on to introduce the three men who Jameel and Dani shook hands with.

'Have you decided to invest in Paul's scheme?' asked the last man to clasp Al Jameel's hand. 'That is, assuming the authorities approve it.'

'Makayla has convinced me it would be a very good investment. If the authorities do approve Paul's application, it's safe to say I will put money in.'

'Excellent!' the man said.

Canning smiled. 'I'll leave you three to carry on talking to Makayla. I've seen another man I want to introduce Isa to.' He'd spotted Eric Blunt strolling around with his wife. She seemed rather tense.

'The man I'm about to introduce you to is Eric Blunt. He's the planning officer,' Canning explained as he steered Al Jameel and Dani towards him.

'Eric! Good to see you here,' Canning said, 'and of course your lovely wife. Can I introduce you to Isa Al Jameel, one of our most important investors.'

Eric and his wife shook hands with Al Jameel and Dani.

Canning noticed Mrs Blunt's eyes light up at the sight of the two Saudis. 'Eric will be speaking on behalf of the council at the public enquiry. We're confident the chairman will recommend approval of the application,' Canning said. 'The secretary of state will make the final decision. He happens to be here as well. I'll introduce you to him next.'

'May I ask why you are happy with Mr Canning's application while local residents oppose it?' Dani asked Blunt.

'There was always a clash of views over what development should take place in the area. Residents and the parish council are wary of major development. We see the bigger picture. Mr Canning's plan is in line with current government requirements,' Blunt replied.

'Am I correct your office would normally approve applications?' Al Jameel asked.

'Yes,' Blunt said. 'But where there are major concerns, I pass the application to the council's planning committee of elected councillors.'

'And you would advise them?'

'That would be normal practice, yes.'

'But not in this case?' Al Jameel pressed.

'No, the parish council wrote to the secretary of state asking him to call in the application, which he's done. That means he will make the final decision.'

Al Jameel nodded. 'I see. But you still have some say in the matter?'

'Yes. I will be pressing hard at the public enquiry to make the case for the application to be approved.'

Canning saw Walter Hammond leaving his wife talking to some of the other guests and head towards him. 'And the very man who will make the final decision is about to join us,' he said.

A smiling Hammond strode over, hand outstretched to Al Jameel. 'Very pleased to meet you,' he said, shaking his hand. He turned to Dani. 'And you look just like your father. Enjoying your stay here?' He didn't wait for an answer. 'Walter Hammond, by the way, secretary of state for housing, communities and local government.'

'Walter and I are old friends from university days,' Canning said.

'Ah, yes, you told me,' Al Jameel said.

Hammond looked at Blunt and Canning. 'Do you mind if I have a private word with Mr Jameel. Government business so to speak.'

'Not at all,' Canning and Blunt echoed.

Canning left them to go and check everyone's glasses were full. He smiled. *Hammond getting cosy with Al Jameel might work in my favour.*

37

Fleming walked down to the incident room after his update meeting with Temple. She'd told him the appointment of a new chief constable was imminent. Pressure was on to get a result on the Slater murder beforehand.

It was on that note Fleming hoped Anderson had something positive to report from her trip to London. He stepped into the incident room to find Logan and Anderson debating who should have the last chocolate biscuit.

'I should have the last one and do you a favour,' Logan said. 'You need to keep trim. It's too late for me.'

'You've already had three,' Anderson protested.

'No, I had two.'

'I put six on the plate and I've only had two. One left. I make it you had three.'

'The maths work,' Logan admitted with a coy smile.

Fleming entered and picked the biscuit up to take a bite. 'Kind of you both to leave one for me. Thought Harry would have scoffed the lot by now.'

Logan and Anderson looked at each other and began to laugh.

Fleming bit on the biscuit. 'Nice.'

'You've just solved the dilemma of who should have the last biscuit,' Anderson said.

Fleming grinned. 'Coffee would be good to go with it.'

Logan and Anderson swapped glances to see who would offer. Fleming shook his head. 'Why don't I get them while you two sort out what you need to tell me that's going to throw new light on the Slater case. Super's chomping at the bit again, so I hope you've got something to offer.'

When Fleming returned with the drinks, he heard Anderson mention Canning's name to Logan.

'Can't quite make up my mind whether he's egotistical or just plain arrogant. Seems like a man who can exude false charm when he likes, but there's a menacing side to him if you ask me,' Logan said.

'Arrogant prat, was my impression,' Anderson said.

'Must be something in the air,' Fleming said with a smile. 'Arguing over a chocolate biscuit and then slagging off a pillar of the community.'

'Don't let Darmont residents hear you call him that,' Logan quipped.

'Okay, frivolity aside, what about Canning?'

'I paid a visit to his London offices and didn't find anything... except this,' Anderson said, fishing into her laptop bag.

'What?' Fleming and Logan asked in unison.

'I found this note in Slater's office desk.' She handed it to Fleming.

'Nice work, Naomi,' Fleming said. 'We now know the two meetings in London were about money... and Slater wanted a larger share.'

'He had gambling debts,' Logan reminded them. 'Maybe he wanted some money to help clear them.'

'Could be,' Fleming agreed. 'But we don't know for sure what it was he wanted more of.'

'Not a lot of use then?' Anderson said.

'Yes, it is,' Fleming said. 'At least we know why Slater went to London for the two mystery meetings. Anything else?'

'I've arranged for Forensics to take Slater's computer away for examination. I asked them to treat it as a priority. Should get the results in a few days. Nothing else from Canning's offices.'

'How did you get on in Edinburgh, boss?' Logan asked.

'Mr Nash's account of why Slater sacked him was that Slater and Canning's accountant stitched him up. They knew he'd had a massive row with Canning over something and Canning had threatened to get rid of him. Seeing an opportunity, they fabricated a story to sack Nash. They then did a bit of creative accounting to put some cash into Slater's personal account and blamed Nash for stealing the money.'

'The gambling debts again,' Logan said.

Fleming nodded. 'That's what Nash thought. Whatever was going on, it's pretty clear Slater needed money.'

'One thing is for sure,' Logan said. 'Nash would not have been happy with Slater if he did frame him. But angry enough to kill him?'

'We need to have a word with Canning's accountant,' Fleming said.

Logan scratched his head. 'There's also the possibility that Slater's killer was someone he owed money to. Someone who asked to meet him at the village hall and who shot him because...'

'Because what?' Fleming asked.

'I have no idea,' Logan replied. 'That's why I didn't finish the sentence. Can't work it out. Why would you kill someone who owed you money.'

'Unless,' Anderson chipped in, 'Slater told the killer he

didn't have it and couldn't get it. The killer sees red and shoots him.'

'Taking a gun with you would suggest that was the intention from the start, not a sudden fit of rage,' Fleming said.

'I suppose so,' Anderson admitted.

'What about the hotel barman, Naomi?'

Anderson pulled her laptop round so Logan and Fleming could see the screen. She selected pictures and found the video of the hotel CCTV footage. 'I showed this to Enrico. He pointed out this man.' Anderson froze the film and aimed a finger at a face. 'He confirmed this is the man Slater met on the two nights he stayed at the London hotel.'

'Did he catch a name for this other man?'

'Afraid not,' Naomi said.

'Hear what they were talking about?'

'No, but whoever he is... he was the person Slater wanted to ask for a larger share.'

'Okay, we need the best copy stills we can get of this man and ask all the people who knew Slater if they recognise him.'

Anderson tapped the heel of her hand against her forehead. 'Ah! Just remembered. There was one more piece of information Enrico gave me... the other man was Italian.'

38

Dunbar was on her way home after seeing Eric Blunt. Darmont wasn't far off her route, so she decided to pay a visit. It was nearing lunchtime. Good chance for a quick drink and a snack at the Down Inn, then a visit to the local butcher. He was sure to know most people in Darmont and would no doubt be up to date with all the village gossip.

She pulled into the Down Inn car park and wandered in through the lounge door. Dunbar had heard the other pub in the village was a popular eating place. But she was more interested in information than good food.

The man behind the counter was a friendly chap who was used to seeing the same customers. 'Passing through?' he asked, trying to make polite conversation.

'I suppose I am,' Dunbar said. 'Just need a bite to eat and a glass of white wine. What do you have on the food front?'

'Fish and chips, burger and chips, egg and–'

'Chips,' Dunbar finished the sentence for him. 'How about a sandwich... not a chip butty though.'

'Cheese and pickle, or ham?'

'Ham, no side chips.'

'Brown or white bread?'

Dunbar smiled. 'Brown. Thin sliced... in case you were about to ask.'

The barman laughed. 'Right. Been anywhere nice?' he asked as he poured the wine into a glass.

'Not exactly. On my way home after a meeting with the area planning officer.'

The friendly look left the barman's face. 'Work for the property developers, do you?'

'No, I'm a freelance investigative reporter. I'm looking into Mr Canning's planning application and the claims of bribery and corruption.'

'Is that so?' The friendly look reappeared. 'There's a lot of talk about it, but I don't think anyone can prove anything. What did the planning officer have to say? I take it you asked him about it?'

'He said there was no impropriety.'

'He would, wouldn't he?' the barman said, handing the ham sandwich order to a colleague heading for the kitchen.

'Were you here the night Vic Quinn had an altercation with Tom Slater?'

'I was. Wasn't a big deal though. Vic came in and did mouth off a bit... aimed at Mr Slater who was drinking with a friend. They left.'

'That was it?'

'I heard there was a bit of a scuffle outside, but that was all.'

'He had a spat with Paul Canning as well. I gather Quinn vandalised his car.'

'Vic came in and told us all about it. Said Canning thrashed the back of his legs with his walking cane.'

'Did he say that was before or after he scratched Canning's car?'

'Come to think about it, no he didn't.'

Dunbar's sandwich arrived complete with a small side salad. She thanked the barman and retreated to a table by the window to enjoy her snack. *Butcher's shop next.*

The shop was tiny. One door in, a long counter, and another door out at the other end. The aroma of cooked pies and pasties filled the air before Dunbar had even entered the shop. She pushed her way through the beaded fly-screen curtain. A giant of a man stood behind the counter wearing a white butcher's coat and white nylon-mesh trilby. *Good, no other customers in.*

He was busy arranging some pork chops on a tray and looked up as she entered. 'Afternoon. What can I get you?' The man narrowed his eyes as though deep in thought. 'I know you're not local, but I seem to think I've seen you before.'

'You may have seen me at the briefing meeting in the village hall.'

'Ah, yes! You asked DCI Fleming some questions. You're a reporter, yes?'

'Freelance. I'm working on a story surrounding the planning application for Darmont. I guess you're one of the few people here who'll be in favour of the housing development.'

The butcher narrowed his eyes. 'How come?'

'Extra business.'

The man frowned. 'I'm a bit ambivalent about the whole thing to be honest. Yes, it'll be good for business, but I feel for the local people who are going to be directly affected by the development.'

'Like Vic Quinn's mother?'

'My, you have been doing your homework. How did you know about her?'

'Asking around. It's what I do for a living. I gather she's had to reduce her selling price because of uncertainty over the development.'

'She's a regular customer of mine, and she's bitter about it. I can understand that.'

'There was some trouble between Mr Canning and Mrs Quinn's son, wasn't there?'

'Yes. Vic can be a bit volatile at times. He's a bit opinionated.'

Dunbar pointed to the tray the butcher had been filling when she came into the shop. 'I'll have one of those pork chops please.'

The butcher picked one up using a piece of brown paper and held it up for Dunbar to see. 'This okay?'

'Fine, and one of those pasties please.' She pointed to a separate counter at the end of the shop.

'You ever had any trouble with him?'

Turning to go and get the pastie, the butcher spoke over his shoulder. 'Who, Vic? Nah. Good customer as well as his mother.' He returned with the pastie in a paper bag. 'Anything else?'

'One more question...'

'I meant anything else to buy.'

Dunbar ignored the remark. 'There's been talk of council officials being on the take. You heard any of that?'

'You mean the *parish* council?' The look on the butcher's face told the story. 'No way! They're opposed to the plans.'

Dunbar had chosen to be vague to see what the response would be. 'No, no... I mean the district council... the planning department.'

'Local people come in here all the time and say there must be shady deals on the go, but there's no proof. Feelings are running a bit high. Is that all?'

'Yes, thank you.' Dunbar paid and left through the end door.

Outside she bumped into Gale Slater who was about to enter the other door.

'Mrs Slater, we haven't actually met. I was at the briefing meeting in the village hall.'

Gale gave her a quizzical look. 'Sorry, I don't...'

'Zoe Dunbar. I'm a reporter. Please accept my condolences on your loss. How are you coping?'

'Okay, I suppose.'

'Have the police made any progress yet, do you know?'

'They haven't said. Look... I must get some shopping, if you don't mind?'

Dunbar realised it wasn't a good time to ask Mrs Slater any questions about her husband's murder. She wished her a good day.

On the drive back home, Dunbar slammed a hand against the steering wheel. *No proof, no story.*

39

The Volvo XC60 was on the way from Zimmerman's country house to Canning's mansion near Henley. 'How come you and Zimmerman knew when this Al Jameel chap and his son were coming to stay and for how long?' Kelso asked Guerra.

'Inside job. Someone in the Canning camp passed the information on. Still don't see why the boss took the risk of breaking you out of prison to do this though. We could have managed.'

'I doubt it. Zimmerman's no fool. He knows what he's doing.'

'More people to split the ransom between is how I look at it. You'd better be worth it.'

'Two million goes a long way. Come to think of it though, Zimmerman never did say how he would split the money.'

'Between the boss, you and me.'

'Can't be in equal amounts. Stands to reason I should get more than you since I'm leading the operation.'

'Huh. I took most of the risk getting you out of prison. There was a cost associated to that. I reckon we should deduct it from your share,' Guerra retorted.

'Only teasing. You're too sensitive, mate.'

'Fuck you!'

Kelso grinned. It was so easy to wind Guerra up. He stayed silent for a while then asked, 'What about your driver mate, Taffy? He not in on it?'

'Not now that *leader* Kelso is on the scene,' Guerra scoffed. 'Taffy's been squeezed out,' he added.

'Does he know about the kidnap plan?'

'Nah, he knows we're planning something big, but he's no idea what it is. Don't worry, he knows when to keep his mouth shut.'

'Just checking.'

'You always so mistrusting?'

'Careful is the word you're looking for.'

Guerra concentrated on his driving for a few minutes, then asked, 'Who was the guy who put you away for the armed robbery?'

'He died. Heart attack, I heard. Saved me the trouble.'

'You'd have killed him?'

'Thought had crossed my mind if I got out of prison. By the way, I hear the detective who's in charge of the Slater murder enquiry is a guy called Fleming. Name rings a bell. He may have questioned me at some stage.'

Guerra frowned. 'I thought the Met dealt with the armed robbery. Fleming's with Thames Valley Police.'

'Must have transferred. He was a DI with the Met.'

'He's a DCI now.'

'How'd you know?'

'In the papers. You should read more. Score to settle there?'

'As I said, I'm careful. Fleming may only have questioned me. If I went after every cop who interviewed me, plus the judge and jury, I'd be in business killing for some time.'

Guerra stifled a laugh. 'You could be one of the most famous serial killers of all time though.'

Kelso shook his head and wondered about Guerra's sanity.

The car slowed as they found the small parking place in the woods off the country lane near Canning's mansion. 'You realise this is the fifth time we've been here,' Guerra complained as he parked the car. 'If it was up to me, we'd have kidnapped the fucking man by now.'

'Something they drummed into me in the army.'

'What?'

'Time spent on reconnaissance is rarely wasted.'

'Okay, but five bloody times, for fuck's sake.'

'First time, I wanted to check the lay of the land before Al Jameel and his son arrived. Second time, we happened to come when Canning had a big garden party on the go. There were too many security men around to hang about.'

'Right, but since then, we've been another twice.'

'We need to check daily routines. That is, if there are any. There may not be. You can't just turn up expecting to find your target in a position where it's going to be possible to abduct them.'

'Okay, we found Al Jameel's son goes for a daily jog round the grounds about nine in the morning. We know he follows the same route, and we know a security guard comes with him. Seen him do that twice. Why do we need to check again?'

'We know they're here for another three days. I want to make sure he does keep to the same routine.'

'What if he doesn't, eh? Have you thought about that? We spend so many fucking days checking, the routine changes, and he leaves before we get a chance to nab him.'

'We'll get him when we're good and ready.'

'I say we move now before it's too late.'

'Are you always so impulsive? What do you want to do... storm the house, guns at the ready, and find the target isn't there?'

'Binoculars. We look first, or... we phone and ask if he's there saying it's a friend from Saudi Arabia who wants to speak to him.'

'Okay. He's there and comes to the phone. What then?'

'We hang up and move in.'

'Alerting the security men that something's wrong. Great idea. I can see why Zimmerman wanted someone in charge who knew what they were doing.'

'You're far too bloody careful if you ask me.'

'I'm not asking you. I'm telling you what we do.'

Debating done, the men got out of the car and walked across the road. There was a small grass verge and a crumbling drystone wall forming the boundary to Canning's land. They climbed over and settled themselves behind a large laurel bush. It was next to the rough path through the woods where Dani Al Jameel usually jogged.

They waited for half an hour before they heard feet pounding the ground and the sound of panting voices.

Guerra hissed, 'Let's get him now!'

40

Fleming could see from the car park that a light was on in Liz Temple's office. He'd arrived for a quick meeting with Logan and Anderson prior going to see Eric Blunt in the council offices.

Before going to see his two colleagues, Fleming decided to call in on Temple. Her door was open and she waved him in. 'Alex, thought you were out today.'

'Yeah, going to speak to Eric Blunt, but wanted to see Logan and Anderson first. See where we are and sort out priorities for this week.'

'Making good progress?'

'Still following up on our two main suspects.'

'I hope you get a breakthrough soon. The new chief constable starts tomorrow. I'm in the middle of preparing a briefing for her.'

'Who is it?'

'Vanita Lazar from West Midlands Police. She was deputy chief constable there. Comes highly rated, they say. She'll want to know about the Slater murder.'

'Best get on with it then,' Fleming said, turning to go.

'Alex?'

'Yes, ma'am?'

'Try to have some positive news for her,' Temple said, going back to her notes.

~

Logan and Anderson were already in the incident room when Fleming arrived. 'I've had a quick word with the super,' he said. 'New chief constable starts tomorrow. Vanita Lazar. She was DCC at West Midlands Police.'

'Don't tell me,' Logan said, 'the super wants to greet her with a result on the Slater case.'

'You've guessed it, Harry. So, let's get started.'

'With coffee and biscuits?' Logan asked.

'He meant work, Sarge,' Anderson said.

'Yeah, yeah. But you know what they say?'

'I'd guess I'm about to hear one of your pearls of wisdom,' Anderson retorted.

'An army marches on its stomach.'

Anderson laughed. 'Some army, three people.'

Fleming raised his eyes to the ceiling. 'Okay, first thing, one of you needs to go and speak to Canning. He told us he knew nothing about the two meetings Slater went to in London. See if he has any idea why Slater would want to ask someone for more money or a larger share.'

'I'll go,' Logan offered.

'Take a photo of the man Slater met at the hotel. See if Canning knows who he is.'

'Okay.'

'Anything back on Slater's computer, Naomi?'

'Nothing. It's all work related. No clues about who he went to meet or who might have wanted to kill him.'

'Didn't expect there would be, but worth checking. Harry, anyone at The Rising Sun recollect Vic Quinn going there for a curry the night of the murder?'

'Yes, he was there and timings check out. His car was picked up on CCTV as well.'

'Anything from the search of Quinn's house?'

'Nothing. No gun, no evidence one was ever there, no bloodstained clothing. What now?' Logan asked.

'All we have on him are the incidents with Slater and Canning, he's a bit volatile, and his fingerprints are on Slater's car door handle. He's explained that, and we can't disprove it. Not enough to arrest him. We just keep an eye on him for now and keep digging.'

'What about Rashad Yousefi, boss? I spoke to the Met and I've got you an interview arranged with him for Tuesday in London. Want me to come with you?'

'Might as well. If I know anything about the Met, they'll be reluctant to lend me one of their CID officers to sit in with me. Not their case.'

'Not even to help out one of their former officers?' Logan queried.

'Doubt it, so it's you.'

'Do you want me to carry on showing the photo of the man Slater saw in London to everyone else who knew Slater?' Anderson asked. 'See if anyone recognises him.'

'Yes, please do.'

'We still need to speak to Canning's accountant,' Logan reminded Fleming.

'You can arrange to see her when you go to see Canning. That it for now?'

Logan and Anderson both nodded their agreement.

'In which case, I'd best be off to see Eric Blunt.'

~

It took Fleming under an hour to get to the council offices. He thought the meeting wouldn't take long. He only wanted to have a quick word with the area planning officer as he had some dealings with Tom Slater.

Fleming parked his Porsche in the large car park. The council building was new by the looks of it. A modern construction which looked to be of more glass than concrete. The entrance led into an open atrium. A reception desk was over to the right.

Fleming walked over and spoke to a young receptionist who looked up at him and smiled as he approached. 'Can I help you?'

'DCI Fleming. I have a meeting with Eric Blunt.'

'Just a moment. I'll let him know you're here.'

Five minutes later, Blunt appeared out of the lifts. He walked across the atrium with his shoes clicking on the large tiled floor. 'DCI Fleming, good to see you. I'm Eric Blunt. Let's go up to my office.'

'Fine,' Fleming said.

'Tea or coffee?' Blunt asked as they sat at a small table across from his desk.

'No, thanks. This won't take long. I just wanted to ask you about Tom Slater. We need to speak to everyone who saw him in the last few weeks.'

'I only met him once. He came here with Paul Canning. They wanted to discuss Canning's planning application.'

'The submission?'

'Yes. They wanted to check what the procedure was.'

'Did Slater seem like a man who was worried or nervous about something?'

'No, not at all.'

'He had a death threat over the application. Did you know that?'

'No, I didn't.'

'Have you had any death threats?'

'Yes. Didn't worry me though. Comes with the job. Angry people always appear when we're considering a planning application. The threats are meant to scare, they're not serious.'

'Except in Tom Slater's case, it seems they were.'

'You think it was one of the protesters?'

'We haven't ruled out the possibility.' Fleming pulled the photo of the man Slater met in London out of his pocket. 'Any idea who he is?'

Blunt looked at the photo and shook his head. 'No, never seen him before.'

'Have you heard of a man called Vic Quinn?'

Blunt smiled. 'Oh, yes! He's one of the more vocal protesters. I heard about the incidents with Mr Slater and Paul Canning. Quinn's led protests out by the main entrance on several occasions, banners and all.'

'Have you met him in person?'

'No, but I was there at a public information meeting in the village hall. As Mr Slater was leaving, Quinn was shouting abuse at him. Said he was a dead man.'

41

Kelso and Guerra had stayed silent as they drove back to Zimmerman's country house after the surveillance on Canning's mansion. Guerra's rashness and willingness to act on impulse was beginning to worry Kelso. He was recalling what he'd said to The Supplier: *There's one weak link, but I can take care of it.*

'Still think we should have nabbed him then when we had the chance,' Guerra said, breaking the silence.

'We weren't ready.'

'You're joking. We've been planning this kidnap from the start. How can you say we weren't ready?'

'It wasn't planned to happen today. In case you've forgotten, Zimmerman is coming over this afternoon to go through the plans. He might have been surprised to find we'd abducted Al Jameel before we'd had a chance to discuss it.'

'My guess is he would have been impressed we seized the moment and took advantage of a good opportunity.'

Kelso glanced sideways at Guerra who was staring straight ahead with his hands gripping the steering wheel.

'Acting on impulse without any thought is usually a bad idea,' Kelso said.

'Okay, know-all. Suppose he changes his routine and doesn't go for a run on the day we go to get him. Got a plan B?'

'I have,' Kelso lied. 'I'll explain all to Zimmerman when he arrives.'

The two men fell silent again for the rest of the journey.

Guerra had dropped Kelso off at the house while he went to fetch Zimmerman. Kelso reckoned he had about three to four hours before they arrived back at the house. He took the opportunity to check over the Glock 17 he'd acquired from The Supplier before hiding it under a pile of clothing in his wardrobe.

After hiding the Glock, he went out to walk round the grounds for some fresh air to clear his head. He needed to work out what his plan B would be and what he was going to tell Zimmerman. Guerra and his mate, Taffy, had been armed during the prison escape, so Kelso assumed Zimmerman would supply guns. The Glock 17 was just in case, but he didn't want Zimmerman and Guerra to know he had it. He would need the gun for his escape after he got his share of the ransom money. Besides, there was also a part of him that didn't trust Guerra. *Need to keep a close eye on him.*

After several rounds of the grounds, Kelso went back into the house to grab a beer from the fridge. It was a hot day, so he took it outside to sit in the patio area at the back of the house. He'd worked out what plan B for the kidnap would be in case Dani didn't stick to his jogging routine, so that was a plus point.

Four hours after Guerra had dropped Kelso off, he returned with Zimmerman. They grabbed some beers and joined Kelso outside. Zimmerman took a swig from his can of beer. 'Everything all planned?' he asked Kelso.

'I've got the actual abduction worked out. But would I be right in assuming you've got arrangements in place for how you'll get the ransom?'

'It's all taken care of. I have a complicated system in place for money laundering. Some of my mules opened loads of different accounts set up by using fake and stolen documents. We get the ransom split up and paid into those accounts. It's then immediately exchanged for convertible currencies, mainly US dollars. By layering, I get the money shuffled around various overseas accounts. That makes it difficult to trace back to me. After a while, it appears in my legitimate accounts as clean money. On the face of it, income earned from investments, rents and sales of goods.'

'Impressive. And how does my share find its way to me?' Kelso asked.

'I make a withdrawal from several of my legitimate accounts and pay you cash.'

'And how, may I ask, are you going to split the two million between the three of us?' Guerra asked.

'I take half on account I planned it and have the means in place to launder the money,' Zimmerman said. 'You two get the other half split between you.'

'Seems a bit weighted in your favour,' Guerra said.

'Take it or leave it, Marco. Half a million for an abduction is enough.'

Guerra shot a glance at Kelso and grinned. 'So much for you expecting a bigger share,' he taunted.

Zimmerman raised an eyebrow and looked at Kelso.

'Just a little joke between Marco and me. I was winding him up saying I should get more because I was leading the kidnap operation.'

Zimmerman narrowed his eyes and glared at the two men. 'I need you two to stop the petty squabbling and concentrate on getting this job done without any hitches. Don't forget, if you don't pull this off, you get nothing.'

Guerra scowled.

'Going back to what I asked,' Zimmerman said, 'all set to go?' he asked Kelso.

'Yeah. We've had Canning's place under surveillance for a few days. Dani Al Jameel has a regular routine. He goes jogging round the grounds with a security guard every morning about nine. Always follows the same route. There's a place we can park in the woods off the country lane which runs by the house.'

'What vehicle are you using?'

'What happened to the van used in my escape?'

Guerra grinned. 'Taffy had it resprayed a different colour and it's got false number plates. Seemed a shame to get rid of it.'

'That's what we'll use then.' Turning to Zimmerman, 'I assume you're supplying us with guns?'

'I have guns for you both, but I'd prefer you don't shoot anyone if you don't have to. Let's keep it simple.'

'Right. We'll be lying in wait inside the grounds for Jameel and the security guard to appear. We hold them up. I keep an eye on them while Marco ties the security guard's and Jameel's hands behind their backs. We leave the guard with his legs tied together and mouth taped so he can't shout for help after we've gone.'

'And if the security guard resists?' Zimmerman asked.

Kelso smiled. 'I smack him on the head with the gun. It'll take us seconds to get Jameel over the road to the van. We drive back here, lock him up and hide the van in the garage until you get a chance to get rid of it.'

'You said you had a plan B in case Jameel doesn't stick to his routine. What is it?' Guerra asked. 'Might be an idea if I knew in advance.'

'We keep an eye on Canning's mansion, all day if necessary.'

'Then what?'

'We make sure we have sight of Jameel, and wait for an opportunity.'

'And if an opportunity doesn't present itself?'

'We come back another day.'

'Leaving it a bit late, isn't it?' Guerra said.

'We have three days left before the Jameels are due to go home. If we don't get him before, we hijack the vehicle they leave in to go to the airport.'

'And run the risk of someone seeing us.'

'Kidnapping is a risky business,' Kelso said. 'Worth a bit of a risk for half a million. Any better ideas?'

Guerra shook his head.

'When do you plan to make the first attempt?' Zimmerman asked.

Kelso downed the last of his beer. 'Tomorrow.'

42

The Met had made sure an interview room was free, but as Fleming had expected, no CID officers were able to attend.

Logan had spoken to Yousefi on his mobile and had requested his presence at the local police station. He'd explained he wasn't under arrest and that he didn't have to attend. Yousefi had declined and told Logan where to go. Logan had then told him he could arrest him on suspicion of murder, in which case he would have no choice in the matter. He also told him they could take his fingerprints and DNA samples and keep him in custody for up to twenty-four hours if he arrested him. Yousefi had agreed to be there.

Interview room three was hot and cramped. The only furniture was a table and four chairs. Fleming and Logan sat on one side of the table. Yousefi sat opposite them, watching the two detectives with anxious eyes.

Logan switched the digital interview recorder on and Fleming stated where they were, the date and time, and who was present. He cautioned Yousefi and explained he was not under arrest and could leave at any time.

Yousefi grunted. 'That a fact?' he asked in disbelief. 'Only your mate here,' he said, pointing at Logan, 'will arrest me if I try to leave. He's already threatened me with that.'

'For the record, and the purposes of the DIR,' Logan said, 'I only told Mr Yousefi what would happen if I arrested him. He agreed to attend.'

Yousefi tapped a heel up and down on the floor and beads of sweat were beginning to form on his forehead. 'Very thoughtful of you,' he mocked.

'As you are under caution you can have free legal advice. Do you wish to have a solicitor present?' Fleming asked.

'I don't need one. I ain't done anything wrong.'

Sweat stains began to appear under the arms of the grey T-shirt Yousefi was wearing.

Fleming opened a folder on the table in front of him and read from his notes. 'When we saw you last, you told us you were in the commune on the night your stepfather was murdered. Is that correct?'

Yousefi said nothing. He just nodded, avoiding eye contact with Fleming.

'For the purposes of the DIR,' Fleming said, 'Mr Yousefi is not answering, but he is nodding in agreement.'

'You're sticking to your story?' Fleming prompted.

'Yes.'

'We have three signed statements from people in the commune where you live. They all confirmed you left there around six in the evening and came back around ten.'

'They must have the wrong night.'

'There's no mistake,' Fleming persisted.

'They're lying.'

'Why would they?'

'To get me into trouble. There are people there I don't get on with.'

'Including your friend with the black car?'

Yousefi shifted in his seat and his eyes darted between Logan and Fleming. 'He told you I went out?'

'He wilted under a bit of pressure and confirmed that you did.'

'Okay, I did go out. I needed to go and see my mother to get some money. She told me my stepfather was out, so my friend took me in the car.'

'What time did you get to your mother's house?'

'We got to Darmont about seven. Didn't stay long in case my stepfather came home.'

'What time did you leave?'

'Around eight.'

'It took you about an hour to get to Darmont. That would put it around nine when you returned to the commune. Where were you until ten?'

Yousefi shrugged. 'Went for a drive.'

'Where?'

Another shrug. 'I wasn't paying any attention. We took the scenic route back. Must have taken longer.'

'Why did you lie about your whereabouts?'

'Wouldn't look good if I was in Darmont, would it?'

Fleming frowned. 'If I find out you've been lying again, I will arrest you. You were in Darmont at roughly the time your stepfather was murdered.'

'I didn't do it!'

'And a witness saw a black car speeding away from near the scene.'

'I swear I had nothing to do with it!'

Fleming reached into his folder again and pulled out the photograph of the man Slater met in London. 'For the purposes of the DIR, I'm showing Mr Yousefi photograph reference P2765/06. Do you recognise this man?'

Yousefi shook his head. 'No.'

Fleming put the photograph back in the folder and closed it. 'Interview terminated at eleven thirty.'

43

The day after questioning Yousefi in London with Fleming, Logan was on his way to see Paul Canning. Fleming and Anderson were going to see Gale Slater to check out her son's version of events. Logan had checked with Yousefi's friend who confirmed they took a longer route back to the commune in London. That didn't count for much in Logan's book though. They would have made sure their stories matched. He'd asked for Forensics to check the car. They found no traces of Slater's DNA, fingerprints, blood, or evidence of a gun.

Logan had decided to leave straight from home in Kidlington to drive to Canning's mansion. In less than an hour, he was pulling up on the gravel outside the front door. He'd phoned to say what time he would arrive and had asked if Makayla Yamamura could be there as well.

Jane Canning let Logan in and led him down the hall. 'Paul's in the dining room checking over his plans,' she said. 'Can I get you anything? Tea, coffee?'

'No, thanks. I won't be long.'

Canning had cleared the dining-room table which had a plan of the development site on it. He was tracing a line across the plan with his walking cane while holding a large glass of brandy in the other hand. A smoking cigar sat in an ashtray he'd used to hold down a corner of the plan.

'DS Logan is here, Paul.'

Canning turned and waved Logan over to the table. 'Just going through my plans and preparing for the public enquiry. Drink?'

'No, thanks. Your wife already offered. I won't take up much of your time.'

'I must admit I was surprised you wanted to see me again. I told you all I knew about Tom.'

'A couple of things have come up I wanted to ask you about.'

'Wouldn't be to do with that bloody upstart Quinn, would it?'

'Any reason you think it might be to do with him?'

'He's a troublemaker, and he vandalised my car.'

'You also assaulted him,' Logan reminded Canning.

'Deserves more than a fucking good thrashing if you ask me,' Canning said, then took a large gulp of his brandy. He picked up his cigar, puffed on it, then blew a cloud of thick white smoke up towards the ceiling. 'Anyway, local police have dealt with that.'

'I didn't come to see you about Quinn. Not my case. The murder of Tom Slater is.'

'Listen, I don't mean to be rude, but I'm a busy man and I've told you all I can. I'm expecting Isa Al Jameel and his son back from London this afternoon and I need to get things ready for them.'

'Seeing the sights while they're here?'

'They're visiting my London office to get a handle on things there.' Canning took another puff of his cigar and blew smoke in Logan's direction. He jutted his chin out. 'So, what are the other things that've come up you want to talk about?'

Logan waved a hand in front of his face to steer the smoke

away. He fished into his jacket pocket to pull out the photograph of the man Slater met at the London hotel. 'Recognise this man?'

Canning sipped at his brandy while he took a look at the photo. He shook his head. 'No idea. Never seen him before. Who is he?'

'That's what we're trying to find out. He's the man Slater met in London. The meetings you said you knew nothing about.'

'I didn't.'

'We've found out why he went to meet this man.'

'You have?'

'He wanted to ask for a bigger share of something. Mean anything to you?'

Canning shook his head. 'Not a thing. I've no idea what that would be about.'

'Sure?'

'Yes. I'm afraid I can't help you with that one. Was there something else?'

'Mr Slater fired a man. Nash. Know why?'

'I heard about it, but I don't get involved with the minutia of running the business.'

'Mr Nash claims he disagreed with you over something and you had a big row. Says you threatened to get rid of him.'

'I have rows with loads of people. I'm running a business, not a fan club. If people don't perform, they get axed.'

'He also claims he was set up, accused of fraud.'

'Rubbish. The man was useless. And, I may say, devious.'

'It seems odd your colleagues accused him of fraud and Slater didn't get the police involved.'

'I would have known if Slater had accused him of fraud. Nash must have made it up. There was no fraud. Tom probably sacked him because he fucked up over something. Bitter people often make wild exaggerated claims.'

'Okay, I won't take up any more of your time.'

'Makayla is in the room Tom used to work from when he was here. I'll take you along,' Canning said.

Yamamura was sitting at a desk, tapping away on the keyboard while watching the computer screen. She got up to shake Logan's hand. 'Take a seat,' she said, waving to another chair by her side. 'I take it you want to ask me about Tom Slater?'

'Yes, but before I do, I'd like you to have a look at this.' Logan took the photo he'd showed to Canning out of his pocket. 'Do you recognise this man?'

Yamamura studied the photo for a few seconds. 'No.'

'He was the man Mr Slater went to see twice in London.'

'Sorry, no idea who he is.'

Logan put the photo back in his pocket. 'I wanted to ask you about a man Mr Slater sacked. A Mr Nash.'

At the mention of the name, Logan thought he detected a glimmer of alarm in Yamamura's eyes. He studied her for a second. 'Do you know what it was over?'

'Something to do with consultants he hired. They made a mess of something and Nash failed to manage it. Tried to cover it up and it cost the business a lot of money.'

'That's not what Mr Nash said.'

'Doesn't surprise me. What did he say?'

'He said you and Mr Slater set him up for a fraud he didn't commit.'

Logan saw Yamamura stiffen.

'That's ridiculous!'

'He reckons you fiddled the books on the consultants' fees and syphoned some money off into Mr Slater's account.'

'What!'

'That's what he's claiming. Reckoned he knew you and Slater were behind the fraud because you didn't call the police.'

'Look, there was no need for us to call the police because there was no fraud. I've explained why Tom fired Nash.'

'So he's lying?'

'Of course he is! Think about it, if he thought I had fiddled the books to pay money into Tom's account, why didn't *he* call the police?'

'Okay. It was just something we needed to clear up. Thank you for your time. I'll let myself out.'

On the way back to the office, Logan supposed Yamamura had a good point. But she had seemed uneasy when he mentioned Nash's name.

44

Canning had taken care to choose a restaurant which MPs tended, in the main, not to frequent. They had their favourite eating places nearer to Westminster. He'd arranged to meet Walter Hammond there for lunch. It was convenient. Hammond wouldn't want to run the risk of other MPs seeing him talking to Canning.

The food had been good. After eating, Canning had ordered brandy. Hammond had settled for another glass of sparkling water. 'The party was a splendid affair, don't you think?' Canning asked.

'It was,' Hammond agreed with a smarmy smile. 'Fantastic weather, and a welcoming host, what more could you want?'

'How did your little chat with Al Jameel go?' Canning asked.

Hammond's unctuous smile widened. 'Very well. He seemed keen to know how talks on the trade and arms deals were going. I told him they were going well. But I had to explain I wasn't involved in the talks. Only had a say in matters as a member of the cabinet.'

Canning took a sip of his brandy and peered over the rim of the glass at Hammond. 'By the way, he's decided to invest in my development plans. It would be a great pity if the application weren't approved, wouldn't it? Al Jameel would be very disappointed. I mean, having seen a sound investment opportunity.'

Hammond frowned. 'Yes, indeed. That would be a shame. Let's hope the chair of the public enquiry recommends approval.'

'Have you appointed a planning inspector to chair the enquiry yet?'

'I have, yes.'

'Someone who might owe you a favour?'

'Not quite.'

'But someone inclined to recommend approval?'

Hammond smiled. 'Let's say I'm in a position to nudge certain things his way that might be to his benefit. May help to persuade him.'

Canning downed the rest of his brandy and ordered another. 'Bloody shame you're not allowed to smoke in restaurants these days. Could do with a cigar to celebrate.'

'Don't get overexcited,' Hammond warned. 'I can't go so far as directing him to recommend approval.'

'But whatever he recommends, the final decision is yours, isn't it?'

'It is, but I do have to take the planning inspector's findings into account. It would be unusual for a minister to ignore their recommendations.'

'I hate to persist, but you are not obliged to do so. Is that correct?'

Hammond studied the water in his glass before answering. 'I would have to have a damned good reason to ignore the findings.'

Canning sipped on his second brandy and viewed Hammond through narrowed eyes. Canning decided to change tack. The gloves were off and it was time to play his final card. 'Remember the times we had at university? We had some fun, didn't we?'

Hammond narrowed his eyes. He laughed nervously. 'We did indeed, but that was a long time ago.'

'I suppose one of the problems of being in the public eye is that the past can sometimes come back to bite you. It can cause embarrassment to a government minister.'

'Paul, if I didn't know better, that sounds rather like a threat. Is it?'

'My dear chap, not at all. I'm trying to protect you. If the press ever found out about your drug taking at uni–'

'You wouldn't,' Hammond cut in.

'Then there's the wild drugs parties at your London house before you became a minister.'

Hammond's mouth dropped open. His face was ashen.

'And if it came out about your fling with the woman who is now the secretary of state for international trade, that would be terrible. Right at the time when the government are in trade talks with Saudi Arabia.'

'You despicable git! I thought you were a friend!'

'Just saying... press would have a field day. It would most likely spell the end of your career, hers as well.'

'I'll... I'll do my best to get your application approved,' Hammond spluttered.

Canning downed the rest of his brandy. He stood to leave and patted Hammond on the shoulder. 'I know you'll do the right thing, Walter.'

On his way back to Henley, Canning smiled to himself. He was sure Hammond would approve his application.

45

Someone had draped a large white cloth banner across one side of the church facing the road. “Save our village from Canning” was written across it in big red letters. Fleming and Anderson were driving into Darmont when they saw it. The vicar was climbing a ladder to take it down.

Fleming stopped the car and turned to Anderson. ‘Wait here. I’ll only be a minute.’ He got out and called over to the vicar. ‘You all right up there? Look a bit unsteady.’

The vicar looked down at Fleming. ‘Oh, hello there. If you could just put a foot on the bottom of the ladder, I’d be grateful. Not very good with heights.’

Fleming smiled. The vicar was only halfway up the ladder and was clutching the sides like his life depended on it. ‘Sure, no problem.’ He put a foot on the bottom rung and held the sides steady.

After a few minutes, the vicar had managed to cut the ties and the banner floated down to the ground. He climbed back down and offered a hand to Fleming. ‘Thank you so much. I did say a prayer before I got the ladder out and, although I had complete trust in God, it was nice to have a bit of extra help.’

'Good job we were passing at the right time.'

Fleming saw realisation dawning in the vicar's eyes.

The vicar laughed. 'Of course! He answered my prayer.'

For a minute Fleming thought he was serious. 'Any idea who put it up?'

'No. I came to do a few things in the church and saw it there.'

'Feelings running high, eh?'

'I have some sympathy with local residents, I must say. They're seeing the worst side of capitalism. The rich reaping profits whatever the environmental damage. No thought for the impact on villagers who see profiteers threatening their tranquil way of life.'

'I suppose the Cannings of this world think they're providing much-needed homes in line with government policy.'

'There's that argument, yes. But people here have no doubt that Mr Canning is more interested in lining his pockets than helping the government out.'

'I'm sure the planning inspector chairing the public enquiry will get both sides of the argument.'

'That I can guarantee,' the vicar said.

'Best let you get on with whatever you were doing.' Fleming made to walk back to the car, then turned. 'Was Mr Slater a churchgoer?'

'He used to attend regularly with his wife, Gale. People regarded him as a quiet, but likeable chap. Kept pretty much to himself. Didn't get very much involved in village life, but then he was a busy working man. Spent a lot of time commuting into London. Stopped coming to church after Mr Canning's planning application. Got angry stares from people and I don't think he and his wife were prepared to run the gauntlet, so to speak.'

'Must have been awkward for them.' Fleming pulled out the photo of the man Slater had met in London. 'Bit of a long shot, but did you ever see Mr Slater with this man?'

The vicar peered at the photo. 'I'm sure I know the faces of all the local people, but I can't say I recognise this man. Pretty sure he's not from round here.'

Fleming put the photo back in his pocket. 'It was worth asking. Long shots sometimes pay off, but not always. Best be on my way. You take care.'

'Good luck with your investigation,' the vicar shouted after him. 'And thanks for your help.'

Fleming waved a hand over his shoulder as he climbed into his Porsche.

A few minutes later, Fleming and Anderson were sitting in Gale Slater's lounge. Fleming was trying to work out if her expression was one of alarm or nervousness. 'Sorry to bother you again, Mrs Slater, but there's a couple of things we need to check with you,' he said.

'Oh, dear. I'm sure I told you everything when you first spoke to me.' Her voice trembled.

Fleming pulled the photo out of his jacket pocket and showed it to Gale. 'This is the man your husband went to see in London. Know who he is?'

Gale took the photo with a shaking hand and looked at it for a second or two. 'I've no idea. Never seen him before. Have you asked Paul?'

'I've got someone speaking to him about it. I'm hoping someone will recognise who the man is soon.'

'Do you think he had something to do with Tom's murder?'

'I don't know. We're following up on every bit of information we have. More often than not, things that look like they might be possible clues turn into dead ends.'

Gale brushed a hair back from her cheek and folded her

arms. 'You said there were a couple of things you needed to check.'

'When we questioned your son, he told us he was in the commune all night on the night your husband was killed.'

Gale stiffened.

'He lied. We have verified witnesses who say he went out. Do you know where he went?'

Gale's face was ashen. 'He came here to see me after ringing me to check Tom wasn't at home.'

'And the purpose of his visit?'

'He needed money.'

'What time did he arrive here?'

'I didn't look at the clock. Don't usually pour wine till after six when I eat. I'd tidied up and was on my second glass, so I guess it would have been around seven.'

'How long did your son stay, Mrs Slater,' Anderson asked.

Fleming thought Gale looked as though she was about to give away state secrets. She hesitated. 'He stayed about an hour.'

'So left about eight?' Anderson prompted.

'I think so.'

'According to the autopsy report, your husband was killed between eight and eleven that night. Did your son mention Tom at all when he was here?' Fleming asked.

'No, he just asked on the phone if Tom was at home. You think Rashad did it?'

'It took his friend an hour to drive Rashad here. Allowing for the same time back to the commune would have got them there by nine. He didn't get back until ten.'

Gale gasped.

'Do you know where he was for the missing hour?'

'No.'

'Why didn't you tell us about this before?'

'I knew it would cast suspicion on Rashad. He might not have got on with Tom, but he would never kill anyone.'

'He told us his friend took him on a drive going the long way back to the commune. His friend confirms his story. At the moment, we can't prove otherwise.'

'What happens now? Will you arrest him?'

'There's a lot of circumstantial evidence, but no forensics to put him at the scene. He denied having anything to do with it. Arresting him would be premature at this stage. Unless we find the gun or forensic evidence... or he confesses.'

They left Gale Slater looking a worried woman.

Anderson had been quiet on the drive back to the office. 'Penny for them,' Fleming said.

Anderson smiled. 'Just thinking outside the box, sir. Sometimes everything seems to point in a particular direction and you get blinded to other possibilities.'

'Go on.'

'Mrs Slater seemed to be on edge today, nervous even.'

'I noticed. Your point?'

'She was in the village that night. There must have been tensions between her and her husband over debts due to Slater's gambling. And... he treated her son badly.'

46

They were working a late shift at HQ. One or two staff sat at their desks looking tired. Temple was still there. Apart from that, it was just Fleming, Logan and Anderson in the incident room. Everyone else had long since gone home.

'How did your little chat with Paul Canning go?' Fleming asked Logan.

'He's not the kind of man I'd take a liking to, that's for sure. He's rude and a bit of an egotistical sod. Still whinging about Vic Quinn.'

'Bet they're not the exact words that went through your mind when you were forming an opinion of Canning,' Anderson teased.

'Naomi, your ability to read minds never ceases to amaze me. Full marks for insight and intuition.'

'Doesn't take much to read your mind, Sarge. I know when you take a dislike to someone your sarcasm comes to the fore.'

'Confidence is one thing, but when someone thinks they have a superior sense of importance, you know they're just plain arrogant. As far as I'm concerned, Canning has crossed the line between being confident and being a conceited git.'

'Anything else nice to say about him, Sarge?' Anderson joked.

'Not that I can think of. Anyway, getting back to the boss's question, I showed Canning the photo of the man Slater met in London. Says he doesn't recognise him. No idea who he is.'

'Did you tell him we'd found out why Slater wanted to meet this man?'

'I did. Reckons he hasn't a clue what it was all about. He also trashed Nash's claim that Slater stitched him up. Reckoned Slater sacked him for incompetence.'

'What did Yamamura have to say about it?'

'Pretty much the same as Canning. Incompetence.'

'How did she respond when you told her Nash's side of the story?'

'Got all indignant. Claimed Nash was lying. Did make a valid point though. She asked why Nash didn't inform the police if he thought she and Slater had committed fraud.'

Fleming frowned. 'I asked him that as well. He reckoned it wouldn't have got him anywhere. Thing is, if Nash wasn't lying, he would have had a serious gripe against Slater, but enough to kill a man for?'

'Known people to kill for less,' Logan remarked.

'And if he was lying, he'd have no gripe we know of against Slater,' Anderson said. 'Except that he sacked him.'

'Did you show her the photo, Harry?'

'Yes. She didn't recognise him.'

'What about the reason for the meeting?'

'She had no idea what it could have been about.'

'Okay, no one so far knows who the man is who Slater met. Nash may or may not have being lying about the reason for his dismissal. He could have had a motive to kill Slater, but it seems a bit thin. I'm afraid our little chat with Gale Slater was just as fruitless.'

'She didn't recognise the man in the photo either?' Logan guessed.

'No, and she confirmed her son's story. Didn't tell us before that her son came to visit her as she knew it would cast suspicion on him.'

'Being in the village around the time of the murder when you have a motive doesn't look good, I agree.' Logan said. 'Motive, opportunity... only the means missing.'

'And any forensic evidence,' Fleming added.

'We need a breakthrough, don't we?' Anderson said. 'We've got suspects in Quinn and Yousefi... maybe Nash, but not enough evidence to charge anyone.'

'Don't forget the outside bets,' Logan said.

'We betting on horses now?' Anderson laughed.

'I think Harry means the man in the photo. Canning's a possibility as well,' Fleming said.

'Canning?' Anderson queried.

'Bit of a long shot, but Gale Slater told us things had become strained between her husband and Canning. He refused to give Slater a pay rise. They weren't getting on.'

'Isn't it more likely Slater would have killed Canning rather than the other way round in that case?' Anderson asked.

'Always keep an open mind, Naomi,' Logan said.

'By the way, thinking about our list of possible suspects and Naomi's intuitive powers, she had a thought as we left Gale Slater's house,' Fleming said.

'Naomi had a thought?' Logan quipped.

Fleming smiled. 'Think about those outside bets, Harry. Naomi thinks we shouldn't disregard Gale Slater as a suspect. Could have been tension between her and her husband over gambling debts. Slater didn't get on with her son. Threw him out. She also happened to be in the village the night her husband was murdered.'

47

When a day starts off on the wrong foot, the rest of the day is sure to get worse. Kelso was afraid that might be the case and wondered whether to call off the kidnap plan for that day.

Guerra was looking awkward. 'It wasn't my fault, Taff–'

'You're a fucking liability,' Kelso cut in. 'And you thought you and your mate could carry this off on your own?'

'We can still do it,' Guerra insisted.

'How the hell did you manage to wreck the van we were going to use?'

'I was reversing out of the garage. Taffy hadn't propped the door open properly and a sudden gust of wind caught one side. It slammed shut against the back of the van. Dented it in and knocked the rear lights out. Back window was also smashed.'

Kelso shook his head in exasperation.

'It's not a big deal,' Guerra insisted. 'We can use my car. I've put stolen number plates on. No one will see the car if we park it where we've been parking in the woods off the road.'

Kelso wasn't happy, but realised they didn't have much choice.

~

They parked the car in the usual place in the woods, near the entrance to Canning's driveway. Checking there was no one about, they crossed the road and hid in the bushes where they had carried out their reconnaissance. Kelso was still fuming with Guerra. Zimmerman had supplied guns as promised. Kelso hadn't brought his Glock 17. He might need it later. They'd brought a large roll of heavy-duty adhesive tape with them and four hoods. Two with eyeholes and two without.

Half an hour went by and there was no sign of Dani Al Jameel coming out for a run.

Guerra looked at Kelso who said nothing.

Another ten minutes went by and there was still no sign of him.

'So much for your time spent on reconnaissance rarely being wasted,' Guerra grumbled. 'Where the fuck is he?'

Kelso cursed. 'We do what I said and keep an eye on the house. See if we get sight of the target.'

'Knew Zimmerman should never have brought you in on this. If I'd had my way the last time we were here, we'd have him by now,' Guerra said.

Kelso ignored the remark and kept his binoculars trained on the mansion. He stiffened. 'There he is!' he whispered.

'Where?' Guerra asked, narrowing his eyes.

'He's carrying a bag of golf clubs to the garage. Maybe he's going out on his own. No... wait... there's a security guard with some clubs as well.'

'So, what do we do now, mastermind?' Guerra mocked.

Kelso's brain was racing. 'Back to the car.'

Guerra frowned. 'We giving up? Why don't we follow the car if they're going for a round of golf? We can hijack them where there's a quiet spot.'

'I've got a better idea. We take your car and park it sideways on in front of the electronic gates, blocking the exit. Lift the boot and the bonnet to make it look like we've broken down. We hide in the bushes by the side of the gates and wait. When the security guard opens the gates, he's sure to have a look at the car, so good job you fitted stolen number plates. That's when we strike.'

'Might work if no one comes by.'

'We'll have to take that chance. It's a quiet country lane so, with a bit of luck, no one will. Let's go!'

Three minutes later, Guerra had parked his car and lifted the boot and bonnet as planned. They donned their hoods, put on gloves, drew their guns and waited behind the bushes by the side of the gates.

After a short while, Kelso heard the crunch of gravel as the car approached. Seconds later, it appeared round a bend in the driveway and stopped behind the gates.

Kelso could see the driver pointing something through the windscreen and the gates swung open.

The driver got out of the car and started to walk towards Guerra's car, looking around for signs of anyone.

Before the security guard had gone through the gates, Kelso and Guerra sprang out of their hiding place, hoods on and guns at the ready.

The man's eyes widened. 'What the–'

'Behind your car!' Kelso snapped at the guard while Guerra got a terrified Al Jameel out of the passenger side.

Kelso kept both men covered while Guerra threw the eyeless hoods over their heads and taped their hands behind their backs.

'Don't shoot,' the security guard pleaded.

'Do as you're told and no one gets hurt,' Kelso said.

Kelso jabbed Al Jameel in the back with his gun. 'Over to our car and climb in the boot.'

Guerra grabbed hold of Al Jameel's arm and marched him over to his car. He manhandled him into the boot, slammed it shut and closed the bonnet.

Meanwhile, Kelso had pulled the guard over to a tree inside the grounds, out of sight of the driveway and road. He wrapped tape round the man's legs and chest to pin him to the tree and put some more over the hood where his mouth was.

Going back to the guard's car, Kelso jumped in, reversed, then drove over the grass to park behind a large bush inside the grounds out of sight of the house and road. He found the gadget for the electronic gates and closed them behind him as he dashed to the Volvo.

Guerra was revving up, ready to go.

Kelso pulled off his hood and climbed into the passenger seat. He hadn't even fastened his seat belt before Guerra set off with wheels spinning in the gravel. 'Take it easy,' he said. 'We'll be back at Zimmerman's long before anyone realises we've got Al Jameel.'

Two minutes later, they were heading up the A4130 when a cyclist appeared from nowhere out of a side road. Guerra was driving too fast and swerved, missing the cyclist by inches. The cyclist fell off his bike, but Guerra kept going.

'I told you to take it easy! You trying to do your best to get us noticed?' Kelso shouted.

The two men stayed silent for the rest of the journey with Kelso deep in thought. *Job done. Now I need to watch my back.*

48

The office was quiet. Most people had long since gone home including Logan and Anderson. They'd briefed Fleming on the progress local forces were making, checking the list of black cars provided by DVLA. So far, no one had emerged as a potential suspect, Vic Quinn being the exception.

Neither had they had any luck finding out who the man was that met Slater in London. In a last-ditch effort, Fleming had asked Anderson to get a copy of the photo pinned on the Darmont village hall noticeboard. He'd also told her to get it out in the national press. Someone had to know who this man was.

Temple had asked Fleming to stay behind. The new chief constable was coming over and wanted to have a word with them. He grabbed a second cup of coffee to take back to his office while he was waiting for Temple to call him. Sitting behind his desk, he looked at his notes and thought about the list of possible suspects. He recalled Anderson's words. *Sometimes everything seems to point in a particular direction... She was in the village that night.*

He looked at his watch. Temple had told him the chief

constable would be there by seven. It was now eight. *Timekeeping is not one of the chief constable's strengths.*

Fleming's phone rang, jolting him out of his thoughts. It was Temple, and she sounded stressed. 'Can you come and join us, Alex?'

As soon as Fleming walked into Temple's office, he sensed something was wrong. The atmosphere was sombre. Both women were standing in the middle of the office. The chief constable had her back to Fleming and turned as he entered.

Vanita Lazar was a tall, slim woman. The epaulettes on the neat-fitting uniform jacket showed high rank. Her face was as colourless as the platinum-blonde hair. It was short and cut across the forehead in a straight fringe. Fleming guessed she was in her early fifties. Piercing blue eyes gazed at Fleming. 'DCI Fleming... good to meet you,' she said, offering a hand. She spoke in a slow, strained voice. Her demeanour seemed almost patronising.

Fleming shook her hand and smiled. 'Pleased to meet you, ma'am.'

Lazar didn't return the smile and kept her eyes locked on Fleming. 'Seems I've arrived under a baptism of fire.'

Fleming wondered what she was referring to. 'You mean the Tom Slater murder?'

Temple cleared her throat. 'No, something else has come up. It's serious. I took the call a little over an hour ago.'

Fleming waited for Temple to continue.

'It appears Isa Al Jameel's son has been abducted. I've explained to the chief constable that Al Jameel is a potential investor in Paul Canning's development plans for Darmont.'

'Liz did tell me you are currently investigating the murder of one of Mr Canning's employees. Tom Slater, I take it?'

'That's right, ma'am.'

'Mr Canning seems to attract controversy, does he not?'

'He does,' Fleming agreed then turned to Temple. 'Have we got any details?'

'Al Jameel's son, Dani, left Canning's house this morning to go for a round of golf. There was a security guard with him.'

'Security guard?' Lazar queried. 'Why would he need one to go and play golf?'

'Al Jameel is a rich Saudi businessman. There have been violent protests over Canning's planning application. Death threats as well. They're taking no chances,' Temple explained.

'I see. And this murder investigation you're working on is to do with the threats?' Lazar asked Fleming.

'We don't know yet. There are several possible suspects. One of them is a key protester.'

'You've questioned this man, I take it?' Lazar asked.

'Yes, but there isn't enough evidence to justify an arrest at this stage. He has an alibi we can't disprove and there's no forensic evidence.'

'I see.' Lazar turned to Temple. 'Sorry, do go on, Liz.'

'They didn't return when expected. Al Jameel tried ringing his son, but there was no answer. Canning tried the security man, and he didn't answer either. He then rang the golf club who told him Dani didn't turn up for his pre-booked game.'

'Do they know for sure he was abducted? Could have been an accident. Has anyone checked local hospitals?' Fleming asked Temple.

'They found the car hidden by the front gates. The kidnappers had tied the security guard to a tree. He was in shock but unharmed. He told the local CID officer who came out that two armed men abducted Dani.'

'Was he able to describe them?'

'Only build and clothes. They wore hoods.'

Lazar looked at Temple. 'DCI Fleming ought to take this on.

He's already involved in a murder enquiry and it looks like there could be a connection.'

'I agree,' Temple said. 'There's one more thing, Alex.'

'Ma'am?'

'I had a call from number ten... and Walter Hammond. There are political sensitivities. They want this resolved quickly.'

'How come? I mean the political interest.'

'Al Jameel is very influential in Saudi Arabia. The government are having talks with the Saudis. They're about to sign a trade and arms deal worth around one and a half billion. Dani's abduction is a big embarrassment.'

'Has there been a ransom demand yet?' Fleming asked.

'No. You should get over to Canning's place tonight in case the kidnappers get in touch,' Temple said.

Lazar looked at Fleming. 'I want you to keep me informed.'

Fleming nodded. 'Yes, ma'am.'

On the way back to his office, Fleming cursed. *We need a breakthrough*, Anderson had said. *Not quite the breakthrough I was expecting.*

49

Before leaving the office to drive down to Canning's place, Fleming pondered over whether to call Logan. It was half past eight. By the time he picked him up from home in Kidlington and drove down to Henley it would be getting on for ten. Be lucky to get him home by midnight. Fleming decided to call to let him know, but he would go on his own to see Canning and Al Jameel.

Logan picked the phone up after two rings. 'Hello?'

'Harry, it's Alex. Something's come up I wanted to let you know about.'

'Don't tell me. You've got the breakthrough Naomi wanted.'

'Not quite. I've just been to see the super and the new chief constable.'

'Something to do with the new chief?'

'No. There's been a kidnap. Two men abducted Isa Al Jameel's son at gunpoint as he was coming out of Canning's place this morning.'

'Bloody hell! You on your way there now?'

'About to leave the office. Thought I'd call you first to let you know.'

'Come and pick me up. I'll be ready.'

'No, don't worry. I can go on my own. It'll be going on for midnight before I got you back home. Thought I'd let you know. Regards to your wife. Catch up in the office tomorrow.'

Fleming ended the call, grabbed his car keys and headed downstairs and out into the car park. It was still daylight, but it would be dark before he arrived at Canning's place.

A uniformed police officer stood in front of the blue-and-white tape stretched across the driveway. Fleming wound down his window and looked up at the officer. He had to shield his eyes from the glare of floodlights attached to the top of high masts. They illuminated the whole area like a football stadium.

The officer approached Fleming's Porsche. 'Sorry, this is a crime scene. No visitors are being allowed.'

Fleming showed his warrant card. 'DCI Fleming.'

'Ah, right, sir. Let me lift the tape so you can get through.'

'Thanks.'

Fleming eased the car under the tape. A group of SOCOs dressed in white overalls were searching the grounds as he drove past.

Two minutes later, a harassed-looking Jane Canning opened the front door. She led Fleming down to the living room where Canning and Al Jameel were sitting. Canning was puffing on a large cigar and had a brandy in his hand. Al Jameel was drinking tea. 'Can I get you a drink?' Jane asked Fleming.

'No, thanks.' He could sense the tension in the air.

Canning remained seated and blew a cloud of white smoke towards the ceiling. He pointed his cigar. 'This is DCI Fleming.'

Al Jameel rose to offer a hand to Fleming. 'Thank you for

coming this evening. Forgive me if I appear rather vague. I am, how do you say, a little anxious.'

Fleming shook Al Jameel's hand. 'Understandable. I see the scene-of-crime officers are hard at work outside. I just need to ask a few questions.'

'Why?' Canning demanded. 'We've already had uniformed police and a local CID officer here. Told them everything we know.'

'That would be DI Oliver,' Fleming explained, looking at Al Jameel rather than Canning. 'He phoned the major crime unit, and we're handling the case.'

'Why can't Oliver handle it?' Canning demanded.

Fleming glanced towards Canning. 'With help from local CID, I was about to add.'

Fleming turned back to face Al Jameel. 'It would be useful, if you don't mind, going over everything for my benefit.'

'Of course. What do you wish to ask?'

'When did you first realise something was wrong?'

'Mid-afternoon. Dani should have been back by then. He didn't arrive. I didn't worry at first as I assumed they'd stayed for a drink after the round of golf.'

'When did you start to get concerned?'

'If you don't mind me saying so, Inspector–'

'Chief Inspector,' Fleming cut in.

'Whatever. How will knowing when we got concerned help find Dani?'

'I'm only trying to establish the timing of events to get a picture of how things happened.'

Al Jameel intervened. 'It would be around four. I tried ringing Dani's mobile, but there was no answer. The security guard didn't answer his phone either.'

'What did you do then?'

'I tried the golf club. They told me Dani hadn't turned up for his round.'

'How did you find out he'd been abducted?'

'Jane took the dog out for a walk round the grounds and it went bounding off,' Canning said. 'Started barking and Jane found the security guard tied to a tree.'

'And the car was hidden from view of the drive and road?'

'Yes. The kidnappers must have driven it there,' Canning said.

'With a bit of luck, the SOCOs may find fingerprints or DNA samples.'

Al Jameel furrowed his brow. 'SOCOs?'

'Scene-of-crime officers,' Fleming explained. 'What did the security guard tell you?'

'He saw a car parked across the driveway outside the electronic gates. The bonnet and boot were both open. There was no sign of anyone there. He opened the gates and started to walk towards the car and two armed men jumped out from behind some bushes.'

'He wasn't able to describe them?'

'They wore hoods.'

'Clothes?'

'Blue jeans, and plain dark T-shirts.'

'Height, build?'

'The guard said they were both tall, one a bit taller than the other. The shorter man was a little chubby. The other one was well-built, muscular.'

'What about the car they took off in?'

'It was a black Volvo.'

'Did he get the registration?'

'No, the car was sideways on to him and he had a hood put over his head.'

'No matter. It would have had false number plates.'

Canning stubbed his cigar out and went to pour himself another brandy.

Fleming looked at him. 'Who all knew Dani and his father were coming here to stay?'

Canning frowned. 'Apart from me... Jane, my accountant, the reporter Zoe Dunbar, Walter Hammond, and Tom Slater. Tom made all the arrangements.'

'Including the security arrangements?'

Canning took a sip from his refilled brandy glass. 'Yes, he did.'

'And who all knew Dani was going out to play golf today?'

'Everyone here.'

'No one from outside the house?'

'No. It was a last-minute decision.'

Al Jameel stroked his beard. 'So how would the kidnappers know Dani would be coming up the drive at that precise moment?'

'Good question,' Fleming said. 'They must have been keeping the house under surveillance which suggests they must have been here every day.'

'How come?' Canning asked, lighting another cigar.

'Be a bit of a coincidence if they turned up for the first time today.'

Fleming looked at Al Jameel. 'Anyone been in touch yet to ask for a ransom?'

Al Jameel shook his head, unable to speak.

'Okay. You need to call me as soon as anyone gets in touch.'

'And in the meantime?' Canning asked.

'I liaise with DI Oliver and start making enquiries.'

Fleming let himself out and made a mental note to check if anyone nearby had seen any suspicious vehicles over the last few days.

50

Zoe Dunbar was in the car on her way to Darmont to speak to Kim Ogilvie when her mobile showed an incoming call: *Bob Inman.*

She was on hands-free so accepted the call. 'Hi, Bob.'

'Hello, Zoe. Just checking how you're getting on with your report.'

'I've spoken to Paul Canning and Eric Blunt, the council planning officer.'

'Find out anything?'

'Loads of ill feeling about, that's for sure. Canning wasn't happy with the last report I did. Thought I painted a skewed picture of his application and unrest in the village.'

'Did you broach the subject of bribery and corruption?'

'I did. Came straight out and asked him if there was any reason to suspect there might be some truth in the allegations.'

'And?'

'Denied there was anything in it. He was more than happy when I told him I wanted to write a report on the positive aspects of the proposed development. Not so when he realised I might cover the bribery and corruption fears again.'

'But still no proof?'

'No.'

'What about the planning officer?'

'Seemed charming, polite and friendly at first. But he became defensive when I asked if there might be any truth in the claims Canning could be bribing someone on the council. He denied it and brought the meeting to an abrupt end.'

'You still have no proof of anything shady going on you can report on. Only local feelings and suspicions.'

'That's about it. I'm on my way to see Kim Ogilvie now. See what she has to say.'

'Who's she?'

'Chair of the parish council.'

Dunbar heard Inman sigh. 'If you can't find actual proof of bribery and corruption, you're going to have to stick to saying local feelings are running high. You could say unsubstantiated claims are being made.'

'I'll keep digging till I find proof.'

'By the way, I heard on the radio that two men have been helping police with their enquiries over the murder of Tom Slater.'

'Have they now? Not arrested?'

'No, but sounds like they were questioned under caution. That's what police usually mean when they say someone has been helping with enquiries.'

'Interesting. I'll be in touch.' Dunbar ended the call.

Dunbar had thought of calling in on Gale Slater to ask about the two men, but then decided against it. *I can always speak to Fleming.*

Kim Ogilvie was sitting at her desk when Dunbar arrived.

The office door was open, Dunbar knocked and stuck her head in. 'Hello. Zoe Dunbar. You're expecting me.'

'Come in. Have a seat. I gather you want to ask about the public enquiry over Paul Canning's planning application?'

'Yes. I'm keen to get a handle of the effect it'll have on local people and the village if it's approved. Government policy to build more houses versus public opinion. That sort of thing.'

'I could have saved you the trouble of a visit. There's not much to tell I couldn't have told you over the phone.'

'I always prefer face-to-face meetings, and I was passing through.'

Ogilvie shrugged. 'Villagers didn't like the plan we put together. They also don't like the council's local one. Neither do we. And we're both united in our opposition to Paul Canning's application. That's it in a nutshell.'

'The council are supporting Canning's application. Right?'

'Yes.'

'Despite the fact the proposed development is on greenfield land?'

'It would appear so.'

'Doesn't it suggest to you that the claims some people are making might have some substance?'

'What claims?'

'That Canning has bribed someone on the council.'

'Quite a claim.'

'Needs checking out though.'

'I'd be careful about writing anything like that without proof.'

'Don't worry. I don't put anything in print I can't prove.'

'Very wise.'

Dunbar rose to leave. 'I take it you'll be opposing Canning's application at the public enquiry?'

'I will, yes.'

'Chances of him being successful?'

'I wouldn't take any bets on it. Final decision will lie with Walter Hammond, and we all know what the government position on the new build is.'

'Well... good luck anyway.'

Dunbar left thinking she would never get the proof she needed, unless someone confessed.

Protests outside the council offices had become a daily occurrence as the day neared for the start of the public enquiry. Protesters milled around the entrance. They waved banners and posed for local press officers to take photographs. A couple of uniformed police had turned up to ensure the protests remained peaceful. Vic Quinn held a placard in front of him inviting Canning to leave Darmont alone.

Dunbar approached him with a microphone aimed at his face. 'I hear some people are claiming council officers must be on the take from Canning. Is that right?'

'Yes.'

'You have proof?'

'I mean, yes, it's right people are claiming there's some shady business going on.'

'Meaning you don't have any proof of bribery or corruption.'

'Look, because we can't prove anything doesn't mean it isn't happening. How come the council have decided to support the application? Stands to reason, doesn't it?' Wouldn't trust the bastards in there as far as I could spit. As for Canning...'

'What about him?'

'People like him make their millions by being ruthless. They trample over anyone who gets in their way. Wouldn't put threats and bribery beyond him.'

'Tom Slater was one of his employees. Do you think someone killed him because he was?'

'Who knows?'

'I heard two men have been helping police with their enquiries. Know who they are?'

'Nosey bitch, aren't you?'

'Just curious. Wondering if either of them were locals.'

Quinn snorted, lifted his placard and pushed his way past Dunbar, heading for the car park.

51

They'd prepared a secure room upstairs for Dani. It was on the other side of the landing opposite the bedroom Kelso was using. They'd locked and boarded up the window which looked out over the lawn to the tall yew hedge. The room was empty apart from one double bed. A small adjoining bathroom contained only a toothbrush, toothpaste and a bar of soap. Kelso had removed anything Dani might try to use as a weapon or means of escape.

'What is to become of me?' Dani had asked.

'You won't come to any harm if your father pays the ransom.'

'You have asked him for money for my release?'

'Not yet. Soon.'

'How much will you ask?'

'A sum your father will be able to pay.'

'And should he refuse to pay?'

'I don't think he will.'

Kelso had offered Dani a can of beer. He'd declined, but accepted a bottle of water. Kelso left a worried-looking Dani and had locked the door behind him.

Zimmerman, Kelso and Guerra were sitting downstairs sipping on cans of beer. 'All went to plan then?' Zimmerman asked.

Kelso was first to speak. 'Not quite. Marco here managed to prang the van we were going to use.'

Guerra looked at the floor. 'Wasn't my fault, boss. The bloody garage doors slammed shut in the wind as I was reversing out the garage.'

'You should have made sure they were propped open with a brick or something instead of leaving them flapping about.'

Zimmerman glared at Guerra. 'So what vehicle did you use?'

'Would you believe, he came in his own fucking car,' Kelso said before Guerra could answer.

Zimmerman frowned. 'You used your own car? Fuck's sake!'

'It's okay. I had false number plates, and in any case, no one saw us.'

'Apart from Dani and the security guard,' Kelso said.

'False plates,' Guerra reminded Kelso.

'You're a complete idiot,' Kelso retorted. 'Colour and make weren't false, were they?'

'Okay,' Zimmerman said. 'Can't be undone, so we have to live with it. Any more hiccups?'

Guerra pointed a finger at Kelso. 'He thinks he's so fucking high and mighty. We almost lost a chance to get Dani due to sticking to his rigid surveillance plan.'

Zimmerman raised an eyebrow. 'Is that right?'

'Marco panics. He's too impulsive. Yeah, there was a slight blip in that Dani didn't keep to his normal jogging routine, but we managed to improvise.'

'We could have had him the day before, but Kelso bottled it.'

'You're treading on thin ice, Marco. I've never shirked anything. I happen to be a little more careful than you, that's all.'

'Oh yeah? We end up carrying out a kidnap in broad daylight right next to the road running past Canning's house.'

'We got away with it, didn't we?' Kelso turned to Zimmerman. 'But then Marco decides to floor it in the car and knocks a cyclist off his bike.'

Zimmerman looked as though he was about to explode. He glared at Guerra. 'You what!'

'He's stirring it!' Guerra spat out. 'I didn't knock him off. I missed him and he fell off.'

'This was by Canning's place, not near here I hope,' Zimmerman said.

'Don't worry, boss. It wasn't anywhere near here. We'd only just nabbed Dani.'

Zimmerman shook his head. 'Let's get one thing straight. I don't want any more squabbling between you two... and I don't want any more fuck-ups, understood?'

'When do you propose to make the ransom demand?' Kelso asked.

'I'll leave Dani's father to sweat it out tonight. Keep him on edge. Might phone tomorrow.'

'Think he'll pay?'

'Police will try to persuade him not to. Their theory is there'll be more kidnaps if people pay ransoms.'

'Doesn't exactly sound encouraging,' Guerra said.

'He'll pay,' Zimmerman assured him.

'How come you're so certain?' Guerra asked.

'I'll tell him we'll send his son back piece by piece if he doesn't.'

'We'd do that?'

'Might not have to send too many pieces before he agrees to pay.'

Kelso finished his beer and rose to get another. 'Want one?' he asked Zimmerman.

'Sure.'

'And me,' Guerra said.

Kelso glowered at Guerra. 'Get your own.'

52

Isa Al Jameel hadn't slept well. He was up until one in the morning. Canning had stayed with him till midnight by which time he'd consumed several more brandies. His wife Jane had gone to bed with a headache at eleven, unable to bear the tension and the strain. Al Jameel, left on his own for an hour before he decided to try to get some sleep, had watched the second hand on the big clock tick by in silence. There was no call.

The morning was a sombre affair. Jane's eyes were red. Canning had a hangover. Jane had cooked a breakfast. Canning ate after swallowing two painkillers with a glass of water. Al Jameel felt sick. His heart was pounding. He picked at his plate.

Al Jameel looked across the table at Jane with a faint smile. 'Sorry, Jane. There's nothing wrong with the food. I don't feel like eating.'

Jane threw a solicitous look back at Al Jameel. 'Don't worry. I wasn't thinking. Shouldn't have bothered cooking. Bad idea.'

'Isa is our guest. We have to make the effort, despite the circumstances,' Canning mumbled through a mouthful of bacon.

Jane gave him a disapproving look.

Al Jameel looked at his watch. Eight o'clock. He picked up his mobile. No messages.

The sudden sharp ring of Canning's landline broke the silence that fell over the table. Al Jameel's cup crashed to the floor. Canning glanced towards the phone then threw a questioning look at Al Jameel. Canning got a nod from his guest. He went over to pick up the phone. Taking a deep breath, he spoke. 'Hello?'

There was a moment's silence while Canning listened. His face contorted into a frown. 'Fuck off,' he shouted, and slammed the phone down. 'One of those bloody cold calls.'

Al Jameel picked his cup up and dabbed at the spilt tea with his napkin. He looked sheepishly at Jane. 'Sorry.'

'Don't worry.' Jane cleared up and went through to the kitchen.

Silence fell once more.

Jameel watched the seconds tick by on the clock.

'Would you like a newspaper?' Canning asked.

Al Jameel shook his head and looked at the clock again.

Kelso knocked on Dani's door. 'We're coming in. Stand at the back of the room,' he shouted through the door. 'Be warned, I'm armed.' He was holding the gun supplied by Zimmerman. Kelso still had the Glock hidden away in his room and wanted to make sure Guerra had no idea he had it.

Guerra unlocked the door and threw it open.

Dani had done as Kelso told him and was standing by the boarded-up window at the other end of the room. He looked wide-eyed at the gun in Kelso's hand as the two men entered.

Kelso saw no threat from Dani and tucked the gun into his

waistband. 'Don't worry. We've brought you some breakfast and a morning paper to read.'

Guerra walked over and put a tray holding some cereal and a mug of tea on the bed.

'We'll leave you in peace to have some breakfast, but we need to take a photo of you first,' Kelso said.

Dani looked confused.

'For your dad,' Kelso explained. 'When we call, he needs to see we have you and that you're okay.'

Dani nodded his understanding.

'Hold the newspaper in front of your chest so I can see the headline and the date.'

'Why do you want me to hold a newspaper?'

'So your father knows we took the photo of you today.'

Dani shrugged and did as Kelso told him.

Guerra took the photograph.

'You'll speak to my father today?' Dani asked.

'That's the plan,' Kelso said.

Three minutes later, Guerra sent the photo with a text message to Zimmerman who had gone back to London the night before.

Zimmerman was in the office of his London club tapping his chin with the burner phone he was using. He'd received the photo of Dani holding that day's newspaper and was now pondering over how to play this.

Having decided, he held the phone in front of him, and tapped in the numbers he'd copied from Dani's phone.

Jane Canning asked Al Jameel if he wanted tea. He shook his head and glanced at the clock again.

Fleming had advised Al Jameel to record any incoming call from the kidnappers, if possible. Al Jameel didn't have the facility on his mobile, but Canning remembered having an old voice recorder. He'd fished it out and got it ready.

Al Jameel paced up and down the living room.

'Try to relax,' Canning advised. 'They're sure to call soon.'

'What if they haven't kidnapped him for money? What if whoever it is just wants to kill him?'

'He's been abducted. No doubt about it. If they wanted to kill him, they'd have done it there and then. They had guns.'

Al Jameel saw that Canning was right and continued pacing.

Canning poured himself a brandy, despite the fact it was still morning.

The clock in the corner chimed. Al Jameel drew in a deep breath and blew out through his lips.

Two minutes later, his mobile rang. Al Jameel looked at the screen: *unknown caller.* He waved at Canning who grabbed the voice recorder, switched it on and brought it over to the phone.

Al Jameel held the device close to his ear and took the call. 'Hello?'

'Am I speaking to Isa Al Jameel?' The voice was low and hoarse.

'You are.'

'I have your son. Two million pounds will secure his release.'

Al Jameel gasped. 'Who are you? How do I know you have Dani?'

'I'll send you a photograph taken this morning. Two million if you want him back.'

'I can't get that sort of money quickly. It's tied up in business accounts and investments.'

'I'm sure a man of your means will find a way. I'll give you three days and call you back. You'll get details on how to pay the money then.'

'And if I can't pay?'

'You'll find a way if I send you one of Dani's fingers. If you need extra persuasion, more will follow. A word of warning, no police. I'll call you back.' The man rang off.

Al Jameel slumped into a chair. 'He wants two million,' he whispered.

'Christ!' Canning took a large gulp of his brandy. 'I'd best get in touch with Fleming.'

53

'One of the kidnappers has been in touch,' Fleming told Temple. 'He phoned Al Jameel this morning. They want two million for his son's release.'

'That's a big ask. I take it you're going down to Canning's place to see him now?'

'I am. I'll go and see DI Oliver, the local CID officer, while I'm down there. He was first on the scene after they abducted Dani. See if he's made any progress with his enquiries.'

'This is all we need on top of Slater's murder. Right when the new chief constable has started.'

'You'll let her know there's been a ransom demand?' Fleming asked.

'Yes. By the way, you ought to know she's been in touch with The National Crime Agency… AKEU.'

Fleming raised an eyebrow.

'The Anti Kidnap and Extortion Unit.'

'I know what it is, ma'am. Just surprised she took it upon herself to contact them without telling me.'

'She told me and now I'm telling you. Is that a problem?'

'No, ma'am.'

'They can provide expert support and tactical advice.'

'But we lead the investigation?'

'You lead it. That's what the chief constable said, isn't it?'

'Right, as long as we know where we stand. How does this work with AKEU? Will they contact me or do I contact them if I need advice?'

'They'll contact you. My guess is they'll want one of their people in to handle any negotiations with the kidnappers.'

'Fine.'

'They have already advised that Al Jameel shouldn't agree to the kidnappers' demands. Although it's not illegal to pay ransom money, it's not recommended on the basis it would encourage further kidnaps.'

Fleming scratched his head. 'If that's the case, how come you think they'd want one of their people to handle negotiations? There won't be any if Al Jameel refuses to pay.'

Temple paused for a second. 'They may want to talk to them to see if they give anything away which identifies them. Might get a clue where they're holding Dani. They could agree to pay, but insist on a method of payment which would allow officers to apprehend the kidnappers.'

'They'll be too smart for that.'

Temple sighed. 'Let's leave it to the experts.'

Fleming left Temple's office to go and find Logan. *Nice to have a vote of confidence.*

Fleming and Logan were speeding to Canning's place. Fleming had decided to use his Porsche as Canning had said the kidnapper had warned Al Jameel not to involve the police. The last thing they needed was to use a marked car in case the kidnappers had eyes on the house. On the way, Fleming took the opportunity to update Logan on Dani Al Jameel's abduction, and his conversation with Temple.

It was late morning when Fleming and Logan arrived at Canning's mansion. Jane let them in and took the two detectives to the living room where they found a worried-looking Al Jameel and Canning.

'How are you bearing up?' Fleming asked Al Jameel who rose to shake Fleming's and Logan's hands.

His reddened eyes told the story. 'Not very well. It's all so unreal. I can't believe this is happening.'

'We'll do everything we can to get your son back,' Fleming assured him. 'The chief constable has been in touch with the National Crime Agency. They have a specialist unit which has experience in securing the safe release of hostages.'

Al Jameel frowned. 'Will they be taking over from you then?'

'No, I'm the officer in charge. They will provide support and advice.'

'I see. What happens now? The kidnapper warned me not to contact the police.'

'Don't worry. We came in an unmarked car.'

'You think they may be watching the house?'

'It's possible. Did you manage to record the call?'

'Yes. The sound quality isn't very good but you can hear what they're saying.'

'May I listen to it?'

Al Jameel produced Canning's voice recorder and pushed the play button.

The voice was a bit muffled, but clear enough to understand.

Fleming listened to the conversation. 'Has the security man who was with Dani when he was abducted heard this?'

Al Jameel looked perplexed. 'No, why?'

'Get him to listen to it. See if he recognises the voice as one of the two men who abducted Dani. Let me know.'

'What good will that do?' Canning demanded.

'If he doesn't recognise the voice, it means we're dealing with at least three men, not two.'

Canning snorted. 'And that gets us closer to finding Dani?'

Fleming shot him a glance. 'It gives us a little more information. At this stage, we need as much as we can get.'

'Did the caller send the photograph he promised?' Logan asked Al Jameel.

Al Jameel took out his mobile, tapped on Messages and showed Fleming and Logan the photo of Dani holding that day's newspaper. There was nothing in the background of the photograph which offered any clue where the kidnappers might have taken it. All that could be seen was a bare white wall and a boarded-up window.

Fleming threw a sympathetic look at Al Jameel. 'I believe the NCA have advised you not to agree to the kidnappers' demands.'

'You heard what the kidnapper said,' Canning butted in. 'If Isa doesn't pay up, he'll cut off Dani's fingers one by one until he does.'

Fleming looked at Al Jameel. 'The Anti Kidnap and Extortion Unit in the NCA are the experts in dealing with kidnap demands. They'll want to have someone here when the kidnapper calls you back.'

'What about the phone call? I thought the police could trace who sent calls,' Canning said.

'Not easy if he used a burner phone, which he is certain to have done.'

'Great. And in the meantime?' Canning asked.

'I speak to the AKEU and the local CID chap, Oliver. I'll be in touch if we find anything to go on.'

'Otherwise?' Canning pressed.

'We wait. Let me know if there are any more developments here. I'll let you know what the AKEU intend to do.'

'Don't think Canning was too impressed,' Logan said as they made their way to see DI Oliver.

'I get the impression he's more worried about losing his potential investment than Dani's welfare,' Fleming said.

'Think the AKEU will stand any chance of getting Dani back in one piece, boss?'

'Let's hope so. In the meantime, we'll see what DI Oliver has to say.'

Fleming had phoned to say they were coming and Oliver was waiting in his office. 'They've made contact then?' he asked Fleming.

'This morning. They want two million.'

Oliver sucked in air. 'Bloody hell!'

'The kidnapper gave him three days to get the money together. He's going to call back with details on how to pay the ransom.'

Oliver sighed. 'Afraid I haven't made much progress with local enquiries. One witness said he saw a black car parked in the woods a few days ago. It was in a small clearing off the road opposite Canning's grounds. Unfortunately, there's no CCTV covering the area.'

'They get the registration number?'

'No. They didn't think anything about it. Thought it was someone who'd parked there to take a dog for a walk.'

'Anything else?'

'A cyclist came forward. A black car driving at speed almost knocked him off his bike.'

'Don't tell me,' Fleming said. 'He didn't get the registration either.'

'Afraid not, he fell off his bike, but did confirm it was a black car heading in a north-westerly direction on the A4130.'

'Not got much to go on, have we?' Logan said.

Fleming shrugged. 'We have two men in a black Volvo... and we know what direction they were heading in.'

54

Zoe Dunbar pulled her car into the council office's car park with minutes to spare. It was the final day of the public enquiry. She'd heard about Dani Al Jameel on the radio. *No proof of bribery, but there is a murder and a kidnap,* she thought as she got out of the car.

There were no protesters outside. They were all inside the meeting room. On the first day of the enquiry, the chairman had warned he would not tolerate any disruption. Were there to be any protests, he would clear the public from the room. There had been heated debates, but no trouble. Even Vic Quinn had remained silent.

Dunbar pushed her way through the large glass doors and crossed the atrium to the meeting room. She found a seat in the area set out for the public where about thirty villagers sat. Kim Ogilvie and her advisors were in front of them, facing the planning inspector's desk at the front of the room.

Over to the right, Canning, Yamamura and their solicitor, Silas Revell QC, sat behind desks covered in folders. Ogilvie stared straight ahead looking pensive. She'd taken a verbal mauling from Revell over the last three days.

Richard Pitt, the planning inspector, waited for the room to fall quiet. 'Can we have the door closed please?' he asked an assistant. Once done, Pitt cleared his throat and spoke. 'Over the last three days we've heard evidence from the parish council, the district council and Mr Canning's solicitor. There has been some rigorous cross-examination.' He gave a knowing glance in Revell's direction before going on. 'Some of it, I have to say, acrimonious. I do hope there will be less rancour today.'

Dunbar hid a smile. It was only a matter of time before Pitt saw fit to clamp down on Revell whose hostile probing of Ogilvie's evidence had been, at times, offensive. He was a tough and ruthless man who showed no mercy.

Pitt looked over to where the public sat. 'Today is the last day of the enquiry. This morning we will hear the closing statements. The parish council, the district council, and Silas Revell QC, acting on behalf of Mr Canning, will each make their case. After lunch, we will be going on a site visit. Any questions?'

Revell looked over his reading glasses at Pitt. 'I take it we are at liberty to interrupt if someone says something which isn't true? I say that because, over the last three days, we have heard some rather dubious claims from the parish council.'

'You may not. If you feel someone is not representing the facts, you are free to mention it in your closing statement. You can also request I expunge certain words from the record if you feel they are offensive or untrue.'

'Fine.' Revell stared in Kim Ogilvie's direction and failed to hide the smirk on his face.

Dunbar felt for Ogilvie. She'd done her best to present a strong case for the parish council and the villagers. But Revell had torn into her at every chance. The previous day, he'd cross-examined her for over an hour. She'd made some valid points about the adverse effect the development would have on the village. Canning was aware she would do this and had made sure Revell could tear apart any arguments against his application.

Pitt looked around. 'If there are no more questions, can we have the parish council's closing statement first please?'

Kim Ogilvie stood, looked at her notes and cleared her throat. 'Thank you. During the course of this enquiry, I've tried to show how the plan we put forward is the best for Darmont. I know it does not have one hundred per cent approval within the village, but there is a majority in favour. Not one single person is in favour of Mr Canning's planning application. In my closing statement, I'll explain why.'

Ogilvie took over half an hour to argue a capable, convincing case. She explained in detail why the secretary of state should quash the application. She sat down to applause from the villagers.

Pitt allowed the applause to continue for a few seconds. 'Can we please have quiet from the public?' He looked at his watch. 'Mr Blunt, are you ready to present the closing statement for the district council?'

'I am,' Blunt said, standing with notes shaking in his hand.

Canning gave him a nod and Revell smiled support. Blunt looked at his notes and began to read. He spent the next forty minutes explaining why the secretary of state should grant the application.

Pitt looked at his watch again. 'We should have a comfort-and-coffee break at this point. Back here in fifteen minutes please.'

Dunbar managed to catch a quick word with Ogilvie in the canteen. 'You've taken some stick over the past three days. Particularly from that rodent, Revell. He's a nasty piece of work.'

'You can say that again. Glad it's now all over for me. I've done my best.'

Dunbar placed a reassuring hand on Ogilvie's arm. 'You did a good job in there. Made a good case.'

'Thanks, but will it be good enough?'

'What do you think?'

Ogilvie pursed her lips. 'I get the feeling it's already been decided.'

'To grant?'

'Yes.'

'What makes you think that?'

'It's only a gut feeling. Best get back in there and hear what the rodent has to say.'

Back in the enquiry room, Pitt waited for everyone to settle down. As silence descended, there was an air of nervous anticipation in the room. Pitt looked across at the Canning desk. Revell was shuffling documents around, peering over the top of his glasses.

'Are you ready to make your closing statement on behalf of Mr Canning's planning application, Mr Revell?'

'I am.' Revell rose to his feet. He looked around the room for several seconds before he spoke. 'We have heard over the last three days some feeble attempts to make a case for why my client's application should not be approved. People have attempted to distort the truth and I have exposed the weaknesses in the parish council and villagers' claims. I have made a robust and convincing case for this development. Today, I will set out why the secretary of state must grant this application.'

Revell went on for a full hour, using every means at his disposal to try to weaken the parish council case. Indeed, some of his remarks were defamatory and insulting towards Ogilvie. He sat down to uproar and turned to speak in Canning's ear.

Ogilvie jumped to her feet. 'I object to some of the remarks made by Mr Revell. That man,' she shouted, pointing at him, 'has made slanderous statements. I want him to apologise and withdraw them.'

Revell looked across at Ogilvie with a wry smile.

Ogilvie looked at Pitt. 'I would like some of Mr Revell's comments expunged from the record, and I would appreciate advice on what legal action I can take against him.'

There were shouts of support from the villagers.

Pitt tried to restore order. 'Please, calm down, everyone, or I will have to clear the room.'

Vic Quinn jumped to his feet. 'Do what you bloody like! We're done here anyway.'

Before Pitt could say anything, Quinn stormed out of the room.

Pitt finally managed to restore order by getting Revell's agreement to certain of his words being expunged. Turning to Ogilvie, Pitt said, 'You must take advice outside this room whether you have a case for legal action.'

Ogilvie sat down to pats on the back from some of the villagers sitting behind her.

As soon as the meeting was over, Canning got out his mobile and tapped in the numbers for Walter Hammond.

He picked up after three rings. 'Hello, Paul, what can I do for you?'

'Public enquiry went well. Relying on you to ensure your planning inspector recommends approval of my application. I know I can count on you.'

55

'What time is she coming?' Logan asked.

'About ten,' Fleming replied.

'Who exactly is she?'

'She's a Grade 2 investigating officer... Unity Elford.'

'And what will she be doing?'

'AKEU are the experts in handling kidnaps. She'll be providing help and support with the investigation and will handle any negotiations with the kidnappers.'

Logan looked at his watch. 'Be here soon. Best leave you to it, unless you want me there.'

'No, I've got a meeting with the super and chief constable afterwards. Got some jobs for you and Naomi to follow up on in the meantime.'

'Okay.'

'Have another word with DI Oliver. See if he's getting anywhere with local enquiries. Check if anyone else saw the black car parked near Canning's house. Get a request out for anyone to come forward who may have seen a speeding black Volvo on the A4130 the morning of the kidnap. See if any speed cameras picked it up.'

'Won't be much use, boss. They're certain to have had stolen number plates on the car.'

'True. But at least we can trace the owner and find out where and when they nicked the plates. Might give us a start.'

'Right.'

'You could also get Naomi to ring round the local forces checking on all the owners of black cars with the partial registration we have. Ask them to concentrate on black Volvos for now.'

'Okay, but they still need to check all cars to see if anyone comes up as a suspect in the Slater case.'

'Agreed. But they might have more luck with the kidnap car. Thinking about Slater though, see if Naomi has had anything back on the photo of the man he met in London. If we're lucky, someone may have recognised him from the copy pinned on the village hall noticeboard. Check if anyone has come forward after the press release of the photo.'

'Anything else?'

'You might check with Canning to see if they've let the security man listen to the recording of the kidnapper's voice. If he recognised it as one of the two men who abducted Dani, it might suggest we're only looking for two men. If he didn't, we're looking for at least three.'

'Okay, I'll get on with all that. Good luck with the super and chief constable.'

Fleming's phone rang as Logan got up to leave.

'Could be your visitor from AKEU,' Logan said.

'Unity Elford, sir,' Anderson announced, showing a burly woman of medium height into Fleming's office. She had short black hair and wore a white shirt under a suit matching the colour of her hair. Fleming guessed Elford was in her forties. Her broad-shouldered frame suggested she might have regular workouts at the gym. Clutching a black leather document holder, she looked very much the professional executive.

Fleming got up from behind his desk and offered a hand. 'Nice to meet you. Come in and have a seat. Coffee?'

'No, thanks. Won't take up much of your time. I'd like to get up to speed on where you're at on the kidnap and let you know how the AKEU can be of help.'

'There's not a great deal I can tell you at this stage. Two men kidnapped Dani Al Jameel at gunpoint a couple of days ago. Yesterday someone rang with a ransom demand of two million. A security guard was with Dani when the kidnappers abducted him. I'm waiting to hear if the guard recognised the caller's voice as one of the two men.'

'The call was recorded?'

'It was.'

'I'd like to hear it.'

'No problem. We do have a copy. But I'll take you over to see Dani's father. You can listen to it there if you want. It'll then still be fresh in your head when the kidnapper rings again. The kidnapper said he would give him three days to get the money arranged. Said he'd call back with details on how to pay. That would be the day after tomorrow.'

'Is it okay with you if I'm there to take the call and handle negotiations?'

'Fine by me. You're the expert at this sort of thing.'

'Anything else I should know?'

'The kidnappers used a black Volvo. Someone saw a black car parked in the woods near Canning's house a few days before. A cyclist also reported a speeding black car heading north-west on the A4130 on the day of the kidnap. It almost hit him and he fell off his bike. It's certain to be the same car.'

'But no registration noted?'

'No.'

Elford rose to go. 'If that's all for now, I'll meet up with you to go to Canning's house on Wednesday. Best be there early. Don't want to miss the call. Let me know if anything else comes to light in the meantime.'

~

Vanita Lazar was already in Temple's office when Fleming turned up for his meeting. 'Sorry I'm a little late. Been talking to Unity Elford, the AKEU officer.'

'How did it go?' Lazar asked.

'Fine. I've brought her up to speed on the kidnap, and we've arranged to meet up to go to Canning's place first thing on Wednesday. That's when the kidnapper said he would call back.'

'Did she say how she was going to handle it?' Lazar asked.

'Only that she would prefer to take the call and deal with negotiations. My guess is she'll try to stall to buy some time. Get the kidnapper talking to see if he gives anything away.'

'And what will you be doing while you wait for the kidnapper to call back?'

'The only clue we have so far is the kidnappers used a black Volvo. There have been two other sightings of a black car, one of them speeding up the A4130 on the morning they abducted Dani.'

'Any luck in tracing the car?'

'No. We don't have the registration, but they would have stolen the number plates anyway. DS Logan is carrying out further checks. The best bet is if speed cameras picked the car up. If they did, we find the owner of the car they stole them from. Once we know that, we should get some clues about how and where the kidnappers stole the plates.'

'You need to move fast on this, Fleming,' Lazar stressed. 'The prime minister and Walter Hammond are getting agitated. The kidnap of the son of a man who has influence in Saudi Arabia at a politically sensitive time is not going down well.'

'We're moving as fast as we can, ma'am. But, with respect, I'm more worried about getting Dani back safely than the concerns of politicians.'

Lazar shot a steely glare at Fleming. 'Chief Inspector, I do not want us to become the cause of political embarrassment. Do I make myself clear?'

'Yes, ma'am.'

'Good. And what about the Slater case. Any progress?'

'I've interviewed two suspects, but I don't yet have enough evidence to make an arrest.'

'And that's it?'

'We also have a photograph of a man Slater met twice in London. We're trying to identify him.'

Fleming turned to Temple who had so far remained quiet. 'On the Slater case, ma'am, I need you to authorise a check of his bank account.'

'Why?'

'Slater had large gambling debts. I'd like to see if he was making payments to anyone.'

'Okay, I'll get it arranged. Anything else?'

'No, ma'am.'

Fleming took his leave. Lazar's eyes were boring into his back.

56

It was the day the kidnapper had said he would call again. Fleming was on his way to Canning's house with Unity Elford. Not taking any chances of the kidnappers seeing a marked car turning up, he was using the Porsche again. He'd been in touch with Canning to let him know about Elford. She would handle the call when it came.

Nothing had surfaced yet on the lines of enquiry Fleming had asked Logan to follow up on. He'd asked him to phone straight away if anything came up. In particular, he was keen to find out if there had been any progress on getting more information on the black Volvo. That, and the prospect of Forensics finding any fingerprints or DNA samples in the dumped security guard's car, was about all they had to go on so far.

Fleming had picked Elford up and forty minutes later they were approaching the driveway to Canning's place. The electronic gates at the entrance swung open as Fleming eased the Porsche towards them. The blue-and-white tape and floodlights had all gone. There was no sign of any police presence.

Fleming parked the car in front of the house and he and Elford climbed out.

Jane Canning appeared at the door. 'Hello. Heard your car on the gravel.'

Fleming noticed the concerned look on her face. 'Hi. Any calls yet?'

'No. I'm afraid things are rather fraught. Paul is being a pain. He's been grumbling all morning.'

Fleming grimaced. The last thing he needed was conflict with Canning. Frayed tempers would not be good if the kidnapper called. Fleming worried Canning might intervene and cause a problem. 'What's he grumbling about?'

'Oh, you know. This whole business. Paul gets impatient and he's getting angry. He's afraid the kidnap might sway Isa's mind about investing.'

'More concerned with that than Dani's welfare, eh?'

Jane smiled. 'The final day of the public enquiry was on Monday. He thinks it went well, but he's very edgy. There's a lot at stake.'

'Even more so with Dani, don't you think?'

'Yes... of course. I'm worried about Paul though. He seems... different.'

'Pressure getting to him?'

'Yes, it is.'

'Okay. By the way, this is Unity Elford from the NCA. Let's go in and we'll see if we can calm things down.'

Jane took Fleming and Elford down to the living room where Al Jameel and Canning sat in silence. The tension in the air was palpable.

Al Jameel rose to greet Fleming and offered a hand. 'Glad you've come, Chief Inspector.'

Fleming smiled. 'Tried to get here as soon as we could. Had a couple of calls to make. This is Unity Elford from the NCA.' He nodded towards Elford.

Elford shook Al Jameel's hand. 'I gather DCI Fleming has told you I'll be handling the call if the kidnapper phones.'

'Yes. I'm glad you are here to do this for me.'

'No problem. Try not to worry.'

Fleming turned to Canning. 'Did you get the security guard to listen to the recording of the phone call?'

'I did. DS Logan has already been on the phone to ask me. Don't you two speak to each other?'

Fleming ignored the niggle. 'Did the guard recognise the voice of the man who called?'

'Didn't Logan tell you?'

Fleming glared at Canning. 'I came straight here this morning. I haven't spoken to him. It would be helpful if you just answered my question now that I'm here.'

Canning pulled one of his large cigars out of a box and lit up. 'He didn't recognise the voice.'

'Thank you.'

Al Jameel was looking awkward. He picked up his mobile phone. 'Do you think the kidnapper will call?'

He'd directed the question at Fleming, but Elford answered. 'He will. The reason they kidnapped your son was to extort money. The only way they'll get it is to ring and tell you how to pay.'

'Would you like to listen to the recording now?' Fleming asked Elford.

'Yes, please.'

Fleming glanced at Canning. 'Do you mind?'

'What?'

Fleming sighed. 'The recording. Can you let Officer Elford listen to the recording of the kidnapper's call?'

As Canning was fishing out the voice recorder, Jane came into the room. 'Anyone for tea?'

'Christ's sake, woman! How can you think of tea at a time like this!' Canning burst out.

'I... I thought...'

'No, we don't want tea, Jane.'

'I'd love a cup,' Elford said. 'Milk, no sugar.'

'Me too,' Al Jameel said.

'Make it three,' Fleming joined in, grateful that Elford had intervened to stick up for poor Jane.

Canning grunted. 'Unbelievable!'

Fleming ignored the outburst. 'If the guard didn't recognise the voice, it means there are at least three men in the kidnap gang.'

'What bloody difference does that make?' Canning blurted out, thrusting the voice recorder at Elford.

Elford took the recorder with a sweet smile. 'Thank you.' She switched it on and listened intently.

While she was listening, Al Jameel jumped as Fleming's mobile rang. Fleming looked at the screen: *Logan.*

'Hi Harry, what's new?'

'Forensics have been on to me. No fingerprints or DNA samples in the security guard's car. They found a few clothes fibres in some bushes, and took photos of footprints.'

'That's it?'

'No. Close examination of the tape they used to bind the guard revealed some DNA samples. They're running a check for any matches on the DNA database.'

'Wow. Result. Thanks, Harry.' He ended the call.

Elford had finished listening to the recording. 'Something come up?'

'Forensics have found traces of DNA on the tape they used to bind the guard.'

'Any matches?'

'They're checking.'

Elford smiled. 'Great.'

Al Jameel's eyes lit up. 'Does that mean they might identify the kidnappers?'

Canning stubbed out his cigar as Jane came back in with a tray of teas. 'What happens next?' he demanded.

'If we get a positive ID, we make an arrest and find out where they're holding Dani,' Fleming said. 'In the meantime, we wait for the call.'

Al Jameel stared at his mobile and almost dropped it on the floor when it vibrated, then rang.

Elford held out a hand. 'I'll take it.' She switched the voice recorder on and answered the call. 'Hello?'

There was a moment's hesitation. 'Who is this?'

'I'm a financial adviser friend of Mr Al Jameel.'

'I want to speak to him.'

'I'm afraid that's not possible. He's ill. It's the stress and worry of it all.'

'Get him on the phone – now!'

'I can't, he's in hospital,' Elford lied.

Fleming guessed Elford would be listening for any background noises while she was talking. Anything that might offer a clue where the kidnapper could be calling from.

'If you want to talk about the ransom,' Elford continued, 'I need to hear Dani's voice. I have to be sure he's still alive.'

There was a long pause. 'I can arrange it, but not now. He's not here.'

'No problem. I'm currently working on getting Al Jameel's cash sorted out. There will be no payments or transfers of money until I speak to Dani though. Is that understood?'

Another long pause. 'This had better not be a trick. Be

assured we will cut Dani's fingers off one by one if there is any attempt to withhold payment.'

'Understood. There's one more thing. You will have to make all future calls to my number.' Elford read it out. 'Got it?'

'Yes. But no tricks... and no police. Is that clear?'

'Yes. I can get the money ready in three days. Call me back then so I can speak to Dani.' Elford ended the call.

'Was that wise?' Al Jameel asked. 'I mean to cut him off?'

'I needed to establish a strong position from which to conduct future negotiations. The number I've given him goes straight to our office. We have all the necessary recording equipment and IT in place there. I've also bought us three more days to try to find the kidnappers and where they're holding Dani.'

57

It was late afternoon when Fleming arrived back at HQ from Canning's house. The second call from the kidnapper had gone as well as expected. Unity Elford had done well to buy some more time. And Forensics had come up with some information.

As he steered his Porsche into his allotted parking space, he saw the silver Audi A5 parked in one of the visitors' spaces. *What the hell is Zoe Dunbar doing here?*

Logan and Anderson were busy at their computers when Fleming came into the office. Logan looked up from his screen. 'Hi, boss, you had a visitor. She was passing and called in on the off-chance she could have a word.'

'Zoe Dunbar... the reporter.'

'How did you know?'

'Recognised the car outside. Where is she?'

'I told her I didn't know what time you'd be back, so she was going to leave. Asked if she could use the loo before she went.'

'What did she want?'

Logan shrugged. 'Could be she has some information.'

'More likely wants some,' Fleming said.

'True, but I also thought you might like to hear some. I could tell you what went on at the public enquiry into the Canning planning application,' Dunbar said, walking up behind him.

Fleming turned to face her. 'Thought you'd left.'

'I was on my way. Had to pay a visit and thought I'd have one more look to see if you were back before I set off for home.'

'I can spare a few minutes if you want to come into my office.'

'Thanks.'

Fleming took a seat behind his desk and waved to Dunbar to help herself to one of the other chairs in the office. He waited until she sat down. 'So, what is it you wanted to tell me about the public enquiry?'

'I'll come to that in a minute, but can I ask how you're getting on with the Slater murder?'

'You were reporting on Canning's proposed development. Are you seeing a connection with that and Tom Slater's murder?'

'Is there?'

'You asked me that at the briefing meeting in the village hall.'

'I did. You said it was a possibility.'

'And have you found out something to suggest it could be the case?'

'I'm keeping an open mind.' Dunbar paused for a second. 'I heard that two men have been helping with enquiries.'

'It's public knowledge we've interviewed two men, yes.'

'Under caution?'

'Yes.'

'But not arrested?'

'No. We've made no arrests so far.'

'Can you give me the names?'

'No.'

Dunbar looked hard into Fleming's eyes. 'Was Vic Quinn one of them, by any chance?'

Fleming furrowed his brow. 'Is there any reason for you to think he might have been?'

Dunbar shrugged. 'Just that he's an angry man and is one of the more vocal protesters.'

'And that makes him a potential murderer?'

'He had a bit of a scuffle outside a pub with Slater. And Quinn's mother is struggling to sell her house because of the proposed development.'

'So are other villagers.'

'I spoke to him at the council offices where there was a protest in full flow. He's convinced Canning is bribing someone on the council.'

'There's no proof. It's only gossip.'

'He got a bit tetchy when I asked him if he thought someone killed Tom Slater because he was one of Canning's employees. Stormed off when I mentioned it was common knowledge that two men were helping police with their enquiries.'

Fleming smiled. 'You do have a propensity to get up people's noses.'

'It's my job to ask questions.'

'Mine too. Speaking of which, what was it you wanted to tell me about the public enquiry?'

'I attended on all four days, but the last day was rather interesting.'

'Go on.'

'It all got a bit heated. Threats of legal action against the solicitor representing Canning. Guy called Revell, Silas Revell. Ever heard of him?'

'Can't say I have, no.'

'Nasty piece of work.' Dunbar hesitated for a second before speaking again. 'And Vic Quinn was there. He got angry when the planning officer threatened to clear the public from the room. Gave him a mouthful and stormed out.'

'The point you're making is?'

'I have every reason to believe he's one of the men helping with enquiries.'

'Persistent as ever. I've already told you I'm not prepared to give names.'

'Okay, but are you anywhere near to making an arrest?'

'I'll let you know when we are.'

'Soon?'

Fleming held up a hand. 'It wouldn't be a good idea to put anything like that in print at this stage. Might raise expectations.'

'Does that mean you're not anywhere near making an arrest?'

'It means the enquiry is progressing.'

'Do you think Dani Al Jameel's abduction is somehow linked to Tom Slater's murder?'

'At present, they are two separate enquiries.' Fleming looked at his watch. 'If you don't mind, I have some work to do. Nice talking to you, but you didn't have much for me by way of information, did you?'

'Only the bit about Vic Quinn and the public enquiry.'

'Interesting though that is, it doesn't help me much.'

'Okay, I won't keep you. One more thing before I go. I saw the newspaper article with the photograph of a man you want to trace. Is he a suspect in the Slater case?'

'He's someone we need to speak to.'

'I could make you an offer to help.'

'How?'

'The national newspaper editor I'm currently working for has loads of contacts. Reporters have a wealth of information. If the man in the photo is a dodgy character, it's possible he could have featured in an old article. In which case, someone may remember him. I could ask the editor to check around to see if there's anyone who recognises him.'

'If you can get me a name, I'd be most grateful. And in return?'

'Usual. You give me a heads-up in front of everyone else on any reportable developments in the Slater murder. And the Al Jameel kidnap case.'

Fleming thought for a second. 'I can do that, but only if you find me a name before I do.'

'Okay. I'll let you get on with your work.' Dunbar rose to go. 'Be in touch.'

Fleming watched as she closed the door. *Will you find a name before I do?*

58

Fleming was at his desk signing overtime forms for Logan and Anderson. Between them, they'd clocked up quite a few extra hours following up on the Slater murder leads. They were both busy at their desks in the open-plan area outside Fleming's office.

After two more minutes of form signing, Logan appeared at Fleming's door. 'Coffee from that swanky new coffee machine you brought in, boss?'

Fleming smiled. He'd finally decided he could no longer settle for the foul-tasting vending-machine coffee. 'Thanks. Could do with a break from paperwork.'

Logan pointed at the papers on Fleming's desk. 'Important though it is.'

'Don't worry, I'm about done. Think I'll wander over to the incident room. Mind bringing my drink?'

'Sure, no problem.'

Fleming was standing in front of the whiteboard, deep in thought when Logan came with his coffee.

'What you thinking, boss?'

Fleming turned and took the steaming cup from Logan.

'Thanks. Thinking over what we have in the Slater case. We seem to have hit a brick wall.'

'Still a few things to follow up on, but I guess you're right. Potential suspects, but not enough evidence or proof to make an arrest.'

Fleming rubbed his chin. 'What's going through your mind, Harry?'

'Vic Quinn is my bet. An angry man with a motive. He had the spat with Slater, and Forensics found his fingerprints on Slater's car door handle.'

'But nothing in his house... and his alibi checked out.'

'Yes, but he did lie about it at first.'

Fleming sipped at his coffee and pointed to Yousefi's name on the whiteboard. 'What about him?'

Logan shrugged. 'No love lost between him and his stepfather. Lied about his alibi, but then was later able to account for his whereabouts. So far, we can't disprove what he's claiming.'

Fleming sighed. 'That's what I mean about hitting a brick wall.'

'We're still trying to identify the man who met Slater in London. It'll throw new light on things if we get a name for him.'

'Speaking of which, Zoe Dunbar has offered to use her press contacts to see if someone can identify him.'

Logan grunted. 'And if she comes up trumps, what does she want?'

'A heads-up before any other reporters get hold of it.'

'Thought as much.' Logan furrowed his brow. He tapped a finger against Nash's name which he'd added to the whiteboard after Fleming's visit to Edinburgh. 'There's also this man. Slater sacked him and he disappeared off up to Scotland soon after the murder.'

Fleming took another sip of his coffee. 'And... he reckoned

Slater had stitched him up for fraud. Keep him on the board for now.'

Logan chuckled.

Fleming shot him a quizzical look. 'What?'

'I've just realised we could add to the suspect list. A name we haven't got on here yet,' Logan said, pointing at the whiteboard.

'Who?'

'Canning.'

'What makes you think of him?'

'Things had become strained between Slater and Canning over Canning's refusal to give Slater a pay rise. Canning was the last man to see Slater alive, in fact only a few hours before the estimated time of death.'

Fleming tilted his head to one side as though considering this. 'Pretty slim motive.'

'Slater went to meet Canning that night. Mrs Slater told you it was a bit odd because he wasn't getting on with Canning. Maybe things got out of hand.'

'How do you explain why Slater left his car in the village hall car park, and was then shot in the woods at the edge of the playing fields?'

Logan exhaled a long breath. 'That's a very good question. Could be there was more than a falling out over pay. Canning could have got Slater to drive them back to Darmont at gunpoint, took him down to the woods and shot him.'

'And how would he get back home?'

'Could have arranged for someone to follow them who then drove Canning home.'

'Or,' Fleming mused, 'Canning arranged someone to call Slater while he was with him. The accomplice asks Slater to meet him at the village hall car park in Darmont saying they had some money for him. Canning follows Slater, kills him and drives home.'

'But the car the witness saw speeding away was a black car. Canning has a blue Land Rover Discovery,' Logan pointed out.

'Could be he has another car,' Fleming suggested. 'Put his name on the board.'

'Okay.'

'While we're thinking of filling the whiteboard with suspects, Naomi had an interesting thought.'

'Oh?'

'She reckons there must have been tensions between Gale Slater and her husband. She wouldn't be happy over the gambling debts he amassed. He also didn't see eye to eye with her son. They argued a lot and he threw him out the house.'

'And she was in the village the night of the murder,' Anderson said, coming up behind them.

'Welcome to the party, Sherlock. We were seeing how much of the whiteboard we could fill with the names of possible suspects,' Logan said.

'Need a bigger board, Sarge.'

'Don't tell me you've got something else to add,' Logan quipped.

'Some dead ends, but a real result.'

'Give us the dead ends first so we end on a positive note, Naomi,' Fleming suggested.

'Okay. No one has come forward yet on the photo of the man Slater met in London. Checked with DI Oliver and he's got nothing else on the black car parked in the woods near Canning's house. Nothing else on the black Volvo seen on the A4130, and there's nothing on any speed cameras. I've got local forces concentrating on owners of black Volvos to check against the partial registration we have. Nothing to report yet.'

'Please tell me that's all the dead ends,' Logan pleaded.

Anderson smiled. 'It is. Been checking through Slater's bank accounts and found the two payments to the London hotel.

There was a recent cash deposit of five thousand pounds. Interesting for someone who was in debt through gambling.'

Fleming clicked his fingers. 'The note you found, Naomi... in Slater's office desk. He wanted to ask for a larger share from the man he was meeting in London. Could the deposit be from our mystery man?'

Logan looked puzzled. 'Payment for what though?'

'Whatever it was, it wasn't the larger share he wanted,' Anderson said.

'How come?' Logan asked.

'Because the five thousand deposit was made before the first meeting.'

Fleming chipped in. 'Right. He received payment for something, then went back to ask for more. We must find who the man is in the photo.'

'There's something else,' Anderson said. 'There's a deposit from one of Canning's business accounts of three thousand.'

'That's the figure Nash reckoned Slater and Yamamura secreted into Slater's account,' Fleming said. 'Seems our man Slater got himself involved in some shady dealings. We need to find out what.'

'You want the real icing on the cake?' Anderson asked.

'Do I need to sit down for this?' Logan joked.

'Probably. You know Forensics were running a check on traces of fingerprints and DNA they found on the tape used to bind the security guard?'

Logan gasped. 'They've got a result?'

'They have.'

'Hang on, didn't the guard say the kidnappers were wearing gloves?' Logan asked Fleming.

'He did, but they obviously didn't when they bought the tape and took it with them.'

Realisation dawned on Logan's face. 'Bloody hell! What did they find, Naomi?'

'The prints and DNA are a match with the guy who escaped from prison... Jack Kelso.'

Fleming's mouth dropped open.

'Bloody hell,' Logan said again.

Fleming looked at Logan. 'Get onto Hertfordshire police and find out who the SIO is investigating the prison escape. We need to speak to whoever it is... find out what they know. Someone must have planned Kelso's escape to carry out the kidnap.'

'Should I let Unity Elford know?' Logan asked.

Fleming thought for a moment. 'No... not yet.'

Something was nagging away in Fleming's head. *Is there a connection between Tom Slater's murder and the kidnap?*

59

The drive down from Long Hanborough to Welwyn Garden City had taken less than an hour and a half. Fleming and Logan were in the office of DI Afia Wacera at Hertfordshire Constabulary HQ. Her section of the major crime unit was leading the investigation into Jack Kelso's prison escape.

'DS Logan said on the phone you had some information on Jack Kelso,' Wacera said.

'We do,' Fleming replied. 'But we're also hoping you might be able to help us.'

'I will if I can, but so far we have little to go on. Kelso seems to have vanished. Mind if I ask what your interest is in him?'

'We believe Kelso was involved in a kidnap case we're working on.'

'How do you know?'

'Forensics found fingerprints and DNA on some tape used in the abduction. We ran checks and there's a match with Kelso.'

'Is that all the info you have for me? There's nothing else?'

'They used a black Volvo, and we know it was heading northwest on the A4130.'

'How do you know?'

'They almost knocked a cyclist off his bike near where the kidnap took place.'

'That's the only lead you have so far?'

'Afraid so. We were hoping you might be able to fill us in on the prison escape. There could be something that'll give us a lead on who else was behind the kidnap. It's possible that whoever it was who helped Kelso to escape did so to assist with the abduction.'

'Who did they kidnap?'

'Man called Dani Al Jameel. He's the son of a wealthy Saudi businessman who plans to invest in a major housing and shopping development.'

'I see. And if you find where they're holding Dani, that's where you guess Kelso will be?'

'Correct.'

'I'll give you all I know, but I want something in return.'

'Which is?'

'As the SIO tasked with putting Kelso back behind bars, I need to be in the loop if you get any info about where he's hiding out.'

Fleming thought for a moment. He sensed Wacera was worried he might find Kelso before she did. 'Okay, but the Anti Kidnap and Extortion Unit and I will be in charge of any rescue attempt.'

Wacera hesitated for a second. 'Fine, but I need to be involved in the operation. Agreed?'

'Okay, but you take a back seat.'

'As long as I get some credit for finding Kelso.'

Fleming pursed his lips. 'There's keen political interest in the kidnap for reasons I don't need to bore you with. What's more important than who takes credit is finding Dani and getting him back safely.'

Wacera smiled. 'We all have our own agendas.'

Logan looked irritated. 'It would help if we could concentrate on finding out how Kelso managed to escape, and who might have been helping him.'

Wacera shot Logan a look.

'If you don't mind,' Fleming prompted.

Wacera frowned. 'Okay, here's what I have. Kelso was working in the textiles workshop. Some inmates created a diversion. He managed to sneak into the stores where other prisoners were loading offcuts into a lorry. He somehow got into one of the sacks and got out through the gates in the back of the lorry.'

'Any suspicion prison officers helped him?' Logan asked.

'We've questioned everyone who was in the workshop. There's nothing to suggest he had inside help other than with the inmates in the storeroom.'

'What about who was in charge of the stores?' Fleming asked.

'It was a civilian storeman. A few inmates were hassling him to add to the commotion going on in the workshop. That's when another inmate must have helped Kelso into the lorry. There's no suspicion the storeman had anything to do with the escape.'

'When was Kelso discovered missing?'

'Almost straight after the ruckus...'

'In which case the lorry couldn't have gone far,' Fleming said.

'No, the prison officers realised what had happened. Someone rang the police and a few officers chased out in their cars after the lorry.'

'They obviously didn't catch it,' Logan observed.

'They caught up with the lorry, but too late. Two men wearing hoods had stopped the driver. They both had guns.'

'I'm assuming you have no idea who these men might have been,' Fleming said.

'The only clue we have is a man calling himself Oscar applied for a visiting order. He'd never visited Kelso before.'

'What address did he give for the VO to be sent to?' Fleming asked.

'Turned out to be a flat in London. It was empty, but this guy, Oscar, must have known of it, used it to get the VO sent to, then broke in to retrieve it.'

Fleming scratched his head. 'Seems likely then that this Oscar lives in London, maybe somewhere near the flat.'

'We did run a check for someone called Oscar, but it was a long shot. There was no way he was going to use his real name.'

'Did he visit once?' Logan asked.

'No, there were a few visits. A prison officer gave us a description, but so far we haven't been able to identify him.'

'Did the lorry driver provide any useful information?' Fleming asked.

'He said they were using a black BMW.'

'Did he get the registration?'

'No, but the number plates were false anyway. Prison officers sped off in the direction the lorry driver told them the car had gone. They found it burning half a mile further up the road.'

'And you have no information about whatever vehicle they must have transferred into?' Fleming guessed.

Wacera sighed and held up her hands as though in surrender. 'Not a clue. We've hit a brick wall. We've no idea where Kelso might have gone. We've alerted all police forces, ports and airports, but so far, nothing... that is until now.'

Fleming shrugged. 'I'm afraid we haven't helped you much. Only that Kelso was one of the kidnappers. Likewise, we have no idea where Kelso is holding Dani.'

'Oh, there was one other thing,' Wacera said. 'The lorry

driver detected what he thought was an Italian accent in one of the hooded men.'

~

On the way back to HQ, Fleming was deep in thought.

'What are you thinking, boss?' Logan asked, breaking the silence.

'Just wondering if it's coincidence.'

'What?'

'Naomi said the receptionist and the barman at the hotel told her the man Slater met could have been Italian.'

60

Anderson was looking worried when Fleming and Logan arrived back in the office.

'Everything okay?' Fleming asked.

'Super was looking for you. Said to tell you to go and see her as soon as you got back. She seemed...'

'Stressed?'

'Yes.'

Fleming groaned. 'Okay, I'd better go and see her.'

Temple's door was open. She had her phone by her ear listening intently when Fleming looked in. She glanced up and waved him in and mouthed, *chief constable.*

Fleming nodded his understanding and waited.

'Very well, ma'am,' Temple said and put the phone down.

'You wanted to see me?' Fleming asked.

'Yes. We have a problem. There's been another murder.'

Fleming knitted his eyebrows. 'In Darmont?'

'Next town.'

'Who?'

'Felicity Blunt. The council planning officer's wife.'

Fleming shook his head. 'What next!'

Temple sounded weary. 'Eric Blunt phoned the police. He found his wife at home when he returned from work late. DI Oliver is at the house now with the SOCOs. He rang to tell me. I asked him to stay put until you got there. Best get over there right away.'

~

A uniformed officer was on guard by the blue-and-white tape stretched across the front of Blunt's house. Flashing blue lights from two police cars reflected off the windows. Curious neighbours huddled in groups in deep conversation across the street. They watched as Fleming pulled up in his car.

Fleming showed his warrant card to the uniformed officer. He donned his protective clothing and ducked under the tape, heading for the front door. Another officer stood guard there. 'DI Oliver still here?' Fleming asked him.

'I'm here,' Oliver said, coming to the door to meet Fleming.

The SOCOs were already at work searching every inch of the house.

'Getting a bit busy in these parts,' Fleming said.

Oliver exhaled a deep breath. 'You're telling me, two murders and a kidnap.'

'All involving people connected to Canning's planning application.'

'Yes, but what's the connection?'

'That's what we need to find out. What happened here?'

'Eric Blunt called 999. He was in a bit of a state according to the officer who took the call in the police control room. Blunt claimed he went home from work late and found his wife. Looks like she was hit on the head by a heavy object.'

'Did the uniforms who arrived on the scene find whatever it was?'

'Afraid not.'

'Is Blunt here?'

'No, he collapsed when the uniforms turned up. They thought he'd had a heart attack and rang for an ambulance. He's in hospital.'

'I'll need to speak to him. Pathologist here yet?'

'No, he's stuck in heavy traffic. Been an accident.'

'Any sign of a forced entry?'

'No, she must have let the attacker in.'

'Which means she knew them, or... her husband killed her.'

'That was my thinking.'

'Did the uniforms see any sign of blood on Blunt when they arrived?'

'They said not.'

'Bit strange.'

'How come?'

'If he arrived home and found his bloodstained wife lying on the floor, he'd have rushed to her to try to revive her. If there was a lot of blood on her, it would seem likely he would have some on him.'

'Hmm. Or he went to change clothes and wash it off.'

'In which case the SOCOs will no doubt find something. Where was the body found?'

'In the living room. Want to have a look?'

'Yes.'

Felicity Blunt was lying on her back on the floor next to a heavy oak coffee table. Her lifeless eyes were staring up at the ceiling. Blood had soaked into the carpet behind her head.

'There's blood on a corner of the coffee table,' Oliver pointed out.

Fleming bent down and had a look. 'She must have hit her head on it as she fell, but something else struck her before then.'

'How do you know that?'

'There's a deep cut on the side of her head that hit the table. But there's another gash, bruising and swelling on the other side.' Fleming bent over the body. 'Looks like something heavy struck her on the head and she fell against the coffee table.'

'Doing my job for me,' came Dr Nathan Kumar's voice from behind him.

'Nathan, good to see you. We seem to be keeping you busy.'

'Sorry I'm a bit late on the scene. Accident on the road here and got stuck in a big traffic jam.'

'No worries. Care to have a look at the body?'

'Sure.'

Fleming left Kumar to it and drew Oliver to one side. 'Can you get your local uniforms to carry out house-to-house enquiries and see if there's any CCTV around?'

'Right. Think this is the work of a protester? Maybe they came looking for Blunt, but he wasn't here.'

'Not so sure about that. No forced entry. Mrs Blunt wouldn't have let them in.'

'Could have knocked on the door and forced their way in when she opened it.'

'Possible. Let's wait until I've had a word with Eric Blunt.'

Fleming turned back to Kumar. 'Think I'm done here, Nathan. Let me have your report asap.'

'As always, Alex. Be as quick as I can.'

'What hospital did they take Blunt to?' Fleming asked Oliver. 'I want to see if they'll let me speak to him.'

61

The sun was shining. There wasn't a cloud in the sky. A slight breeze ruffled the leaves on the trees. The sound of birds chirping came from the hedges surrounding the back garden of Zimmerman's country retreat.

Kelso was sitting in a deckchair sipping on a can of beer. The gun Zimmerman had supplied was on a table next to him. Guerra had grumbled about the heat and had gone inside.

Dani Al Jameel shuffled up and down the patio a few yards from Kelso, dragging a chain attached to his ankle. Kelso had fixed the other end to a pillar at the base of a small concrete statue. Playing safe, Kelso made sure the deckchair he was sitting on was out of Dani's reach. For good measure, Kelso had taped Dani's hands behind his back. The fact that Kelso also had a gun made it unlikely Dani would make any attempt at escape.

Dani had pleaded with Kelso to let him out of his room for some fresh air, even if for only an hour. A heated argument had ensued between Guerra and Kelso. Guerra had been against it, but Kelso had agreed. Maybe another reason why Guerra had disappeared inside.

Dani stopped a few yards in front of Kelso. 'You've spoken to my father?'

'We have contacted him. The boss gave him three days to get the money together.'

'But three days have passed.'

'True. There's a slight hiccup.'

Dani's eyes opened wide in concern. 'What... what has happened?'

'It seems your father has taken ill. He's in hospital.'

'Is he... is he seriously ill?'

'Don't know. Someone else is handling the money transaction. They want to hear your voice – make sure you're still alive.'

Dani slumped down on the patio wall. 'I'll never see him again, will I?'

'Don't worry. I'm sure it'll all work out,' Kelso said, not believing his own words. He'd already started planning for his escape if this went wrong.

'When do I get to speak to this other person?'

'Soon, but not today.'

'And if they can't get the money?'

'They will. You've had enough fresh air. Let's get you back to your room.'

Kelso had locked Dani back in his room and found Guerra sitting at the kitchen table, swigging beer from a can. 'Don't know why you took the chance of letting him out,' Guerra said. 'What if someone had come round to the back of the house?'

'Like who?'

'A postman, delivery man... how the fuck should I know?'

'Why would Zimmerman get anything delivered to this address when he's not here?'

Guerra shrugged. 'Just saying you took an unnecessary risk.'

'I've nothing against Dani. A condemned man deserves a bit of slack.'

'How'd you mean – condemned? You thinking his father won't pay up?'

'It makes no difference, does it?'

Guerra took a swig of his beer and belched. 'I'm not with you.'

'You're an idiot, Guerra. You really think Zimmerman is going to let Dani go even if his father coughs up?'

Guerra scowled at Kelso. 'Call me an idiot again and I'll...'

'What?' Kelso snapped.

Guerra took a last swig of his beer, crushed the can in his hand and stood up, pushing the chair away with the back of his legs. 'Just watch yourself, that's all,' he said, swaying on his feet. He paused for a second. 'Why won't Zimmerman let Dani go if we get the ransom?'

Kelso shook his head. 'You *are* an idiot. Haven't thought this through, have you? Dani can describe us and the house we kept him in. Letting him go is as good as inviting the cops to find us.'

'Call me an idiot one more time and you'll regret it!' Guerra shouted. He stamped on the pedal bin to throw his empty can in.

Kelso watched as it landed on top of a screwed-up newspaper. 'That yesterday's?' He pointed at the paper.

Guerra shrugged. 'What if it is?'

'I haven't read it.'

'Nothing in it anyway. Wouldn't bother.'

Kelso ignored him and pulled it out.

Guerra tried to take it off him. 'I said there was nothing in it!'

Kelso pushed him away. 'Something you don't want me to

see, is there?' He flattened the beer-stained paper out on the kitchen table and read the headline. He glowered at Guerra. 'I knew you were a fucking liability!'

'It's not a big deal,' Guerra mumbled.

'Not a big deal! Front-page headline about the kidnap, and the cops know they're looking for a black Volvo! Christ!'

Guerra jutted his chin out at Kelso. 'And how many black Volvos do you think there are in England, eh?'

Kelso stabbed a finger at the article. 'Driving at speed up the A4130! Give me strength!'

'You're forgetting, the car had false number plates.'

'Why doesn't that make me feel any better? Zimmerman know about this?'

'Didn't want to panic him.'

'Hmm, more like you didn't want to let him know how you managed to fuck things up.'

'Calm down. If it'll make you feel happier, I'll get rid of the Volvo. I can use Zimmerman's old Range Rover in the garage until I get another car.'

Kelso watched as Guerra pulled another can of beer out of the fridge. 'Give me one good reason why I shouldn't break your fucking neck.'

Guerra smirked. 'Chill... Once we get the ransom money, I'll be able to afford a swanky new car... you too.'

Kelso decided to go back outside. He'd had enough of Guerra for one day. *I'll need the Glock at this rate.*

62

As Fleming drove over to the hospital where they'd taken Eric Blunt, Fleming wondered what was going to happen next. No wonder Temple looked stressed out. The chief constable had wasted no time in ringing her. No sooner does Vanita Lazar take up the post and there's a murder, a kidnap, and now another murder on her patch.

The hospital car park was full. It came as no surprise to Fleming. Parking in hospitals always seemed to be a problem these days. He finally managed to find a space as someone waved to say they were leaving. The sun had sunk below the horizon and the air felt cooler as Fleming walked over to the entrance. The automatic glass doors swung open as he approached. Following the signs, he made his way to A and E.

Fleming showed his warrant card at the reception desk. 'DCI Fleming. You had a man admitted this evening, Eric Blunt. Can I have a word with him?'

'Just a moment. I'll check,' the receptionist said. She tapped on a computer and after a few seconds looked up at Fleming. 'They've kept him in for observation overnight. He's in ward eight. Upstairs on the second floor.'

'Thanks.'

Fleming took the stairs rather than the lift and found an overweight ward sister sitting in the office by the entrance. 'He showed his warrant card again. 'DCI Fleming. I'd like to speak to Eric Blunt if I may.'

'A and E phoned to say you were coming up. You can see him, but don't stay too long.'

'Okay. Is there anywhere we can talk in private?'

'I'm about to do my rounds. You can use this office if you like. I'll send Mr Blunt to you.'

'Thanks. Appreciate it.'

Blunt appeared at the door dressed in a hospital-issue blue-and-green-diamond gown. He looked gaunter than when Fleming first met him. The grey stubble beard seemed even greyer. 'You wanted to speak to me?'

'Yes. Come in and take a seat.'

Blunt shuffled in and sat at the end of the desk.

Fleming thought the man did look ill. 'I'm sorry about your wife and to have to trouble you right now. You'll appreciate it's critical we get information as soon as we can.'

'I understand,' Blunt mumbled.

'Sure you're okay to answer a few questions?'

Blunt's head sank to his chest. 'Yes.'

'What did they say when they brought you in?'

'Thought I'd had a heart attack. They gave me an ECG, but everything was okay. They're keeping me in overnight for observation.'

'How do you feel now?'

'Okay I suppose. Still in shock.'

'I understand that. Can you tell me what happened?'

Blunt drew in a deep breath. 'I was working a bit late. When I got home, I found Felicity on the floor. Her head was covered in blood.'

'Was the front door open?'

'I... I don't think so.'

'Only there was no sign of a forced entry.'

'Sorry... I'm not thinking straight. It might have been open. I didn't have to use my key to get in.'

'Could it have been on the latch?'

'I suppose so.'

'Was that something your wife did when you were out?'

'Er, she may have done from time to time.'

'She felt safe doing that, even after you'd had a death threat?'

'We weren't too worried. Didn't think too much about it. But you're right, I doubt she had it on the latch. Someone must have knocked on the door, she opened it and they forced her inside.'

'You said the front door wasn't open when you got home. If it wasn't on the latch you would have to have used your key to get in.'

'It's all a bit of a blur I'm afraid. I could have used my key to get in. I can't remember.'

'Okay. What did you do when you found your wife?'

'Called out her name and dashed over to her. Her eyes were staring... lifeless. I felt for a pulse. There was nothing.'

'What did you do then?'

'Rang 999 and asked for the police.'

'Not an ambulance as well?'

'Er... no. I was sure she was dead.'

'There was a lot of blood on your wife and the carpet. Did you get any on you when you were checking for a pulse?'

'Yes... yes, I did.'

'The police who arrived on the scene reckoned you didn't.'

'Couldn't stand the sight of it on my clothes and went to change while I was waiting for them to turn up.'

'Okay. Was anything missing from the house?'

'You think it was a robbery?'

'Trying to look at all possibilities. Was there?'

'What?'

'Anything missing?'

'I… I don't know. Didn't think to look.'

'I need you to check when they let you go home.'

Blunt nodded. 'Okay.'

'What happened when the police arrived?'

'It was all a bit confusing. I let them in, tried to explain what had happened, and then collapsed. Came to on the floor. Next thing I knew, they were rushing me off in an ambulance.'

'Okay, Mr Blunt. That's all for now. Thank you for talking to me. I'll need to speak to you again.'

'It was one of the protesters. I'm sure of it. You need to speak to them. Especially that man Quinn. He's dangerous.'

Fleming left the hospital with Blunt's words ringing in his ears. Somehow, he wasn't convinced by Blunt's account of things.

63

The main visitor entrance to the prison was set in a red-brick building. A high wire-mesh fence with razor wire on top surrounded the perimeter. Thunder rumbled overhead and the first spots of rain began to fall from a black sky as Fleming made his way from the car park to the entrance.

He walked in and held his warrant card up to a prison officer standing behind an impact-resistant window. 'DCI Fleming,' he said into the integral speech panel. 'I've a meeting with the governor.'

'Ah, right, sir. Just one moment.'

A second or two later, an electronic door slid open. Fleming walked through into a small corridor with a staircase leading up to the right. A door opened from the gatehouse office and another uniformed officer came out. 'If you'd like to follow me, sir, I'll take you up to the governor's office.'

'This is the admin block,' the officer explained as he led Fleming up the stairs and down a long corridor. A sign warning of a polished floor was in front of an inmate who was busy with a rotary electric polisher. At the end of the passageway, the officer pulled out a large set of keys from his pocket as they came to a locked metal door. He slid his hand up the chain attaching them to his belt and selected a key. There was a loud metallic click and the door opened into another corridor.

'This way,' the officer said, turning to his left. Halfway along they came to a door with a sign telling him this was the governor's office. The officer knocked and opened the door. 'DCI Fleming, governor,' he announced.

A tall man with receding grey hair rose from behind his desk and walked over to greet Fleming. 'Come in and have a seat,' he said, offering a hand.

Fleming shook hands. 'Thanks. Good of you to see me.'

The governor returned to his desk. 'My secretary told me you wanted to ask about Jack Kelso's escape,' he said.

Fleming took the seat in front of the governor's desk. 'Yes, it appears Kelso is one of two men involved in a kidnap case I'm working on.'

The governor's eyebrows rose. 'Are you thinking that's why he escaped? To carry out the kidnap?'

'It's a distinct possibility. I need to find out as much as I can about the escape. Whoever helped him more than likely planned the kidnap.'

'I see. DI Wacera from Hertfordshire police has already been here questioning everyone.'

'I've spoken to her. She told me about a visiting order for a man called Oscar who had started to visit Kelso.'

'Ah... yes, the VO. She's convinced he's the man who helped Kelso.'

'It seems likely. If he did, it's fairly certain he was Kelso's accomplice. That's why I wanted to see you. I need a description of this Oscar. He arranged for the prison to send the VO to an address in London. It was an empty flat, but I'm assuming Oscar lives in London.'

'Big place to find a man who is sure to have used a fictitious name,' the governor observed.

'Yes, but as it happens, I'm looking for someone else who may live in London. He's a person I want to question in connection with another case. It might be the same man.'

'A related case?'

'It's possible. Someone murdered a man called Slater. He was an employee of a property developer. The kidnapped man is the son of a wealthy businessman who wants to invest in the developer's plans. Maybe too much of a coincidence.'

'I see. How can I help?'

'I need to speak to any of your officers who would have seen this Oscar when he visited Kelso.'

'I can arrange that. Bear with me.' The governor picked up his phone and tapped in three numbers. He waited a few seconds. 'Get the visitors senior officer to come up to my office now please.'

Five minutes later, a worried-looking man was standing in the governor's office. 'You wanted to see me, sir?'

'Yes. DCI Fleming here wants to ask you about the man called Oscar who had visited Kelso.'

The officer turned to Fleming looking relieved. An unexpected summons to the governor's office was not always good news. 'How can I help, sir?'

'Can you describe the man called Oscar?'

The officer scratched his chin. 'We'll have him on CCTV if you want to look. But to save time, he was tall. Not quite as tall as you. Thick curly hair... black, not long. Bit chubby, but not fat, if you know what I mean.'

'Dress?'

'Casual. Jeans and shirt. Not scruffy. Oh... and he had what I took to be an Italian accent.'

Fleming recognised the description and fished out the

photograph of the man Slater had met at the London hotel. 'Is that him?'

The officer looked for a second. 'Yes, that's him.'

'Sure?'

'Positive.'

'Thank you. That's all I want to know.'

The officer turned to the governor. 'Anything else, sir?'

'No, that's all, thank you.' The governor smiled at Fleming. 'Looks like you've identified your man.'

'I knew the man in the photo met Slater a couple of times in London. It was just before someone killed Slater. Now I know it was the same man who helped Kelso to escape. Problem is... I still don't know who he is.'

'You think he could be the murderer?'

'I don't know. Slater had gambling debts. He used to live in London and had several regular haunts there. Maybe Slater owed the man in the photo some money. It could have been the reason for the meetings. He's just someone I need to eliminate from my enquiries.'

'Bit of a coincidence, isn't it? He meets Slater, and helps Kelso to escape.'

'Maybe. Could be the man in the photo is in a London gang and they wanted Kelso out of prison to help with the kidnap.'

'Well, good luck with your enquiries.'

Fleming thanked the governor for his time and left. He made a mental note to get Anderson to check with the Met. It would be useful to find out if any of the owners of black Volvos they were checking in London was Italian.

64

It had been a long day and Fleming was struggling.

The day before, after going to Blunt's house to check the scene of crime, he'd gone straight to the hospital to talk to Blunt. He'd gone home late and had three large glasses of whisky while thinking things through.

First thing this morning, he'd set off for the prison to speak to the governor about Kelso's escape. Afterwards, on his way to the council offices to see Blunt's boss, he picked up a sandwich, bottle of water and a pack of painkillers for a throbbing head.

Fleming had arrived back in the office half an hour ago after a stop-off for a black coffee. Logan popped his head round the door. 'Briefing meeting still on?'

'Yeah, sure. Be with you soon. I want to see the super first.'

Temple was feeling the strain. The new chief constable had been on her back wanting to know whether there had been any developments on the kidnap. 'Any news?' Temple asked Fleming.

'We have a bit of a result. Forensics have matched fingerprints and DNA found on tape used to bind a security guard during the kidnap to Jack Kelso.'

'You think someone broke him out of prison to do the kidnap?'

'Seems like it.'

'But you've no idea where he might be holding Dani?'

'Afraid not, ma'am. But there is something else.'

'What?'

'We now know the man who met Slater in London is the same man who helped Kelso to escape.'

Temple shook her head. 'This is getting very interesting indeed. Any progress on Slater?'

'We found some deposits in his bank account, but nothing that helps point to who the killer was.'

'What about Felicity Blunt?'

'Still early, but I have doubts about her husband's version of events.'

'All right, Alex. Keep digging. Chief constable's getting impatient. I'll keep her informed, but be good if you could make more progress.'

Fleming left Temple's office and found Logan and Anderson in the incident room engaged in yet another bout of light-hearted banter.

'You okay?' Logan asked. 'Look a bit peaky.'

'Fine. Been a long day. Let's see what we have. Slater case first.'

'Been a couple of interesting developments while you've been out of the office,' Logan said. 'Seems Rashad Yousefi has gone off the radar. He's disappeared from the commune.'

'Check with Gale Slater. See if she knows where he's gone,' Fleming said.

'Right. Naomi also got an anonymous tip-off.'

'Yes,' Anderson confirmed. 'Someone called to claim he overheard Vic Quinn in a pub boasting he knew how to get a gun and how he'd like to use it on a local traitor.'

'Did you ask who was calling?'

'Yes, but he said he wanted to remain anonymous for fear of reprisals.'

'Did he say which pub?'

'The Down Inn.'

'Check with the pub. See if anyone else heard that.'

Logan flicked through his notes. 'That's about it on the Slater case.'

'Not quite. I have a couple of things,' Fleming said. 'I followed up on what DI Wacera told us about the man called Oscar who had visited Kelso. It's certain he was one of the men who helped with the prison escape and most likely the kidnap. If he was, we could be a step nearer to finding Kelso and wherever they're holding Dani if we could find out who this man is.'

'And?' Logan queried.

'I went to speak to the prison governor this morning. The officer in charge of visiting recognised the man called Oscar. Turns out it's the man who met Slater in London.'

'He recognised the photo?' Logan prompted.

'Yes... and he confirmed he had an Italian accent. Same as the barman at the hotel told Naomi.'

'But we still don't know who he is,' Anderson said with a frown.

'We have the photo, know he's Italian, most likely lives in London and, if he was involved in the kidnap, drives a black Volvo. Check with the Met to see if they've questioned anyone like that while they've been checking owners of black cars.'

Anderson made a note in her notebook.

'Should I let Unity Elford in the AKEU know about the Kelso connection?' Logan asked.

'Okay,' Fleming agreed.

'How did you get on with Blunt and his boss?' Logan asked.

'Blunt was taken to hospital with a suspected heart attack. Collapsed when police arrived at his house. Turned out it wasn't and I spoke to him at the hospital.'

'Is he a suspect?' Logan asked.

'I wasn't convinced by his account of what happened. He was a bit vague over whether the front door was open or unlocked. Kept changing his story. Didn't know if anything was missing from the house. I've asked him to check when he gets home.'

'You think it could have been a robbery that went wrong?' Logan asked.

'He claimed it was one of the protesters. Pointed the finger at Vic Quinn.'

'But without a shred of evidence to back it up,' Logan guessed.

'I have my doubts about Blunt, I have to say. He said he was working late. But when I spoke to his boss at the council offices this afternoon, he said he had no recollection of it. In fact, he told me he was working a bit late himself and saw Blunt's office lights out when he left.'

'Hmm, beginning to have severe doubts about Blunt myself,' Logan said. 'Vague story and lying are not the traits of an innocent man.'

'His boss also told me something interesting. He was aware there was some sort of problem at home. Blunt had been acting a bit strange lately... seemed distracted, anxious. He didn't know the details and didn't want to pry. He suggested I speak to Felicity Blunt's sister. Said she might know what the problem was.'

'Want me to find out where she lives, sir?' Anderson asked.

'Yes, please. And check with DI Oliver. I asked him to get local uniforms to carry out house-to-house and see if there's any CCTV covering the area. A neighbour may have seen or heard something.'

65

The car park at HQ was almost empty as Fleming finally left the office. But in the far corner there was a car he recognised. It was the silver Audi A5. Zoe Dunbar was sitting behind the wheel.

Fleming walked over as she wound down the window. 'Don't tell me – your satnav got you to take a wrong turning and you happened to turn up here.'

'No, right place, and just the person I wanted to see.'

Fleming sighed. 'Can't keep you away, can I?'

'Are you always so pleased to see a friend?'

'Didn't know we'd become friends.'

'Okay – an exaggeration. More like fellow professionals?'

'It's been a long day. All I want to do is go home. Whatever it is you want can wait for another day.'

'You don't want to hear if I've found anything out about your man in the photo?'

Fleming pricked up his ears. 'You've found a name?'

Dunbar smiled. 'Thought that would get your attention. Fancy a drink?'

'Last thing I need right now.'

Dunbar looked at Fleming through narrowed eyes. 'Rough day? You look a bit the worse for wear.'

'Thanks.'

'No problem.' Dunbar hesitated. 'Would I be right in thinking you had too much last night? That why you don't want a drink?'

'Maybe I just don't need an inquisitive reporter trying to get information out of me.'

'I'll buy. Get you something to eat as well. Save you going home to cook. Or is there someone there to cook for you?'

'Subtle as an air raid as usual. Long story, but no there isn't.'

'Sorry, didn't mean to pry.'

'Look, have you got a name for me?'

'Droll.'

Fleming sighed. 'I meant the man in the photo.'

'Okay, I won't keep you in suspense. No... I don't have a name.'

Fleming tapped the roof of Dunbar's car. 'Right, I'm off.' He turned to go.

'But I could be near to it.'

Fleming turned back.

Dunbar continued. 'There's a reporter I know who thinks the face is familiar. It was a case he worked on some years ago. Something to do with drugs and petty crime in the London gangland scene. It all came to nothing – no evidence. He's going to look through all his old notes to see if he can put a name to the photo.'

'Why didn't you say so at the start instead of pussyfooting around?'

'Sorry. I'll get back to you if I get the name.'

'Thanks.' Fleming turned to go again.

'Any developments with the two men helping with your enquiries on the Slater murder?'

Fleming had started back to his car.

'Anything on the Al Jameel kidnap?'

Fleming ignored the questions and kept walking.

'Want some information on Canning?' Dunbar called after him.

Fleming stopped and turned to face her again. 'You never give up, do you?'

'Persistence is a trait of mine. It's why I'm an investigative reporter.'

Fleming walked back to her car.

'Fancy a drink now?' Dunbar asked.

'Persistent to the point of being a pain in the neck. Just tell me what you've found out.'

'I did a bit of research and found Walter Hammond and Canning were friends at university.'

'So?'

'Hammond is the secretary of state for housing, communities and local government.'

'I do know that.'

'He'll have the final say on the outcome of the public enquiry into Canning's planning application.'

'Still thinking there's bribery and corruption involved in this, eh?'

'Can't prove it, but I do know Hammond attended the welcoming party Canning held at his mansion for Isa Al Jameel and his son. All a bit cosy, don't you think?'

'How did you know that?'

'I'm an investigative reporter. Finding out things is what I do.'

'So you keep telling me.'

'Canning also went to London recently to see Hammond after the garden party. They had lunch together.'

'My, you have been busy, haven't you? How on earth did you find out?'

'I'm convinced something shady is going on. Had one of my reporter friends keep an eye on Hammond and he saw them. He took photos which I have.'

'And you're going to publish them?'

'Not yet. I want more proof before I go into print over corruption claims.'

'Right. That all you have for me? Or have you got some other gem you want to impart?'

'You must think there's a connection between all this.'

'What?'

'One of Canning's employees murdered, the son of one of Canning's possible investors kidnapped, and now the planning officer's wife murdered. All coincidence?'

'Let me know if you get that name,' Fleming said, turning to walk back to his car.

He sat for a moment and watched Dunbar drive off, giving him a wave as she passed.

Fleming turned on the ignition and put his car in gear. *Something ties it all together, but what?*

66

Logan and Anderson were already at their desks when Fleming arrived in the office. He looked a little better than he had the day before. Logan looked up from his computer. 'See you had a visitor in the car park last night when you left. What did Zoe Dunbar want this time?'

'Fishing for information as usual, but she did have something for me.'

'She did?' Logan asked. 'Anything useful?'

'Reckons a reporter friend of hers thought the face was familiar when she showed him the photo of the man who met Slater. He's searching through all his old notes to see if he can put a name to the face.'

'That would be a result,' Logan said.

'She also had some information on Canning. Seems he and Walter Hammond were friends at university.'

'How does that help us?' Anderson asked.

'Not sure it does on the Slater murder,' Fleming said. 'But Hammond attended the party Canning arranged at his mansion to welcome Al Jameel.'

'Suggesting?' Logan queried.

'Dunbar is convinced there's shady goings-on surrounding Canning's planning application. She found out Canning later had lunch with Hammond in London.'

'But what has that to do with Slater and the kidnap?' Anderson asked.

'Good question, Naomi. Probably nothing. But we can't rule out that there may be some sort of connection if Dunbar is right about something dodgy going on involving Canning.'

'And,' Logan reminded them, 'we now have Felicity Blunt's murder.'

'Speaking of which,' Anderson said, 'want an update on where we are with that, sir?'

'Go ahead.'

'SOCOs found a wine bottle in the recycling bin outside Blunt's house. Forensics found traces of Felicity Blunt's blood on it. Looked like someone made an attempt to wash it, but there were a few minor traces left.'

'Has to be her husband,' Logan reasoned. 'Why would a killer go to the trouble of trying to disguise the fact they'd hit Felicity with a bottle, try to clean it and then throw it in the recycling bin?'

'They find any fingerprints on it?' Fleming asked.

Anderson looked at her notes. 'Just traces of Blunt's and his wife's.'

'I rest my case,' Logan said.

'And,' Anderson continued, 'they found some of Blunt's clothes with bloodstains on them in the washing basket.'

'Do we need any more?' Logan asked. 'Why don't we pick him up now?'

'Not so fast, Harry. Don't forget, he admitted to me he'd got blood on his clothes and went to change.'

Logan snorted. 'Convenient.'

'Dr Kumar's report came in,' Anderson said. 'Lot of technical detail, but cause of death was a sharp blow to the head with a heavy blunt object, the table. The blow to the other side of the head, the bottle, was a contributory factor.'

'Estimated time of death?' Fleming asked.

'Between five and eight pm.'

'I checked with Blunt, and he says nothing was missing from the house,' Logan said. 'Still claiming Vic Quinn did it.'

'Anything from DI Oliver on the house-to-house?' Fleming asked, looking at Anderson.

'No CCTV, but a neighbour reckons she saw Blunt's car pull onto the driveway about five thirty.'

Logan closed his notebook and placed his pen on it. 'Evidence mounting up.'

'Timings not conclusive,' Fleming reminded Logan. 'It's possible Mrs Blunt could have been killed just before her husband got home.'

'Going to pull him in for further questioning?' Logan asked.

'Yes, but there's something else I want to check out first.'

'What's that?'

'I want to find out what Blunt's boss was talking about when he told me he thought Blunt had some sort of problem at home. Did you manage to find out where Felicity Blunt's sister lives, Naomi?'

'Yes.' Anderson flicked through her notes. 'Lymington.'

Logan's eyes lit up. 'Trip to the seaside. Want me to go?'

Fleming smiled. 'Nice try, Harry. Got another job for you. I want you and Naomi to chase something up. Where are we on the check of owners of all black cars which meet the partial description we have – especially black Volvos?'

67

Fleming told Logan he thought he could be in Lymington in under two hours. Anderson had checked Felicity Blunt's sister would be at home. She was going to be out in the morning, so Fleming had arranged to see her sometime after lunch.

'Are you sure you don't want me to drive down to see her?' Logan asked. 'Don't forget, this is the third day after the kidnapper's last call. Unity Elford will be waiting for him to ring again. Won't she want you there?'

'Nothing I can do about it,' Fleming said. 'There's no point in me sitting in Elford's office waiting all day for the kidnapper to ring. She's in charge of negotiations.'

'Speaking of which,' Logan replied, 'what will her negotiating strategy be?'

'Not sure. She bought us three days in which to try to find Dani, but we're nowhere near to it.'

'Not looking good for Dani's fingers, is it? Kidnapper threatened to cut them off one by one if Al Jameel delayed on paying the ransom.'

'All she can do is try to find a way to buy more time.'

'Not sure how she'll do that,' Logan said.

Fleming wasn't sure either, but AKEU were the experts.

An hour later, Fleming was on his way. Traffic on the A34, M3 and M27 had been heavy. It was less so on the A337 down to Lymington, but slow.

The bed and breakfast place Ivy Povey and her husband ran was near the centre of Lymington. It was an old red-brick building offering seven guest bedrooms. Fleming found a parking space in front of the house and rang the doorbell.

A man in his early fifties opened the door. 'I guess you must be DCI Fleming.'

Fleming showed his warrant card anyway. 'Yes, Ivy Povey is expecting me.'

'Sure, my wife's sitting out the back.'

Ivy's husband led Fleming down a long hallway to the back of the house and out onto a large patio area. Trees and tall shrubs bordered the garden, offering total seclusion. Ivy Povey was sitting in an outdoor weave lounge chair reading a book. 'DCI Fleming is here,' her husband announced.

Pushing herself up from the chair, Ivy offered Fleming a hand. 'Hello. How was your journey down?'

'Busy,' Fleming said. 'Thank you for seeing me at short notice.' Fleming put Ivy in her mid-forties. She was wearing a light summer dress and had long auburn hair which was showing signs of greying.

'Can my husband get you something? Tea, coffee?'

'A glass of water would be great,' Fleming said.

Mr Povey smiled. 'Or a cold beer?'

'No, water is fine. Thank you.'

'Come and have a seat,' Ivy said, waving a hand at the other weave chair. 'How can I help you?'

'I'm sorry about your sister. Must have come as a shock.'

Ivy took a deep breath. 'Yes, it did. It was awful.'

'Indeed. I'd like to ask a few questions about Felicity and her husband if I may.'

'We weren't very close... I mean Felicity and me. We didn't see so much of each other once we moved down here to take over the bed and breakfast business. Not much chance to get up to see her in the summer months.'

'They didn't get down to see you?'

Ivy sighed. 'No, Eric always seemed to be so busy.'

'Felicity didn't come on her own?'

'I suppose she could have, but she didn't. We had a slight difference of opinion over something.'

'Mind if I ask what that was?'

'Felicity was always a bit envious when we took over the bed and breakfast business by the sea.'

'And you reckon that's why she didn't visit?' Fleming asked as Ivy's husband appeared with a glass of iced water.

Fleming took the glass, looked up and smiled. 'Thank you. Perfect on a hot day like this.'

'Cold beer for me,' Mr Povey said, and disappeared back indoors.

Fleming took a long sip of water before prompting Ivy. 'You were saying Felicity was envious, but what was it you didn't agree about?'

'She had this idea she could go one better and wanted to run a hotel.'

'As a manager?'

'No, she was always very headstrong, impulsive. She wanted to buy one.'

'How did her husband feel about it?'

'Eric was dead against it. Said it wouldn't pay.'

'There was friction between them?'

Ivy looked alarmed. 'Oh, my goodness, you don't think Eric had anything to do with Felicity's death, do you?'

'I just need to get a feel for how things were between them. Eric's boss thought there was some sort of problem at home. He reckoned Eric had seemed anxious... distracted lately.'

'It would be the worry over finances.'

'You mean how to finance the hotel business?' Fleming said before taking another long sip of water.

'Felicity had a friend who reckoned she could help with some of the money in return for a share in the business.'

'And the rest of the money?'

'She took out a loan.'

'They don't have a hotel. What happened?'

'That was where we had a difference of opinion. I thought she was putting too much trust in this friend. Her friend got cold feet and pulled out.'

'Then what did she do?'

'As I said, Felicity was impulsive. She took out another loan thinking she could repay it when the business took off.'

'And it didn't?'

'Far from it. It failed, as Eric said it would. The banks called in the loans and Felicity had to sell the hotel at a loss.'

'Did she get enough to repay the loans?'

'No. Eric had a lot of investments from money his parents left him. He had to cash them all in to help pay off the debts.'

Fleming thanked Ivy for her time and took his leave. On the drive back to the office, he was thinking about Blunt needing money to pay off his wife's debts. He recalled Dunbar's words: *I want more proof before I go into print over corruption claims.*

68

Traffic had slowed to a walking pace on the A34 going north. A low-flying helicopter buzzed overhead. *Must be an accident.* Fleming had seen a sign about a mile back for a service station and saw the slip road up ahead. He decided to pull off for a drink and a break until the traffic cleared. Half the cars on the road had decided to do the same.

Twenty minutes later, he was in the car park sipping on a takeaway coffee when his mobile indicated an incoming call: *Unity Elford.* Fleming took the call. 'Hello?'

'Alex, is that you? It's Unity.'

'Yes. Any news?'

'Yes. The kidnapper called back.'

'And?'

'He put Dani on so at least we know he's alive.'

'How did you know it was him?'

'His father told me to ask Dani what nickname he gave him as a young boy. He knew the answer.'

'Good. How did the rest of the call go?'

'I told him I needed a few more days to arrange the money transfers because Dani's father was still in hospital and that the bank was being cautious about transferring such large sums to different accounts.'

'What was his reaction?'

'He wasn't happy. Threatened to send one of Dani's fingers to Canning's address to help focus attention on getting this done.'

'How did you respond?'

'I stressed I was making every effort to cut through the red tape and get the monies transferred. Assured him it would all click into place.'

'Did he swallow that?'

'I called his bluff. Told him there would be no payments if any harm came to Dani.'

'How much time do we have to find Dani?'

'Another three days. Best I could do.'

'You did a good job. Well done. All we need to do now is find him somehow.' Fleming ended the call, then tapped in the numbers for Logan. 'Hi, Harry, I'm on my way back, but there's been an accident or something on the A34. Might be a bit late.'

Fleming was in the incident room with Logan and Anderson. He'd briefed Temple on the state of play over the kidnap so she could update the chief constable. Logan and Anderson were also up to speed on events.

'We're running out of time,' Fleming said. 'Anything back from the Met on Italian owners of black Volvos in London, Naomi?'

'Yes. I emailed them a copy of the photo of the man who met Slater in London. They confirmed they had questioned someone who looks like him and he ticks all the boxes.'

Fleming sucked in air. 'Who?'

'Man called Marco Guerra. Suspected of being mixed up in the London gangland scene, but no criminal record.'

Fleming slapped a hand on the table. 'Result! Good chance he's one of the kidnappers. He helped Kelso escape. Get on to Elford and the Met and arrange for them to put him under surveillance. He could lead us to Dani.'

'I'll do that right now,' Anderson said and set off back to her desk.

'Is this too much of a coincidence?' Logan wondered.

'What?' Fleming asked.

'Guerra meets Slater in London and helps Kelso escape. He has a black car meeting the partial registration seen in Darmont around the time of Slater's murder. Has to be him, doesn't it? Slater's murder, the prison escape and the kidnap all connected somehow.'

'My thoughts exactly,' Fleming confirmed. 'And now we have Felicity Blunt's murder.'

'You see that connected as well?'

'There's a thread that runs through all this. Slater was one of Canning's employees. Someone kidnaps the son of a potential investor in Canning's development plans. Guerra knew Slater and helped Kelso escape. And Kelso and Guerra were sure to be behind the kidnap.'

'Slater couldn't have had anything to do with the kidnap though,' Logan pointed out. 'We know he had debts and needed money, but he was killed before Dani's abduction.'

'Maybe he was involved in part of the planning and was silenced for some reason.'

Logan whistled. 'That would fit. What about Felicity Blunt?'

'Haven't worked that one out yet. But I found out from Felicity's sister that Eric Blunt was angry because his wife got them into debt over a failed business enterprise. I need to pull him in for questioning.'

Fleming's mobile rang: *Zoe Dunbar.* Fleming answered. 'Hello, what can I do for you?'

'It's more what I can do for you,' Dunbar said.

'Oh?'

'I've got a name for you. My reporter friend came up trumps. The guy in your photo is Marco Guerra. Small-time crook. Arrested a few times but never charged and convicted.'

Fleming laughed.

'What?'

'You're too late. I'd already found that out.'

There was a moment's silence before Dunbar spoke again. 'You serious? You're not just saying that to get out of your promise?'

'What promise?'

'You'd give me a heads-up on any developments on the Slater murder case and the kidnap if I found a name for you.'

'Tell you what, because you put the effort in, I'll stick to my promise. How's that?'

'Fair enough. Anything to tell?'

'Not yet.' Fleming ended the call.

'What was all that about, boss?' Logan asked.

'Dunbar found out that Guerra was the man in the photo. Beat her to it though.'

'What was the promise?'

'To give her a chance to get her story out first on the Slater case and the kidnap once we can go public. But right now, let's go and pull Blunt in.'

69

The crushed beer can hit the far wall of the kitchen and splashes of frothy beer trickled down the paintwork. 'Didn't go too well then?' Kelso guessed. 'Or was the beer not cold enough?'

Zimmerman's right eye was as dark as the patch over his left eye. He glared at Kelso and kicked a chair across the floor. 'I'm paying you to be the brawn behind this operation, not a fucking comedian.'

'Just trying to lighten the mood.'

Zimmerman gave a thin smile. 'Won't do your mood any good if we don't get paid,' he mumbled in a rasping voice.

'Going to tell me what happened when you called them?'

'I don't like the way this is going. They've got someone standing in for Al Jameel. She reckons he's in hospital, but I don't believe it.'

'Who are you talking to?'

'Spoke to Al Jameel himself the first time I called. I gave him three days to get the money sorted out.'

'So who are you speaking to now?'

'No idea. Someone who said she was a financial adviser. Not

convinced though. I'm beginning to think she's an experienced negotiator.'

'What makes you say that?'

'She told me she had to speak to Dani to make sure he was okay and it would take three days to get the money sorted out.'

'Three days seems reasonable... given the amount we're talking about.'

'Okay, but she also insisted I call back on her number. Smacks of a professional negotiator to me.'

'Or just convenient if Al Jameel is in hospital.'

Zimmerman shrugged. 'Maybe. I called the number she gave me and let her speak to Dani.'

'What didn't go to plan then?'

'She tried to assure me everything is being arranged to make the money transfers, but she needs a few more days.'

'Give a reason?'

'Because Dani's father is still in hospital and the banks are being difficult.'

'Red tape, I suppose. You know what banks are like. You'd think the money was theirs.'

'I threatened to send them one of Dani's fingers if they kept stalling.'

'That didn't work?'

'This is where she gets a bit cute. Called my bluff.'

'You were bluffing?'

'No, I wasn't.'

'But?'

'She said they wouldn't make any payments at all if any harm came to Dani.'

Kelso frowned. 'She's bluffing. She knows full well we'll kill him if they don't pay up.'

'We're going to kill him in any case,' Zimmerman said. 'He's seen you and Guerra and can describe the house we're keeping him in.'

'Right. They'll know that as well. So they're stalling for time hoping to find Dani.'

'I don't like how this is going. They're not going to pay if they think we'll kill Dani anyway.'

'How do we get round that?'

'She asked for another three days. I could try to assure her no harm will come to Dani.'

'Think she'll believe you?'

'I'll tell her we intend to skip the country as soon as we get the money and we'll leave Dani someplace where they can find him.'

'So it doesn't matter if Dani can describe us and the house,' Kelso suggested. 'Flimsy, but might work.'

'One more thing. An associate of mine tells me the Met questioned him. He happens to own a black Volvo. It was a junior detective constable who saw him. He didn't seem too interested. Said they were going through the motions of checking everyone in London who owned a black Volvo with a partial registration they had. He seemed to think it was a complete waste of time.'

'Hang on. How did they know to check London?'

'Beats me. But I want you to ask Guerra when he gets back from his little shopping trip if anyone has questioned him.'

'Okay.'

Zimmerman pointed at the beer-stained wall. 'Best be on my way. Be a good chap and clean that up.'

Kelso was wiping the kitchen wall down when Guerra returned.

'Didn't know you were the cleaning type,' Guerra taunted.

'It'll be your blood I'm cleaning off the wall next if you give me any more lip.'

'Bad mood, eh?' Guerra gave Kelso a quizzical look. 'Zimmerman gone?'

'Yeah. He's the one in a foul mood.'

'After the phone call?'

'It didn't quite go to plan. They're stalling over paying the ransom.'

'Who's going to cut a finger off then?'

'They said they wouldn't pay any money if any harm came to Dani.'

'They're bullshitting!'

'Zimmerman isn't taking any chances. He's given them another three days.'

Guerra thumped his bag full of groceries and beer cans onto the kitchen table. 'Fuck!'

'Something you're not telling me?'

'What do you mean?'

'About the car?'

'What about it? I told you I was going to get rid of it.'

Kelso narrowed his eyes. 'Have the Met questioned you yet?'

Guerra's face turned pale. 'What... what the hell makes you say that?'

'Because they're trying to speak to everyone with a black Volvo who lives in London.'

'Okay, so they did. Routine, they said. They were checking hundreds. Asked where I was on the day of the kidnap.'

Kelso grabbed hold of Guerra's head with both hands. 'You idiot. You're doing your best to get us caught. I should break your fucking neck!'

Guerra's eyes flashed with fear. 'Don't worry. I told them I was with my mate, Taffy. You know, the guy who drove the van after your prison escape. Said we were down in Brighton for the day. Taffy will confirm if they bother asking him. Doubt it though. The officer who phoned me seemed to think he was wasting his time.'

Kelso pushed Guerra away. 'You'd better stay out of sight in case the cops want to see you again.' He grabbed a can of beer from Guerra's bag and pointed it at Guerra's face. 'And keep out of my sight as well!'

70

It was hot and stuffy in police interview room one. Eric Blunt was facing Fleming and Logan across a small table. Canning had offered Blunt the legal services of his solicitor, Silas Revell, who sat next to Blunt. Logan switched on the digital recording machine and Fleming went through introductions. He cautioned Blunt and was about to start questioning him when Revell butted in.

'I need to advise my client that, as you have not arrested him, he is free to leave at any time,' Revell said.

'Thank you, I was about to tell him.'

'Also, he should know you cannot take his fingerprints and DNA unless you do arrest him.'

'That's true as well, but he may choose to agree if I ask him. I might well do that when I've finished questioning him.'

Revell grunted and turned to Blunt. 'You don't need to answer any questions if you don't want to. A "no comment" answer is acceptable.'

Fleming tapped a pen on the folder in front of him. 'Now your client is fully briefed, can we make a start?'

Revell glowered at Fleming and sat back in his chair, arms folded.

Fleming looked across at Blunt. 'How are you? Hospital let you home the next day after you were admitted?'

'Yes. They gave me the all-clear. No heart problem. I'm fine.'

'Good. You told me at the hospital you found your wife when you arrived home after working late.'

'Yes, that's right.'

'I spoke to your boss. He said he was working late and noticed your office lights were out when he left.'

'He must have worked a bit later than me.'

'What time did you get home?'

Blunt looked at the ceiling as though looking for the answer. 'I guess it would be around eight.'

Fleming opened the folder on his desk. 'I have a statement from a neighbour who says she saw your car pull onto your driveway around five thirty.'

'She must be mistaken.'

'When I saw you at the hospital, you were vague over whether the front door was open or closed when you arrived home.'

'I... I was confused. My mind went blank after I saw Felicity lying there.'

'At first you said the front door might have been closed.'

'Did I?'

'But when I reminded you there was no sign of a forced entry, you said it could have been open.'

'I... I couldn't remember.'

'You did recall not having to use your key to get in. You're sure about that?'

Blunt hesitated for a second before answering. 'Yes, pretty sure.'

'Meaning the door was either on the latch, or your wife let the killer in and left the door open.'

'I guess so.'

'Wouldn't it be unlikely for your wife to keep the door on the latch after you'd had a death threat?'

'I told you, she must have answered the door and someone forced her inside.'

'You claimed there was nothing missing from the house.'

'There wasn't. My guess is Vic Quinn came looking for me. I'm sure it was him who sent the death threat. Everyone knows he's a volatile character opposed to the development. He had run-ins with Tom Slater and Paul Canning.'

'Forensics found traces of your wife's blood on some of your clothes. Can you explain how it got there?'

'I told you at the hospital. I got blood on me and went to change.'

'Your boss thought you'd been acting a bit out of character lately. He said you seemed anxious, not quite with it. Why was that?'

'Don't know what he's talking about. Pressure of work can get to you sometimes.'

'I spoke to your wife's sister. She told me about the failed hotel business.'

Blunt gasped. 'What did she tell you?'

'Your wife agreed to go into a partnership with a friend who offered to put up some of the money, but she pulled out. Your wife had also taken out a loan, then took out another one when her friend pulled out.'

Blunt's face had turned ashen.

'The business failed and your wife had to sell the hotel at a loss to pay off the loans.'

'I was always against it. Knew it wouldn't work.'

'Felicity's sister told me you had to cash in some investments to pay off the debts.'

'That's personal! She had no right to tell you!'

'You must have been angry your wife had got into this mess, especially when you advised against it.'

'I was... but I didn't kill her if that's what you're about to suggest.'

'A wine bottle was found in the recycling bin with traces of your wife's blood on it.'

Blunt put his hands on the table and clasped them together to stop them shaking. 'The killer must have used it to hit Felicity.'

'The only fingerprints on it were yours and your wife's.'

'I–'

'There were no other prints or DNA in the house,' Fleming cut in.

Blunt said nothing.

'You arrived home around five thirty according to your neighbour. The estimated time of death is between five and eight.'

Blunt stared at the whites of his knuckles on his clenched fists and stayed silent.

'You had a row with your wife when you got home, didn't you? Maybe got out of hand. Is that what happened?'

Revell glanced sideways at Blunt. 'I don't think you should answer any more questions right now,' he advised. Turning to face Fleming. 'If you are not arresting my client, we're leaving.'

Fleming looked at Blunt who took his head in his hands and sobbed. 'It was an accident.'

'Don't say any more,' Revell warned.

'Okay,' Fleming said. 'Want to tell me what happened?'

'I came home. She'd been drinking. An empty wine bottle was on the coffee table. We had a heated row. I was in serious financial difficulties due to her stupidity. Paul Canning somehow found out and offered me five thousand pounds.'

'In return for?'

'Approving his planning application. But then it went to the public enquiry.'

Beads of sweat appeared on Revell's brow. 'We should stop this here!'

Fleming ignored Revell and held Blunt's eyes. 'Your wife knew you'd accepted a bribe?'

'Called me stupid. She picked up the bottle and tried to hit me with it. A red mist came over me. She was the one who got us into this mess. I snatched the bottle out of her hand. Didn't think what I was doing. I lashed out. It caught her on the side of the head and she crashed into the edge of the coffee table as she fell. I froze for a while. She didn't move. I checked for a pulse but there was nothing.'

71

It only took half an hour to get to the motorway services at the Welcome Break, Oxford. Kelso had phoned Zimmerman and said he wanted to meet him to discuss something of the utmost importance. Guerra had asked why Kelso needed to use the Range Rover Zimmerman kept at the house where they were holding Dani. 'Someone I need to see to help with my escape once we get the ransom money,' Kelso had lied.

Before leaving the house, Kelso had slipped a small digital voice recorder into his pocket and had taken the Glock out of his wardrobe to check it over. He didn't trust Guerra and wanted to find somewhere else to hide it. Guerra was sure to search his bedroom while he was out. Zimmerman had boarded over some joists in the garage roof to provide storage space. In the far corner, Kelso had found an empty toolbox. He'd wrapped the gun in an old rag before padlocking the toolbox with a lock he'd found in a kitchen drawer.

It was a sunny morning as Kelso drove into the car park. It was filling up fast. There had been a lot of coverage in the newspapers about the prison escape. Photos of Kelso were all over the front pages. As time had passed, reporting on the escape had dwindled and editors had consigned reports to the inside pages. They'd found new things to cover, like Dani Al Jameel's kidnap. Despite having grown a beard, wearing dark sunglasses and a baseball cap, Kelso was being careful about exposure to the public. He was taking no chances of anyone recognising him, especially motorway police.

As arranged, Kelso parked at the far end of the car park furthest away from the retail and catering outlets. There was no sign of Zimmerman's black Mercedes-Benz GLA 200. Kelso parked where he could see cars arriving. He resisted the temptation to get out and go for a takeaway coffee.

After waiting for fifteen minutes, Kelso was beginning to wonder if Zimmerman was going to turn up. Then he saw what he didn't want to see. A police patrol car was cruising up between the rows of parked cars. Kelso pulled the baseball cap over his eyes and tipped his seat back as though he were having a nap.

He froze when there was a knock on the driver's side window. He tipped the baseball cap up and glanced out, expecting to see a policeman. It was Zimmerman. Kelso wound the window down. 'Fuck's sake, Ulrick, you just about gave me a heart attack!'

Zimmerman smiled. 'Having a wee nap, were we?'

'Police patrol car went by. Trying to keep out of sight.'

Zimmerman walked round the front of the car and climbed in beside Kelso. 'What's so important you need to have a clandestine meeting?'

Kelso made sure Zimmerman didn't notice him switching on the voice recorder. 'It's Guerra. He's in danger of fucking this whole operation up. Where did you get him from?'

'He was a small-time crook looking for work. Advantage was, he has no criminal record. Started working for me as a driver after you ended up in prison. He's a bit cocky and impulsive.

Didn't think he was the right man to lead on the kidnap. Needed an ex-military man, hence your escape from prison. And I owed you one for keeping quiet over my part in planning the armed robbery you got nicked for.'

'Never mind lead on it... he's the wrong man to have anything to do with it!'

'Okay, what's the problem?'

'You wanted me to ask him if the police had questioned him because he owns a black Volvo.'

Zimmerman raised an enquiring eyebrow. 'Have they?'

'Yeah. I told you he was a liability when he pranged the van we were going to use for the kidnap and we ended up using his Volvo.'

Zimmerman rubbed his chin. 'We can't afford to run the risk of the police questioning him again.'

'He reckoned it was only routine. They were going through hundreds of them. He told me he had an alibi arranged for the day of the kidnap.'

'Which was?'

'Told them he was in Brighton for the day with his mate, Taffy.'

'I can't let the police track him back to me if they do question him again.'

'I told him to keep low in case the cops put him under surveillance.'

'You think they might do that?'

'It's possible if they don't believe his story.'

'His Volvo might be our undoing,' Zimmerman said.

'He said he was going to get rid of it.'

'And draw attention to it when it's all over the papers that a black Volvo was used in the kidnap.'

'So what do you suggest we do?'

'If he's keeping a low profile away from his flat it'll look like he's done a runner. We need to make sure he isn't found.'

'Are you suggesting what I think you are?' Kelso asked.

'We don't need him anymore. He's becoming a problem. One we need to remove.'

'Care to define what you mean by remove?'

'You need to kill him.'

72

Fleming and Logan had taken an early morning train down to London to see Unity Elford in the AKEU. On the way down Logan asked, 'Think Blunt will plead guilty to murder or manslaughter?'

'He'll maybe get away with manslaughter, but there's also the charge of bribery to be taken into account.'

'Looks like Dunbar was right all along about bribery and corruption. Wonder if Canning's solicitor knew about it.'

'Anybody's guess,' Fleming said. 'I've been in touch with the Serious Fraud Office. They're taking a special interest due to the close connection between Walter Hammond and Canning. They'll always want to know when politicians could be implicated.'

'Reputation and integrity of government, eh?'

'Something like that. They want to be informed after I've brought Canning in for questioning.'

'Going to arrest him?'

'No. All we have is Blunt's word. Canning will deny he bribed Blunt. We'll see how the questioning goes.'

Logan nodded. 'Guess we'll have to find proof.'

'Or the Serious Fraud Office will decide to investigate further, after which they may ask me to arrest Canning.'

'Oh, talking of which, things are going to get interesting. Have you heard the news?'

'What?'

'It was on the radio. There's uproar in Darmont. The inspector in charge of the public enquiry recommended Hammond should approve Canning's planning application.'

'And he has?'

'Yes. What'll happen to it now?'

'It'll no doubt be overturned if the SFO conclude there was bribery and corruption involved.'

Logan fell silent for a while then remembered a couple of things. 'By the way, the Met found Rashad Yousefi. I asked Gale Slater if she knew where he'd gone and she told me he'd met some girl, but she didn't know where she lived. Anyway, turns out he had left the commune to shack up with this girl. Bobbies on the beat were looking out for him and found him coming out of a pub near her flat.'

'And the other thing?'

'Naomi asked around at the Down Inn. Regulars were reticent about confirming that Quinn said he knew how to get a gun.'

'Thought that might turn out to be the case. Villagers sticking together.'

'Naomi pressed them. Threatened to charge them with obstructing a police officer in the course of her duties.'

Fleming smiled. 'Good for her. Get any result?'

'Two men did confirm Quinn had said he knew where to get a gun and how he'd like to use it on what he called a local traitor.'

'We need to speak to him again.'

~

It took just over an hour to get from Oxford to London Paddington. Fleming and Logan took the Bakerloo Line from there to Oxford Circus where they changed to the Victoria Line to Vauxhall. It was an eight-minute walk from there to Tinworth Street. Elford's office was there in the central London hub of the AKEU, not far from the headquarters of MI6.

They showed their warrant cards at a reception desk. 'We have a meeting with Unity Elford,' Fleming said.

'If you'll take a seat,' the woman behind a glass screen said, 'I'll ring through for her to come and get you.'

Five minutes later, Elford appeared. 'Sorry to keep you waiting.'

They followed Elford through security glass doors and took the lift up to the second floor. Her office was small, but there was enough room for a desk, a small meeting table and four chairs.

'How much of your time do you spend here, and how much out and about?' Fleming asked.

'Varies. On call for twenty-four-seven customer support. Anything can happen at any time. I can be travelling abroad in hours if need be. I often have to go to conferences and meetings and do the odd bit of training.'

'Keeps you busy then,' Logan observed.

'It does. I spend a lot of my time on tactical advice and support.'

'Which is why we're here,' Fleming said.

'Right. Nothing has happened since the last call, but thank you for letting me know you've probably identified two of the kidnappers.'

'Forensics found traces of fingerprints and DNA on tape used to bind a security guard. They were a match to the escaped prisoner, Jack Kelso. We also happen to be working on a murder case and we had a photograph of a man who met the victim, but we didn't know who he was. Turns out he's the same man who visited Kelso in prison and most likely helped him to escape.'

'And was more likely than not involved in the kidnap,' Elford added. 'Marco Guerra, the man you wanted put under surveillance.'

'Yes. Anything on that front?' Fleming asked.

'Nothing. He's not been seen at his flat since I asked the Met for help on this.'

'Police questioned him as part of a routine check of all London owners of black Volvos. They were checking everyone who had a car that matched a partial registration number we got from a witness in the murder case,' Fleming said.

'Maybe he's taken fright and decided to lie low for a while,' Logan suggested.

'Which doesn't help us find Dani,' Elford said.

'How much time have we got before the kidnapper calls back expecting the ransom to be ready?' Fleming asked.

'He's due to call tomorrow.'

'How many more times do you think you can stall?'

Elford sucked in air. 'Not much more, I'm afraid. He's already getting impatient and cagey. I could say the banks are aiming to release some of the money to one of the accounts he gave which they've checked out. But because of the large sum involved, it'll take three to four days for it to appear.'

'Think that'll work?' Fleming asked.

'It'll have to. It's the last chance we've got.'

73

'The boss called me,' Guerra said.

Kelso had been expecting it, but feigned surprise. 'What did he want?'

'Wants me to meet him in some derelict warehouse in west London with someone he knows.'

'What for?'

'The guy wants my Volvo.'

'You're joking!'

'I told you I'd get rid of it, didn't I? You should have had more trust in me.'

'Should never have doubted you,' Kelso said. *Trust in you is the last thing I have.*

'This guy intends to do a respray job on it and put a new set of false number plates on for a robbery he's planning.'

Kelso knew full well why Zimmerman had picked the location. It was in a run-down old industrial area with no houses or retail outlets anywhere near the old warehouse. 'Strange place to meet. Why there?'

'Boss wants to make sure no one sees us. Makes sense.'

'Right. And how will you get back here?' *Only you won't be coming back.*

'The boss has worked it all out.'

I know.

'You follow me in the Range Rover.'

'Didn't tell me that,' Kelso lied. He knew all along what the plan was.

'Must have been leaving it to me to tell you.'

'Guess so. When do we leave?'

'Should be going in the next hour.'

'Okay. I'll see to Dani and make sure everything is locked up.' *And I'll collect the Glock.*

Finding the warehouse was a nightmare, but after a few wrong turns they found the place. The two cars pulled off a narrow potholed road onto a tarmac area in front of the building. Large painted iron gates had once blocked the entrance, but now they were rusting and open. It had been raining and the two cars splashed through puddles on the surface. Someone had long since boarded up the broken windows in the building.

Guerra's car was in front. He drove round to the back and parked facing a low wall bordering the Thames. Kelso pulled up next to the Volvo. He grabbed the Glock out of the glove compartment and tucked it behind him, in his jeans. Getting out of the car to join Guerra, he made sure he kept a safe distance.

Guerra was leaning on the wall looking out over the murky river. 'Where the fuck is he? We had further to come and we're here before him.'

'He's not coming.'

'What?'

'I said he's not coming.'

Guerra looked puzzled. 'What do you mean, he's not coming? How the fuck do you know?'

'Because he told me. Nobody wants your bloody Volvo.'

A worried look crossed Guerra's face. 'What the hell is going on here?'

'Zimmerman wants you out of the way. He panicked when he found out the Met had questioned you over the Volvo.'

'How'd he find out?'

'I told him.'

'You bastard!'

'Thing is, he thinks you're a liability. Could blow the whole kidnap operation if the police question you again and you talk.'

'Whoa, hold on there. I wouldn't talk. No way!'

'He's not taking any chances.'

'So what does he want me to do?'

'He wants a guarantee you can't talk.'

'I can promise him that.'

Kelso smiled. 'So can I.'

'What you mean?'

'He wants a cast-iron guarantee.'

Realisation seemed to dawn on Guerra. His eyes flashed from side to side as though looking for a way to escape. He reached behind his back where he'd tucked the Beretta Zimmerman had supplied for the kidnap.

Kelso saw the move and pulled out the Glock and pointed it at Guerra's head. 'Put your hands in front of you where I can see them.'

Sweat glistened on Guerra's forehead as he did as Kelso told him. 'He wanted me here so you could kill me!'

'Good guess.'

'Please,' Guerra pleaded, 'you don't need to do this! We can come to an arrangement.'

'What did you have in mind?'

'You could tell him you killed me and tossed my body in the river.'

'Then what?'

'We leave the Volvo here. You can tie me up and take me back to the house where we have Dani. You ask Zimmerman for my share of the ransom as the fee for killing me. Once you get your money, you can let me go when you make your escape. How about it, Jack?'

'Sorry, no deal. I don't trust you. Never did. Never liked you either. I did have a feeling you would try to kill me so you could get my share of the ransom.'

'No way! I promise!'

'Was that a gun you were reaching behind your back for?'

'Okay. I have a gun on me. It's the one Zimmerman supplied. I always carry it.' Guerra licked his lips. 'Here, I'll hand it over to you.' He made to put a hand behind his back.

Kelso didn't hesitate. He shot Guerra once in the chest.

Guerra was flung against the wall and slid down with a confused look on his face.

Kelso put another bullet between Guerra's eyes to make sure. He had intended to pull Guerra over the wall and dump his body in the Thames. But plans always seem to have a way of going wrong.

He heard the music first, then saw it. A sleek white cruiser was sailing slowly upriver against the ebbing tide. There was no way Kelso could throw Guerra's body over the wall without someone on the boat seeing him. Neither did he want to hang around waiting for the boat to pass. He jumped in his car and drove off, wheels spinning on loose gravel on the tarmac.

74

The chief constable was in Temple's office when Fleming called in to brief the super on the state of play. Lazar was getting impatient and her visits to Temple's office were becoming more frequent. Fleming had taken the opportunity to bring them both up to speed on everything. Lazar was more interested in the kidnap on account of the political interest.

'You know the names of two of the kidnappers, but you've no idea where they are,' Lazar said. 'That's all you have?'

'Apart from the fact they used a black Volvo seen driving up the A4130.'

'Two names, a car, and an identified road and you still can't find the kidnappers,' Lazar fumed.

'Kelso has been on the run since escaping prison. So far, police have had no sightings of him. He could be anywhere.'

'I take it you've had cars patrolling up and down the A4130 to see if they can spot this black Volvo?'

'We have. Nothing so far.'

'And the surveillance on this chap, Marco Guerra, has come up with nothing?'

'I spoke to Unity Elford this morning down in the AKEU HQ. Guerra hasn't been near his flat.'

'Which suggests he's hiding out wherever they're holding Al Jameel,' Lazar said. 'Probably somewhere off the A4130.'

'Seems likely, but the road is a bit short of a distance of thirty miles... and they could have turned off anywhere.'

'How long have you got before the kidnapper calls again?' Temple chipped in.

'He's due to ring Elford tomorrow.'

'She can't pay,' Lazar said.

'She's going to tell him the bank has released some money to one of the accounts, but it'll take three to four days to appear. Best she can do.'

'You'd better find Dani in the next four days then,' Lazar said.

'What about this business about a gun and Vic Quinn?' Temple asked.

'Spoke to him about that. Searched his house again. We found nothing. He laughed it off and said he was bragging after having too much to drink.'

Temple looked at Lazar whose face had set into a deep frown. 'We do have a confession on the Felicity Blunt murder,' Temple said.

'Her husband claimed it was an accident,' Fleming added. 'Also said Paul Canning had bribed him over his planning application. I'm going to speak to Canning about that later.'

'SFO advised?' Lazar asked.

'Yes. They wanted me to keep them informed after I questioned Canning. They've asked for a transcript of the interview.'

'Then they'll decide whether to investigate further?' Lazar asked.

'That's about it, ma'am,' Fleming confirmed.

~

Logan drove the squad car past the open electronic gates and up the gravel driveway to Canning's mansion and parked in front of the house. Fleming got out of the passenger seat and walked over to ring the bell.

Jane Canning arrived at the door looking concerned. 'He's round the back. I can show you through the house, or you can walk round the path.'

'The path is fine. He's expecting us?'

'Yes. Your colleague, a lady I spoke to, said you wanted to ask him a few questions.'

'Just routine. We'll go and find your husband.'

'Can I get you a cold drink? It's been a hot day. Paul is past what he calls gin o'clock time. He's having one with ice. I don't suppose you...'

'No, thanks. On duty.'

'Of course. Water?'

'That'll be fine,' Fleming said.

Jane looked at Logan.

'Same,' he said.

They found Canning sitting in a chair next to the swimming pool. He was holding a large gin and tonic in one hand and a cigar in the other. He raised his glass in salute to the two detectives. 'Come and have a seat.'

Fleming and Logan pulled up chairs and sat by a table facing Canning.

'Thank you for agreeing to see us,' Fleming said. 'You do understand I'm going to question you under caution due to the allegations made against you?'

'The officer who phoned me said I could attend a police station voluntarily. I'd much rather answer your questions here. Far more civilised, don't you think?'

'Did she say you could have a solicitor present?'

'Yes. Not necessary. I have nothing to hide.'

'And, as I'm not arresting you, you can refuse to answer my questions at any time. Do you understand?'

'Yes.'

'Okay. You do not have to say anything. But it may harm your defence if you do not mention when questioned something which you later rely on in court. Anything you do say may be given in evidence.'

Canning blew a cloud of smoke up into the air and took a sip of his gin. 'I understand.'

Logan had his notebook out at the ready.

'You had a meeting with Eric Blunt and Tom Slater at the council offices. Is that right?'

'Yes.'

'What was it about?'

'My planning application.'

'How many other times had you met Blunt?'

'He was at the planning information meeting in the village hall, but I hadn't arranged to meet him there.'

'Blunt has confessed to killing his wife. Claims it was an accident.'

'Dreadful business.' Canning puffed on his cigar and took another sip of gin.

Before Fleming could ask another question, Jane appeared with two glasses of iced water. Fleming thanked her and turned back to Canning. 'You only had the one meeting with Blunt?'

'Yes,' Canning said.

Fleming thought he was lying. 'And yet you offered the services of your solicitor to him when I questioned him over the death of his wife.'

'Least I could do to help.'

'Did you know Blunt had serious financial difficulties?'

'Did he?'

'He claimed he accepted a bribe of five thousand pounds from you in return for supporting your application.'

'Preposterous! I deny that!'

'We could get forensic accountants to check your accounts for any hidden payments.'

Canning stubbed his cigar out with more force than was necessary. 'Do what you like.'

'Walter Hammond has approved your application. I gather you were friends at university. Is that correct?'

Canning shifted in his chair. 'We were.'

'He attended the welcoming party you threw here for Al Jameel.'

Canning said nothing.

'You also met Hammond afterwards for lunch in London. Any particular reason?'

'I think our little chat is over,' Canning said.

'Fine,' Fleming said. He and Logan, who'd been taking copious notes of the conversation, rose to go. 'By the way, the Serious Fraud Office will want to speak to you and Hammond.'

75

'Alex. Thank God you're in. My office, now!' Temple said over the phone.

Fleming sensed the urgency and wondered if the kidnapper had called Elford early. He dashed out of his office and made for Temple's.

Logan was shouting after him, 'Where's the fire?'

'Super wants to see me right away. Something's up,' Fleming called back over his shoulder.

Temple was standing at her door waiting for him. 'There's been a major development. Marco Guerra's been found.'

Fleming gasped. 'Where? Was he with Dani?'

'No, Dani wasn't with him. Guerra's been murdered.'

It took a second for this to sink in. 'What! Where?'

'Back of a disused warehouse on an old industrial site in west London. The Met are there now.'

'I need to get down there to speak to them today and search Guerra's flat.'

'I can get you there sooner than you think,' Temple said.

Fleming looked perplexed.

'Chief constable has pulled rank and she's found an NPAS helicopter which is at Oxford Airport.'

'Thought the nearest National Police Air Service base is at Benson.'

'It is, but there happens to be one of their helicopters at Oxford. Lazar has commandeered it. It's on its way here to pick you up. Should be here any minute.'

'That's service. I thought budget cuts had reduced the number of helicopters they had.'

The loud throbbing of helicopter rotor blades partially drowned out Temple's reply. 'There have been cuts. Lazar played the political interest card though. She said we wanted the murdered man in connection with a high-profile kidnap.'

Temple went over to her window. 'Better get down there. Your helicopter has landed.'

Fleming rushed back to his office to grab his coat. 'Going on a helicopter ride,' he shouted to a bemused-looking Logan.

The distinctive black-and-yellow Eurocopter EC135 was idling in a space the pilot had found in the car park. Fleming dashed across and climbed in. 'Hi, DCI Fleming. Know where we're going?'

The pilot checked his instruments and opened the throttle on the collective lever to his left. 'West London. I'm in radio contact with the Met. They'll guide us to the exact location as we get nearer.' There was a loud whining noise which increased in volume as the speed of the rotors picked up.

Fleming watched as the pilot pulled the collective up at the same time as operating the foot pedals. As the engine noise increased, the lift produced by the rotors exceeded the weight of the helicopter and it lifted slowly into the air. At a height of about fifty feet, the pilot used the cyclic pitch control to swing the helicopter round to head for London.

As they picked up speed, the pilot spoke into his radio to say they were on their way and set out his flight path. 'ETA about thirty minutes,' he said, glancing sideways at Fleming.

There were a few garbled messages on the radio on the way to London. As they neared the site, the person on the other end directed the pilot to the old warehouse. He hovered over the large parking area at the rear of the building. Below, Fleming could see men in white overalls searching every inch of the ground. As the pilot manoeuvred the helicopter to land, the rotor downdraught fanned ripples across the nearby Thames.

The helicopter touched the ground with a slight bump and the whine of the rotors wound down as the pilot switched the engine off.

A man dressed in civilian clothes came across to meet Fleming as he got out of the helicopter. 'Hi, DCI Fleming I presume?' he said, holding out a hand. 'DI Ireland... Met.'

Fleming shook hands. 'I take it you've been briefed on what my interest in this man is?'

'Wanted in connection with a kidnap.'

'Yes. Afraid I didn't have time to collect my protective clothing so you'll have to tell me what you've found.'

'Had his driving licence on him so we got an immediate ID. His mobile was in the glove compartment and we found a Beretta tucked in his jeans behind him. The killer shot him in the chest and once between the eyes. Gangland killing if you ask me.'

'Or connected to the kidnap,' Fleming guessed. 'Did you know your guys were working with the AKEU keeping his flat under surveillance?'

'Yeah, I did.'

'I'll want to search it next.'

'Sure, no problem.'

Fleming fished in his pocket and pulled out a card. 'Email me all the contacts on his mobile.' He glanced across at the black Volvo. 'I'll also need details of anything Forensics find in the car.'

'Right.'

'Any CCTV?'

Ireland waved a hand round the place and grinned. 'Look at it. Why would anyone want CCTV here?'

'Looks like Guerra came here to meet someone. Probably why the killer picked it,' Fleming guessed. 'Who discovered the body?'

'Anonymous. The officer who took the call reckons it's a place where pushers go to collect and deliver drugs, hence no name given.'

'Okay. Can you take me to have a look at Guerra's flat?'

'Sure. We can go in my car.'

Fleming looked over to the helicopter pilot. He pointed a finger at Ireland's car, indicating it was his next mode of transport.

The pilot gave him a thumbs up and the rotors started to turn with a loud whine. Fleming and Ireland shielded their eyes against the dust kicked up by the rotors as the helicopter took off into the London sky.

76

It took an hour for Ireland's car and a squad car with two uniformed officers to get to Peckham from the old warehouse. Guerra's flat was above a small run-down shop. Access was through a door to the right of the shop and up some old stone stairs. Flaking blue paint hung off the door, and the landing outside had the distinct smell of urine. Ireland checked some keys they'd found in Guerra's pocket, but none of them fitted. He turned to one of the uniformed officers. 'Get the Enforcer.'

A few minutes later, the officer returned carrying the large battering ram. It didn't take long before the splintered door was hanging off its hinges. 'Needn't worry about protective clothing,' Ireland said. 'It's not a crime scene.'

The flat had a small living room, a tiny kitchen, one bathroom and one bedroom. Ireland disappeared into the kitchen while Fleming looked round the living room. It was grubby, and there was nothing much by way of furniture. Wallpaper was peeling off and an empty beer can lay on the floor under a small coffee table. An ashtray containing the butts of some spliffs was on top of the table. A stained mug sat next to the ashtray.

There was no TV and no landline phone. Guerra's mobile seemed to be his main means of communication. Two old newspapers were on the floor beside an armchair. One carried news of the Kelso prison escape. The other had headlines on the Al Jameel kidnap. Guerra must have wanted to check if the police had any leads.

Fleming's eyes focussed on a small bureau in the corner. It looked old and uncared for. The wood stain had all but gone and there was no sign Guerra had ever polished it. Fleming walked over and pulled the top open. Inside, there was an array of old bills, betting slips, a few receipts and a notepad. A jar contained a few pens and pencils. Fleming flicked through the receipts and found one for the hotel where Guerra had met Slater.

'Find anything?' Ireland shouted through from the kitchen. 'Nothing but dirty dishes and filth in here. Doubt he ever did any cleaning.'

'Nothing yet,' Fleming called back. He knew the hotel receipt would be of no interest to Ireland.

There was a sudden crash of breaking glass.

'Oops!' Ireland exclaimed. 'Too much bloody clutter in here!'

Fleming smiled and continued looking through the papers in the top of the bureau. He opened a small envelope and found a prison visiting order Guerra hadn't used. There had been no need. The date on it was after the date Kelso had escaped. Underneath a narrow shelf at the back of the bureau, there was a small pull-out drawer. Fleming pulled it open and found some business cards. Most were for tradesmen, but one caught Fleming's eye. It was a card for the owner of a London nightclub, Ulrick Zimmerman.

Ireland appeared through the door to the kitchen holding a sealed glass jar. 'This was in the back of a cupboard.'

Fleming took one look. 'Cannabis?'

'More of this than food by the look of things in there,' Ireland said. 'You found anything of interest?'

Fleming showed Ireland the business card. 'Ever heard of him?'

Ireland shook his head. 'Can't say I have. I'll check back at the office. See if anyone else has.'

'Or if he has any record,' Fleming prompted.

'That as well.'

'If you take the bathroom, I'll check the bedroom,' Fleming suggested.

'Okay. Mind you, given the state of the kitchen, I hate to think what the bathroom will be like,' Ireland grumbled. 'Sure you don't want to check it?'

'Bedroom is fine for me.'

'Right. I'll get on with it then.'

Fleming grinned and went to the bedroom. He pushed the door open to find the room in pretty much the same unkempt state as the living room. There was an unmade double bed, a rickety wooden chair, a single wardrobe, and a set of bedside drawers. There was a musty smell and there were holes in the threadbare carpet. An old blanket served as a curtain.

Fleming walked over to the wardrobe and held his breath as he opened the door. Two pairs of shoes and a duffle bag littered the bottom. A few pairs of trousers, jeans and shirts hung from hangers. The top shelf contained a few extra blankets. Fleming lifted them up and found two spare Beretta magazines for a nine-millimetre gun.

Fleming went over to sit on the edge of the bed and pulled open the bedside drawer. All he found was a charger for a mobile phone and Guerra's passport. 'You won't be needing that,' Fleming muttered to himself and made his way back to the living room.

Ireland had finished his search of the bathroom. 'Nothing.'

'Think you can get the contacts off Guerra's mobile and any forensic results to me by tomorrow?'

'I'll do my best.'

'And anything you can find on this guy, Zimmerman.'

'That I can promise.'

'You'll need to get the SOCOs over here to carry out a thorough check.'

'Already done. They're on their way. How are you getting back to your HQ?'

Fleming shrugged. 'Lift to a station? Then train, I guess.'

77

'Boss took time off for a trip in a helicopter yesterday,' Logan told Anderson when Fleming arrived in the office.

'This one of your jokes, Sarge?'

'No... he did. Chief constable commandeered one for him. That right, boss?'

'She did.'

Anderson looked doubtful. 'You're both having me on.'

'It wasn't exactly time off for a jolly.' Fleming laughed. 'She wanted me in London in double quick time.'

'I guessed something was in the offing... way you dashed off to see the super, then ran out of the office,' Logan said. 'What was the panic?'

'The Met have found our man, Guerra.'

'With Dani?' Logan asked.

'Afraid not. Guerra's been murdered.'

Anderson looked shocked. 'Oh, my god! What's happening here? First, Tom Slater, then the kidnap, Felicity Blunt, and now this!'

'Keeps us busy,' Logan said.

'Sarge! You shouldn't be so flippant. This is serious stuff.'

Logan looked suitably chastised. 'Yeah, sorry, you're right. Super up to speed?' he asked Fleming.

'Spoke to her last night when I got back from London... by train this time.'

'Didn't say a word,' Logan said.

'She phoned the chief constable who's getting agitated. Expected more news after commandeering a helicopter. Bottom line is, we are no nearer to finding Dani, though I'm hoping to get more information from the Met today.'

'Talking about Dani,' Logan said. 'Elford rang while you were down in London. Kidnapper phoned again.'

'What'd she tell him?'

'Told him some of the money was on its way to one of the accounts, but it would take a few days to appear.'

'Did he buy that?'

'She reckoned he was getting twitchy. Pissed off, if you'll excuse the expression. The caller shouted down the phone that the money had better appear, or they'd start cutting Dani's fingers off. Then he hung up.'

'She'd told him before that there would be no payments made if any harm came to Dani,' Fleming reminded Logan.

'I guess he's getting impatient. Anger can get in the way of clear thinking.'

'We don't need an angry kidnapper. This could end badly if we don't get a clue where they're holding Dani pretty damned quick.'

Anderson sighed. 'If Guerra was one of the kidnappers, who would have killed him?'

'He *was* definitely one of the kidnappers. He was driving a black Volvo.'

'But *why* would someone want to kill him?'

'That's what I'm hoping to find out. Seems too much of a coincidence for his murder not to be connected somehow.'

'This is all becoming a bit of a puzzle,' Logan said. 'Slater meets Guerra in a couple of clandestine meetings in London which no one knows anything about. Someone murders Slater soon after. Guerra is one of the kidnappers and someone kills him while negotiations over payment of the ransom are going on.'

'What about Felicity Blunt?' Anderson asked.

Logan shook his head. 'Blunt admitted to killing her. Claims it was an accident. Either way, it was to do with a heated argument over finances and the fact Blunt had accepted a bribe from Canning. I think we can rule it out of the kidnap equation.'

Fleming was thoughtful. 'We've already concluded Slater couldn't have been part of the actual kidnap. But he *was* in a position to know of the arrangements for Al Jameel's visit while Canning still employed him. Could be that's what the meeting with Guerra was all about. Could he have known about the plan to kidnap Dani and threatened to go to the police?'

'That's it!' Logan exclaimed. 'Slater needed money to pay off gambling debts. He asked Canning for a pay rise which Canning refused. Could be Guerra approached Slater to get information about Al Jameel's visit and offered money in exchange. Slater asks for more or threatens to go to the police. Guerra kills him after getting the information he needed.'

'Sounds plausible,' Anderson agreed, 'but what about Guerra? Who killed him?'

Fleming was about to answer when his phone rang. 'Back in a min,' he said, heading for his office door.

'Fleming.'

'Hi, it's DI Ireland. I have some information for you. I've emailed you a list of all the contacts on Guerra's mobile.'

'Thanks.'

'Met Forensics have pulled out all the stops. They've been in touch with your Forensics guys and compared notes over what they found in Guerra's car and your kidnap case. Kelso's fingerprints are all over Guerra's car and they found traces of DNA in the boot which matched the samples taken from Dani Al Jameel's clothes your guys checked in Canning's house.'

'Anything else?'

'Your Forensics said you were also working on a murder enquiry and guess what?'

'What?'

'Fibres taken from Guerra's clothing match fibres your Forensics guys found at the scene of the Tom Slater murder. And... your chaps reckon a nine-millimetre handgun was used to kill Slater. Guerra's gun is a nine-millimetre Beretta.'

'Confirms our suspicions that Guerra killed Slater.'

'There's more... Guerra's fingerprints are a match with ones found on Slater's car.'

'Anything on Zimmerman?'

'Yes. Turns out police questioned him over the armed robbery they nicked Jack Kelso for. Met thought he might have been the mastermind behind it. Not enough evidence to link him to it though. He walked free while Kelso served time... until he escaped.'

'Thanks. You've been a great help. Let me know if you get any leads on who might have killed Guerra.'

'Sure.'

Fleming ended the call and looked up his emails to get the list of Guerra's contacts. Kelso's was there... and something else sent Fleming's pulse racing. He dashed back out to where Logan and Anderson were sitting. 'Just had the Met on. It's more or less confirmed Guerra killed Slater. His fingerprints were on Slater's car. Clothing fibres found at the scene match with Guerra's, and he had a nine-millimetre gun.'

Logan whistled. 'Wow, that is a result.'

'And... I found a business card for a guy called Zimmerman

in Guerra's flat. I received a list of all the contacts on Guerra's mobile and Zimmerman's is there, with an address for a holiday home.'

'What's the relevance?' Logan asked.

'We have a link between Zimmerman and Kelso. A witness saw the black Volvo used for Dani's abduction driving up the A4130 away from Henley. The road ends around the junction to the A34. North from there takes you to Oxford, hang a left from there on the A40 and that's where Zimmerman's holiday home is!'

'You think it's where they might be holding Dani?' Logan asked.

'Get onto the Met and ask them to bring Zimmerman in. I need to question him,' Fleming said. 'And get the house under covert surveillance.'

78

Fleming had left Logan to brief Temple on the latest development so she could update the chief constable. He'd decided it would be pushing it to ask for another helicopter to take him down to London and had caught a train. Ireland had confirmed he would pick Zimmerman up and hold him until Fleming arrived.

After a quick coffee, Fleming and Ireland joined Zimmerman and his solicitor in interview room two. It was a cramped room with blue painted walls and green carpet tiles. The only furniture was a table and four chairs. A single pendant ceiling light with a domed shade hung over the table.

Fleming and Ireland sat opposite Zimmerman and his solicitor. Ireland switched on the digital recording machine. Zimmerman tapped his fingers on the table while Fleming went through the introductions. He then cautioned Zimmerman and read him his rights.

Zimmerman was wearing a white shirt, a cream blazer, and matching casual trousers. The black patch over his left eye was in stark contrast, but somehow didn't seem out of place. He'd declined the invitation to attend the police station so Ireland had arrested him. The clock was now ticking. They could only hold Zimmerman for twenty-four hours before either charging or releasing him.

Preliminaries and Zimmerman's finger-tapping over, Fleming launched into his first question. 'Do you know a man called Marco Guerra?'

Zimmerman glanced at his solicitor who gave an imperceptible nod. 'Yes.'

'In what capacity?'

'He works for me from time to time.'

'Doing what?'

'I own a few nightclubs. He runs errands, fetches and carries, drives, cleans up. Sometimes works behind the bar if I'm short of staff.'

'What sort of errands did he run for you?'

'You said did.'

'You haven't heard then?'

'What?'

'Someone's murdered him.' Fleming looked for a sign of reaction from Zimmerman, but saw none.

'How? When?'

It was the lack of any emotion that convinced Fleming that Zimmerman already knew. 'Yesterday. He was shot.'

'Oh my god!'

The sudden attempt to register shock didn't convince Fleming. 'His body was found at the back of a disused warehouse in west London. Know any places like that?'

'Can't say I do.'

'Going back to my question about errands he ran for you. What exactly did that entail?'

'Shopping, collecting supplies, delivering flyers for club events. That sort of thing.'

'Fetching and carrying involve drugs?'

Zimmerman smiled. 'Never.'

'We found cannabis in his flat.'

'Must have been for personal use. Nothing to do with me, I can assure you.'

'Did he work for you every day?'

'More or less.'

'You didn't think it strange he didn't turn up for work yesterday or today?'

'Not really.'

'He wasn't a good timekeeper?'

'I did say he worked for me more or less every day. I wasn't too concerned he didn't come in.'

'Did you try contacting him?'

'No.'

'How well did you know Guerra?'

'Knew him for about five years.'

'You don't seem particularly upset to find out someone you knew for so long has been murdered.'

Zimmerman smirked. 'I keep my emotions in check. Doesn't pay for a London nightclub owner to go about crying.'

'Neither did you show any concern he didn't turn up for work. Is that because you knew he wouldn't?'

'Are you accusing my client of having something to do with Guerra's murder?' the solicitor asked. 'He was arrested for a kidnap he knows nothing about. You must keep your line of questioning to that.'

'You said Guerra did some driving for you. Did he use his black Volvo?'

Zimmerman shifted uneasily in his seat at the mention of the Volvo. 'Yes,' he admitted.

'A black Volvo was used to kidnap Dani Al Jameel.'

Zimmermann snorted. 'Must be thousands of them.'

'Police interviewed you years ago about an armed robbery. Is that correct?'

Zimmerman looked to his solicitor for help.

'I insist you confine your questions to the kidnap,' the solicitor said. 'This has no relevance whatsoever.'

'Oh, but it has,' Fleming argued. 'We have evidence Jack Kelso and Guerra were the two men who kidnapped Al Jameel. Kelso was convicted for the armed robbery and he refused to disclose the name of the man who planned it.'

Zimmerman shrugged. 'So?'

'We also have evidence it was Guerra who helped Kelso escape from prison.'

'Your point being?' the solicitor asked.

'Guerra worked for your client. He had his and Kelso's contact details on his mobile. Was one of the errands Guerra ran for you to break Kelso out of prison to help with the kidnap? Did you also arrange Kelso's escape to repay the debt you owed him for not naming you in connection with the armed robbery?'

'Ridiculous!'

'There's an address for your holiday home near Oxford on Guerra's mobile.'

'What of it? I have a second home. Good to get out of London for a break from time to time. I also use it for corporate entertainment.'

'Its location happens to coincide with the general direction the kidnappers took from Paul Canning's place. Is that where you're holding Dani?'

'No... no.'

'We have the place under surveillance as we speak. Any chance Kelso and Dani will be there?'

A look of panic crossed Zimmerman's face.

'I'm about to give the order for armed police to raid the house.'

'Okay, okay! It's not what you think. If I tell you what happened, will you go easy on me?'

'Depends what you tell me.'

'Guerra asked if he could use the house to hide out for a while. Some drug dealers had threatened him. I went up to see him and found he and Kelso were holding Dani there. It was nothing to do with me! I couldn't say anything due to being implicated. They were using my house, for God's sake!'

'You didn't make the calls to ask for the ransom?'

'No... no. It must have been one of them. Look... I can tell you something else if it'll help me.'

'Go on.'

'Guerra told me it was Tom Slater who gave him the information about Al Jameel's visit. He paid him, but Slater came back asking for more. He threatened to go to the police, so Guerra killed him.'

'And you chose not to report all this.'

'I told you. I couldn't, due to being implicated.'

'Anything else you want to tell me?'

'Guerra told me he thought Kelso was planning to kill him so he could take his share of the ransom. I reckon he did.'

79

Fleming was on the phone to Logan as soon as he'd finished questioning Zimmerman. 'Harry? It's me. I need you to go and see the super. Tell her I've questioned Zimmerman and he's admitted Kelso is holding Dani at his holiday home near Oxford.'

'He admitted it... just like that?'

'Long story. He's trying to claim he didn't know Guerra and Kelso had planned the kidnap, but found out they were using his house. Tell you about it when I get back.'

'Right. Want me to arrange a raid on the house?'

'Yes. Speak to Temple. Get her to authorise an armed response unit. She can tell the chief constable what's happening. If they catch Kelso, get them to take him to the police station in Oxford. I'm on my way back so I can question him there.'

'What about Zimmerman?'

'We can keep him in custody until noon tomorrow. I can be back in London first thing to charge him before the twenty-four-hour clock stops ticking.'

'And DI Wacera, what do you want me to do about her? You

told her she could be involved in the bid to free Dani if Kelso had him.'

'Forget that. Don't want her holding things up. Anyway, she was more interested in getting personal credit for finding Kelso than Dani's welfare.'

'She won't be happy.'

'Tough. We'll say it all happened so fast and there was no time to contact her. We'll tell her superiors she helped with our enquiries.'

'Right. Elford?'

'Better let her know.'

'Got it. On my way to see the super.'

'Thanks.' Fleming ended the call.

Kelso had a bad feeling. Things weren't going to plan. Zimmerman was getting edgy. He was sure the woman handling the negotiations for Al Jameel was stringing him along. Maybe the police were on to them and thought they might be able to find Dani before Al Jameel paid any ransom. Could be they were just playing for time.

Then there was Guerra. The Met had questioned him over ownership of a black Volvo and Zimmerman had panicked. Guerra had to go, he'd told Kelso. Not that Kelso had any qualms about killing Guerra. The man was a liability and he didn't trust him. And... it meant he'd get a bigger share of the ransom.

The Supplier had been in touch to say Kelso's false ID papers and passport were ready. Kelso had told him there was a delay in getting the money and that he would contact him soon. But he was beginning to wonder if he would ever see any money. Kelso sat in the kitchen for a while and thought about grabbing his bag and the Glock.

~

The armed response unit vehicles stopped near Zimmerman's driveway. There were three vehicles containing an inspector, sergeant and ten armed constables.

The ARU had been in radio contact with the surveillance officers. One of them was waiting near the entrance to the driveway out of sight of the house. The inspector wound down his window. 'Any sign of life?'

'Just one kidnapper we could see through a downstairs window. No sign of Dani.'

'Okay. We have confirmation he is in there so we're going in.' He got out of the car and went to speak to the sergeant who was in the second vehicle. 'Might only be one kidnapper in there with Dani. We'll approach on foot. Get a couple of armed officers round the back to cover any rear exit. The rest of us go straight through the front door. Ground level first, then upstairs.'

'Right.'

The inspector, sergeant and the armed constables lined either side of the gravel driveway. They kept to the grass to avoid any crunching underfoot. Each wore black overalls over bulletproof vests, black helmets and goggles. They all had Glock 17 pistols strapped to their legs. The ten constables carried Heckler and Koch MP5 carbines. One of the men had an Enforcer battering ram slung over his shoulder.

Keeping behind whatever cover there was, the twelve men made their way towards the house. The constables took the lead with carbines trained in front of them, eyes glued to the windows. Reaching the front door without incident, the sergeant indicated for two men to go to the back of the house.

The rest of the men waited for a few seconds while the

inspector tried the door. Locked. He nodded to the man with the battering ram and signalled for the others to be ready to enter.

The door burst open with a loud crash. All ten men dashed inside. The constables swung their carbines from side to side. There was no sign of the kidnapper. The inspector could see one door on the right-hand side of the central staircase. He held three fingers up showing he wanted three men to follow him. Pointing to the sergeant, he signalled he wanted him to search the other downstairs rooms with the rest of the men.

The inspector had his Glock in one hand and, standing to one side, threw open the kitchen door. The three constables burst in, carbines pointed straight ahead.

Kelso was pulling his Glock out of a drawer and was starting to swing round to aim at the constables.

'Police. Freeze!' the inspector shouted.

Kelso ignored him and raised his gun.

One constable fired and a bullet caught Kelso in his arm. Blood spurted from the wound and the gun dropped to the floor. Kelso yelped in pain and leant against the kitchen worktop holding his arm.

'Where's Dani?' the inspector shouted.

Kelso jerked his head upwards to show he was upstairs.

'Anyone else up there?'

Kelso shook his head.

The sergeant and other constables had come running at the sound of the shot.

'Get the medical kit,' the inspector told one of the men. He slapped handcuffs on Kelso's wrists. 'Dani's upstairs,' the inspector told the sergeant. He nodded towards Kelso. 'He reckons there's no one else up there,' he said. 'But be careful. Take three men with you.'

A minute later, the inspector heard the sergeant shout, 'Police!' There was a crash as a locked door burst open.

After a short while, a pale-faced Dani appeared on shaky legs.

'Looks like your lucky day, Dani,' Kelso said.

80

Fleming and Logan were at St Aldates Police Station in Oxford having a cup of tea, going over the day's events. Kelso was waiting in interview room one. He'd been taken to hospital to have his right arm seen to. The wound hadn't been too bad in the end. It was only a deep graze. They'd patched him up, put his arm in a sling, and gave him painkillers.

'How long do we leave him to stew before we go in to question him?' Logan asked.

'We'll go in as soon as we finish our tea.'

'You were saying Zimmerman claimed he had nothing to do with the kidnap. He just happened to find out Kelso and Guerra were using his holiday home. Bit far-fetched, isn't it?'

'He owned up to it when I told him we had his place under surveillance and were about to raid it.'

'Didn't have much choice. He's obviously the brains behind it.'

'He also claimed Guerra told him he'd killed Tom Slater.'

'Why?'

'Thought he could get off more lightly if he offered information.'

'I meant why did Guerra kill Slater?'

'Zimmerman reckons Slater gave Guerra information about the arrangements for Al Jameel's visit. Guerra paid him, but then Slater asked for more. Threatened to go to the police if he didn't get it.'

'Think Guerra told Kelso?'

'Who knows? I'll ask him.' Fleming finished his tea. 'Zimmerman also reckoned Kelso killed Guerra.'

'Loyal to his mates, eh?'

'Could get Kelso talking if I tell him Zimmerman pointed the finger at him.' Fleming nodded towards the interview-room door. 'Ready?'

Kelso looked up as Fleming and Logan entered. They took their seats opposite Kelso while Logan switched on the digital recorder.

Fleming looked across the table at Kelso and spoke. 'This interview is being recorded. We are in interview room one at St Aldates Police Station, Oxford. It's seven thirty-two pm. This is an interview with...' Fleming indicated for Kelso to confirm his name.

'Jack Kelso.'

'Your address.'

'No fixed address.'

'I am DCI Fleming. Also present is DS Logan. There are no other persons present.' Fleming paused for a second. 'You do not have to say anything, but it may harm your defence if you do not mention when questioned something which you later rely on in court. Anything you do say may be given in evidence. Do you wish to have a solicitor?'

'Don't think I need bother with that now,' Kelso said.

'How's the arm?'

'Sore.'

'You're facing a long time in prison for attempting to shoot a police officer and kidnap. You might help yourself if you tell us everything.'

Kelso shrugged.

'You'll also have to serve the rest of your prison sentence for armed robbery, plus some extra time.'

Kelso didn't respond.

'We know Marco Guerra helped you escape from prison. Anyone else involved?'

'No comment.'

'Guerra was identified as the man who had visited you in prison. We also identified him as the same person who met a man called Tom Slater in London. Slater ended up dead shortly afterwards. Know anything about that?'

'No.'

'Apart from finding you holding Dani Al Jameel, we have forensic evidence proving you were one of the kidnappers.'

'What evidence?'

'Your prints and DNA were found on tape used to bind the security guard.'

'How careless of me.'

'Someone shot Guerra dead. Was it you?'

'No.'

'Forensics found your fingerprints and DNA in Guerra's car. They also found traces of Dani's DNA in Guerra's car boot.'

'Okay. So we kidnapped him, but I don't know anything about Slater or Guerra.'

'Know a man called Ulrick Zimmerman?'

'No.'

'His contact details were on Guerra's mobile with yours.'

'Doesn't mean I know him.' Kelso rubbed his beard. 'Out of interest, how did you find out where we were holding Dani?'

'Zimmerman. He told me everything.'

Kelso's eyes darkened.

'He told me about the house, how you and Guerra had planned Dani's abduction. Said he had nothing to do with it and had only agreed to let Guerra use the house because he wanted to lie low for a while. Says he had to keep quiet because you were using his house.'

'The scheming bastard!'

'He told me Guerra had killed Slater and that you were planning to kill Guerra so you could get all the ransom money.'

Kelso slammed a fist on the table. 'To think I covered up for him all these years ago over the armed robbery, and he walked free while I did time.'

'So he was the mastermind behind that?'

'Yes. No way I'll cover for him this time!'

'Did he plan the kidnap?'

'Of course he bloody did! Planned my escape to help with it because he didn't trust Guerra to do it on his own.'

'Anything else you want to tell me?'

'Zimmerman paid Slater for information about Al Jameel's visit. When Slater asked for more money or he would go to the police, Zimmerman got Guerra to kill him.'

'And Guerra?'

'I've nothing to lose now. I'll get life anyway. Zimmerman's not going to get off this time. Guerra was becoming a liability. Zimmerman told me to kill him.'

81

Fleming and Logan were back at HQ after terminating the interview with Kelso. Temple was surprised how quickly things had happened. The news that Dani was safe had brought a smile to her face. She'd congratulated Fleming over Kelso's arrest. That he'd all but wrapped up the murders of Tom Slater, Felicity Blunt and Marco Guerra was icing on the cake. She wanted to waste no time in letting the chief constable know. Fleming had left her to it.

'How's the super?' Logan asked as Fleming came back to his office. 'Happy?'

'She was. Listen, I want to go and give Elford a call. Let her know what's happened. I need you to make another call while I do that.'

'Who to?'

'DI Wacera. Tell her I'm sorry there wasn't time to get her involved in Dani's rescue and Kelso's arrest.'

'She won't be happy.'

'Tell her I'll buy her a drink next time I'm over in Hertfordshire and we'll mention how she helped us.'

'Sure you don't want to make that call?'

'You've got a thick skin, Harry. Just be your pleasant self.'

'Thanks a lot, boss.'

Fleming smiled and went into his office. Elford picked up after three rings. 'Elford, AKEU.'

'Hi, Unity. It's Fleming. We got Dani and Jack Kelso has been arrested.'

'Is he okay?'

'Dani is. Kelso was shot in the arm, but he's okay.'

'How did you find him?'

'The other kidnapper, Marco Guerra was shot dead in London. He had a business card for a guy called Zimmerman who has a holiday home near Oxford. I questioned him and he admitted that's where they were holding Dani when I told him we were going to raid the place.'

'Wow, things have moved fast.'

'Just as well. We were running out of time.'

'Have you arrested this Zimmerman?'

'He's under arrest, yes. He's being held in custody in London. I'm going back down there first thing to question him again. I've got until midday to either charge or release him.'

'Well, good luck with that, and... thanks for letting me know.'

Fleming sat next to Ireland in interview room two facing Zimmerman and his solicitor across the table. Ireland had switched on the DIR. After a night in custody, Zimmerman's clothes were looking creased and grubby. He was already under arrest for the kidnap of Dani Al Jameel. Kelso's prison escape, the murders of Slater and Guerra, and planning the old armed robbery had been added.

Having gone through the usual process, Fleming was ready

to start questioning. Ireland had reminded him they had until midday to either charge or release Zimmerman. It was ten thirty and the clock was ticking fast.

'Do you know a man known as Taffy?'

'Never heard of him.'

'We traced all Guerra's contacts to question them about Jack Kelso's escape and the kidnap.'

'I told you yesterday I had nothing to do with it.'

Fleming continued. 'Taffy was on the list. Panicked when questioned. He was told he was facing two to five years for aiding and abetting a prison escape, but that the judge might be more lenient if he talked.'

Zimmerman said nothing.

'He said you and Guerra planned the prison escape and the kidnap.'

'He's lying.'

'Dani was found at your holiday home. Police arrested Kelso. I questioned him last night. He also says you planned the kidnap and arranged his escape from prison.'

Zimmerman pulled out a handkerchief and dabbed at sweat on his forehead.

'We searched your London flat. Found a burner phone. You used it to make the ransom demand, didn't you?'

'No! I keep telling you, I had nothing to do with the kidnap. They were using my Oxfordshire house without my prior knowledge.'

'The number you were given to call back on was a direct line into the Anti Kidnap and Extortion Unit.'

'I didn't make any calls.'

'They have all the state-of-the-art equipment there. Forensic voice-recognition experts checked the caller's voice against the recording of your voice taken when I questioned you yesterday.'

'Doubt that's conclusive.'

'Why should you be worried if you didn't make the calls?'

'I meant I suspect these things aren't always accurate. Doesn't matter to me of course.' Zimmerman smirked. 'Unless they wrongly match the kidnapper's voice with mine.'

'I'm told it is accurate. They use fine-grained phonetic analysis. It determines the probability of a speaker's identity by comparing with a known reference. There's no doubt it's your voice.'

Zimmerman glanced at his solicitor who shook his head.

'No comment,' Zimmerman whispered.

'Kelso also claims you got Guerra to kill Tom Slater. Did you?'

'No!'

'Slater's phone number was found in your flat. Why did you have his number?'

'No comment.'

'Your bank statements show a cash withdrawal of five thousand pounds a few days before Slater made a similar cash deposit in his account. It was payment for information on Al Jameel's visit, wasn't it?'

'No comment.'

'He threatened to go to the police if you didn't pay him more and you had Guerra kill him, didn't you?'

'No comment.'

'Kelso also admitted to killing Guerra. Claimed you asked him to do it because you thought we were getting closer to Guerra.'

'That's not true!'

'Kelso had a small voice recorder. He had it on when you admitted to planning the armed robbery, his escape, the kidnap, and when you asked him to kill Guerra.'

'You're lying!'

'Want to hear it?'

Zimmerman shook his head.

Fleming looked at the clock. It was eleven forty-five.

'I've spoken to the CPS. They've confirmed I should charge you with several offences. Planning an armed robbery and a prison escape for a start. Then a kidnap, and arranging the murders of Tom Slater and Marco Guerra. You'll be remanded in custody.'

Zimmerman's one eye flashed in panic. He turned to his solicitor who shook his head.

Fleming charged Zimmerman and looked towards the DIR. 'Interview terminated at eleven forty-six.'

82

It was late afternoon and the sun still had some heat in it. Fleming, Logan and Anderson were sitting under a parasol on the terrace of The Trout Inn. Below the terrace wall, the light shimmered off the surface of the slow-flowing Thames. Two people in canoes paddled around and waved to some friends up on the terrace.

Fleming raised his glass. 'Cheers. Here's to the speedy and successful conclusion to our recent cases. The super and chief constable pass on their thanks. Cash in the kitty came from them.'

'Very generous,' Logan said, then took a sip of his pint. 'Is there enough to get some nosh as well?'

Anderson smiled. 'True to form, Sarge.'

'What do you mean, Naomi?'

'Thinking of your stomach.'

'Wasn't suggesting a meal. Just a few chips.'

'I'll order some when I get the next drinks in,' Fleming said.

Logan took another sip of beer, swallowed. 'Police work has suddenly become much more appealing.'

Anderson looked at Fleming. 'I see you kept your promise to

Zoe Dunbar,' she said. 'I read her articles on the Slater case and Dani's abduction. Got news scoops before anyone else got their story out.'

'She did try to help. Least I could do.'

'She can be a bit of a pain,' Logan said, 'but she does have her uses at times.'

'Did you see the other article she wrote?' Anderson said.

'She wrote more than two?' Logan asked.

'Don't you read the papers, Sarge?'

'Try not to. Full of bad news.'

'Editors print what's likely to sell papers,' Fleming pointed out.

'Okay,' Logan said, 'what was in the other article?'

'It was about Eric Blunt's confession that he killed his wife. And his claim Canning had bribed him to approve his planning application.'

'Hang on,' Logan said. 'I thought it went to a public enquiry and Walter Hammond approved it.'

'He did, but that was after the council had approved the plan and the parish council applied for the application to be called in.'

'Ah, got it,' Logan said, taking the last sip of his beer.

'Blunt pleaded guilty to manslaughter, didn't he?' Anderson asked.

'Yes,' Fleming confirmed. 'He's facing at least two concurrent five-year sentences for that and for accepting a bribe in public office.' He downed the rest of his pint. 'Ready for another?'

'Yes please,' Logan and Anderson replied in unison.

'And a couple of plates of chips, I guess,' Fleming said, looking at Logan.

'One would do, boss.'

'I was thinking Naomi and I could have some as well, if that's okay,' Fleming said with a broad smile.

Anderson grinned as Fleming got up to go and order the food and drinks.

When he returned, Anderson and Logan were laughing at the antics of the two canoeists. They'd almost capsized after bumping into each other.

Fleming put the drinks on the table. 'Chips will be on their way soon.'

Anderson smiled. 'Looks like Dunbar's article confirms the claims of bribery and corruption were justified,' she said. 'We've got Blunt admitting that Canning bribed him. The photos of Canning having lunch with Walter Hammond look dubious as well.'

'I have some news on that front. Just found out this morning,' Fleming said.

'What?' Logan asked.

'The SFO are going to investigate Canning, his accountant and his solicitor. Walter Hammond as well.'

'Let's hope they all get what they deserve,' Logan said as the chips arrived.

'And...' Fleming continued, 'the prime minister has sacked Hammond.'

'What happened to being innocent before being proved guilty?' Logan asked.

'Doesn't work like that in politics, Harry. The mere fact the SFO are going to investigate him is enough to cause embarrassment to the government. Ministers have been sacked for much less.'

'Rat race,' Logan muttered.

Fleming smiled. 'The parish council are also taking legal action against Canning's solicitor, Silas Revell,' Fleming said.

'What for?' Logan asked, digging into some chips.

'He said something at the public enquiry which upset Kim

Ogilvie. She reckoned he made some insulting and slanderous statements about her.'

'Doesn't surprise me. He's a slimy little worm,' Logan said, putting a chip in his mouth.

'So what will happen to Canning's planning application now?' Anderson asked.

'It'll be thrown out,' Fleming guessed.

Anderson had grabbed some chips before Logan finished them. 'Isa Al Jameel hasn't waited to see what happens.'

'How'd you know?' Logan asked.

'It was in Zoe Dunbar's article about alleged corruption. Al Jameel said he was no longer interested in investing in Canning's plans. It had all gone wrong, and he was sure the authorities would throw the application out anyway. He thanked the police for finding his son and said they were returning home.'

Fleming held up his glass and examined the golden chilled beer. He sipped at it through the layer of froth on top. 'Nice pint.'

'Thought whisky was your tipple,' Logan said.

'It is if I have a drink after dinner, but on a hot day like today, cold beer is great.'

'What do you think Zimmerman will get?' Anderson asked.

'I guess he'll get life. Accessory to two murders, kidnap, and planning a prison escape,' Fleming said. 'Oh... and the armed robbery he was behind four years ago.'

'What about Kelso?'

'Most likely the same, life for kidnap and killing Guerra.'

Anderson swilled the rest of her drink round in her glass. 'The villagers in Darmont will no doubt be relieved Canning's plans are in disarray.'

'I gather the old chief constable isn't too happy though,' Fleming said.

'Why?' Anderson asked.

'The people he was planning to buy a house from took their house off the market, then put it back on at a higher price.'

'Because the threat of the housing and shopping development has gone,' Logan guessed. 'Wonder if he'll pay the extra.'

Fleming shrugged. 'Who knows? But the threat of development isn't over.'

'How come?'

'The dispute between locals and the council won't go away. There has to be more housing. Government policy. Someone else could slap in a planning application.'

'Sounds like we might end up with another case at this rate. Think another plan is likely?'

'Highly. Doubt Isa Al Jameel will be interested though.'

THE END

A NOTE FROM THE PUBLISHER

Thank you for reading this book. If you enjoyed it please do consider leaving a review on Amazon to help others find it too.

We hate typos. All of our books have been rigorously edited and proofread, but sometimes mistakes do slip through. If you have spotted a typo, please do let us know and we can get it amended within hours.

info@bloodhoundbooks.com

Printed in Great Britain
by Amazon